THE LIFE OF
GEORGE WASHINGTON

Washington Irving

THE LIFE OF
GEORGE WASHINGTON

VOLUME I

BIBLIOBAZAAR

THE LIFE OF
GEORGE WASHINGTON

CONTENTS

CHAPTER I.

GENEALOGY OF THE WASHINGTON FAMILY.

The Washington family is of an ancient English stock, the genealogy of which has been traced up to the century immediately succeeding the Conquest. At that time it was in possession of landed estates and manorial privileges in the county of Durham, such as were enjoyed only by those, or their descendants, who had come over from Normandy with the Conqueror, or fought under his standard. When William the Conqueror laid waste the whole country north of the Humber, in punishment of the insurrection of the Northumbrians, he apportioned the estates among his followers, and advanced Normans and other foreigners to the principal ecclesiastical dignities. One of the most wealthy and important sees was that of Durham. Hither had been transported the bones of St. Cuthbert from their original shrine at Lindisfarne, when it was ravaged by the Danes. That saint, says Camden, was esteemed by princes and gentry a titular saint against the Scots.[1] His shrine, therefore, had been held in peculiar reverence by the Saxons, and the see of Durham endowed with extraordinary privileges.

William continued and increased those privileges. He needed a powerful adherent on this frontier to keep the restless Northumbrians in order, and check Scottish invasion; and no doubt considered an enlightened ecclesiastic, appointed by the crown, a safer depositary of such power than an hereditary noble.

Having placed a noble and learned native of Loraine in the diocese, therefore, he erected it into a palatinate, over which the bishop, as Count Palatine, had temporal, as well as spiritual jurisdiction. He built a strong castle for his protection, and to serve

---

1   Camden, Brit. iv., 349.

as a barrier against the Northern foe. He made him lord high-admiral of the sea and waters adjoining his palatinate,—lord warden of the marches, and conservator of the league between England and Scotland. Thenceforth, we are told, the prelates of Durham owned no earthly superior within their diocese, but continued for centuries to exercise every right attached to an independent sovereign.[2]

The bishop, as Count Palatine, lived in almost royal state and splendor. He had his lay chancellor, chamberlains, secretaries, steward, treasurer, master of the horse, and a host of minor officers. Still he was under feudal obligations. All landed property in those warlike times, implied military service. Bishops and abbots, equally with great barons who held estates immediately of the crown, were obliged, when required, to furnish the king with armed men in proportion to their domains; but they had their feudatories under them to aid them in this service.

The princely prelate of Durham had his barons and knights, who held estates of him on feudal tenure, and were bound to serve him in peace and war. They sat occasionally in his councils, gave martial splendor to his court, and were obliged to have horse and weapon ready for service, for they lived in a belligerent neighborhood, disturbed occasionally by civil war, and often by Scottish foray. When the banner of St. Cuthbert, the royal standard of the province, was displayed, no armed feudatory of the bishop could refuse to take the field.[3]

Some of these prelates, in token of the warlike duties of their diocese, engraved on their seals a knight on horseback armed at all points, brandishing in one hand a sword, and holding forth in the other the arms of the see.[4]

Among the knights who held estates in the palatinate on these warlike conditions, was WILLIAM DE HERTBURN, the progenitor of the Washingtons. His Norman name of William would seem to point out his national descent; and the family long continued to have Norman names of baptism. The surname of De Hertburn was taken from a village on the palatinate which he held of the bishop in knight's fee; probably the same now called Hartburn

2   Annals of Roger de Hovedon. Hutchinson's Durham, vol. ii. Collectanea Curiosa, vol. ii., p. 83.

3   Robert de Graystanes, Ang. Sac., p. 746.

4   Camden, Brit. iv., 349.

on the banks of the Tees. It had become a custom among the Norman families of rank about the time of the Conquest, to take surnames from their castles or estates; it was not until some time afterwards that surnames became generally assumed by the people.[5]

How or when the De Hertburns first acquired possession of their village is not known. They may have been companions in arms with Robert de Brus (or Bruce) a noble knight of Normandy, rewarded by William the Conqueror with great possessions in the North, and among others, with the lordships of Hert and Hertness in the county of Durham.

The first actual mention we find of the family is in the Bolden Book, a record of all the lands appertaining to the diocese in 1183. In this it is stated that William de Hertburn had exchanged his village of Hertburn for the manor and village of Wessyngton, likewise in the diocese; paying the bishop a quitrent of four pounds, and engaging to attend him with two greyhounds in grand hunts, and to furnish a man at arms whenever military aid should be required of the palatinate.[6]

The family changed its surname with its estate, and thenceforward assumed that of DE WESSYNGTON.[7] The

5   Lower on Surnames, vol. i., p. 43. Fuller says, that the custom of surnames was brought from France in Edward the Confessor's time, about fifty years before the Conquest; but did not become universally settled until some hundred years afterwards. At first they did not descend hereditarily on the family.—*Fuller, Church History. Roll Battle Abbey.*

6   THE BOLDEN BOOK. As this ancient document gives the first trace of the Washington family, it merits especial mention. In 1183, a survey was made by order of Bishop de Pusaz of all the lands of the see held in demesne, or by tenants in villanage. The record was entered in a book called the Bolden Buke; the parish of Bolden occurring first in alphabetical arrangement. The document commences in the following manner: Incipit liber qui vocatur Bolden Book. Anno Dominice Incarnationis, 1183, &c.

      The following is the memorandum in question:—

      Willus de Herteburn habet Wessyngton (excepta ecclesia et terra ecclesie partinen) ad excamb. pro villa de Herteburn quam pro hac quietam clamavit: Et reddit 4 L. Et vadit in *magna caza* cum 2 Leporar. Et quando commune auxilium venerit debet dare 1 Militem ad plus de auxilio, &c.—*Collectanea Curiosa*, vol. ii., p. 89.

      The Bolden Buke is a small folio, deposited in the office of the bishop's auditor, at Durham.

7   The name is probably of Saxon origin. It existed in England prior to the Conquest. The village of Wassengtone is mentioned in a Saxon charter as granted by king Edgar in 973 to Thorney Abbey.—*Collectanea Topographica*, iv., 55.

condition of military service attached to its manor will be found to have been often exacted, nor was the service in the grand hunt an idle form. Hunting came next to war in those days, as the occupation of the nobility and gentry. The clergy engaged in it equally with the laity. The hunting establishment of the Bishop of Durham was on a princely scale. He had his forests, chases and parks, with their train of foresters, rangers, and park keepers. A grand hunt was a splendid pageant in which all his barons and knights attended him with horse and hound. The stipulations with the Seignior of Wessyngton show how strictly the rights of the chase were defined. All the game taken by him in going to the forest belonged to the bishop; all taken on returning belonged to himself.[8]

Hugh de Pusaz (or De Pudsay) during whose episcopate we meet with this first trace of the De Wessyngtons, was a nephew of king Stephen, and a prelate of great pretensions; fond of appearing with a train of ecclesiastics and an armed retinue. When Richard Coeur de Lion put every thing at pawn and sale to raise funds for a crusade to the Holy Land, the bishop resolved to accompany him. More wealthy than his sovereign, he made magnificent preparations. Besides ships to convey his troops and retinue, he had a sumptuous galley for himself, fitted up with a throne or episcopal chair of silver, and all the household, and even culinary, utensils, were of the same costly material. In a word, had not the prelate been induced to stay at home, and aid the king with his treasures, by being made one of the regents of the kingdom, and Earl of Northumberland for life, the De Wessyngtons might have followed the banner of St. Cuthbert to the Holy wars.

Nearly seventy years afterwards we find the family still retaining its manorial estate in the palatinate. The names of Bondo de Wessyngton and William his son appear on charters of land, granted in 1257 to religious houses. Soon after occurred the wars of the barons, in which the throne of Henry III was shaken by the De Mountforts. The chivalry of the palatinate rallied under the royal standard. On the list of loyal knights who fought for their sovereign in the disastrous battle of Lewes (1264), in which the

---

8   Hutchinson's Durham vol. ii., p. 489.

king was taken prisoner, we find the name of William Weshington, of Weshington.[9]

During the splendid pontificate of Anthony Beke (or Beak), the knights of the palatinate had continually to be in the saddle, or buckled in armor. The prelate was so impatient of rest that he never took more than one sleep, saying it was unbecoming a man to turn from one side to another in bed. He was perpetually, when within his diocese, either riding from one manor to another, or hunting and hawking. Twice he assisted Edward I. with all his force in invading Scotland. In the progress northward with the king, the bishop led the van, marching a day in advance of the main body, with a mercenary force, paid by himself, of one thousand foot and five hundred horse. Besides these he had his feudatories of the palatinate; six bannerets and one hundred and sixty knights, not one of whom, says an old poem, but surpassed Arthur himself, though endowed with the charmed gifts of Merlin.[10] We presume the De Wessyngtons were among those preux chevaliers, as the banner of St. Cuthbert had been taken from its shrine on the occasion, and of course all the armed force of the diocese was bound to follow. It was borne in front of the army by a monk of Durham. There were many rich caparisons, says the old poem, many beautiful pennons, fluttering from lances, and much neighing of steeds. The hills and valleys were covered with sumpter horses and waggons laden with tents and provisions. The Bishop of Durham in his warlike state appeared, we are told, more like a powerful prince, than a priest or prelate.[11]

At the surrender of the crown of Scotland by John Baliol, which ended this invasion, the bishop negotiated on the part of England. As a trophy of the event, the chair of Schone used on the inauguration of the Scottish monarchs, and containing the stone on

---

9   This list of knights was inserted in the Bolden Book as an additional entry. It is cited at full length by Hutchinson.—*Hist. Durham*, vol. i., p. 220.

10   Onques Artous pour touz ces charmes,
Si beau prisent ne ot de Merlyn.

SIEGE OF KARLAVEROCK; *an old Poem in Norman French.*

11   Robert de Graystanes, Ang. Sac., p. 746, cited by Hutchinson, vol. i. p. 239.

which Jacob dreamed, the palladium of Scotland, was transferred to England and deposited in Westminster Abbey.[12]

In the reign of Edward III. we find the De Wessyngtons still mingling in chivalrous scenes. The name of Sir Stephen de Wessyngton appears on a list of knights (nobles chevaliers) who were to tilt at a tournament at Dunstable in 1334. He bore for his device a golden rose on an azure field.[13]

He was soon called to exercise his arms on a sterner field. In 1346, Edward and his son, the Black Prince, being absent with the armies in France, king David of Scotland invaded Northumberland with a powerful army. Queen Philippa, who had remained in England as regent, immediately took the field, calling the northern prelates and nobles to join her standard. They all hastened to obey. Among the prelates was Hatfield, the Bishop of Durham. The sacred banner of St. Cuthbert was again displayed, and the chivalry of the palatinate assisted at the famous battle of Nevil's cross, near Durham, in which the Scottish army was defeated and king David taken prisoner.

Queen Philippa hastened with a victorious train to cross the sea at Dover, and join king Edward in his camp before Calais. The prelate of Durham accompanied her. His military train consisted of three bannerets, forty-eight knights, one hundred and sixty-four esquires, and eighty archers, on horseback.[14] They all arrived to

---

12 An extract from an inedited poem, cited by Nicolas in his translation of the Siege of Carlavarock, gives a striking picture of the palatinate in these days of its pride and splendor:—

There valour bowed before the rood and book,
    And kneeling knighthood served a prelate lord,
Yet little deigned he on such train to look,
    Or glance of ruth or pity to afford.

There time has heard the peal rung out at night,
    Has seen from every tower the cressets stream,
When the red bale fire on yon western height
    Had roused the warder from his fitful dream.

Has seen old Durham's lion banner float
    O'er the proud bulwark, that, with giant pride
And feet deep plunged amidst the circling moat,
    The efforts of the roving Scot defied.

13 Collect. Topog. et Genealog. T. iv., p. 395.
14 Collier's Eccles. Hist., Book VI., Cent. XIV.

witness the surrender of Calais, (1346) on which occasion queen Philippa distinguished herself by her noble interference in saving the lives of its patriot citizens.

Such were the warlike and stately scenes in which the De Wessyngtons were called to mingle by their feudal duties as knights of the palatinate. A few years after the last event (1350), William, at that time lord of the manor of Wessyngton, had license to settle it and the village upon himself, his wife, and "his own right heirs." He died in 1367, and his son and heir, William, succeeded to the estate. The latter is mentioned under the name of Sir William de Weschington, as one of the knights who sat in the privy council of the county during the episcopate of John Fordham.[15] During this time the whole force of the palatinate was roused to pursue a foray of Scots, under Sir William Douglas, who, having ravaged the country, were returning laden with spoil. It was a fruit of the feud between the Douglases and the Percys. The marauders were overtaken by Hotspur Percy, and then took place the battle of Otterbourne, in which Percy was taken prisoner and Douglas slain.[16]

For upwards of two hundred years the De Wessyngtons had now sat in the councils of the palatinate; had mingled with horse and hound in the stately hunts of its prelates, and followed the banner of St. Cuthbert to the field; but Sir William, just mentioned, was the last of the family that rendered this feudal service. He was the last male of the line to which the inheritance of the manor, by the license granted to his father, was confined. It passed away from the De Wessyngtons, after his death, by the marriage of his only daughter and heir, Dionisia, with Sir William Temple of Studley. By the year 1400 it had become the property of the Blaykestons.[17]

But though the name of De Wessyngton no longer figured on the chivalrous roll of the palatinate, it continued for a time to flourish in the cloisters. In the year 1416, John de Wessyngton was elected prior of the Benedictine convent, attached to the cathedral.

---

15   Hutchinson, vol. ii.

16   Theare the Dowglas lost his life,
        And the Percye was led away.

                              FORDUN. *Quoted by Surtee's Hist. Durham,* vol i.

17   Hutchinson's Durham, vol. ii., p. 489.

The monks of this convent had been licensed by Pope Gregory VII. to perform the solemn duties of the cathedral in place of secular clergy, and William the Conqueror had ordained that the priors of Durham should enjoy all the liberties, dignities and honors of abbots; should hold their lands and churches in their own hands and free disposition, and have the abbot's seat on the left side of the choir—thus taking rank of every one but the bishop.[18]

In the course of three centuries and upwards, which had since elapsed, these honors and privileges had been subject to repeated dispute and encroachment, and the prior had nearly been elbowed out of the abbot's chair by the archdeacon. John de Wessyngton was not a man to submit tamely to such infringements of his rights. He forthwith set himself up as the champion of his priory, and in a learned tract, *de Juribus et Possessionibus Ecclesiae Dunelm*, established the validity of the long controverted claims, and fixed himself firmly in the abbot's chair. His success in this controversy gained him much renown among his brethren of the cowl, and in 1426 he presided at the general chapter of the order of St. Benedict, held at Northampton.

The stout prior of Durham had other disputes with the bishop and the secular clergy touching his ecclesiastical functions, in which he was equally victorious, and several tracts remain in manuscript in the dean and chapter's library; weapons hung up in the church armory as memorials of his polemical battles.

Finally, after fighting divers good fights for the honor of his priory, and filling the abbot's chair for thirty years, he died, to use an ancient phrase, "in all the odor of sanctity," in 1446, and was buried like a soldier on his battle-field, at the door of the north aisle of his church, near to the altar of St. Benedict. On his tombstone was an inscription in brass, now unfortunately obliterated, which may have set forth the valiant deeds of this Washington of the cloisters.[19]

By this time the primitive stock of the De Wessyngtons had separated into divers branches, holding estates in various parts of England; some distinguishing themselves in the learned professions, others receiving knighthood for public services. Their names are to be found honorably recorded in county histories, or engraved on

---

18   Dugdale Monasticon Anglicanum. T. i., p. 231. London ed. 1846.

19   Hutchinson's Durham, vol. ii., passim.

monuments in time-worn churches and cathedrals, those garnering places of English worthies. By degrees the seignorial sign of *de* disappeared from before the family surname, which also varied from Wessyngton to Wassington, Wasshington, and finally, to Washington.[20]

A parish in the county of Durham bears the name as last written, and in this probably the ancient manor of Wessyngton was situated. There is another parish of the name in the county of Sussex.

The branch of the family to which our Washington immediately belongs sprang from Laurence Washington, Esquire, of Gray's Inn, son of John Washington, of Warton in Lancashire. This Laurence Washington was for some time mayor of Northampton, and on the dissolution of the priories by Henry VIII. he received, in 1538, a grant of the manor of Sulgrave, in Northamptonshire, with other lands in the vicinity, all confiscated property formerly belonging to the monastery of St. Andrew's.

Sulgrave remained in the family until 1620, and was commonly called "Washington's manor."[21]

One of the direct descendants of the grantee of Sulgrave was Sir William Washington, of Packington, in the county of Kent.

---

20 "The de came to be omitted," says an old treatise, "when Englishmen and English manners began to prevail upon the recovery of lost credit."—*Restitution of decayed intelligence in antiquities.* Lond. 1634.

About the time of Henry VI., says another treatise, the de or d' was generally dropped from surnames, when the title of *armiger, esquier,* amongst the heads of families, and *generosus,* or *gentylman,* among younger sons was substituted.—*Lower on Surnames,* vol i.

21 The manor of Garsdon in Wiltshire has been mentioned as the homestead of the ancestors of our Washington. This is a mistake. It was the residence of Sir Laurence Washington, second son of the above-mentioned grantee of Sulgrave. Elizabeth, granddaughter of this Sir Laurence, married Robert Shirley, Earl Ferrers and Viscount of Tamworth. Washington became a baptismal name among the Shirleys—several of the Earls Ferrers have borne it.

The writer of these pages visited Sulgrave a few years since. It was in a quiet rural neighborhood, where the farm-houses were quaint and antiquated. A part only of the manor house remained, and was inhabited by a farmer. The Washington crest, in colored glass, was to be seen in a window of what was now the buttery. A window on which the whole family arms was emblazoned had been removed to the residence of the actual proprietor of the manor. Another relic of the ancient manor of the Washingtons was a rookery in a venerable grove hard by. The rooks, those stanch adherents to old family abodes, still hovered and cawed about their hereditary nests. In the pavement of the parish church we were shown a stone slab bearing effigies on plates of brass of Laurence Wasshington, gent., and Anne his wife, and their four sons and eleven daughters. The inscription in black letter was dated 1564.

He married a sister of George Villiers, Duke of Buckingham, the unfortunate favorite of Charles I. This may have attached the Sulgrave Washingtons to the Stuart dynasty, to which they adhered loyally and generously throughout all its vicissitudes. One of the family, Lieutenant Colonel James Washington, took up arms in the cause of king Charles, and lost his life at the siege of Pontefract castle. Another of the Sulgrave line, Sir Henry Washington, son and heir of Sir William, before mentioned, exhibited in the civil wars the old chivalrous spirit of the knights of the palatinate. He served under prince Rupert at the storming of Bristol, in 1643, and when the assailants were beaten off at every point, he broke in with a handful of infantry at a weak part of the wall, made room for the horse to follow, and opened a path to victory.[22]

He distinguished himself still more in 1646, when elevated to the command of Worcester, the governor having been captured by the enemy. It was a time of confusion and dismay. The king had fled from Oxford in disguise and gone to the parliamentary camp at Newark. The royal cause was desperate. In this crisis Sir Henry received a letter from Fairfax, who, with his victorious army, was at Haddington, demanding the surrender of Worcester. The following was Colonel Washington's reply:

SIR,

It is acknowledged by your books and by report of your own quarter, that the king is in some of your armies. That granted, it may be easy for you to procure his Majesty's commands for the disposal of this garrison. Till then I shall make good the trust reposed in me. As for conditions, if I shall be necessitated, I shall make the best I can. The worst I know and fear not; if I had, the profession of a soldier had not been begun, nor so long continued by your Excellency's humble servant,

HENRY WASHINGTON.[23]

---

22 Clarendon, Book vii.
23 Greene's Antiquities of Worcester, p. 273.

In a few days Colonel Whalley invested the city with five thousand troops. Sir Henry dispatched messenger after messenger in quest of the king to know his pleasure. None of them returned. A female emissary was equally unavailing. Week after week elapsed, until nearly three months had expired. Provisions began to fail. The city was in confusion. The troops grew insubordinate. Yet Sir Henry persisted in the defence. General Fairfax, with 1,500 horse and foot, was daily expected. There was not powder enough for an hour's contest should the city be stormed. Still Sir Henry "awaited his Majesty's commands."

At length news arrived that the king had issued an order for the surrender of all towns, castles, and forts. A printed copy of the order was shown to Sir Henry, and on the faith of that document he capitulated (19th July, 1646) on honorable terms, won by his fortitude and perseverance. Those who believe in hereditary virtues may see foreshadowed in the conduct of this Washington of Worcester, the magnanimous constancy of purpose, the disposition to "hope against hope," which bore our Washington triumphantly through the darkest days of our revolution.

We have little note of the Sulgrave branch of the family after the death of Charles I. and the exile of his successor. England, during the protectorate, became an uncomfortable residence to such as had signalized themselves as adherents to the house of Stuart. In 1655, an attempt at a general insurrection drew on them the vengeance of Cromwell. Many of their party who had no share in the conspiracy, yet sought refuge in other lands, where they might live free from molestation. This may have been the case with two brothers, John and Andrew Washington, great-grandsons of the grantee of Sulgrave, and uncles of Sir Henry, the gallant defender of Worcester. John had for some time resided at South Cave, in the East Riding of Yorkshire;[24] but now emigrated with his brother to Virginia; which colony, from its allegiance to the exiled monarch and the Anglican Church had become a favorite resort of the Cavaliers. The brothers arrived in Virginia in 1657, and purchased lands in Westmoreland County, on the northern neck, between the Potomac

---

24   South Cave is near the Humber. "In the vicinity is Cave Castle, an embattled edifice. It has a noble collection of paintings, including a portrait of General Washington, whose ancestors possessed a portion of the estate."—*Lewes, Topog. Dict.* vol. i., p. 530.

and Rappahannock rivers. John married a Miss Anne Pope, of the same county, and took up his residence on Bridges Creek, near where it falls into the Potomac. He became an extensive planter, and, in process of time, a magistrate and member of the House of Burgesses. Having a spark of the old military fire of the family, we find him, as Colonel Washington, leading the Virginia forces, in co-operation with those of Maryland, against a band of Seneca Indians, who were ravaging the settlements along the Potomac. In honor of his public services and private virtues the parish in which he resided was called after him, and still bears the name of Washington. He lies buried in a vault on Bridges Creek, which, for generations, was the family place of sepulture.

The estate continued in the family. His grandson Augustine, the father of our Washington, was born there in 1694. He was twice married; first (April 20th, 1715), to Jane, daughter of Caleb Butler, Esq., of Westmoreland County, by whom he had four children, of whom only two, Lawrence and Augustine, survived the years of childhood; their mother died November 24th, 1728, and was buried in the family vault.

On the 6th of March, 1730, he married in second nuptials, Mary, the daughter of Colonel Ball, a young and beautiful girl, said to be the belle of the Northern Neck. By her he had four sons, George, Samuel, John Augustine, and Charles; and two daughters, Elizabeth, or Betty, as she was commonly called, and Mildred, who died in infancy.

George, the eldest, the subject of this biography, was born on the 22d of February (11th, O. S.), 1732, in the homestead on Bridges Creek. This house commanded a view over many miles of the Potomac, and the opposite shore of Maryland. It had probably been purchased with the property, and was one of the primitive farm-houses of Virginia. The roof was steep, and sloped down into low projecting eaves. It had four rooms on the ground floor, and others in the attic, and an immense chimney at each end. Not a vestige of it remains. Two or three decayed fig trees, with shrubs and vines, linger about the place, and here and there a flower grown wild serves "to mark where a garden has been." Such at least, was the case a few years since; but these may have likewise passed away.

A stone[25] marks the site of the house, and an inscription denotes its being the birthplace of Washington.

We have entered with some minuteness into this genealogical detail; tracing the family step by step through the pages of historical documents for upwards of six centuries; and we have been tempted to do so by the documentary proofs it gives of the lineal and enduring worth of the race. We have shown that, for many generations, and through a variety of eventful scenes, it has maintained an equality of fortune and respectability, and whenever brought to the test has acquitted itself with honor and loyalty. Hereditary rank may be an illusion; but hereditary virtue gives a patent of innate nobleness beyond all the blazonry of the Herald's College.

---

25   Placed there by George W. P. Custis, Esq.

CHAPTER II.

THE HOME OF WASHINGTON'S BOYHOOD—HIS
EARLY EDUCATION—LAWRENCE WASHINGTON AND
HIS CAMPAIGN IN THE WEST INDIES—DEATH OF
WASHINGTON'S FATHER—THE WIDOWED MOTHER
AND HER CHILDREN—SCHOOL EXERCISES.

Not long after the birth of George, his father removed to an estate in Stafford County, opposite Fredericksburg. The house was similar in style to the one at Bridges Creek, and stood on a rising ground overlooking a meadow which bordered the Rappahannock. This was the home of George's boyhood; the meadow was his playground, and the scene of his early athletic sports; but this home, like that in which he was born, has disappeared; the site is only to be traced by fragments of bricks, china, and earthenware.

In those days the means of instruction in Virginia were limited, and it was the custom among the wealthy planters to send their sons to England to complete their education. This was done by Augustine Washington with his eldest son Lawrence, then about fifteen years of age, and whom he no doubt considered the future head of the family. George was yet in early childhood: as his intellect dawned he received the rudiments of education in the best establishment for the purpose that the neighborhood afforded. It was what was called, in popular parlance, an "old field schoolhouse;" humble enough in its pretensions, and kept by one of his father's tenants named Hobby, who moreover was sexton of the parish. The instruction doled out by him must have been of the simplest kind, reading, writing, and ciphering, perhaps; but George had the benefit of mental and moral culture at home, from an excellent father.

Several traditional anecdotes have been given to the world, somewhat prolix and trite, but illustrative of the familiar and practical manner in which Augustine Washington, in the daily intercourse of domestic life, impressed the ductile mind of his child with high maxims of religion and virtue, and imbued him with a spirit of justice and generosity, and above all a scrupulous love of truth.

When George was about seven or eight years old his brother Lawrence returned from England, a well-educated and accomplished youth. There was a difference of fourteen years in their ages, which may have been one cause of the strong attachment which took place between them. Lawrence looked down with a protecting eye upon the boy whose dawning intelligence and perfect rectitude won his regard; while George looked up to his manly and cultivated brother as a model in mind and manners. We call particular attention to this brotherly interchange of affection, from the influence it had on all the future career of the subject of this memoir.

Lawrence Washington had something of the old military spirit of the family, and circumstances soon called it into action. Spanish depredations on British commerce had recently provoked reprisals. Admiral Vernon, commander-in-chief in the West Indies, had accordingly captured Porto Bello, on the Isthmus of Darien. The Spaniards were preparing to revenge the blow; the French were fitting out ships to aid them. Troops were embarked in England for another campaign in the West Indies; a regiment of four battalions was to be raised in the colonies and sent to join them at Jamaica. There was a sudden outbreak of military ardor in the province; the sound of drum and fife was heard in the villages with the parade of recruiting parties. Lawrence Washington, now twenty-two years of age, caught the infection. He obtained a captain's commission in the newly raised regiment, and embarked with it for the West Indies in 1740. He served in the joint expeditions of Admiral Vernon and General Wentworth, in the land forces commanded by the latter, and acquired the friendship and confidence of both of those officers. He was present at the siege of Carthagena, when it was bombarded by the fleet, and when the troops attempted to escalade the citadel. It was an ineffectual attack; the ships could not get near enough to throw their shells into the town, and the scaling ladders proved too short. That part of the attack, however, with which

Lawrence was conc[...]istinguished itself by its bravery. The troops sustained unflinching a destructive fire for several hours, and at length retired with honor, their small force having sustained a loss of about six hundred in killed and wounded.

We have here the secret of that martial spirit so often cited of George in his boyish days. He had seen his brother fitted out for the wars. He had heard by letter and otherwise of the warlike scenes in which he was mingling. All his amusements took a military turn. He made soldiers of his schoolmates; they had their mimic parades, reviews, and sham fights; a boy named William Bustle was sometimes his competitor, but George was commander-in-chief of Hobby's school.

Lawrence Washington returned home in the autumn of 1742, the campaigns in the West Indies being ended, and Admiral Vernon and General Wentworth being recalled to England. It was the intention of Lawrence to rejoin his regiment in that country, and seek promotion in the army, but circumstances completely altered his plans. He formed an attachment to Anne, the eldest daughter of the Honorable William Fairfax, of Fairfax County; his addresses were well received, and they became engaged. Their nuptials were delayed by the sudden and untimely death of his father, which took place on the 12th of April, 1743, after a short but severe attack of gout in the stomach, and when but forty-nine years of age. George had been absent from home on a visit during his father's illness, and just returned in time to receive a parting look of affection.

Augustine Washington left large possessions, distributed by will among his children. To Lawrence, the estate on the banks of the Potomac, with other real property, and several shares in iron works. To Augustine, the second son by the first marriage, the old homestead and estate in Westmoreland. The children by the second marriage were severally well provided for, and George, when he became of age, was to have the house and lands on the Rappahannock.

In the month of July the marriage of Lawrence with Miss Fairfax took place. He now gave up all thoughts of foreign service, and settled himself on his estate on the banks of the Potomac, to which he gave the name of MOUNT VERNON, in honor of the admiral.

Augustine took up his abode at the homestead on Bridges Creek, and married Anne, daughter and co-heiress of William Aylett, Esquire, of Westmoreland County.

George, now eleven years of age, and the other children of the second marriage, had been left under the guardianship of their mother, to whom was intrusted the proceeds of all their property until they should severally come of age. She proved herself worthy of the trust. Endowed with plain, direct good sense, thorough conscientiousness, and prompt decision, she governed her family strictly, but kindly, exacting deference while she inspired affection. George, being her eldest son, was thought to be her favorite, yet she never gave him undue preference, and the implicit deference exacted from him in childhood continued to be habitually observed by him to the day of her death. He inherited from her a high temper and a spirit of command, but her early precepts and example taught him to restrain and govern that temper, and to square his conduct on the exact principles of equity and justice.

Tradition gives an interesting picture of the widow, with her little flock gathered round her, as was her daily wont, reading to them lessons of religion and morality out of some standard work. Her favorite volume was Sir Matthew Hale's Contemplations, moral and divine. The admirable maxims therein contained, for outward action as well as self-government, sank deep into the mind of George, and, doubtless, had a great influence in forming his character. They certainly were exemplified in his conduct throughout life. This mother's manual, bearing his mother's name, Mary Washington, written with her own hand, was ever preserved by him with filial care, and may still be seen in the archives of Mount Vernon. A precious document! Let those who wish to know the moral foundation of his character consult its pages.

Having no longer the benefit of a father's instructions at home, and the scope of tuition of Hobby, the sexton, being too limited for the growing wants of his pupil, George was now sent to reside with Augustine Washington, at Bridges Creek, and enjoy the benefit of a superior school in that neighborhood, kept by a Mr. Williams. His education, however, was plain and practical. He never attempted the learned languages, nor manifested any inclination for rhetoric or belles-lettres. His object, or the object of his friends, seems to have been confined to fitting him for ordinary business. His manuscript school books still exist, and are models of neatness and accuracy. One of them, it is true, a ciphering book, preserved in the library at Mount Vernon, has some school-boy attempts at calligraphy; nondescript birds, executed with a flourish of the pen, or profiles of faces, probably intended for those of his schoolmates; the rest are all grave and business-like. Before he was thirteen years of age he had copied into a volume forms for all kinds of mercantile and legal papers; bills of exchange, notes of hand, deeds, bonds, and the like. This early self-tuition gave him throughout life a lawyer's skill in drafting documents, and a merchant's exactness in keeping accounts; so that all the concerns of his various estates; his dealings with his domestic stewards and foreign agents; his accounts with government, and all his financial transactions are to this day to be seen posted up in books, in his own handwriting, monuments of his method and unwearied accuracy.

He was a self-disciplinarian in physical as well as mental matters, and practised himself in all kinds of athletic exercises, such as running, leaping, wrestling, pitching quoits and tossing bars. His frame even in infancy had been large and powerful, and he now excelled most of his playmates in contests of agility and strength. As a proof of his muscular power, a place is still pointed out at Fredericksburg, near the lower ferry, where, when a boy, he flung a stone across the Rappahannock. In horsemanship too he already excelled, and was ready to back, and able to manage the most fiery steed. Traditional anecdotes remain of his achievements in this respect.

Above all, his inherent probity and the principles of justice on which he regulated all his conduct, even at this early period of life, were soon appreciated by his schoolmates; he was referred to as an umpire in their disputes, and his decisions were never reversed. As he had formerly been military chieftain, he was now legislator of the school; thus displaying in boyhood a type of the future man.

CHAPTER III.

PATERNAL CONDUCT OF AN ELDER BROTHER—
THE FAIRFAX FAMILY—WASHINGTON'S CODE OF
MORALS AND MANNERS—SOLDIERS' TALES—THEIR
INFLUENCE—WASHINGTON PREPARES FOR THE
NAVY—A MOTHER'S OBJECTIONS—RETURN TO
SCHOOL—STUDIES AND EXERCISES—A SCHOOL-
BOY PASSION—THE LOWLAND BEAUTY—LOVE
DITTIES AT MOUNT VERNON—VISIT TO BELVOIR—
LORD FAIRFAX—HIS CHARACTER—FOX-HUNTING
A REMEDY FOR LOVE—PROPOSITION FOR A
SURVEYING EXPEDITION.

The attachment of Lawrence Washington to his brother George seems to have acquired additional strength and tenderness on their father's death; he now took a truly paternal interest in his concerns, and had him as frequently as possible a guest at Mount Vernon. Lawrence had deservedly become a popular and leading personage in the country. He was a member of the House of Burgesses, and Adjutant General of the district, with the rank of major, and a regular salary. A frequent sojourn with him brought George into familiar intercourse with the family of his father-in-law, the Hon. William Fairfax, who resided at a beautiful seat called Belvoir, a few miles below Mount Vernon, and on the same woody ridge bordering the Potomac.

William Fairfax was a man of liberal education and intrinsic worth; he had seen much of the world, and his mind had been enriched and ripened by varied and adventurous experience. Of an ancient English family in Yorkshire, he had entered the army at the age of twenty-one; had served with honor both in the East and West Indies, and officiated as governor of New Providence, after having aided in rescuing it from pirates. For some years past he had resided in Virginia, to manage the immense landed estates of his cousin, Lord Fairfax, and lived at Belvoir in the style of an English country gentleman, surrounded by an intelligent and cultivated family of sons and daughters.

An intimacy with a family like this, in which the frankness and simplicity of rural and colonial life were united with European refinement, could not but have a beneficial effect in moulding the character and manners of a somewhat homebred schoolboy. It was probably his intercourse with them, and his ambition to acquit himself well in their society, that set him upon compiling a code of morals and manners which still exists in a manuscript in his own handwriting, entitled "rules for behavior in company and conversation." It is extremely minute and circumstantial. Some of the rules for personal deportment extend to such trivial matters, and are so quaint and formal, as almost to provoke a smile; but in the main, a better manual of conduct could not be put into the hands of a youth. The whole code evinces that rigid propriety and self control to which he subjected himself, and by which he brought all the impulses of a somewhat ardent temper under conscientious government.

Other influences were brought to bear on George during his visit at Mount Vernon. His brother Lawrence still retained some of his military inclinations, fostered no doubt by his post of Adjutant General. William Fairfax, as we have shown, had been a soldier, and in many trying scenes. Some of Lawrence's comrades of the provincial regiment, who had served with him in the West Indies, were occasional visitors at Mount Vernon; or a ship of war, possibly one of Vernon's old fleet, would anchor in the Potomac, and its officers be welcome guests at the tables of Lawrence and his father-in-law. Thus military scenes on sea and shore would become the topics of conversation. The capture of Porto Bello; the bombardment of Carthagena; old stories of cruisings in the East and West Indies, and campaigns against the pirates. We can picture to ourselves George, a grave and earnest boy, with an expanding intellect, and a deep-seated passion for enterprise, listening to such conversations with a kindling spirit and a growing desire for military life. In this way most probably was produced that desire to enter the navy which he evinced when about fourteen years of age. The opportunity for gratifying it appeared at hand. Ships of war frequented the colonies, and at times, as we have hinted, were anchored in the Potomac. The inclination was encouraged by Lawrence Washington and Mr. Fairfax. Lawrence retained pleasant recollections of his cruisings in the fleet of Admiral Vernon, and considered the naval service a popular path to fame and fortune. George was at a suitable age to enter the navy. The great difficulty was to procure the assent of his mother. She was brought, however, to acquiesce; a midshipman's warrant was obtained, and it is even said that the luggage of the youth was actually on board of a man of war, anchored in the river just below Mount Vernon.

At the eleventh hour the mother's heart faltered. This was her eldest born. A son, whose strong and steadfast character promised to be a support to herself and a protection to her other children. The thought of his being completely severed from her and exposed to the hardships and perils of a boisterous profession, overcame even her resolute mind, and at her urgent remonstrances the nautical scheme was given up.

To school, therefore, George returned, and continued his studies for nearly two years longer, devoting himself especially to mathematics, and accomplishing himself in those branches calculated to fit him either for civil or military service. Among these, one of the most important in the actual state of the country was land surveying. In this he schooled himself thoroughly, using the highest processes of the art; making surveys about the neighborhood, and keeping regular field books, some of which we have examined, in which the boundaries and measurements of the fields surveyed were carefully entered, and diagrams made, with a neatness and exactness as if the whole related to important land transactions instead of being mere school exercises. Thus, in his earliest days, there was perseverance and completeness in all his undertakings. Nothing was left half done, or done in a hurried and slovenly manner. The habit of mind thus cultivated continued throughout life; so that however complicated his tasks and overwhelming his cares, in the arduous and hazardous situations in which he was often placed, he found time to do every thing, and to do it well. He had acquired the magic of method, which of itself works wonders.

In one of these manuscript memorials of his practical studies and exercises, we have come upon some documents singularly in contrast with all that we have just cited, and, with his apparently unromantic character. In a word, there are evidences in his own handwriting, that, before he was fifteen years of age, he had conceived a passion for some unknown beauty, so serious as to disturb his otherwise well-regulated mind, and to make him really unhappy. Why this juvenile attachment was a source of unhappiness we have no positive means of ascertaining. Perhaps the object of it may have considered him a mere school-boy, and treated him as such; or his own shyness may have been in his way, and his "rules for behavior and conversation" may as yet have sat awkwardly on him, and rendered him formal and ungainly when he most sought to please. Even in later years he was apt to be silent and embarrassed in female society. "He was a very bashful young man," said an old lady, whom he used to visit when they were both in their nonage. "I used often to wish that he would talk more."

Whatever may have been the reason, this early attachment seems to have been a source of poignant discomfort to him. It clung to him after he took a final leave of school in the autumn of 1747, and went to reside with his brother Lawrence at Mount Vernon. Here he continued his mathematical studies and his practice in surveying, disturbed at times by recurrences of his unlucky passion. Though by no means of a poetical temperament, the waste pages of his journal betray several attempts to pour forth his amorous sorrows in verse. They are mere common-place rhymes, such as lovers at his age are apt to write, in which he bewails his "poor restless heart, wounded by Cupid's dart," and "bleeding for one who remains pitiless of his griefs and woes."

The tenor of some of his verses induce us to believe that he never told his love; but, as we have already surmised, was prevented by his bashfulness.

"Ah, woe is me, that I should love and conceal;
Long have I wished and never dare reveal."

It is difficult to reconcile one's self to the idea of the cool and sedate Washington, the great champion of American liberty, a woe-worn lover in his youthful days, "sighing like furnace," and inditing plaintive verses about the groves of Mount Vernon. We are glad of an opportunity, however, of penetrating to his native feelings, and finding that under his studied decorum and reserve he had a heart of flesh throbbing with the warm impulses of human nature.

Being a favorite of Sir William Fairfax, he was now an occasional inmate of Belvoir. Among the persons at present residing there was Thomas, Lord Fairfax, cousin of William Fairfax, and of whose immense landed property the latter was the agent. As this nobleman was one of Washington's earliest friends, and, in some degree the founder of his fortunes, his character and history are worthy of especial note.

Lord Fairfax was now nearly sixty years of age, upwards of six feet high, gaunt and raw-boned, near-sighted, with light gray eyes, sharp features and an aquiline nose. However ungainly his present appearance, he had figured to advantage in London life in his younger days. He had received his education at the university of Oxford, where he acquitted himself with credit. He afterwards held a commission, and remained for some time in a regiment of horse called the Blues. His title and connections, of course, gave him access to the best society, in which he acquired additional currency by contributing a paper or two to Addison's Spectator, then in great vogue.

In the height of his fashionable career, he became strongly attached to a young lady of rank; paid his addresses, and was accepted. The wedding day was fixed; the wedding dresses were provided; together with servants and equipages for the matrimonial establishment. Suddenly the lady broke her engagement. She had been dazzled by the superior brilliancy of a ducal coronet.

It was a cruel blow, alike to the affection and pride of Lord Fairfax, and wrought a change in both character and conduct. From that time he almost avoided the sex, and became shy and embarrassed in their society, excepting among those with whom he was connected or particularly intimate. This may have been among the reasons which ultimately induced him to abandon the gay world and bury himself in the wilds of America. He made a voyage to Virginia about the year 1739, to visit his vast estates there. These he inherited from his mother, Catharine, daughter of Thomas, Lord Culpepper, to whom they had been granted by Charles II. The original grant was for all the lands lying between the Rappahannock and Potomac rivers; meaning thereby, it is said, merely the territory on the northern neck, east of the Blue Ridge. His lordship, however, discovering that the Potomac headed in the Allegany Mountains, returned to England and claimed a correspondent definition of his grant. It was arranged by compromise; extending his domain into the Allegany Mountains, and comprising, among other lands, a great portion of the Shenandoah Valley.

Lord Fairfax had been delighted with his visit to Virginia. The amenity of the climate, the magnificence of the forest scenery, the abundance of game,—all pointed it out as a favored land. He was pleased, too, with the frank, cordial character of the Virginians, and their independent mode of life; and returned to it with the resolution of taking up his abode there for the remainder of his days. His early disappointment in love was the cause of some eccentricities in his conduct; yet he was amiable and courteous in his manners, and of a liberal and generous spirit.

Another inmate of Belvoir at this time was George William Fairfax, about twenty-two years of age, the eldest son of the proprietor. He had been educated in England, and since his return had married a daughter of Colonel Carey, of Hampton, on James River. He had recently brought home his bride and her sister to his father's house.

The merits of Washington were known and appreciated by the Fairfax family. Though not quite sixteen years of age, he no longer seemed a boy, nor was he treated as such. Tall, athletic, and manly for his years, his early self-training, and the code of conduct he had devised, gave a gravity and decision to his conduct; his frankness and modesty inspired cordial regard, and the melancholy, of which he speaks, may have produced a softness in his manner calculated to win favor in ladies' eyes. According to his own account, the female society by which he was surrounded had a soothing effect on that melancholy. The charms of Miss Carey, the sister of the bride, seem even to have caused a slight fluttering in his bosom; which, however, was constantly rebuked by the remembrance of his former passion—so at least we judge from letters to his youthful confidants, rough drafts of which are still to be seen in his tell-tale journal.

To one whom he addresses as his dear friend Robin, he writes: "My residence is at present at his lordship's, where I might, was my heart disengaged, pass my time very pleasantly, as there's a very agreeable young lady lives in the same house (Col. George Fairfax's wife's sister); but as that's only adding fuel to fire, it makes me the more uneasy, for by often and unavoidably being in company with her, revives my former passion for your Lowland Beauty; whereas was I to live more retired from young women, I might in some measure alleviate my sorrows, by burying that chaste and troublesome passion in the grave of oblivion," &c.

Similar avowals he makes to another of his young correspondents, whom he styles, "Dear friend John;" as also to a female confidant, styled "Dear Sally," to whom he acknowledges that the company of the "very agreeable young lady, sister-in-law of Col. George Fairfax," in a great measure cheers his sorrow and dejectedness.

The object of this early passion is not positively known. Tradition states that the "lowland beauty" was a Miss Grimes, of Westmoreland, afterwards Mrs. Lee, and mother of General Henry Lee, who figured in revolutionary history as Light Horse Harry, and was always a favorite with Washington, probably from the recollections of his early tenderness for the mother.

Whatever may have been the soothing effect of the female society by which he was surrounded at Belvoir, the youth found a more effectual remedy for his love melancholy in the company of Lord Fairfax. His lordship was a staunch fox-hunter, and kept horses and hounds in the English style. The hunting season had arrived. The neighborhood abounded with sport; but fox-hunting in Virginia required bold and skilful horsemanship. He found Washington as bold as himself in the saddle, and as eager to follow the hounds. He forthwith took him into peculiar favor; made him his hunting companion; and it was probably under the tuition of this hard-riding old nobleman that the youth imbibed that fondness for the chase for which he was afterwards remarked.

Their fox-hunting intercourse was attended with more important results. His lordship's possessions beyond the Blue Ridge had never been regularly settled nor surveyed. Lawless intruders— squatters, as they were called—were planting themselves along the finest streams and in the richest valleys, and virtually taking possession of the country. It was the anxious desire of Lord Fairfax to have these lands examined, surveyed, and portioned out into lots, preparatory to ejecting these interlopers or bringing them to reasonable terms. In Washington, notwithstanding his youth, he beheld one fit for the task—having noticed the exercises in surveying which he kept up while at Mount Vernon, and the aptness and exactness with which every process was executed. He was well calculated, too, by his vigor and activity, his courage and hardihood, to cope with the wild country to be surveyed, and with its still wilder inhabitants. The proposition had only to be offered to Washington to be eagerly accepted. It was the very kind of occupation for which he had been diligently training himself. All the preparations required by one of his simple habits were soon made, and in a very few days he was ready for his first expedition into the wilderness.

CHAPTER IV.

EXPEDITION BEYOND THE BLUE RIDGE—THE
VALLEY OF THE SHENANDOAH—LORD HALIFAX—
LODGE IN THE WILDERNESS—SURVEYING—LIFE
IN THE BACKWOODS—INDIANS—WAR DANCE—
GERMAN SETTLERS—RETURN HOME—WASHINGTON
AS PUBLIC SURVEYOR—SOJOURN AT GREENWAY
COURT—HORSES, HOUNDS, AND BOOKS—RUGGED
EXPERIENCE AMONG THE MOUNTAINS.

It was in the month of March (1748), and just after he had
completed his sixteenth year, that Washington set out on horseback
on this surveying expedition, in company with George William
Fairfax. Their route lay by Ashley's Gap, a pass through the Blue
Ridge, that beautiful line of mountains which, as yet, almost formed
the western frontier of inhabited Virginia. Winter still lingered
on the tops of the mountains, whence melting snows sent down
torrents, which swelled the rivers and occasionally rendered them
almost impassable. Spring, however, was softening the lower parts
of the landscape and smiling in the valleys.

They entered the great valley of Virginia, where it is about
twenty-five miles wide; a lovely and temperate region, diversified
by gentle swells and slopes, admirably adapted to cultivation. The
Blue Ridge bounds it on one side, the North Mountain, a ridge
of the Alleganies, on the other; while through it flows that bright
and abounding river, which, on account of its surpassing beauty,
was named by the Indians the Shenandoah—that is to say, "the
daughter of the stars."

The first station of the travellers was at a kind of lodge in
the wilderness, where the steward or land-bailiff of Lord Halifax
resided, with such negroes as were required for farming purposes,

and which Washington terms "his lordship's quarter." It was situated not far from the Shenandoah, and about twelve miles from the site of the present town of Winchester.

In a diary kept with his usual minuteness, Washington speaks with delight of the beauty of the trees and the richness of the land in the neighborhood, and of his riding through a noble grove of sugar maples on the banks of the Shenandoah; and at the present day, the magnificence of the forests which still exist in this favored region justifies his eulogium.

He looked around, however, with an eye to the profitable rather than the poetical. The gleam of poetry and romance, inspired by his "lowland beauty," occurs no more. The real business of life has commenced with him. His diary affords no food for fancy. Every thing is practical. The qualities of the soil, the relative value of sites and localities, are faithfully recorded. In these his early habits of observation and his exercises in surveying had already made him a proficient.

His surveys commenced in the lower part of the valley, some distance above the junction of the Shenandoah with the Potomac, and extended for many miles along the former river. Here and there partial "clearings" had been made by squatters and hardy pioneers, and their rude husbandry had produced abundant crops of grain, hemp, and tobacco; civilization, however, had hardly yet entered the valley, if we may judge from the note of a night's lodging at the house of one of the settlers—Captain Hite, near the site of the present town of Winchester. Here, after supper, most of the company stretched themselves in backwood style, before the fire; but Washington was shown into a bed-room. Fatigued with a hard day's work at surveying, he soon undressed; but instead of being nestled between sheets in a comfortable bed, as at the maternal home, or at Mount Vernon, he found himself on a couch of matted straw, under a threadbare blanket, swarming with unwelcome bedfellows. After tossing about for a few moments, he was glad to put on his clothes again, and rejoin his companions before the fire.

Such was his first experience of life in the wilderness; he soon, however, accustomed himself to "rough it," and adapt himself to fare of all kinds, though he generally preferred a bivouac before a fire, in the open air, to the accommodations of a woodman's cabin. Proceeding down the valley to the banks of the Potomac, they found that river so much swollen by the rain which had fallen among the Alleganies, as to be unfordable. To while away the time until it should subside, they made an excursion to examine certain warm springs in a valley among the mountains, since called the Berkeley Springs. There they camped out at night, under the stars; the diary makes no complaint of their accommodations; and their camping-ground is now known as Bath, one of the favorite watering-places of Virginia. One of the warm springs was subsequently appropriated by Lord Fairfax to his own use, and still bears his name.

After watching in vain for the river to subside, they procured a canoe, on which they crossed to the Maryland side; swimming their horses. A weary day's ride of forty miles up the left side of the river, in a continual rain, and over what Washington pronounces the worst road ever trod by man or beast, brought them to the house of a Colonel Cresap, opposite the south branch of the Potomac, where they put up for the night.

Here they were detained three or four days by inclement weather. On the second day they were surprised by the appearance of a war party of thirty Indians, bearing a scalp as a trophy. A little liquor procured the spectacle of a war-dance. A large space was cleared, and a fire made in the centre, round which the warriors took their seats. The principal orator made a speech, reciting their recent exploits, and rousing them to triumph. One of the warriors started up as if from sleep, and began a series of movements, half-grotesque, half-tragical; the rest followed. For music, one savage drummed on a deerskin, stretched over a pot half filled with water; another rattled a gourd, containing a few shot, and decorated with a horse's tail. Their strange outcries, and uncouth forms and garbs, seen by the glare of the fire, and their whoops and yells, made them appear more like demons than human beings. All this savage gambol was no novelty to Washington's companions, experienced in frontier life; but to the youth, fresh from school, it was a strange spectacle, which he sat contemplating with deep interest, and carefully noted down in his journal. It will be found that he soon made himself acquainted with the savage character, and became expert at dealing with these inhabitants of the wilderness.

From this encampment the party proceeded to the mouth of Patterson's Creek, where they recrossed the river in a canoe, swimming their horses as before. More than two weeks were now passed by them in the wild mountainous regions of Frederick County, and about the south branch of the Potomac, surveying lands and laying out lots, camped out the greater part of the time, and subsisting on wild turkeys and other game. Each one was his own cook; forked sticks served for spits, and chips of wood for dishes. The weather was unsettled. At one time their tent was blown down; at another they were driven out of it by smoke; now they were drenched with rain, and now the straw on which Washington was sleeping caught fire, and he was awakened by a companion just in time to escape a scorching.

The only variety to this camp life was a supper at the house of one Solomon Hedge, Esquire, his majesty's justice of the peace, where there were no forks at table, nor any knives, but such as the guests brought in their pockets. During their surveys they were followed by numbers of people, some of them squatters, anxious, doubtless, to procure a cheap title to the land they had appropriated; others, German emigrants, with their wives and children, seeking a new home in the wilderness. Most of the latter could not speak English; but when spoken to, answered in their native tongue. They appeared to Washington ignorant as Indians, and uncouth, but "merry, and full of antic tricks." Such were the progenitors of the sturdy yeomanry now inhabiting those parts, many of whom still preserve their strong German characteristics.

"I have not slept above three or four nights in a bed," writes Washington to one of his young friends at home, "but after walking a good deal all the day I have lain down before the fire upon a little straw or fodder, or a bear skin, whichever was to be had, with man, wife, and children, like dogs and cats; and happy is he who gets the berth nearest the fire."

Having completed his surveys, he set forth from the south branch of the Potomac on his return homeward; crossed the mountains to the great Cacapehon; traversed the Shenandoah valley; passed through the Blue Ridge, and on the 12th of April found himself once more at Mount Vernon. For his services he received, according to his note-book, a doubloon per day when actively employed, and sometimes six pistoles.[26]

---

26   A pistole is $3.60.

The manner in which he had acquitted himself in this arduous expedition, and his accounts of the country surveyed, gave great satisfaction to Lord Fairfax, who shortly afterwards moved across the Blue Ridge, and took up his residence at the place heretofore noted as his "quarters." Here he laid out a manor, containing ten thousand acres of arable grazing lands, vast meadows, and noble forests, and projected a spacious manor house, giving to the place the name of Greenway Court.

It was probably through the influence of Lord Fairfax that Washington received the appointment of public surveyor. This conferred authority on his surveys, and entitled them to be recorded in the county offices, and so invariably correct have these surveys been found that, to this day, wherever any of them stand on record, they receive implicit credit.

For three years he continued in this occupation, which proved extremely profitable, from the vast extent of country to be surveyed and the very limited number of public surveyors. It made him acquainted, also, with the country, the nature of the soil in various parts, and the value of localities; all which proved advantageous to him in his purchases in after years. Many of the finest parts of the Shenandoah valley are yet owned by members of the Washington family.

While thus employed for months at a time surveying the lands beyond the Blue Ridge, he was often an inmate of Greenway Court. The projected manor house was never even commenced. On a green knoll overshadowed by trees was a long stone building one story in height, with dormer windows, two wooden belfries, chimneys studded with swallow and martin coops, and a roof sloping down in the old Virginia fashion, into low projecting eaves that formed a verandah the whole length of the house. It was probably the house originally occupied by his steward or land agent, but was now devoted to hospitable purposes, and the reception of guests. As to his lordship, it was one of his many eccentricities, that he never slept in the main edifice, but lodged apart in a wooden house not much above twelve feet square. In a small building was his office, where quitrents were given, deeds drawn, and business transacted with his tenants.

About the knoll were out-houses for his numerous servants, black and white, with stables for saddle-horses and hunters, and kennels for his hounds, for his lordship retained his keen hunting propensities, and the neighborhood abounded in game. Indians, half-breeds, and leathern-clad woodsmen loitered about the place, and partook of the abundance of the kitchen. His lordship's table was plentiful but plain, and served in the English fashion.

Here Washington had full opportunity, in the proper seasons, of indulging his fondness for field sports, and once more accompanying his lordship in the chase. The conversation of Lord Fairfax, too, was full of interest and instruction to an inexperienced youth, from his cultivated talents, his literary taste, and his past intercourse with the best society of Europe, and its most distinguished authors. He had brought books, too, with him into the wilderness, and from Washington's diary we find that during his sojourn here he was diligently reading the history of England, and the essays of the Spectator.

Such was Greenway Court in these its palmy days. We visited it recently and found it tottering to its fall, mouldering in the midst of a magnificent country, where nature still flourishes in full luxuriance and beauty.

Three or four years were thus passed by Washington, the greater part of the time beyond the Blue Ridge, but occasionally with his brother Lawrence at Mount Vernon. His rugged and toilsome expeditions in the mountains, among rude scenes and rough people, inured him to hardships, and made him apt at expedients; while his intercourse with his cultivated brother, and with the various members of the Fairfax family, had a happy effect in toning up his mind and manners, and counteracting the careless and self-indulgent habitudes of the wilderness.

CHAPTER V.

ENGLISH AND FRENCH CLAIMS TO THE OHIO
VALLEY—WILD STATE OF THE COUNTRY—
PROJECTS OF SETTLEMENTS—THE OHIO
COMPANY—ENLIGHTENED VIEWS OF LAWRENCE
WASHINGTON—FRENCH RIVALRY—CELERON DE
BIENVILLE—HIS SIGNS OF OCCUPATION—HUGH
CRAWFORD—GEORGE CROGHAN, A VETERAN
TRADER, AND MONTOUR, HIS INTERPRETER—THEIR
MISSION FROM PENNSYLVANIA TO THE OHIO
TRIBES—CHRISTOPHER GIST, THE PIONEER OF THE
YADKIN—AGENT OF THE OHIO COMPANY—HIS
EXPEDITION TO THE FRONTIER—REPROBATE
TRADERS AT LOGSTOWN—NEGOTIATIONS WITH
THE INDIANS—SCENES IN THE OHIO COUNTRY—
DIPLOMACY AT PIQUA—KEGS OF BRANDY AND
ROLLS OF TOBACCO—GIST'S RETURN ACROSS
KENTUCKY—A DESERTED HOME—FRENCH
SCHEMES—CAPTAIN JONCAIRE, A DIPLOMAT OF THE
WILDERNESS—HIS SPEECH AT LOGSTOWN—THE
INDIANS' LAND—"WHERE?"

During the time of Washington's surveying campaigns among
the mountains, a grand colonizing scheme had been set on foot,
destined to enlist him in hardy enterprises, and in some degree to
shape the course of his future fortunes.

The treaty of peace concluded at Aix-la-Chapelle, which
had put an end to the general war of Europe, had left undefined
the boundaries between the British and French possessions in
America; a singular remissness, considering that they had long
been a subject in dispute, and a cause of frequent conflicts in the

colonies. Immense regions were still claimed by both nations, and each was now eager to forestall the other by getting possession of them, and strengthening its claim by occupancy.

The most desirable of these regions lay west of the Allegany Mountains, extending from the lakes to the Ohio, and embracing the valley of that river and its tributary streams. An immense territory, possessing a salubrious climate, fertile soil, fine hunting and fishing grounds, and facilities by lakes and rivers for a vast internal commerce.

The French claimed all this country quite to the Allegany mountains by the right of discovery. In 1673, Padre Marquette, with his companion, Joliet, of Quebec, both subjects of the crown of France, had passed down the Mississippi in a canoe quite to the Arkansas, thereby, according to an alleged maxim in the law of nations, establishing the right of their sovereign, not merely to the river so discovered and its adjacent lands, but to all the country drained by its tributary streams, of which the Ohio was one; a claim, the ramifications of which might be spread, like the meshes of a web, over half the continent.

To this illimitable claim the English opposed a right derived, at second hand, from a traditionary Indian conquest. A treaty, they said, had been made at Lancaster, in 1744, between commissioners from Pennsylvania, Maryland, and Virginia, and the Iroquois, or Six Nations, whereby the latter, for four hundred pounds, gave up all right and title to the land west of the Allegany Mountains, even to the Mississippi, which land, *according to their traditions*, had been conquered by their forefathers.

It is undoubtedly true that such a treaty was made, and such a pretended transfer of title did take place, under the influence of spirituous liquors; but it is equally true that the Indians in question did not, at the time, possess an acre of the land conveyed; and that the tribes actually in possession scoffed at their pretensions, and claimed the country as their own from time immemorial.

Such were the shadowy foundations of claims which the two nations were determined to maintain to the uttermost, and which ripened into a series of wars, ending in a loss to England of a great part of her American possessions, and to France of the whole.

As yet in the region in question there was not a single white settlement. Mixed Iroquois tribes of Delawares, Shawnees, and

Mingoes, had migrated into it early in the century from the French settlements in Canada, and taken up their abodes about the Ohio and its branches. The French pretended to hold them under their protection; but their allegiance, if ever acknowledged, had been sapped of late years by the influx of fur traders from Pennsylvania. These were often rough, lawless men; half Indians in dress and habits, prone to brawls, and sometimes deadly in their feuds. They were generally in the employ of some trader, who, at the head of his retainers and a string of pack-horses, would make his way over mountains and through forests to the banks of the Ohio, establish his head-quarters in some Indian town, and disperse his followers to traffic among the hamlets, hunting-camps and wigwams, exchanging blankets, gaudy colored cloth, trinketry, powder, shot, and rum, for valuable furs and peltry. In this way a lucrative trade with these western tribes was springing up and becoming monopolized by the Pennsylvanians.

To secure a participation in this trade, and to gain a foothold in this desirable region, became now the wish of some of the most intelligent and enterprising men of Virginia and Maryland, among whom were Lawrence and Augustine Washington. With these views they projected a scheme, in connection with John Hanbury, a wealthy London merchant, to obtain a grant of land from the British government, for the purpose of forming settlements or colonies beyond the Alleganies. Government readily countenanced a scheme by which French encroachments might be forestalled, and prompt and quiet possession secured of the great Ohio valley. An association was accordingly chartered in 1749, by the name of "the Ohio Company," and five hundred thousand acres of land was granted to it west of the Alleganies; between the Monongahela and Kanawha rivers; though part of the land might be taken up north of the Ohio, should it be deemed expedient. The company were to pay no quitrent for ten years; but they were to select two fifths of their lands immediately; to settle one hundred families upon them within seven years; to build a fort at their own expense, and maintain a sufficient garrison in it for defence against the Indians.

Mr. Thomas Lee, president of the council of Virginia, took the lead in the concerns of the company at the outset, and by many has been considered its founder. On his death, which soon took place, Lawrence Washington had the chief management. His enlightened mind and liberal spirit shone forth in his earliest arrangements. He wished to form the settlements with Germans from Pennsylvania. Being dissenters, however, they would be obliged, on becoming residents within the jurisdiction of Virginia, to pay parish rates, and maintain a clergyman of the Church of England, though they might not understand his language nor relish his doctrines. Lawrence sought to have them exempted from this double tax on purse and conscience.

"It has ever been my opinion," said he, "and I hope it ever will be, that restraints on conscience are cruel in regard to those on whom they are imposed, and injurious to the country imposing them. England, Holland, and Prussia I may quote as examples, and much more Pennsylvania, which has nourished under that delightful liberty, so as to become the admiration of every man who considers the short time it has been settled. . . . This colony (Virginia) was greatly settled in the latter part of Charles the First's time, and during the usurpation by the zealous churchmen; and that spirit, which was then brought in, has ever since continued; so that, except a few Quakers, we have no dissenters. But what has been the consequence? We have increased by slow degrees, whilst our neighboring colonies, whose natural advantages are greatly inferior to ours, have become populous."

Such were the enlightened views of this brother of our Washington, to whom the latter owed much of his moral and mental training. The company proceeded to make preparations for their colonizing scheme. Goods were imported from England suited to the Indian trade, or for presents to the chiefs. Rewards were promised to veteran warriors and hunters among the natives acquainted with the woods and mountains, for the best route to the Ohio. Before the company had received its charter, however, the French were in the field. Early in 1749, the Marquis de la Galisonniere, Governor of Canada, despatched Celeron de Bienville, an intelligent officer, at the head of three hundred men, to the banks of the Ohio, to make peace, as he said, between the tribes that had become embroiled with each other during the late war, and to renew the French possession of the country. Celeron de Bienville distributed presents among the Indians, made speeches reminding them of former friendship, and warned them not to trade with the English.

He furthermore nailed leaden plates to trees, and buried others in the earth, at the confluence of the Ohio and its tributaries, bearing inscriptions purporting that all the lands on both sides of the rivers to their sources appertained, as in foregone times, to the crown of France.[27] The Indians gazed at these mysterious plates with wondering eyes, but surmised their purport. "They mean to steal our country from us," murmured they; and they determined to seek protection from the English.

Celeron finding some traders from Pennsylvania trafficking among the Indians, he summoned them to depart, and wrote by them to James Hamilton, Governor of Pennsylvania, telling him the object of his errand to those parts, and his surprise at meeting with English traders in a country to which England had no pretensions; intimating that, in future, any intruders of the kind would be rigorously dealt with.

His letter, and a report of his proceedings on the Ohio, roused the solicitude of the governor and council of Pennsylvania, for the protection of their Indian trade. Shortly afterwards, one Hugh Crawford, who had been trading with the Miami tribes on the Wabash, brought a message from them, speaking of the promises and threats with which the French were endeavoring to shake their faith, but assuring the governor that their friendship for the English "would last while the sun and moon ran round the world." This message was accompanied by three strings of wampum.

Governor Hamilton knew the value of Indian friendship, and suggested to the assembly that it would be better to clinch it with presents, and that as soon as possible. An envoy accordingly was sent off early in October, who was supposed to have great influence among the western tribes. This was one George Croghan, a veteran trader, shrewd and sagacious, who had been frequently to the Ohio country with pack-horses and followers, and made himself popular among the Indians by dispensing presents with a lavish hand. He was accompanied by Andrew Montour, a Canadian of half Indian descent, who was to act as interpreter. They were provided with a small present for the emergency; but were to convoke a meeting of all the tribes at Logstown, on the Ohio, early in the ensuing

---

27   One of these plates, bearing date August 16, 1749, was found in recent years at the confluence of the Muskingum with the Ohio.

spring, to receive an ample present which would be provided by the assembly.

It was some time later in the same autumn that the Ohio company brought their plans into operation, and despatched an agent to explore the lands upon the Ohio and its branches as low as the Great Falls, take note of their fitness for cultivation, of the passes of the mountains, the courses and bearings of the rivers, and the strength and disposition of the native tribes. The man chosen for the purpose was Christopher Gist, a hardy pioneer, experienced in woodcraft and Indian life, who had his home on the banks of the Yadkin, near the boundary line of Virginia and North Carolina. He was allowed a woodsman or two for the service of the expedition. He set out on the 31st of October, from the banks of the Potomac, by an Indian path which the hunters had pointed out, leading from Wills' Creek, since called Fort Cumberland, to the Ohio. Indian paths and buffalo tracks are the primitive highways of the wilderness. Passing the Juniata, he crossed the ridges of the Allegany, arrived at Shannopin, a Delaware village on the south-east side of the Ohio, or rather of that upper branch of it, now called the Allegany, swam his horses across that river, and descending along its valley arrived at Logstown, an important Indian village a little below the site of the present city of Pittsburg. Here usually resided Tanacharisson, a Seneca chief of great note, being head sachem of the mixed tribes who had migrated to the Ohio and its branches. He was generally surnamed the half-king, being subordinate to the Iroquois confederacy. The chief was absent at this time, as were most of his people, it being the hunting season. George Croghan, the envoy from Pennsylvania, with Montour his interpreter, had passed through Logstown a week previously, on his way to the Twightwees and other tribes, on the Miami branch of the Ohio. Scarce any one was to be seen about the village but some of Croghan's rough people, whom he had left behind—"reprobate Indian traders," as Gist terms them. They regarded the latter with a jealous eye, suspecting him of some rivalship in trade, or designs on the Indian lands; and intimated significantly that "he would never go home safe."

Gist knew the meaning of such hints from men of this stamp in the lawless depths of the wilderness; but quieted their suspicions by letting them know that he was on public business, and on good terms with their great man, George Croghan, to whom he despatched a letter. He took his departure from Logstown, however, as soon as possible, preferring, as he said, the solitude of the wilderness to such company.

At Beaver Creek, a few miles below the village, he left the river and struck into the interior of the present State of Ohio. Here he overtook George Croghan at Muskingum, a town of Wyandots and Mingoes. He had ordered all the traders in his employ who were scattered among the Indian villages, to rally at this town, where he had hoisted the English flag over his residence, and over that of the sachem. This was in consequence of the hostility of the French who had recently captured, in the neighborhood, three white men in the employ of Frazier, an Indian trader, and had carried them away prisoners to Canada.

Gist was well received by the people of Muskingum. They were indignant at the French violation of their territories, and the capture of their "English brothers." They had not forgotten the conduct of Celeron de Bienville in the previous year, and the mysterious plates which he had nailed against trees and sunk in the ground. "If the French claim the rivers which run into the lakes," said they, "those which run into the Ohio belong to us and to our brothers the English." And they were anxious that Gist should settle among them, and build a fort for their mutual defence.

A council of the nation was now held, in which Gist invited them, in the name of the Governor of Virginia, to visit that province, where a large present of goods awaited them, sent by their father, the great king, over the water to his Ohio children. The invitation was graciously received, but no answer could be given until a grand council of the western tribes had been held, which was to take place at Logstown in the ensuing spring.

Similar results attended visits made by Gist and Croghan to the Delawares and the Shawnees at their villages about the Scioto River; all promised to be at the gathering at Logstown. From the Shawnee village, near the mouth of the Scioto, the two emissaries shaped their course north two hundred miles, crossed the Great Moneami, or Miami River, on a raft, swimming their horses; and on the 17th of February arrived at the Indian town of Piqua.

These journeyings had carried Gist about a wide extent of country beyond the Ohio. It was rich and level, watered with streams and rivulets, and clad with noble forests of hickory, walnut, ash, poplar, sugar-maple, and wild cherry trees. Occasionally there were spacious plains covered with wild rye; natural meadows, with blue grass and clover; and buffaloes, thirty and forty at a time, grazing on them, as in a cultivated pasture. Deer, elk, and wild turkeys abounded. "Nothing is wanted but cultivation," said Gist, "to make this a most delightful country." Cultivation has since proved the truth of his words. The country thus described is the present State of Ohio.

Piqua, where Gist and Croghan had arrived, was the principal town of the Twightwees or Miamis; the most powerful confederacy of the West, combining four tribes, and extending its influence even beyond the Mississippi. A king or sachem of one or other of the different tribes presided over the whole. The head chief at present was the king of the Piankeshas.

At this town Croghan formed a treaty of alliance in the name of the Governor of Pennsylvania with two of the Miami tribes. And Gist was promised by the king of the Piankeshas that the chiefs of the various tribes would attend the meeting at Logstown to make a treaty with Virginia.

In the height of these demonstrations of friendship, two Ottawas entered the council-house, announcing themselves as envoys from the French Governor of Canada to seek a renewal of ancient alliance. They were received with all due ceremonial; for none are more ceremonious than the Indians. The French colors were set up beside the English, and the ambassadors opened their mission. "Your father, the French king," said they, "remembering his children on the Ohio, has sent them these two kegs of milk," here, with great solemnity, they deposited two kegs of brandy,— "and this tobacco;":—here they deposited a roll ten pounds in weight. "He has made a clean road for you to come and see him and his officers; and urges you to come, assuring you that all past differences will be forgotten."

The Piankesha chief replied in the same figurative style. "It is true our father has sent for us several times, and has said the road was clear; but I understand it is not clear—it is foul and bloody, and the French have made it so. We have cleared a road for our brothers, the English; the French have made it bad, and have taken some of our brothers prisoners. This we consider as done to ourselves." So saying, he turned his back upon the ambassadors, and stalked out of the council-house.

In the end the ambassadors were assured that the tribes of the Ohio and the Six Nations were hand in hand with their brothers, the English; and should war ensue with the French, they were ready to meet it.

So the French colors were taken down; the "kegs of milk" and roll of tobacco were rejected; the grand council broke up with a war-dance, and the ambassadors departed, weeping and howling, and predicting ruin to the Miamis.

When Gist returned to the Shawnee town, near the mouth of the Scioto, and reported to his Indian friends there the alliance he had formed with the Miami confederacy, there was great feasting and speech-making, and firing of guns. He had now happily accomplished the chief object of his mission—nothing remained but to descend the Ohio to the Great Falls. This, however, he was cautioned not to do. A large party of Indians, allies of the French, were hunting in that neighborhood, who might kill or capture him. He crossed the river, attended only by a lad as a travelling companion and aid, and proceeded cautiously down the east side until within fifteen miles of the Falls. Here he came upon traps newly set, and Indian footprints not a day old; and heard the distant report of guns. The story of Indian hunters then was true. He was in a dangerous neighborhood. The savages might come upon the tracks of his horses, or hear the bells put about their necks, when turned loose in the wilderness to graze.

Abandoning all idea, therefore, of visiting the Falls, and contenting himself with the information concerning them which he had received from others, he shaped his course on the 18th of March for the Cuttawa, or Kentucky River. From the top of a mountain in the vicinity he had a view to the southwest as far as the eye could reach, over a vast woodland country in the fresh garniture of spring, and watered by abundant streams; but as yet only the hunting-ground of savage tribes, and the scene of their sanguinary combats. In a word, Kentucky lay spread out before him in all its wild magnificence; long before it was beheld by Daniel Boone.

For six weeks was this hardy pioneer making his toilful way up the valley of the Cuttawa, or Kentucky River, to the banks of the Blue Stone; often checked by precipices, and obliged to seek fords at the heads of tributary streams; and happy when he could find a buffalo path broken through the tangled forests, or worn into the everlasting rocks.

On the 1st of May he climbed a rock sixty feet high, crowning a lofty mountain, and had a distant view of the great Kanawha, breaking its way through a vast sierra; crossing that river on a raft of his own construction, he had many more weary days before him, before he reached his frontier abode on the banks of the Yadkin. He arrived there in the latter part of May, but there was no one to welcome the wanderer home. There had been an Indian massacre in the neighborhood, and he found his house silent and deserted. His heart sank within him, until an old man whom he met near the place assured him his family were safe, having fled for refuge to a settlement thirty-five miles off, on the banks of the Roanoke. There he rejoined them on the following day.

While Gist had been making his painful way homeward, the two Ottawa ambassadors had returned to Fort Sandusky, bringing word to the French that their flag had been struck in the council-house at Piqua, and their friendship rejected and their hostility defied by the Miamis. They informed them also of the gathering of the western tribes that was to take place at Logstown, to conclude a treaty with the Virginians.

It was a great object with the French to prevent this treaty, and to spirit up the Ohio Indians against the English. This they hoped to effect through the agency of one Captain Joncaire, a veteran diplomatist of the wilderness, whose character and story deserve a passing notice.

He had been taken prisoner when quite young by the Iroquois, and adopted into one of their tribes. This was the making of his fortune. He had grown up among them, acquired their language, adapted himself to their habits, and was considered by them as one of themselves. On returning to civilized life he became a prime instrument in the hands of the Canadian government, for managing and cajoling the Indians. Sometimes he was an ambassador to the Iroquois; sometimes a mediator between the jarring tribes; sometimes a leader of their warriors when employed by the French. When in 1728 the Delawares and Shawnees migrated to the banks of the Ohio, Joncaire was the agent who followed them, and prevailed on them to consider themselves under French protection.

When the French wanted to get a commanding site for a post on the Iroquois lands, near Niagara, Joncaire was the man to manage it. He craved a situation where he might put up a wigwam, and dwell among his Iroquois brethren. It was granted of course, "for was he not a son of the tribe—was he not one of themselves?" By degrees his wigwam grew into an important trading post; ultimately it became Fort Niagara. Years and years had elapsed; he had grown gray in Indian diplomacy, and was now sent once more to maintain French sovereignty over the valley of the Ohio.

He appeared at Logstown accompanied by another Frenchman, and forty Iroquois warriors. He found an assemblage of the western tribes, feasting and rejoicing, and firing of guns, for George Croghan and Montour the interpreter were there, and had been distributing presents on behalf of the Governor of Pennsylvania.

Joncaire was said to have the wit of a Frenchman, and the eloquence of an Iroquois. He made an animated speech to the chiefs in their own tongue, the gist of which was that their father Onontio (that is to say, the Governor of Canada) desired his children of the Ohio to turn away the Indian traders, and never to deal with them again on pain of his displeasure; so saying, he laid down a wampum belt of uncommon size, by way of emphasis to his message.

For once his eloquence was of no avail; a chief rose indignantly, shook his finger in his face, and stamping on the ground, "This is our land," said he. "What right has Onontio here? The English are our brothers. They shall live among us as long as one of us is alive. We will trade with them, and not with you;" and so saying he rejected the belt of wampum.

Joncaire returned to an advanced post recently established on the upper part of the river, whence he wrote to the Governor of Pennsylvania: "The Marquis de la Jonquiere, Governor of New France, having ordered me to watch that the English make no treaty in the Ohio country, I have signified to the traders of your government to retire. You are not ignorant that all these lands belong to the King of France, and that the English have no right to trade in them." He concluded by reiterating the threat made two years previously by Celeron de Bienville against all intruding fur traders.

In the mean time, in the face of all these protests and menaces, Mr. Gist, under sanction of the Virginia Legislature, proceeded in the same year to survey the lands within the grant of the Ohio company, lying on the south side of the Ohio river, as far down as the great Kanawha. An old Delaware sachem, meeting him while thus employed, propounded a somewhat puzzling question. "The French," said he, "claim all the land on one side of the Ohio, the English claim all the land on the other side—now where does the Indians' land lie?"

Poor savages! Between their "fathers," the French, and their "brothers," the English, they were in a fair way of being most lovingly shared out of the whole country.

CHAPTER VI.

PREPARATIONS FOR HOSTILITIES—WASHINGTON
APPOINTED DISTRICT ADJUTANT GENERAL—MOUNT
VERNON A SCHOOL OF ARMS—ADJUTANT MUSE A
VETERAN CAMPAIGNER—JACOB VAN BRAAM THE
MASTER OF FENCE—ILL HEALTH OF WASHINGTON'S
BROTHER LAWRENCE—VOYAGE WITH HIM TO THE
WEST INDIES—SCENES AT BARBADOES—TROPICAL
FRUITS—BEEFSTEAK AND TRIPE CLUB—RETURN
HOME OF WASHINGTON—DEATH OF LAWRENCE.

The French now prepared for hostile contingencies. They
launched an armed vessel of unusual size on Lake Ontario; fortified
their trading house at Niagara; strengthened their outposts, and
advanced others on the upper waters of the Ohio. A stir of warlike
preparation was likewise to be observed among the British colonies.
It was evident that the adverse claims to the disputed territories, if
pushed home, could only be settled by the stern arbitrament of the
sword.

In Virginia, especially, the war spirit was manifest. The
province was divided into military districts, each having an adjutant-
general, with the rank of major, and the pay of one hundred and
fifty pounds a year, whose duty was to attend to the organization
and equipment of the militia.

Such an appointment was sought by Lawrence Washington
for his brother George. It shows what must have been the maturity
of mind of the latter, and the confidence inspired by his judicious
conduct and aptness for business, that the post should not only be
sought for him, but readily obtained; though he was yet but nineteen
years of age. He proved himself worthy of the appointment.

He now set about preparing himself, with his usual method and assiduity, for his new duties. Virginia had among its floating population some military relics of the late Spanish war. Among these was a certain Adjutant Muse, a Westmoreland volunteer, who had served with Lawrence Washington in the campaigns in the West Indies, and had been with him in the attack on Carthagena. He now undertook to instruct his brother George in the art of war; lent him treatises on military tactics; put him through the manual exercise, and gave him some idea of evolutions in the field. Another of Lawrence's campaigning comrades was Jacob Van Braam, a Dutchman by birth; a soldier of fortune of the Dalgetty order; who had been in the British army, but was now out of service, and, professing to be a complete master of fence, recruited his slender purse in this time of military excitement, by giving the Virginian youth lessons in the sword exercise.

Under the instructions of these veterans Mount Vernon, from being a quiet rural retreat, where Washington, three years previously, had indited love ditties to his "lowland beauty," was suddenly transformed into a school of arms, as he practised the manual exercise with Adjutant Muse, or took lessons on the broadsword from Van Braam.

His martial studies, however, were interrupted for a time by the critical state of his brother's health. The constitution of Lawrence had always been delicate, and he had been obliged repeatedly to travel for a change of air. There were now pulmonary symptoms of a threatening nature, and by advice of his physicians he determined to pass a winter in the West Indies, taking with him his favorite brother George as a companion.

They accordingly sailed for Barbadoes on the 28th of September, 1751. George kept a journal of the voyage with logbook brevity; recording the wind and weather, but no events worth citation. They landed at Barbadoes on the 3d of November. The resident physician of the place gave a favorable report of Lawrence's case, and held out hopes of a cure. The brothers were delighted with the aspect of the country, as they drove out in the cool of the evening, and beheld on all sides fields of sugar cane, and Indian corn, and groves of tropical trees, in full fruit and foliage.

They took up their abode at a house pleasantly situated about a mile from town, commanding an extensive prospect of sea and land, including Carlyle bay and its shipping, and belonging to Captain Crofton, commander of James Fort.

Barbadoes had its theatre, at which Washington witnessed for the first time a dramatic representation, a species of amusement of which he afterwards became fond. It was in the present instance the doleful tragedy of George Barnwell. "The character of Barnwell, and several others," notes he in his journal, "were said to be well performed. There was music adapted and regularly conducted." A safe but abstemious criticism.

Among the hospitalities of the place the brothers were invited to the house of a Judge Maynards, to dine with an association of the first people of the place, who met at each other's house alternately every Saturday, under the incontestably English title of "The Beefsteak and Tripe Club." Washington notes with admiration the profusion of tropical fruits with which the table was loaded, "the granadilla, sapadella, pomegranate, sweet orange, water-lemon, forbidden fruit, and guava." The homely prosaic beefsteak and tripe must have contrasted strangely, though sturdily, with these magnificent poetical fruits of the tropics. But John Bull is faithful to his native habits and native dishes, whatever may be the country or clime, and would set up a chop-house at the very gates of paradise.

The brothers had scarcely been a fortnight at the island when George was taken down by a severe attack of small-pox. Skilful medical treatment, with the kind attentions of friends, and especially of his brother, restored him to health in about three weeks; but his face always remained slightly marked.

After his recovery he made excursions about the island, noticing its soil, productions, fortifications, public works, and the manners of its inhabitants. While admiring the productiveness of the sugar plantations, he was shocked at the spendthrift habits of the planters, and their utter want of management.

"How wonderful," writes he, "that such people should be in debt, and not be able to indulge themselves in all the luxuries, as well as the necessaries of life. Yet so it happens. Estates are often alienated for debts. How persons coming to estates of two, three, and four hundred acres can want, is to me most wonderful." How much does this wonder speak for his own scrupulous principle of always living within compass.

The residence at Barbadoes failed to have the anticipated effect on the health of Lawrence, and he determined to seek the sweet climate of Bermuda in the spring. He felt the absence from his wife, and it was arranged that George should return to Virginia, and bring her out to meet him at that island. Accordingly, on the 22d of December, George set sail in the Industry, bound to Virginia, where he arrived on the 1st February, 1752, after five weeks of stormy winter seafaring.

Lawrence remained through the winter at Barbadoes; but the very mildness of the climate relaxed and enervated him. He felt the want of the bracing winter weather to which he had been accustomed. Even the invariable beauty of the climate; the perpetual summer, wearied the restless invalid. "This is the finest island of the West Indies," said he; "but I own no place can please me without a change of seasons. We soon tire of the same prospect." A consolatory truth for the inhabitants of more capricious climes.

Still some of the worst symptoms of his disorder had disappeared, and he seemed to be slowly recovering; but the nervous restlessness and desire of change, often incidental to his malady, had taken hold of him, and early in March he hastened to Bermuda. He had come too soon. The keen air of early spring brought on an aggravated return of his worst symptoms. "I have now got to my last refuge," writes he to a friend, "where I must receive my final sentence, which at present Dr. Forbes will not pronounce. He leaves me, however, I think, like a criminal condemned, though not without hopes of reprieve. But this I am to obtain by meritoriously abstaining from flesh of every sort, all strong liquors, and by riding as much as I can bear. These are the only terms on which I am to hope for life."

He was now afflicted with painful indecision, and his letters perplexed his family, leaving them uncertain as to his movements, and at a loss how to act. At one time he talked of remaining a year at Bermuda, and wrote to his wife to come out with George and rejoin him there; but the very same letter shows his irresolution and uncertainty, for he leaves her coming to the decision of herself and friends. As to his own movements, he says, "Six weeks will determine me what to resolve on. Forbes advises the south of France, or else Barbadoes." The very next letter, written shortly afterwards in a moment of despondency, talks of the possibility of "hurrying home to his grave!"

The last was no empty foreboding. He did indeed hasten back, and just reached Mount Vernon in time to die under his own roof, surrounded by his family and friends, and attended in his last moments by that brother on whose manly affection his heart seemed to repose. His death took place on the 26th July, 1752, when but thirty-four years of age. He was a noble-spirited, pure-minded, accomplished gentleman; honored by the public, and beloved by his friends. The paternal care ever manifested by him for his youthful brother, George, and the influence his own character and conduct must have had upon him in his ductile years, should link their memories together in history, and endear the name of Lawrence Washington to every American.

Lawrence left a wife and an infant daughter to inherit his ample estates. In case his daughter should die without issue, the estate of Mount Vernon, and other lands specified in his will, were to be enjoyed by her mother during her lifetime, and at her death to be inherited by his brother George. The latter was appointed one of the executors of the will; but such was the implicit confidence reposed in his judgment and integrity, that, although he was but twenty years of age, the management of the affairs of the deceased were soon devolved upon him almost entirely. It is needless to say that they were managed with consummate skill and scrupulous fidelity.

CHAPTER VII.

COUNCIL OF THE OHIO TRIBES AT LOGSTOWN—
TREATY WITH THE ENGLISH—GIST'S SETTLEMENT—
SPEECHES OF THE HALF-KING AND THE FRENCH
COMMANDANT—FRENCH AGGRESSIONS—THE RUINS
OF PIQUA—WASHINGTON SENT ON A MISSION TO
THE FRENCH COMMANDER—JACOB VAN BRAAM, HIS
INTERPRETER—CHRISTOPHER GIST, HIS GUIDE—HALT
AT THE CONFLUENCE OF THE MONONGAHELA
AND ALLEGANY—PROJECTED FORT—SHINGISS, A
DELAWARE SACHEM—LOGSTOWN—THE HALF KING—
INDIAN COUNCILS—INDIAN DIPLOMACY—RUMORS
CONCERNING JONCAIRE—INDIAN ESCORTS—THE
HALF-KING, JESKAKAKE AND WHITE THUNDER.

The meeting of the Ohio tribes, Delawares, Shawnees, and
Mingoes, to form a treaty of alliance with Virginia, took place at
Logstown, at the appointed time. The chiefs of the Six Nations
declined to attend. "It is not our custom," said they proudly, "to
meet to treat of affairs in the woods and weeds. If the Governor
of Virginia wants to speak with us, and deliver us a present from
our father (the King), we will meet him at Albany, where we expect
the Governor of New York will be present."[28]

At Logstown, Colonel Fry and two other commissioners
from Virginia, concluded a treaty with the tribes above named; by
which the latter engaged not to molest any English settlers south
of the Ohio. Tanacharisson, the half-king, now advised that his
brothers of Virginia should build a strong house at the fork of
the Monongahela, to resist the designs of the French. Mr. Gist

---

28   Letter of Col. Johnson to Gov. Clinton.—Doc. Hist. N. Y. ii., 624.

was accordingly instructed to lay out a town and build a fort at Chartier's Creek, on the east side of the Ohio, a little below the site of the present city of Pittsburg. He commenced a settlement, also, in a valley just beyond Laurel Hill, not far from the Youghiogeny, and prevailed on eleven families to join him. The Ohio Company, about the same time, established a trading post, well stocked with English goods, at Wills' Creek (now the town of Cumberland).

The Ohio tribes were greatly incensed at the aggressions of the French, who were erecting posts within their territories, and sent deputations to remonstrate, but without effect. The half-king, as chief of the western tribes, repaired to the French post on Lake Erie, where he made his complaint in person.

"Fathers," said he, "you are the disturbers of this land by building towns, and taking the country from us by fraud and force. We kindled a fire a long time since at Montreal, where we desired you to stay and not to come and intrude upon our land. I now advise you to return to that place, for this land is ours.

"If you had come in a peaceable manner, like our brothers the English, we should have traded with you as we do with them; but that you should come and build houses on our land, and take it by force, is what we cannot submit to. Both you and the English are white. We live in a country between you both; the land belongs to neither of you. The Great Being allotted it to us as a residence. So, fathers, I desire you, as I have desired our brothers the English, to withdraw, for I will keep you both at arm's length. Whichever most regards this request, that side will we stand by and consider friends. Our brothers the English have heard this, and I now come to tell it to you, for I am not afraid to order you off this land."

"Child," replied the French commandant, "you talk foolishly. You say this land belongs to you; there is not the black of my nail yours. It is my land, and I will have it, let who will stand up against me. I am not afraid of flies and mosquitoes, for as such I consider the Indians. I tell you that down the river I will go, and build upon it. If it were blocked up I have forces sufficient to burst it open and trample down all who oppose me. My force is as the sand upon the sea-shore. Therefore here is your wampum; I fling it at you."

Tanacharisson returned, wounded at heart, both by the language and the haughty manner of the French commandant. He saw the ruin impending over his race, but looked with hope and trust to the English as the power least disposed to wrong the red man.

French influence was successful in other quarters. Some of the Indians who had been friendly to the English showed signs of alienation. Others menaced hostilities. There were reports that the French were ascending the Mississippi from Louisiana. France, it was said, intended to connect Louisiana and Canada by a chain of military posts, and hem the English within the Allegany Mountains.

The Ohio Company complained loudly to the Lieutenant-Governor of Virginia, the Hon. Robert Dinwiddie, of the hostile conduct of the French and their Indian allies. They found in Dinwiddie a ready listener; he was a stockholder in the company.

A commissioner, Captain William Trent, was sent to expostulate with the French commander on the Ohio for his aggressions on the territory of his Britannic majesty; he bore presents also of guns, powder, shot, and clothing for the friendly Indians.

Trent was not a man of the true spirit for a mission to the frontier. He stopped a short time at Logstown, though the French were one hundred and fifty miles further up the river, and directed his course to Piqua, the great town of the Twightwees, where Gist and Croghan had been so well received by the Miamis, and the French flag struck in the council house. All now was reversed. The place had been attacked by the French and Indians; the Miamis defeated with great loss; the English traders taken prisoners; the Piankesha chief, who had so proudly turned his back upon the Ottawa ambassadors, had been sacrificed by the hostile savages, and the French flag hoisted in triumph on the ruins of the town. The whole aspect of affairs was so threatening on the frontier, that Trent lost heart, and returned home without accomplishing his errand.

Governor Dinwiddie now looked round for a person more fitted to fulfil a mission which required physical strength and moral energy; a courage to cope with savages, and a sagacity to negotiate with white men. Washington was pointed out as possessed of those requisites. It is true he was not yet twenty-two years of age, but public confidence in his judgment and abilities had been manifested a second time, by renewing his appointment of adjutant-general, and assigning him the northern division. He was acquainted too with the matters in litigation, having been in the bosom councils of his deceased brother. His woodland experience fitted him for an expedition through the wilderness; and his great discretion and self-command for a negotiation with wily commanders and fickle savages. He was accordingly chosen for the expedition.

By his letter of instructions he was directed to repair to Logstown, and hold a communication with Tanacharisson, Monacatoocha, alias Scarooyadi, the next in command, and the other sachems of the mixed tribes friendly to the English; inform them of the purport of his errand, and request an escort to the head-quarters of the French commander. To that commander he was to deliver his credentials, and the letter of Governor Dinwiddie, and demand an answer in the name of his Britannic majesty; but not to wait for it beyond a week. On receiving it, he was to request a sufficient escort to protect him on his return.

He was, moreover, to acquaint himself with the numbers and force of the French stationed on the Ohio and in its vicinity; their capability of being reinforced from Canada; the forts they had erected; where situated, how garrisoned; the object of their advancing into those parts, and how they were likely to be supported.

Washington set off from Williamsburg on the 30th of October (1753), the very day on which he received his credentials. At Fredericksburg he engaged his old "master of fence," Jacob Van Braam, to accompany him as interpreter; though it would appear from subsequent circumstances, that the veteran swordsman was but indifferently versed either in French or English.

Having provided himself at Alexandria with necessaries for the journey, he proceeded to Winchester, then on the frontier, where he procured horses, tents, and other travelling equipments, and then pushed on by a road newly opened to Wills' Creek (town of Cumberland), where he arrived on the 14th of November.

Here he met with Mr. Gist, the intrepid pioneer, who had explored the Ohio in the employ of the company, and whom he engaged to accompany and pilot him in the present expedition. He secured the services also of one John Davidson as Indian interpreter, and of four frontiersmen, two of whom were Indian traders. With this little band, and his swordsman and interpreter, Jacob Van Braam, he set forth on the 15th of November, through a wild country, rendered almost impassable by recent storms of rain and snow.

At the mouth of Turtle Creek, on the Monongahela, he found John Frazier the Indian trader, some of whose people, as heretofore stated, had been sent off prisoners to Canada. Frazier himself had recently been ejected by the French from the Indian village of Venango, where he had a gunsmith's establishment. According to his account the French general who had commanded on this frontier was dead, and the greater part of the forces were retired into winter quarters.

As the rivers were all swollen so that the horses had to swim them, Washington sent all the baggage down the Monongahela in a canoe under care of two of the men, who had orders to meet him at the confluence of that river with the Allegany, where their united waters form the Ohio.

"As I got down before the canoe," writes he in his journal, "I spent some time in viewing the rivers, and the land at the Fork, which I think extremely well situated for a fort, as it has the absolute command of both rivers. The land at the point is twenty or twenty-five feet above the common surface of the water, and a considerable bottom of flat, well timbered land all around it, very convenient for building. The rivers are each a quarter of a mile or more across, and run here very nearly at right angles; Allegany bearing north-east, and Monongahela south-east. The former of these two is a very rapid and swift-running water, the other deep and still, without any perceptible fall." The Ohio company had intended to build a fort about two miles from this place, on the south-east side of the river; but Washington gave the fork the decided preference. French engineers of experience proved the accuracy of his military eye, by subsequently choosing it for the site of Fort Duquesne, noted in frontier history.

In this neighborhood lived Shingiss, the king or chief sachem of the Delawares. Washington visited him at his village, to invite him to the council at Logstown. He was one of the greatest warriors of his tribe, and subsequently took up the hatchet at various times against the English, though now he seemed favorably disposed, and readily accepted the invitation.

They arrived at Logstown after sunset on the 24th of November. The half-king was absent at his hunting lodge on Beaver

Creek, about fifteen miles distant; but Washington had runners sent out to invite him and all the other chiefs to a grand talk on the following day.

In the morning four French deserters came into the village. They had deserted from a company of one hundred men, sent up from New Orleans with eight canoes laden with provisions. Washington drew from them an account of the French force at New Orleans, and of the forts along the Mississippi, and at the mouth of the Wabash, by which they kept up a communication with the lakes; all which he carefully noted down. The deserters were on their way to Philadelphia, conducted by a Pennsylvania trader.

About three o'clock the half-king arrived. Washington had a private conversation with him in his tent, through Davidson, the interpreter. He found him intelligent, patriotic, and proudly tenacious of his territorial rights. We have already cited from Washington's papers, the account given by this chief in this conversation, of his interview with the late French commander. He stated, moreover, that the French had built two forts, differing in size, but on the same model, a plan of which he gave, of his own drawing. The largest was on Lake Erie, the other on French Creek, fifteen miles apart, with a waggon road between them. The nearest and levellest way to them was now impassable, lying through large and miry savannas; they would have, therefore, to go by Venango, and it would take five or six sleeps (or days) of good travelling to reach the nearest fort.

On the following morning at nine o'clock, the chiefs assembled at the council house; where Washington, according to his instructions, informed them that he was sent by their brother, the Governor of Virginia, to deliver to the French commandant a letter of great importance, both to their brothers the English and to themselves; and that he was to ask their advice and assistance, and some of their young men to accompany and provide for him on the way, and be his safeguard against the "French Indians" who had taken up the hatchet. He concluded by presenting the indispensable document in Indian diplomacy a string of wampum.

The chiefs, according to etiquette, sat for some moments silent after he had concluded, as if ruminating on what had been said, or to give him time for further remark.

The half-king then rose and spoke in behalf of the tribes, assuring him that they considered the English and themselves brothers, and one people; and that they intended to return the French the "speech-belts," or wampums, which the latter had sent them. This, in Indian diplomacy, is a renunciation of all friendly relations. An escort would be furnished to Washington composed of Mingoes, Shannoahs, and Delawares, in token of the love and loyalty of those several tribes; but three days would be required to prepare for the journey.

Washington remonstrated against such delay; but was informed, that an affair of such moment, where three speech-belts were to be given up, was not to be entered into without due consideration. Besides, the young men who were to form the escort were absent hunting, and the half-king could not suffer the party to go without sufficient protection. His own French speech-belt, also, was at his hunting lodge, where he must go in quest of it. Moreover, the Shannoah chiefs were yet absent and must be waited for. In short, Washington had his first lesson in Indian diplomacy, which for punctilio, ceremonial, and secret manoeuvring, is equal at least to that of civilized life. He soon found that to urge a more speedy departure would be offensive to Indian dignity and decorum, so he was fain to await the gathering together of the different chiefs with their speech-belts.

In fact there was some reason for all this caution. Tidings had reached the sachems that Captain Joncaire had called a meeting at Venango, of the Mingoes, Delawares, and other tribes, and made them a speech, informing them that the French, for the present, had gone into winter quarters, but intended to descend the river in great force, and fight the English in the spring. He had advised them, therefore, to stand aloof, for should they interfere, the French and English would join, cut them all off, and divide their land between them.

With these rumors preying on their minds, the half-king and three other chiefs waited on Washington in his tent in the evening, and after representing that they had complied with all the requisitions of the Governor of Virginia, endeavored to draw from the youthful ambassador the true purport of his mission to the French commandant. Washington had anticipated an inquiry of the kind, knowing how natural it was that these poor people should regard, with anxiety and distrust, every movement of two formidable powers thus pressing upon them from opposite sides, he managed, however, to answer them in such a manner as to allay their solicitude without transcending the bounds of diplomatic secrecy.

After a day or two more of delay and further consultations in the council house, the chiefs determined that but three of their number should accompany the mission, as a greater number might awaken the suspicions of the French. Accordingly, on the 30th of November, Washington set out for the French post, having his usual party augmented by an Indian hunter, and being accompanied by the half-king, an old Shannoah sachem named Jeskakake, and another chief, sometimes called Belt of Wampum, from being the keeper of the speech-belts, but generally bearing the sounding appellation of White Thunder.

CHAPTER VIII.

ARRIVAL AT VENANGO—CAPTAIN JONCAIRE—
FRONTIER REVELRY—DISCUSSIONS OVER THE
BOTTLE—THE OLD DIPLOMATIST AND THE YOUNG—
THE HALF-KING, JESKAKAKE, AND WHITE THUNDER
STAGGERED—THE SPEECH-BELT—DEPARTURE—LA
FORCE, THE WILY COMMISSARY—FORT AT FRENCH
CREEK—THE CHEVALIER LEGARDEUR DE ST.
PIERRE, KNIGHT OF ST. LOUIS—CAPTAIN REPARTI—
TRANSACTIONS AT THE FORT—ATTEMPTS TO
SEDUCE THE SACHEMS—MISCHIEF BREWING ON THE
FRONTIER—DIFFICULTIES AND DELAYS IN PARTING—
DESCENT OF FRENCH CREEK—ARRIVAL AT VENANGO.

Although the distance to Venango, by the route taken, was not
above seventy miles, yet such was the inclemency of the weather
and the difficulty of travelling, that Washington and his party did
not arrive there until the 4th of December. The French colors
were flying at a house whence John Frazier, the English trader,
had been driven. Washington repaired thither, and inquired of
three French officers whom he saw there where the commandant
resided. One of them promptly replied that he "had the command
of the Ohio." It was, in fact, the redoubtable Captain Joncaire, the
veteran intriguer of the frontier. On being apprised, however, of
the nature of Washington's errand, he informed him that there was
a general officer at the next fort, where he advised him to apply for
an answer to the letter of which he was the bearer.

In the mean time, he invited Washington and his party
to a supper at head quarters. It proved a jovial one, for Joncaire
appears to have been somewhat of a boon companion, and there
is always ready though rough hospitality in the wilderness. It is

true, Washington, for so young a man, may not have had the most convivial air, but there may have been a moist look of promise in the old soldier Van Braam.

Joncaire and his brother officers pushed the bottle briskly. "The wine," says Washington, "as they dosed themselves pretty plentifully with it, soon banished the restraint which at first appeared in their conversation, and gave a license to their tongues to reveal their sentiments more freely. They told me that it was their absolute design to take possession of the Ohio, and by G——they would do it; for that although they were sensible the English could raise two men for their one, yet they knew their motions were too slow and dilatory to prevent any undertaking. They pretend to have an undoubted right to the river from a discovery made by one La Salle sixty years ago, and the rise of this expedition is to prevent our settling on the river or the waters of it, as they heard of some families moving out in order thereto."

Washington retained his sobriety and his composure throughout all the rodomontade and bacchanalian outbreak of the mercurial Frenchmen; leaving the task of pledging them to his master of fence, Van Braam, who was not a man to flinch from potations. He took careful note, however, of all their revelations, and collected a variety of information concerning the French forces; how and where they were distributed; the situations and distances of their forts, and their means and mode of obtaining supplies. If the veteran diplomatist of the wilderness had intended this revel for a snare, he was completely foiled by his youthful competitor.

On the following day there was no travelling on account of excessive rain. Joncaire, in the mean time, having discovered that the half-king was with the mission, expressed his surprise that he had not accompanied it to his quarters on the preceding day. Washington, in truth, had feared to trust the sachem within the reach of the politic Frenchman. Nothing would do now but Joncaire must have the sachems at head-quarters. Here his diplomacy was triumphant. He received them with open arms. He was enraptured to see them. His Indian brothers! How could they be so near without coming to visit him? He made them presents; but, above all, plied them so potently with liquor, that the poor half-king, Jeskakake, and White Thunder forgot all about their wrongs, their speeches, their speech-belts, and all the business they had come upon; paid no heed to the repeated cautions of their English friends, and were soon in a complete state of frantic extravagance or drunken oblivion.

The next day the half-king made his appearance at Washington's tent, perfectly sober and very much crestfallen. He declared, however, that he still intended to make his speech to the French, and offered to rehearse it on the spot; but Washington advised him not to waste his ammunition on inferior game like Joncaire and his comrades, but to reserve it for the commandant. The sachem was not to be persuaded. Here, he said, was the place of the council fire, where they were accustomed to transact their business with the French; and as to Joncaire, he had all the management of French affairs with the Indians.

Washington was fain to attend the council fire and listen to the speech. It was much the same in purport as that which he had made to the French general, and he ended by offering to return the French speech-belt; but this Joncaire refused to receive, telling him to carry it to the commander at the fort.

All that day and the next was the party kept at Venango by the stratagems of Joncaire and his emissaries to detain and seduce the sachems. It was not until 12 o'clock on the 7th of December, that Washington was able to extricate them out of their clutches and commence his journey.

A French commissary by the name of La Force, and three soldiers, set off in company with him. La Force went as if on ordinary business, but he proved one of the most active, daring, and mischief-making of those anomalous agents employed by the French among the Indian tribes. It is probable that he was at the bottom of many of the perplexities experienced by Washington at Venango, and now travelled with him for the prosecution of his wiles. He will be found, hereafter, acting a more prominent part, and ultimately reaping the fruit of his evil doings.

After four days of weary travel through snow and rain, and mire and swamp, the party reached the fort. It was situated on a kind of island on the west fork of French Creek, about fifteen miles south of Lake Erie, and consisted of four houses, forming a hollow square, defended by bastions made of pallisades twelve feet high, picketed, and pierced for cannon and small arms. Within the bastions were a guard-house, chapel, and other buildings, and outside were stables, a smith's forge, and log-houses covered with bark, for the soldiers.

On the death of the late general, the fort had remained in charge of one Captain Reparti until within a week past, when the Chevalier Legardeur de St. Pierre had arrived, and taken command.

The reception of Washington at the fort was very different from the unceremonious one experienced at the outpost of Joncaire and his convivial messmates. When he presented himself at the gate, accompanied by his interpreter, Van Braam, he was met by the officer second in command and conducted in due military form to his superior; an ancient and silver-haired chevalier of the military order of St. Louis, courteous but ceremonious, mingling the polish of the French gentleman of the old school with the precision of the soldier.

Having announced his errand through his interpreter, Van Braam, Washington offered his credentials and the letter of Governor Dinwiddie, and was disposed to proceed at once to business with the prompt frankness of a young man unhackneyed in diplomacy. The chevalier, however, politely requested him to retain the documents in his possession until his predecessor, Captain Reparti, should arrive, who was hourly expected from the next post.

At two o'clock the captain arrived. The letter and its accompanying documents were then offered again, and received in due form, and the chevalier and his officers retired with them into a private apartment, where the captain, who understood a little English, officiated as translator. The translation being finished, Washington was requested to walk in and bring his translator Van Braam, with him, to peruse and correct it, which he did.

In this letter, Dinwiddie complained of the intrusion of French forces into the Ohio country, erecting forts and making settlements in the western parts of the colony of Virginia, so notoriously known to be the property of the crown of Great Britain. He inquired by whose authority and instructions the French Commander-general had marched this force from Canada, and made this invasion; intimating that his own action would be regulated by the answer he should receive, and the tenor of the commission with which he was honored. At the same time he required of the commandant his peaceable departure, and that he would forbear to prosecute a purpose "so interruptive of the harmony and good understanding which his majesty was desirous to continue and cultivate with the most catholic king."

The latter part of the letter related to the youthful envoy. "I persuade myself you will receive and entertain Major Washington with the candor and politeness natural to your nation, and it will give me the greatest satisfaction if you can return him with an answer suitable to my wishes for a long and lasting peace between us."

The two following days were consumed in councils of the chevalier and his officers over the letter and the necessary reply. Washington occupied himself in the mean time in observing and taking notes of the plan, dimensions, and strength of the fort, and of every thing about it. He gave orders to his people, also, to take an exact account of the canoes in readiness, and others in the process of construction, for the conveyance of troops down the river in the ensuing spring.

As the weather continued stormy, with much snow, and the horses were daily losing strength, he sent them down, unladen, to Venango, to await his return by water. In the mean time, he discovered that busy intrigues were going on to induce the half-king and the other sachems to abandon him, and renounce all friendship with the English. Upon learning this, he urged the chiefs to deliver up their "speech-belts" immediately, as they had promised, thereby shaking off all dependence upon the French. They accordingly pressed for an audience that very evening. A private one was at length granted them by the commander, in presence of one or two of his officers. The half-king reported the result of it to Washington. The venerable but astute chevalier cautiously evaded the acceptance of the proffered wampum; made many professions of love and friendship, and said he wished to live in peace and trade amicably with the tribes of the Ohio, in proof of which he would send down some goods immediately for them to Logstown.

As Washington understood, privately, that an officer was to accompany the man employed to convey these goods, he suspected that the real design was to arrest and bring off all straggling English traders they might meet with. What strengthened this opinion was a frank avowal which had been made to him by the chevalier, that he had orders to capture every British subject who should attempt to trade upon the Ohio or its waters.

Captain Reparti, also, in reply to his inquiry as to what had been done with two Pennsylvania traders, who had been taken with all their goods, informed him that they had been sent to Canada, but had since returned home. He had stated, furthermore, that during the time he held command, a white boy had been carried captive past the fort by a party of Indians, who had with them, also, two or three white men's scalps.

All these circumstances showed him the mischief that was brewing in these parts, and the treachery and violence that pervaded the frontier, and made him the more solicitous to accomplish his mission successfully, and conduct his little band in safety out of a wily neighborhood.

On the evening of the 14th, the Chevalier de St. Pierre delivered to Washington his sealed reply to the letter of Governor Dinwiddie. The purport of previous conversations with the chevalier, and the whole complexion of affairs on the frontier, left no doubt of the nature of that reply.

The business of his mission being accomplished, Washington prepared on the 15th to return by water to Venango; but a secret influence was at work which retarded every movement.

"The commandant," writes he, "ordered a plentiful store of liquor and provisions to be put on board our canoes, and appeared to be extremely complaisant, though he was exerting every artifice which he could invent to set our Indians at variance with us, to prevent their going until after our departure; presents, rewards, and every thing which could be suggested by him or his officers. I cannot say that ever in my life I suffered so much anxiety as I did in this affair. I saw that every stratagem which the most fruitful brain could invent was practised to win the half-king to their interests, and that leaving him there was giving them the opportunity they aimed at. I went to the half-king, and pressed him in the strongest terms to go; he told me that the commandant would not discharge him until the morning. I then went to the commandant and desired him to do their business, and complained to him of ill treatment; for, keeping them, as they were a part of my company, was detaining me. This he promised not to do, but to forward my journey as much as he could. He protested he did not keep them, but was ignorant of the cause of their stay; though I soon found it out. He had promised them a present of guns if they would wait until the morning. As I was very much pressed by the Indians to wait this day for them, I consented, on the promise that nothing should hinder them in the morning."

The next morning (16th) the French, in fulfilment of their promise, had to give the present of guns. They then endeavored to detain the sachems with liquor, which at any other time might have prevailed, but Washington reminded the half-king that his royal word was pledged to depart, and urged it upon him so closely that exerting unwonted resolution and self-denial, he turned his back upon the liquor and embarked.

It was rough and laborious navigation. French Creek was swollen and turbulent, and full of floating ice. The frail canoes were several times in danger of being staved to pieces against rocks. Often the voyagers had to leap out and remain in the water half an hour at a time, drawing the canoes over shoals, and at one place to carry them a quarter of a mile across a neck of land, the river being completely dammed by ice. It was not until the 22d that they reached Venango.

Here Washington was obliged, most unwillingly, to part company with the sachems. White Thunder had hurt himself and was ill and unable to walk, and the others determined to remain at Venango for a day or two and convey him down the river in a canoe. There was danger that the smooth-tongued and convivial Joncaire would avail himself of the interval to ply the poor monarchs of the woods with flattery and liquor. Washington endeavored to put the worthy half-king on his guard, knowing that he had once before shown himself but little proof against the seductions of the bottle. The sachem, however, desired him not to be concerned; he knew the French too well for any thing to engage him in their favor; nothing should shake his faith to his English brothers; and it will be found that in these assurances he was sincere.

CHAPTER IX.

RETURN FROM VENANGO—A TRAMP ON FOOT—
MURDERING TOWN—THE INDIAN GUIDE—
TREACHERY—AN ANXIOUS NIGHT—PERILS ON THE
ALLEGANY RIVER—QUEEN ALIQUIPPA—THE OLD
WATCH-COAT—RETURN ACROSS THE BLUE RIDGE.

On the 25th of December, Washington and his little party set out by land from Venango on their route homeward. They had a long winter's journey before them, through a wilderness beset with dangers and difficulties. The packhorses, laden with tents, baggage, and provisions, were completely jaded; it was feared they would give out. Washington dismounted, gave up his saddle-horse to aid in transporting the baggage, and requested his companions to do the same. None but the drivers remained in the saddle. He now equipped himself in an Indian hunting-dress, and with Van Braam, Gist, and John Davidson, the Indian interpreter, proceeded on foot.

The cold increased. There was deep snow that froze as it fell. The horses grew less and less capable of travelling. For three days they toiled on slowly and wearily. Washington was impatient to accomplish his journey, and make his report to the governor; he determined, therefore, to hasten some distance in advance of the party, and then strike for the Fork of the Ohio by the nearest course directly through the woods. He accordingly put the cavalcade under the command of Van Braam, and furnished him with money for expenses; then disencumbering himself of all superfluous clothing, buckling himself up in a watch-coat, strapping his pack on his shoulders, containing his papers and provisions, and taking gun in hand, he left the horses to flounder on, and struck manfully ahead, accompanied only by Mr. Gist, who had equipped himself in like manner.

At night they lit a fire, and "camped" by it in the woods. At two o'clock in the morning they were again on foot, and pressed forward until they struck the south-east fork of Beaver Creek, at a place bearing the sinister name of Murdering Town; probably the scene of some Indian massacre.

Here Washington, in planning his route, had intended to leave the regular path, and strike through the woods for Shannopins Town, two or three miles above the fork of the Ohio, where he hoped to be able to cross the Allegany River on the ice.

At Murdering Town he found a party of Indians, who appeared to have known of his coming, and to have been waiting for him. One of them accosted Mr. Gist, and expressed great joy at seeing him. The wary woodsman regarded him narrowly, and thought he had seen him at Joncaire's. If so, he and his comrades were in the French interest, and their lying in wait boded no good. The Indian was very curious in his inquiries as to when they had left Venango; how they came to be travelling on foot; where they had left their horses, and when it was probable the latter would reach this place. All these questions increased the distrust of Gist, and rendered him extremely cautious in reply.

The route hence to Shannopins Town lay through a trackless wild, of which the travellers knew nothing; after some consultation, therefore, it was deemed expedient to engage one of the Indians as a guide. He entered upon his duties with alacrity, took Washington's pack upon his back, and led the way by what he said was the most direct course. After travelling briskly for eight or ten miles Washington became fatigued, and his feet were chafed; he thought, too, they were taking a direction too much to the north-east; he came to a halt, therefore, and determined to light a fire, make a shelter of the bark and branches of trees, and encamp there for the night. The Indian demurred; he offered, as Washington was fatigued, to carry his gun, but the latter was too wary to part with his weapon. The Indian now grew churlish. There were Ottawa Indians in the woods, he said, who might be attracted by their fire, and surprise and scalp them; he urged, therefore, that they should continue on: he would take them to his cabin, where they would be safe.

Mr. Gist's suspicions increased, but he said nothing. Washington's also were awakened. They proceeded some distance further: the guide paused and listened. He had heard, he said, the report of a gun toward the north; it must be from his cabin; he accordingly turned his steps in that direction.

Washington began to apprehend an ambuscade of savages. He knew the hostility of many of them to the English, and what a desirable trophy was the scalp of a white man. The Indian still kept on toward the north; he pretended to hear two whoops—they were from his cabin—it could not be far off.

They went on two miles further, when Washington signified his determination to encamp at the first water they should find. The guide said nothing, but kept doggedly on. After a little while they arrived at an opening in the woods, and emerging from the deep shadows in which they had been travelling, found themselves in a clear meadow, rendered still more light by the glare of the snow upon the ground. Scarcely had they emerged when the Indian, who was about fifteen paces ahead, suddenly turned, levelled his gun, and fired. Washington was startled for an instant, but, feeling that he was not wounded, demanded quickly of Mr. Gist if he was shot. The latter answered in the negative. The Indian in the mean time had run forward, and screened himself behind a large white oak, where he was reloading his gun. They overtook, and seized him. Gist would have put him to death on the spot, but Washington humanely prevented him. They permitted him to finish the loading of his gun; but, after he had put in the ball, took the weapon from him, and let him see that he was under guard.

Arriving at a small stream they ordered the Indian to make a fire, and took turns to watch over the guns. While he was thus occupied, Gist, a veteran woodsman, and accustomed to hold the life of an Indian rather cheap, was somewhat incommoded by the scruples of his youthful commander, which might enable the savage to carry out some scheme of treachery. He observed to Washington that, since he would not suffer the Indian to be killed, they must manage to get him out of the way, and then decamp with all speed, and travel all night to leave this perfidious neighborhood behind them; but first it was necessary to blind the guide as to their intentions. He accordingly addressed him in a friendly tone, and adverting to the late circumstance, pretended to suppose that he had lost his way, and fired his gun merely as a signal. The Indian, whether deceived or not, readily chimed in with the explanation. He said he now knew the way to his cabin, which was at no great distance. "Well then," replied Gist, "you can go home, and as we are tired we will remain here for the night, and follow your track at daylight. In the mean time here is a cake of bread for you, and you must give us some meat in the morning."

Whatever might have been the original designs of the savage, he was evidently glad to get off. Gist followed him cautiously for a distance, and listened until the sound of his footsteps died away; returning then to Washington, they proceeded about half a mile, made another fire, set their compass and fixed their course by the light of it, then leaving it burning, pushed forward, and travelled as fast as possible all night, so as to gain a fair start should any one pursue them at daylight. Continuing on the next day they never relaxed their speed until nightfall, when they arrived on the banks of the Allegany River, about two miles above Shannopins Town.

Washington had expected to find the river frozen completely over; it was so only for about fifty yards from either shore, while great quantities of broken ice were driving down the main channel. Trusting that he had out-travelled pursuit, he encamped on the border of the river; still it was an anxious night, and he was up at daybreak to devise some means of reaching the opposite bank. No other mode presented itself than by a raft, and to construct this they had but one poor hatchet. With this they set resolutely to work and labored all day, but the sun went down before their raft was finished. They launched it, however, and getting on board, endeavored to propel it across with setting poles. Before they were half way over the raft became jammed between cakes of ice, and they were in imminent peril. Washington planted his pole on the bottom of the stream, and leaned against it with all his might, to stay the raft until the ice should pass by. The rapid current forced the ice against the pole with such violence that he was jerked into the water, where it was at least ten feet deep, and only saved himself from being swept away and drowned by catching hold of one of the raft logs.

It was now impossible with all their exertions to get to either shore; abandoning the raft therefore, they got upon an island, near which they were drifting. Here they passed the night exposed to intense cold by which the hands and feet of Mr. Gist were frozen. In the morning they found the drift ice wedged so closely together, that they succeeded in getting from the island to the opposite side of the river; and before night were in comfortable quarters at the house of Frazier, the Indian trader, at the mouth of Turtle Creek on the Monongahela.

Here they learned from a war party of Indians that a band of Ottawas, a tribe in the interest of the French, had massacred a whole family of whites on the banks of the great Kanawha River.

At Frazier's they were detained two or three days endeavoring to procure horses. In this interval Washington had again occasion to exercise Indian diplomacy. About three miles distant, at the mouth of the Youghiogeny River, dwelt a female sachem, Queen Aliquippa, as the English called her, whose sovereign dignity had been aggrieved, that the party on their way to the Ohio, had passed near her royal wigwam without paying their respects to her.

Aware of the importance, at this critical juncture, of securing the friendship of the Indians, Washington availed himself of the interruption of his journey, to pay a visit of ceremony to this native princess. Whatever anger she may have felt at past neglect, it was readily appeased by a present of his old watch-coat; and her good graces were completely secured by a bottle of rum, which, he intimates, appeared to be peculiarly acceptable to her majesty.

Leaving Frazier's on the 1st of January, they arrived on the 2d at the residence of Mr. Gist, on the Monongahela. Here they separated, and Washington having purchased a horse, continued his homeward course, passing horses laden with materials and stores for the fort at the fork of the Ohio, and families going out to settle there.

Having crossed the Blue Ridge and stopped one day at Belvoir to rest, he reached Williamsburg on the 16th of January, where he delivered to Governor Dinwiddie the letter of the French commandant, and made him a full report of the events of his mission.

We have been minute in our account of this expedition as it was an early test and development of the various talents and characteristics of Washington.

The prudence, sagacity, resolution, firmness, and self-devotion manifested by him throughout; his admirable tact and self-possession in treating with fickle savages and crafty white men; the soldier's eye with which he had noticed the commanding and defensible points of the country, and every thing that would bear upon military operations; and the hardihood with which he had acquitted himself during a wintry tramp through the wilderness, through constant storms of rain and snow; often sleeping on the ground without a tent in the open air, and in danger from treacherous foes,—all pointed him out, not merely to the governor, but to the public at large, as one eminently fitted, notwithstanding his youth, for important trusts involving civil as well as military duties. It is an expedition that may be considered the foundation of his fortunes. From that moment he was the rising hope of Virginia.

CHAPTER X.

REPLY OF THE CHEVALIER DE ST. PIERRE—TRENT'S
MISSION TO THE FRONTIER—WASHINGTON
RECRUITS TROOPS—DINWIDDIE AND THE HOUSE
OF BURGESSES—INDEPENDENT CONDUCT OF THE
VIRGINIANS—EXPEDIENTS TO GAIN RECRUITS—
JACOB VAN BRAAM IN SERVICE—TOILFUL MARCH
TO WILLS' CREEK—CONTRECOEUR AT THE FORK OF
THE OHIO—TRENT'S REFRACTORY TROOPS.

The reply of the Chevalier de St. Pierre was such as might have been expected from that courteous, but wary commander. He should transmit, he said, the letter of Governor Dinwiddie to his general, the Marquis du Quesne, "to whom," observed he, "it better belongs than to me to set forth the evidence and reality of the rights of the king, my master, upon the lands situated along the river Ohio, and to contest the pretensions of the King of Great Britain thereto. His answer shall be a law to me. . . . As to the summons you send me to retire, I do not think myself obliged to obey it. Whatever may be your instructions, I am here by virtue of the orders of my general; and I entreat you, sir, not to doubt one moment but that I am determined to conform myself to them with all the exactness and resolution which can be expected from the best officer." . . .

"I made it my particular care," adds he, "to receive Mr. Washington with, a distinction suitable to your dignity, as well as his own quality and great merit. I flatter myself that he will do me this justice before you, sir, and that he will signify to you, in the manner I do myself, the profound respect with which I am, sir," &c.[29]

---

29   London Mag., June, 1754.

This soldier-like and punctilious letter of the chevalier was considered evasive, and only intended to gain time. The information given by Washington of what he had observed on the frontier convinced Governor Dinwiddie and his council that the French were preparing to descend the Ohio in the spring, and take military possession of the country. Washington's journal was printed, and widely promulgated throughout the colonies and England, and awakened the nation to a sense of the impending danger, and the necessity of prompt measures to anticipate the French movements.

Captain Trent was despatched to the frontier, commissioned to raise a company of one hundred men, march with all speed to the Fork of the Ohio, and finish as soon as possible the fort commenced there by the Ohio Company. He was enjoined to act only on the defensive, but to capture or destroy whoever should oppose the construction of the works, or disturb the settlements. The choice of Captain Trent for this service, notwithstanding his late inefficient expedition, was probably owing to his being brother-in-law to George Croghan, who had grown to be quite a personage of consequence on the frontier, where he had an establishment or trading-house, and was supposed to have great influence among the western tribes, so as to be able at any time to persuade many of them to take up the hatchet.

Washington was empowered to raise a company of like force at Alexandria; to procure and forward munitions and supplies for the projected fort at the Fork, and ultimately to have command of both companies. When on the frontier he was to take council of George Croghan and Andrew Montour the interpreter, in all matters relating to the Indians, they being esteemed perfect oracles in that department.

Governor Dinwiddie in the mean time called upon the governors of the other provinces to make common cause against the foe; he endeavored, also, to effect alliances with the Indian tribes of the south, the Catawbas and Cherokees, by way of counterbalancing the Chippewas and Ottawas, who were devoted to the French.

The colonies, however, felt as yet too much like isolated territories; the spirit of union was wanting. Some pleaded a want of military funds; some questioned the justice of the cause; some declined taking any hostile step that might involve them in a war, unless they should have direct orders from the crown.

Dinwiddie convened the House of Burgesses to devise measures for the public security. Here his high idea of prerogative and of gubernatorial dignity met with a grievous countercheck from the dawning spirit of independence. High as were the powers vested in the colonial government of Virginia, of which, though but lieutenant-governor, he had the actual control; they were counterbalanced by the power inherent in the people, growing out of their situation and circumstances, and acting through their representatives.

There was no turbulent factious opposition to government in Virginia; no "fierce democracy," the rank growth of crowded cities, and a fermenting populace; but there was the independence of men, living apart in patriarchal style on their own rural domains; surrounded by their families, dependants and slaves, among whom their will was law,—and there was the individuality in character and action of men prone to nurture peculiar notions and habits of thinking, in the thoughtful solitariness of country life.

When Dinwiddie propounded his scheme of operations on the Ohio, some of the burgesses had the hardihood to doubt the claims of the king to the disputed territory; a doubt which the governor reprobated as savoring strongly of a most disloyal French spirit; he fired, as he says, at the thought "that an English legislature should presume to doubt the right of his majesty to the interior parts of this continent, the back part of his dominions!"

Others demurred to any grant of means for military purposes which might be construed into an act of hostility. To meet this scruple it was suggested that the grant might be made for the purpose of encouraging and protecting all settlers on the waters of the Mississippi. And under this specious plea ten thousand pounds were grudgingly voted; but even this moderate sum was not put at the absolute disposition of the governor. A committee was appointed with whom he was to confer as to its appropriation.

This precaution Dinwiddie considered an insulting invasion of the right he possessed as governor to control the purse as well as the sword; and he complained bitterly of the assembly, as deeply tinctured with a republican way of thinking, and disposed to encroach on the prerogative of the crown, "which he feared would render them more and more difficult to be *brought to order*."

Ways and means being provided, Governor Dinwiddie augmented the number of troops to be enlisted to three hundred, divided into six companies. The command of the whole, as before, was offered to Washington, but he shrank from it, as a charge too great for his youth and inexperience. It was given, therefore, to Colonel Joshua Fry, an English gentleman of worth and education, and Washington was made second in command, with the rank of lieutenant-colonel.

The recruiting, at first, went on slowly. Those who offered to enlist, says Washington, were for the most part loose idle persons without house or home, some without shoes or stockings, some shirtless, and many without coat or waistcoat.

He was young in the recruiting service, or he would have known that such is generally the stuff of which armies are made. In this country especially it has always been difficult to enlist the active yeomanry by holding out merely the pay of a soldier. The means of subsistence are too easily obtained by the industrious, for them to give up home and personal independence for a mere daily support. Some may be tempted by a love of adventure; but in general, they require some prospect of ultimate advantage that may "better their condition."

Governor Dinwiddie became sensible of this, and resorted to an expedient rising out of the natural resources of the country, which has since been frequently adopted, and always with efficacy. He proclaimed a bounty of two hundred thousand acres of land on the Ohio River, to be divided among the officers and soldiers who should engage in this expedition; one thousand to be laid off contiguous to the fort at the fork, for the use of the garrison. This was a tempting bait to the sons of farmers, who readily enlisted in the hope of having, at the end of a short campaign, a snug farm of their own in this land of promise.

It was a more difficult matter to get officers than soldiers. Very few of those appointed made their appearance; one of the captains had been promoted; two declined; Washington found himself left, almost alone, to manage a number of self-willed, undisciplined recruits. Happily he had with him, in the rank of lieutenant, that soldier of fortune, Jacob Van Braam, his old "master of fence," and travelling interpreter.

In his emergency he forthwith nominated him captain, and wrote to the governor to confirm the appointment, representing him as the oldest lieutenant, and an experienced officer.

On the 2d of April Washington set off from Alexandria for the new fort, at the fork of the Ohio. He had but two companies with him, amounting to about one hundred and fifty men; the remainder of the regiment was to follow under Colonel Fry with the artillery, which was to be conveyed up the Potomac. While on the march he was joined by a detachment under Captain Adam Stephen, an officer destined to serve with him at distant periods of his military career.

At Winchester he found it impossible to obtain conveyances by gentle means, and was obliged reluctantly to avail himself of the militia law of Virginia, and impress horses and waggons for service; giving the owners orders on government for their appraised value. Even then, out of a great number impressed, he obtained but ten, after waiting a week; these, too, were grudgingly furnished by farmers with their worst horses, so that in steep and difficult passes they were incompetent to the draught, and the soldiers had continually to put their shoulders to the wheels.

Thus slenderly fitted out, Washington and his little force made their way toilfully across the mountains, having to prepare the roads as they went for the transportation of the cannon, which were to follow on with the other division under Colonel Fry. They cheered themselves with the thoughts that this hard work would cease when they should arrive at the company's trading-post and store-house at Wills' Creek, where Captain Trent was to have packhorses in readiness, with which they might make the rest of the way by light stages. Before arriving there they were startled by a rumor that Trent and all his men had been captured by the French. With regard to Trent, the news soon proved to be false, for they found him at Wills' Creek on the 20th of April. With regard to his men there was still an uncertainty. He had recently left them at the fork of the Ohio, busily at work on the fort, under the command of his lieutenant, Frazier, late Indian trader and gunsmith, but now a provincial officer. If the men had been captured, it must have been since the captain's departure. Washington was eager to press forward and ascertain the truth, but it was impossible. Trent, inefficient as usual, had failed to provide packhorses. It was necessary to send to Winchester, forty miles distant, for baggage waggons, and await their arrival. All uncertainty as to the fate of the men, however, was brought to a close by their arrival, on the 25th, conducted by an ensign, and bringing with them their working implements. The French might well boast that they had again been too quick for the English. Captain Contrecoeur, an alert officer, had embarked about a thousand men with field-pieces, in a fleet of sixty bateaux and three hundred canoes, dropped down the river from Venango, and suddenly made his appearance before the fort, on which the men were working, and which was not half completed. Landing, drawing up his men, and planting his artillery, he summoned the fort to surrender, allowing one hour for a written reply.

What was to be done! the whole garrison did not exceed fifty men. Captain Trent was absent at Wills' Creek; Frazier, his lieutenant, was at his own residence at Turtle Creek, ten miles distant. There was no officer to reply but a young ensign of the name of Ward. In his perplexity he turned for counsel to Tanacharisson, the half-king, who was present in the fort. The chief advised the ensign to plead insufficiency of rank and powers, and crave delay until the arrival of his superior officer. The ensign repaired to the French camp to offer this excuse in person, and was accompanied by the half-king. They were courteously received, but Contrecoeur was inflexible. There must be instant surrender, or he would take forcible possession. All that the ensign could obtain was permission to depart with his men, taking with them their working tools. The capitulation ended. Contrecoeur, with true French gayety, invited the ensign to sup with him; treated him with the utmost politeness, and wished him a pleasant journey, as he set off the next morning with his men laden with their working tools.

Such was the ensign's story. He was accompanied by two Indian warriors, sent by the half-king to ascertain where the detachment was, what was its strength, and when it might be expected at the Ohio. They bore a speech from that sachem to Washington, and another, with a belt of wampum for the Governor of Virginia. In these he plighted his steadfast faith to the English, and claimed assistance from his brothers of Virginia and Pennsylvania.

One of these warriors Washington forwarded on with the speech and wampum to Governor Dinwiddie. The other he prevailed on to return to the half-king, bearing a speech from him, addressed to the "Sachems, warriors of the Six United Nations, Shannoahs and Delawares, our friends and brethren." In this he informed them that he was on the advance with a part of the army, to clear the road for a greater force coming with guns, ammunition, and provisions; and he invited the half-king and another sachem, to meet him on the road as soon as possible to hold a council.

In fact, his situation was arduous in the extreme. Regarding the conduct of the French in the recent occurrence an overt act of war, he found himself thrown with a handful of raw recruits far on a hostile frontier, in the midst of a wilderness, with an enemy at hand greatly superior in number and discipline; provided with artillery, and all the munitions of war, and within reach of constant supplies and reinforcements. Beside the French that had come from Venango, he had received credible accounts of another party ascending the Ohio; and of six hundred Chippewas and Ottawas marching down Scioto Creek to join the hostile camp. Still, notwithstanding the accumulating danger, it would not do to fall back, nor show signs of apprehension. His Indian allies in such case might desert him. The soldiery, too, might grow restless and dissatisfied. He was already annoyed by Captain Trent's men, who, having enlisted as volunteers, considered themselves exempt from the rigor of martial law; and by their example of loose and refractory conduct, threatened to destroy the subordination of his own troops.

In this dilemma he called a council of war, in which it was determined to proceed to the Ohio Company store-houses, at the mouth of Redstone Creek; fortify themselves there, and wait for reinforcements. Here they might keep up a vigilant watch upon the enemy, and get notice of any hostile movement in time for defence, or retreat; and should they be reinforced sufficiently to enable them to attack the fort, they could easily drop down the river with their artillery.

With these alternatives in view, Washington detached sixty men in advance to make a road; and at the same time wrote to Governor Dinwiddie for mortars and grenadoes, and cannon of heavy metal.

Aware that the Assembly of Pennsylvania was in session, and that the Maryland Assembly would also meet in the course of a few days, he wrote directly to the governors of those provinces, acquainting them with the hostile acts of the French, and with his perilous situation; and endeavoring to rouse them to cooperation in the common cause. We will here note in advance that his letter was laid before the Legislature of Pennsylvania, and a bill was about to be passed making appropriations for the service of the king; but it fell through, in consequence of a disagreement between the Assembly and the governor as to the mode in which the money should be raised; and so no assistance was furnished to Washington from that quarter. The youthful commander had here a foretaste, in these his incipient campaigns, of the perils and perplexities which awaited him from enemies in the field, and lax friends in legislative councils in the grander operations of his future years. Before setting off for Redstone Creek, he discharged Trent's refractory men from his detachment, ordering them to await Colonel Fry's commands; they however, in the true spirit of volunteers from the backwoods, dispersed to their several homes.

It may be as well to observe, in this place, that both Captain Trent and Lieutenant Frazier were severely censured for being absent from their post at the time of the French summons. "Trent's behavior," said Washington, in a letter to Governor Dinwiddie, "has been very tardy, and has convinced the world of what they before suspected—his great timidity. Lieutenant Frazier, though not altogether blameless, is much more excusable, for he would not accept of the commission until he had a promise from his captain that he should not reside at the fort, nor visit it above once a week, or as he saw necessity." In fact, Washington, subsequently recommended Frazier for the office of adjutant.

CHAPTER XI.

MARCH TO THE LITTLE MEADOWS—RUMORS FROM
THE OHIO—CORRESPONDENCE FROM THE BANKS OF
THE YOUGHIOGENY—ATTEMPT TO DESCEND THAT
RIVER—ALARMING REPORTS—SCOUTING PARTIES—
PERILOUS SITUATION OF THE CAMP—GIST AND LA
FORCE—MESSAGE FROM THE HALF-KING—FRENCH
TRACKS—THE JUMONVILLE SKIRMISH—TREATMENT
OF LA FORCE—POSITION AT THE GREAT MEADOWS—
BELLIGERENT FEELINGS OF A YOUNG SOLDIER.

On the 29th of April Washington set out from Wills' Creek at the head of one hundred and sixty men. He soon overtook those sent in advance to work the road; they had made but little progress. It was a difficult task to break a road through the wilderness sufficient for the artillery coming on with Colonel Fry's division. All hands were now set to work, but with all their labor they could not accomplish more than four miles a day. They were toiling through Savage Mountain and that dreary forest region beyond it, since bearing the sinister name of "The Shades of Death." On the 9th of May they were not further than twenty miles from Wills' Creek, at a place called the Little Meadows.

Every day came gloomy accounts from the Ohio; brought chiefly by traders, who, with packhorses bearing their effects, were retreating to the more settled parts of the country. Some exaggerated the number of the French, as if strongly reinforced. All represented them as diligently at work constructing a fort. By their account Washington perceived the French had chosen the very place which he had noted in his journal as best fitted for the purpose.

One of the traders gave information concerning La Force the French emissary, who had beset Washington when on his mission to the frontier, and acted, as he thought, the part of a spy. He had been at Gist's new settlement beyond Laurel Hill, and was prowling about the country with four soldiers at his heels on a pretended hunt after deserters. Washington suspected him to be on a reconnoitering expedition.

It was reported, moreover, that the French were lavishing presents on the Indians about the lower part of the river, to draw them to their standard. Among all these flying reports and alarms Washington was gratified to learn that the half-king was on his way to meet him at the head of fifty warriors.

After infinite toil through swamps and forests, and over rugged mountains, the detachment arrived at the Youghiogeny River, where they were detained some days constructing a bridge to cross it.

This gave Washington leisure to correspond with Governor Dinwiddie, concerning matters which had deeply annoyed him. By an ill-judged economy of the Virginia government at this critical juncture, its provincial officers received less pay than that allowed in the regular army. It is true the regular officers were obliged to furnish their own table, but their superior pay enabled them to do it luxuriously; whereas the provincials were obliged to do hard duty on salt provisions and water. The provincial officers resented this inferiority of pay as an indignity, and declared that nothing prevented them from throwing up their commissions but unwillingness to recede before approaching danger.

Washington shared deeply this feeling. "Let him serve voluntarily, and he would with the greatest pleasure in life devote his services to the expedition—but to be slaving through woods, rocks, and mountains, for the shadow of pay—" writes he, "I would rather toil like a day laborer for a maintenance, if reduced to the necessity, than serve on such ignoble terms." Parity of pay was indispensable to the dignity of the service.

Other instances of false economy were pointed out by him, forming so many drags upon the expedition, that he quite despaired of success. "Be the consequence what it will, however," adds he, "I am determined not to leave the regiment, but to be among the last men that leave the Ohio; even if I serve as a private volunteer, which I greatly prefer to the establishment we are upon. . . . I have a constitution hardy enough to encounter and undergo the most severe trials, and I flatter myself resolution to face what any man dares, as shall be proved when it comes to the test."

And in a letter to his friend Colonel Fairfax—"For my own part," writes he, "it is a matter almost indifferent whether I serve for full pay or as a generous volunteer; indeed, did my circumstances correspond with my inclinations, I should not hesitate a moment to prefer the latter; *for the motives that have led me here are pure and noble. I had no view of acquisition but that of honor, by serving faithfully my king and country.*"

Such were the noble impulses of Washington at the age of twenty-two, and such continued to actuate him throughout life. We have put the latter part of the quotation in italics, as applicable to the motives which in after life carried him into the Revolution.

While the bridge over the Youghiogeny was in the course of construction, the Indians assured Washington he would never be able to open a waggon-road across the mountains to Redstone Creek; he embarked therefore in a canoe with a lieutenant, three soldiers, and an Indian guide, to try whether it was possible to descend the river. They had not descended above ten miles before the Indian refused to go further. Washington soon ascertained the reason. "Indians," said he, "expect presents—nothing can be done without them. The French take this method. If you want one or more to conduct a party, to discover the country, to hunt, or for any particular purpose, they must be bought; their friendship is not so warm as to prompt them to these services gratis." The Indian guide in the present instance, was propitiated by the promise of one of Washington's ruffled shirts, and a watch-coat.

The river was bordered by mountains and obstructed by rocks and rapids. Indians might thread such a labyrinth in their light canoes, but it would never admit the transportation of troops and military stores. Washington kept on for thirty miles, until he came to a place where the river fell nearly forty feet in the space of fifty yards. There he ceased to explore, and returned to camp, resolving to continue forward by land.

On the 23d Indian scouts brought word that the French were not above eight hundred strong, and that about half their number had been detached at night on a secret expedition. Close upon this report came a message from the half-king, addressed "to the first of his majesty's officers whom it may concern."

"It is reported," said he, "that the French army is coming to meet Major Washington. Be on your guard against them, my brethren, for they intend to strike the first English they shall see. They have been on their march two days. I know not their number. The half-king and the rest of the chiefs will be with you in five days to hold a council."

In the evening Washington was told that the French were crossing the ford of the Youghiogeny about eighteen miles distant. He now hastened to take a position in a place called the Great Meadows, where he caused the bushes to be cleared away, made an intrenchment and prepared what he termed "a charming field for an encounter."

A party of scouts were mounted on waggon horses, and sent out to reconnoitre. They returned without having seen an enemy. A sensitiveness prevailed in the camp. They were surrounded by forests, threatened by unseen foes, and hourly in danger of surprise. There was an alarm about two o'clock in the night. The sentries fired upon what they took to be prowling foes. The troops sprang to arms, and remained on the alert until daybreak. Not an enemy was to be seen. The roll was called. Six men were missing, who had deserted.

On the 25th. Mr. Gist arrived from his place, about fifteen miles distant. La Force had been there at noon on the previous day, with a detachment of fifty men, and Gist had since come upon their track within five miles of the camp. Washington considered La Force a bold, enterprising man, subtle and dangerous; one to be particularly guarded against. He detached seventy-five men in pursuit of him and his prowling band.

About nine o'clock at night came an Indian messenger from the half-king, who was encamped with several of his people about six miles off. The chief had seen tracks of two Frenchmen, and was convinced their whole body must be in ambush near by.

Washington considered this the force which had been hovering about him for several days, and determined to forestall their hostile designs. Leaving a guard with the baggage and ammunition, he set out before ten o'clock, with forty men, to join his Indian ally. They groped their way in single file, by footpaths through the woods, in a heavy rain and murky darkness, tripping occasionally and stumbling over each other, sometimes losing the track for fifteen or twenty minutes, so that it was near sunrise when they reached the camp of the half-king.

That chieftain received the youthful commander with, great demonstrations of friendship, and engaged to go hand in hand with him against the lurking enemy. He set out accordingly, accompanied by a few of his warriors and his associate sachem Scarooyadi or Monacatoocha, and conducted Washington to the tracks which he had discovered. Upon these he put two of his Indians. They followed them up like hounds, and brought back word that they had traced them to a low bottom surrounded by rocks and trees, where the French were encamped, having built a few cabins for shelter from the rain.

A plan was now concerted to come upon them by surprise; Washington with, his men on the right; the half-king with his warriors on the left; all as silently as possible. Washington was the first upon the ground. As he advanced from among the rocks and trees at the head of his men, the French caught sight of him and ran to their arms. A sharp firing instantly took place, and was kept up on both sides for about fifteen minutes. Washington and his party were most exposed and received all the enemy's fire. The balls whistled around him; one man was killed close by him, and three others wounded. The French at length, having lost several of their number, gave way and ran. They were soon overtaken; twenty-one were captured, and but one escaped, a Canadian, who carried the tidings of the affair to the fort on the Ohio. The Indians would have massacred the prisoners had not Washington prevented them. Ten of the French had fallen in the skirmish, and one been wounded. Washington's loss was the one killed and three wounded which we have mentioned. He had been in the hottest fire, and having for the first time heard balls whistle about him, considered his escape miraculous. Jumonville, the French leader, had been shot through the head at the first fire. He was a young officer of merit, and his fate was made the subject of lamentation in prose and verse—chiefly through political motives.

Of the twenty-one prisoners the two most important were an officer of some consequence named Drouillon, and the subtle and redoubtable La Force. As Washington considered the latter an arch mischief-maker, he was rejoiced to have him in his power. La Force and his companion would fain have assumed the sacred character of ambassadors, pretending they were coming with a summons to him to depart from the territories belonging to the crown of France.

Unluckily for their pretensions, a letter of instructions, found on Jumonville, betrayed their real errand, which was to inform themselves of the roads, rivers, and other features of the country as far as the Potomac; to send back from time to time, by fleet messengers, all the information they could collect, and to give word of the day on which they intended to serve the summons.

Their conduct had been conformable. Instead of coming in a direct and open manner to his encampment, when they had ascertained where it was, and delivering their summons, as they would have done had their designs been frank and loyal, they had moved back two miles, to one of the most secret retirements, better for a deserter than an ambassador to encamp in, and staid there, within five miles of his camp, sending spies to reconnoitre it, and despatching messengers to Contrecoeur to inform him of its position and numerical strength, to the end, no doubt, that he might send a sufficient detachment to enforce the summons as soon as it should be given. In fact, the footprints which had first led to the discovery of the French lurking-place, were those of two "runners" or swift messengers, sent by Jumonville to the fort on the Ohio.

It would seem that La Force, after all, was but an instrument in the hands of his commanding officers, and not in their full confidence; for when the commission and instructions found on Jumonville were read before him, he professed not to have seen them before, and acknowledged, with somewhat of an air of ingenuousness, that he believed they had a hostile tendency.[30]

Upon the whole, it was the opinion of Washington and his officers that the summons, on which so much stress was laid, was a mere specious pretext to mask their real designs and be used as occasion might require. "That they were spies rather than any thing else," and were to be treated as prisoners of war.

---

30   Washington's letter to Dinwiddie, 29th May, 1754.

The half-king joined heartily in this opinion; indeed, had the fate of the prisoners been in his hands, neither diplomacy nor any thing else would have been of avail. "They came with hostile intentions," he said; "they had bad hearts, and if his English brothers were so foolish as to let them go, he would never aid in taking another Frenchman."

The prisoners were accordingly conducted to the camp at the Great Meadows, and sent on the following day (29th), under a strong escort to Governor Dinwiddie, then at Winchester. Washington had treated them with great courtesy; had furnished Drouillon and La Force with clothing from his own scanty stock, and, at their request, given them letters to the governor, bespeaking for them "the respect and favor due to their character and personal merit."

A sense of duty, however, obliged him, in his general despatch, to put the governor on his guard against La Force. "I really think, if released, he would do more to our disservice than fifty other men, as he is a person whose active spirit leads him into all parties, and has brought him acquainted with all parts of the country. Add to this a perfect knowledge of the Indian tongue, and great influence with the Indians."

After the departure of the prisoners, he wrote again respecting them: "I have still stronger presumption, indeed almost confirmation, that they were sent as spies, and were ordered to wait near us till they were fully informed of our intentions, situation, and strength, and were to have acquainted their commander therewith, and to have been lurking here for reinforcements before they served the summons, if served at all.

"I doubt not but they will endeavor to amuse you with many smooth stories, as they did me; but they were confuted in them all, and, by circumstances too plain to be denied, almost made ashamed of their assertions.

"I have heard since they went away, they should say they called on us not to fire; but that I know to be false, for I was the first man that approached them, and the first whom they saw, and immediately they ran to their arms, and fired briskly till they were defeated." . . . "I fancy they will have the assurance of asking the privileges due to an embassy, when in strict justice they ought to be hanged as spies of the worst sort."

The situation of Washington was now extremely perilous. Contrecoeur, it was said, had nearly a thousand men with him at the fort, beside Indian allies; and reinforcements were on the way to join him. The messengers sent by Jumonville, previous to the late affair, must have apprised him of the weakness of the encampment on the Great Meadows, Washington hastened to strengthen it. He wrote by express also to Colonel Fry, who lay ill at Wills' Creek, urging instant reinforcements; but declaring his resolution to "fight with very unequal numbers rather than give up one inch of what he had gained."

The half-king was full of fight. He sent the scalps of the Frenchmen slain in the late skirmish, accompanied by black wampum and hatchets, to all his allies, summoning them to take up arms and join him at Redstone Creek, "for their brothers, the English, had now begun in earnest." It is said he would even have sent the scalps of the prisoners had not Washington interfered.[31] He went off for his home, promising to send down the river for all the Mingoes and Shawnees, and to be back at the camp on the 30th, with thirty or forty warriors, accompanied by their wives and children. To assist him in the transportation of his people and their effects thirty men were detached, and twenty horses.

"I shall expect every hour to be attacked," writes Washington to Governor Dinwiddie, on the 29th, "and by unequal numbers, which I must withstand, if there are five to one, for I fear the consequence will be that we shall lose the Indians if we suffer ourselves to be driven back. Your honor may depend I will not be surprised, let them come at what hour they will, and this is as much as I can promise; but my best endeavors shall not be wanting to effect more. I doubt not, if you hear I am beaten, but you will hear at the same time that we have done our duty in fighting as long as there is a shadow of hope."

The fact is, that Washington was in a high state of military excitement. He was a young soldier; had been for the first time in action, and been successful. The letters we have already quoted show, in some degree, the fervor of his mind, and his readiness to brave the worst; but a short letter, written to one of his brothers, on the 31st, lays open the recesses of his heart.

---

31   Letter from Virginia.—London Mag., 1754.

"We expect every hour to be attacked by superior force; but if they forbear but one day longer we shall be prepared for them. . . . We have already got intrenchments, and are about a palisade, which, I hope, will be finished today. The Mingoes have struck the French, and, I hope, will give a good blow before they have done. I expect forty odd of them here tonight, which, with our fort, and some reinforcements from Colonel Fry, will enable us to exert our noble courage with spirit."

Alluding in a postscript to the late affair, he adds: "I fortunately escaped without any wound; for the right wing, where I stood, was exposed to, and received, all the enemy's fire; and it was the part where the man was killed and the rest wounded. *I heard the bullets whistle, and, believe me, there is something charming in the sound.*"

This rodomontade, as Horace Walpole terms it, reached the ears of George II. "He would not say so," observed the king, dryly, "if he had been used to hear many."[32]

Washington himself thought so when more experienced in warfare. Being asked, many years afterwards, whether he really had made such a speech about the whistling of bullets, "If I said so," replied he quietly, "it was when I was young."[33] He was, indeed, but twenty-two years old when he said it; it was just after his first battle; he was flushed with success, and was writing to a brother.

---

32   This anecdote has hitherto rested on the authority of Horace Walpole, who gives it in his memoirs of George II., and in his correspondence. He cites the rodomontade as contained in the express despatched by Washington, whom he pronounces a "brave braggart." As no despatch of Washington contains any rodomontade of the kind; as it is quite at variance with the general tenor of his character; and as Horace Walpole is well known to have been a "great gossip dealer," apt to catch up any idle rumor that would give piquancy to a paragraph, the story has been held in great distrust. We met with the letter recently, however, in a column of the London Magazine for 1754, page 370, into which it must have found its way not long after it was written.

33   Gordon, Hist. Am. War, vol. ii., p. 203.

CHAPTER XII.

SCARCITY IN THE CAMP—DEATH OF COLONEL
FRY—PROMOTIONS—MACKAY AND HIS
INDEPENDENT COMPANY—MAJOR MUSE—INDIAN
CEREMONIALS—PUBLIC PRAYERS IN CAMP—
ALARMS—INDEPENDENCE OF AN INDEPENDENT
COMPANY—AFFAIRS AT THE GREAT MEADOWS—
DESERTION OF THE INDIAN ALLIES—CAPITULATION
OF FORT NECESSITY—VAN BRAAM AS AN
INTERPRETER—INDIAN PLUNDERERS—RETURN
TO WILLIAMSBURG—VOTE OF THANKS OF THE
HOUSE OF BURGESSES—SUBSEQUENT FORTUNES OF
THE HALF-KING—COMMENTS ON THE AFFAIR OF
JUMONVILLE AND THE CONDUCT OF VAN BRAAM.

Scarcity began to prevail in the camp. Contracts had been made with George Croghan for flour, of which he had large quantities at his frontier establishment; for he was now trading with the army as well as with the Indians. None, however, made its appearance. There was mismanagement in the commissariat. At one time the troops were six days without flour; and even then had only a casual supply from an Ohio trader. In this time of scarcity the half-king, his fellow sachem, Scarooyadi, and thirty or forty warriors, arrived, bringing with them their wives and children—so many more hungry mouths to be supplied. Washington wrote urgently to Croghan to send forward all the flour he could furnish.

News came of the death of Colonel Fry at Wills' Creek, and that he was to be succeeded in the command of the expedition by Colonel Innes of North Carolina, who was actually at Winchester with three hundred and fifty North Carolina troops. Washington, who felt the increasing responsibilities and difficulties of his situation, rejoiced at the prospect of being under the command of an experienced officer, who had served in company with his brother Lawrence at the siege of Carthagena. The colonel, however, never came to the camp, nor did the North Carolina troops render any service in the campaign—the fortunes of which might otherwise have been very different.

By the death of Fry, the command of the regiment devolved on Washington. Finding a blank major's commission among Fry's papers, he gave it to Captain Adam Stephen, who had conducted himself with spirit. As there would necessarily be other changes, he wrote to Governor Dinwiddie in behalf of Jacob Van Braam. "He has acted as captain ever since we left Alexandria. He is an experienced officer, and worthy of the command he has enjoyed."

The palisaded fort was now completed, and was named Fort Necessity, from the pinching famine that had prevailed during its construction. The scanty force in camp was augmented to three hundred, by the arrival from Wills' Creek of the men who had been under Colonel Fry. With them came the surgeon of the regiment, Dr. James Craik, a Scotchman by birth, and one destined to become a faithful and confidential friend of Washington for the remainder of his life.

A letter from Governor Dinwiddie announced, however, that Captain Mackay would soon arrive with an independent company of one hundred men, from South Carolina.

The title of independent company had a sound ominous of trouble. Troops of the kind, raised in the colonies, under direction of the governors, were paid by the Crown, and the officers had king's commissions; such, doubtless, had Captain Mackay. "I should have been particularly obliged," writes Washington to Governor Dinwiddie, "if you had declared whether he was under my command, or independent of it. I hope he will have more sense than to insist upon any unreasonable distinction, because he and his officers have commissions from his majesty. Let him consider, though we are greatly inferior in respect to advantages of profit, yet we have the same spirit to serve our gracious king as they have, and are as ready and willing to sacrifice our lives for our country's good. And here, once more, and for the last time, I must say, that it will be a circumstance which will act upon some officers of this regiment, above all measure, to be obliged to serve upon such different terms, when their lives, their fortunes, and their operations are equally, and, I dare say, as effectually exposed as those of others, who are happy enough to have the king's commission."

On the 9th arrived Washington's early instructor in military tactics, Adjutant Muse, recently appointed a major in the regiment. He was accompanied by Montour, the Indian interpreter, now a provincial captain, and brought with him nine swivels, and a small supply of powder and ball. Fifty or sixty horses were forthwith sent to Wills' Creek, to bring on further supplies, and Mr. Gist was urged to hasten forward the artillery.

Major Muse was likewise the bearer of a belt of wampum and a speech, from Governor Dinwiddie to the half-king; with medals for the chiefs, and goods for presents among the friendly Indians, a measure which had been suggested by Washington. They were distributed with that grand ceremonial so dear to the red man. The chiefs assembled, painted and decorated in all their savage finery; Washington wore a medal sent to him by the governor for such occasions. The wampum and speech having been delivered, he advanced, and with all due solemnity, decorated the chiefs and warriors with the medals, which they were to wear in remembrance of their father the King of England.

Among the warriors thus decorated was a son of Queen Aliquippa, the savage princess whose good graces Washington had secured in the preceding year, by the present of an old watchcoat, and whose friendship was important, her town being at no great distance from the French fort. She had requested that her son might be admitted into the war councils of the camp, and receive an English name. The name of Fairfax was accordingly given to him, in the customary Indian form; the half-king being desirous of like distinction, received the name of Dinwiddie. The sachems returned the compliment in kind, by giving Washington the name of Connotaucarius; the meaning of which is not explained.

William Fairfax, Washington's paternal adviser, had recently counselled him by letter, to have public prayers in his camp; especially when there were Indian families there; this was accordingly done at the encampment in the Great Meadows, and it certainly was not one of the least striking pictures presented in this wild campaign— the youthful commander, presiding with calm seriousness over a motley assemblage of half-equipped soldiery, leathern-clad hunters and woodsmen, and painted savages with their wives and children, and uniting them all in solemn devotion by his own example and demeanor.

On the 10th there was agitation in the camp. Scouts hurried in with word, as Washington understood them, that a party of ninety Frenchmen were approaching. He instantly ordered out a hundred and fifty of his best men; put himself at their head, and leaving Major Muse with the rest, to man the fort and mount the swivels, sallied forth "in the full hope" as he afterwards wrote to Governor Dinwiddie, "of procuring him another present of French prisoners."

It was another effervescence of his youthful military ardor, and doomed to disappointment. The report of the scouts had been either exaggerated or misunderstood. The ninety Frenchmen in military array dwindled down into nine French deserters.

According to their account, the fort at the fork was completed, and named Duquesne, in honor of the Governor of Canada, It was proof against all attack, excepting with bombs, on the land side. The garrison did not exceed five hundred, but two hundred more were hourly expected, and nine hundred in the course of a fortnight.

Washington's suspicions with respect to La Force's party were justified by the report of these deserters; they had been sent out as spies, and were to show the summons if discovered or overpowered. The French commander, they added, had been blamed for sending out so small a party.

On the same day Captain Mackay arrived, with his independent company of South Carolinians. The cross-purposes which Washington had apprehended, soon manifested themselves. The captain was civil and well disposed, but full of formalities and points of etiquette. Holding a commission direct from the king, he could not bring himself to acknowledge a provincial officer as his superior. He encamped separately, kept separate guards, would not agree that Washington should assign any rallying place for his men in case of alarm, and objected to receive from him the parole and countersign, though necessary for their common safety.

Washington conducted himself with circumspection, avoiding every thing that might call up a question of command, and reasoning calmly whenever such question occurred; but he urged the governor by letter, to prescribe their relative rank and authority. "He thinks you have not a power to give commissions that will command him. If so, I can very confidently say that his absence would tend to the public advantage."

On the 11th of June, Washington resumed the laborious march for Redstone Creek. As Captain Mackay could not oblige his men to work on the road unless they were allowed a shilling sterling a day; and as Washington did not choose to pay this, nor to suffer them to march at their ease while his own faithful soldiers were laboriously employed; he left the captain and his Independent company as a guard at Fort Necessity, and undertook to complete the military road with his own men.

Accordingly, he and his Virginia troops toiled forward through the narrow defiles of the mountains, working on the road as they went. Scouts were sent out in all directions, to prevent surprise. While on the march he was continually beset by sachems, with their tedious ceremonials and speeches, all to very little purpose. Some of these chiefs were secretly in the French interest; few rendered any real assistance, and all expected presents.

At Gist's establishment, about thirteen miles from Fort Necessity, Washington received certain intelligence that ample reinforcements had arrived at Fort Duquesne, and a large force would instantly be detached against him. Coming to a halt, he began to throw up intrenchments, calling in two foraging parties, and sending word to Captain Mackay to join him with all speed. The captain and his company arrived in the evening; the foraging parties the next morning. A council of war was held, in which the idea of awaiting the enemy at this place was unanimously abandoned.

A rapid and toilsome retreat ensued. There was a deficiency of horses. Washington gave up his own to aid in transporting the military munitions, leaving his baggage to be brought on by soldiers, whom he paid liberally. The other officers followed his example. The weather was sultry; the roads were rough; provisions were scanty, and the men dispirited by hunger. The Virginian soldiers took turns to drag the swivels, but felt almost insulted by the conduct of the South Carolinians, who, piquing themselves upon their assumed privileges as "king's soldiers," sauntered along at their ease; refusing to act as pioneers, or participate in the extra labors incident to a hurried retreat.

On the 1st of July they reached the Great Meadows. Here the Virginians, exhausted by fatigue, hunger, and vexation, declared they would carry the baggage and drag the swivels no further. Contrary to his original intentions, therefore, Washington determined to halt here for the present, and fortify, sending off expresses to hasten supplies and reinforcements from Wills' Creek, where he had reason to believe that two independent companies from New York, were by this time arrived.

The retreat to the Great Meadows had not been in the least too precipitate. Captain de Villiers, a brother-in-law of Jumonville, had actually sallied forth from Fort Duquesne at the head of upwards of five hundred French, and several hundred Indians, eager to avenge the death of his relative. Arriving about dawn of day at Gist's plantation, he surrounded the works which Washington had hastily thrown up there, and fired into them. Finding them deserted, he concluded that those of whom he came in search had made good their retreat to the settlements, and it was too late to pursue them. He was on the point of returning to Fort Duquesne, when a deserter arrived, who gave word that Washington had come to a halt in the Great Meadows, where his troops were in a starving condition; for his own part, he added, hearing that the French were coming, he had deserted to them to escape starvation.

De Villiers ordered the fellow into confinement; to be rewarded if his words proved true, otherwise to be hanged. He then pushed forward for the Great Meadows.[34]

In the mean time Washington had exerted himself to enlarge and strengthen Fort Necessity, nothing of which had been done by Captain Mackay and his men, while encamped there. The fort was about a hundred feet square, protected by trenches and palisades. It stood on the margin of a small stream, nearly in the centre of the Great Meadows, which is a grassy plain, perfectly level, surrounded by wooded hills of a moderate height, and at that place about two hundred and fifty yards wide. Washington asked no assistance from the South Carolina troops, but set to work with his Virginians, animating them by word and example; sharing in the labor of felling trees, hewing off the branches, and rolling up the trunks to form a breastwork.

---

34   Hazard's Register of Pennsylvania, vol. iv., p. 22.

At this critical juncture he was deserted by his Indian allies. They were disheartened at the scanty preparations for defence against a superior force, and offended at being subjected to military command. The half-king thought he had not been sufficiently consulted, and that his advice had not been sufficiently followed; such, at least, were some of the reasons which he subsequently gave for abandoning the youthful commander on the approach of danger. The true reason was a desire to put his wife and children in a place of safety. Most of his warriors followed his example; very few, and those probably who had no families at risk, remained in the camp.

Early in the morning of the 3d, while Washington and his men were working on the fort, a sentinel came in wounded and bleeding, having been fired upon. Scouts brought word shortly afterwards that the French were in force, about four miles off. Washington drew up his men on level ground outside of the works, to await their attack. About 11 o'clock there was a firing of musketry from among trees on rising ground, but so distant as to do no harm; suspecting this to be a stratagem designed to draw his men into the woods, he ordered them to keep quiet, and refrain from firing until the foe should show themselves, and draw near.

The firing was kept up, but still under cover. He now fell back with his men into the trenches, ordering them to fire whenever they could get sight of an enemy. In this way there was skirmishing throughout the day; the French and Indians advancing as near as the covert of the woods would permit, which in the nearest place was sixty yards, but never into open sight. In the meanwhile the rain fell in torrents; the harassed and jaded troops were half drowned in their trenches, and many of their muskets were rendered unfit for use.

About eight at night the French requested a parley. Washington hesitated. It might be a stratagem to gain admittance for a spy into the fort. The request was repeated, with the addition that an officer might be sent to treat with them, under their parole for his safety. Unfortunately the Chevalier de Peyrouney, engineer of the regiment, and the only one who could speak French correctly, was wounded and disabled. Washington had to send, therefore, his ancient swordsman and interpreter, Jacob Van Braam. The captain returned twice with separate terms, in which the garrison was required to surrender; both were rejected. He returned a third time, with written articles of capitulation. They were in French. As no implements for writing were at hand, Van Braam undertook to translate them by word of mouth. A candle was brought, and held close to the paper while he read. The rain fell in torrents; it was difficult to keep the light from being extinguished. The captain rendered the capitulation, article by article, in mongrel English, while Washington and his officers stood listening, endeavoring to disentangle the meaning. One article stipulated that on surrendering the fort they should leave all their military stores, munitions, and artillery in possession of the French. This was objected to, and was readily modified.

The main articles, as Washington and his officers understood them, were, that they should be allowed to return to the settlements without molestation from French or Indians. That they should march out of the fort with the honors of war, drums beating and colors flying, and with all their effects and military stores excepting the artillery, which should be destroyed. That they should be allowed to deposit their effects in some secret place, and leave a guard to protect them until they could send horses to bring them away; their horses having been nearly all killed or lost during the action. That they should give their word of honor not to attempt any buildings or improvements on the lands of his most Christian Majesty, for the space of a year. That the prisoners taken in the skirmish of Jumonville should be restored, and until their delivery Captain Van Braam and Captain Stobo should remain with the French as hostages.[35]

The next morning accordingly, Washington and his men marched out of their forlorn fortress with the honors of war, bearing with them their regimental colors, but leaving behind a large flag, too cumbrous to be transported. Scarcely had they begun their march, however, when, in defiance of the terms of capitulation, they were beset by a large body of Indians, allies of the French, who began plundering the baggage, and committing other irregularities. Seeing that the French did not, or could not, prevent them, and that all the baggage which could not be transported on the shoulders of his troops would fall into the hands of these savages, Washington ordered it to be destroyed, as well as the artillery, gunpowder, and

---

35   Horace Walpole, in a flippant notice of this capitulation, says: "The French have tied up the hands of an excellent *fanfaron*, a Major Washington, whom they took and engaged not to serve for one year." (Correspondence, vol. iii., p. 73.) Walpole, at this early date, seems to have considered Washington a perfect fire-eater.

other military stores. All this detained him until ten o'clock, when he set out on his melancholy march. He had not proceeded above a mile when two or three of the wounded men were reported to be missing. He immediately detached a few men back in quest of them, and continued on until three miles from Fort Necessity, where he encamped for the night, and was rejoined by the stragglers.

In this affair, out of the Virginia regiment, consisting of three hundred and five men, officers included, twelve had been killed, and forty-three wounded. The number killed and wounded in Captain Mackay's company is not known. The loss of the French and Indians is supposed to have been much greater.

In the following days' march the troops seemed jaded and disheartened; they were encumbered and delayed by the wounded; provisions were scanty, and they had seventy weary miles to accomplish before they could meet with supplies. Washington, however, encouraged them by his own steadfast and cheerful demeanor, and by sharing all their toils and privations; and at length conducted them in safety to Wills' Creek, where they found ample provisions in the military magazines. Leaving them here to recover their strength, he proceeded with Captain Mackay to Williamsburg, to make his military report to the governor.

A copy of the capitulation was subsequently laid before the Virginia House of Burgesses, with explanations. Notwithstanding the unfortunate result of the campaign, the conduct of Washington and his officers was properly appreciated, and they received a vote of thanks for their bravery, and gallant defence of their country. Three hundred pistoles (nearly eleven hundred dollars) also were voted to be distributed among the privates who had been in action.

From the vote of thanks, two officers were excepted; Major Stobo, who was charged with cowardice, and Washington's unfortunate master of fence and blundering interpreter, Jacob Van Braam, who was accused of treachery, in purposely misinterpreting the articles of capitulation.

In concluding this chapter, we will anticipate dates to record the fortunes of the half-king after his withdrawal from the camp. He and several of his warriors, with their wives and children, retreated to Aughquick, in the back part of Pennsylvania, where George Croghan had an agency, and was allowed money from time to time for the maintenance Of Indian allies. By the by, Washington, in his letter to William Fairfax, expressed himself much disappointed in Croghan and Montour, who proved, he said, to be great pretenders, and by vainly boasting of their interest with the Indians, involved the country in great calamity, causing dependence to be placed where there was none.[36] For, with all their boast, they never could induce above thirty fighting men to join the camp, and not more than half of those rendered any service.

As to the half-king, he expressed himself perfectly disgusted with the white man's mode of warfare. The French, he said, were cowards; the English, fools. Washington was a good man, but wanted experience: he would not take advice of the Indians and was always driving them to fight according to his own notions. For this reason he (the half-king) had carried off his wife and children to a place of safety.

After a time the chieftain fell dangerously ill, and a conjurer or "medicine man" was summoned to inquire into the cause or nature of his malady. He gave it as his opinion that the French had bewitched him, in revenge for the great blow he had struck them in the affair of Jumonville; for the Indians gave him the whole credit of that success, he having sent round the French scalps as trophies. In the opinion of the conjurer all the friends of the chieftain concurred, and on his death, which took place shortly afterwards, there was great lamentation, mingled with threats of immediate vengeance. The foregoing particulars are gathered from a letter written by John Harris, an Indian trader, to the Governor of Pennsylvania, at the request of the half-king's friend and fellow sachem, Monacatoocha, otherwise called Scarooyadi. "I humbly presume," concludes John Harris, "that his death is a very great loss, especially at this critical time."[37]

NOTE.

We have been thus particular in tracing the affair of the Great Meadows, step by step, guided by the statements of Washington himself and of one of his officers, present in the engagement, because it is another of the events in the early stage

36 Letter to W. Fairfax, Aug. 11th, 1754.
37 Pennsylvania Archives, vol. ii., p. 178.

of his military career, before the justice and magnanimity of his character were sufficiently established which have been subject to misrepresentation. When the articles of capitulation came to be correctly translated and published, there were passages in them derogatory to the honor of Washington and his troops, and, which, it would seem, had purposely been inserted for their humiliation by the French commander; but which, they protested, had never been rightly translated by Van Braam. For instance, in the written articles, they were made to stipulate that for the space of a year, they would not work on any establishment beyond the mountains; whereas it had been translated by Van Braam "on any establishment *on the lands of the King of France*" which was quite another thing, as most of the land beyond the mountains was considered by them as belonging to the British crown. There were other points, of minor importance, relative to the disposition of the artillery; but the most startling and objectionable one was that concerning the previous skirmish in the Great Meadows. This was mentioned in the written articles as *l'assassinat du Sieur de Jumonville*, that is to say, the *murder* of De Jumonville; an expression from which Washington and his officers would have revolted with scorn and indignation; and which, if truly translated, would in all probability have caused the capitulation to be sent back instantly to the French commander. On the contrary, they declared it had been translated to them by Van Braam the *death* of De Jumonville.

M. de Villiers, in his account of this transaction to the French government, avails himself of these passages in the capitulation to cast a slur on the conduct of Washington. He says, "We made the English consent to sign that they had assassinated my brother in his camp."—"We caused them to abandon the lands belonging to the king.—We obliged them to leave their cannon, which consisted of nine pieces, &c." He further adds: "The English, struck with panic, took to flight, and left their flag and one of their colors." We have shown that the flag left was the unwieldy one belonging to the fort; too cumbrous to be transported by troops who could not carry their own necessary baggage. The regimental colors, as honorable symbols, were scrupulously carried off by Washington, and retained by him in after years.

M. de Villiers adds another incident intended to degrade his enemy. He says, "One of my Indians took ten Englishmen, whom he brought to me, and whom I sent back by another." These, doubtless, were the men detached by Washington in quest of the wounded loiterers; and who, understanding neither French nor Indian, found a difficulty in explaining their peaceful errand. That they were captured by the Indian seems too much of a gasconade.

The public opinion at the time was that Van Braam had been suborned by De Villiers to soften the offensive articles of the capitulation in translating them, so that they should not wound the pride nor awaken the scruples of Washington and his officers, yet should stand on record against them. It is not probable that a French officer of De Villiers' rank would practise such a base perfidy, nor does the subsequent treatment experienced by Van Braam from the French corroborate the charge. It is more than probable the inaccuracy of translation originated in his ignorance of the precise weight and value of words in the two languages, neither of which was native to him, and between which he was the blundering agent of exchange.

CHAPTER XIII.

FOUNDING OF PORT CUMBERLAND—SECRET LETTER
OF STOBO—THE INDIAN MESSENGER—PROJECT
OF DINWIDDIE—HIS PERPLEXITIES—A TAINT OF
REPUBLICANISM IN THE COLONIAL ASSEMBLIES—
DINWIDDIE'S MILITARY MEASURES—WASHINGTON
QUITS THE SERVICE—OVERTURES OF GOVERNOR
SHARPE, OF MARYLAND—WASHINGTON'S DIGNIFIED
REPLY—QUESTIONS OF RANK BETWEEN ROYAL AND
PROVINCIAL TROOPS—TREATMENT OF THE FRENCH
PRISONERS—FATE OF LA FORCE—ANECDOTES OF
STOBO AND VAN BRAAM.

Early in August Washington rejoined his regiment, which
had arrived at Alexandria by the way of Winchester. Letters
from Governor Dinwiddie urged him to recruit it to the former
number of three hundred men, and join Colonel Innes at Wills'
Creek, where that officer was stationed with Mackay's independent
company of South Carolinians, and two independent companies
from New York; and had been employed in erecting a work to
serve as a frontier post and rallying point; which work received the
name of Fort Cumberland, in honor of the Duke of Cumberland,
captain-general of the British army.

In the mean time the French, elated by their recent triumph,
and thinking no danger at hand, relaxed their vigilance at Fort
Duquesne. Stobo, who was a kind of prisoner at large there,
found means to send a letter secretly by an Indian, dated July
28, and directed to the commander of the English troops. It was
accompanied by a plan of the fort. "There are two hundred men
here," writes he, "and two hundred expected; the rest have gone off
in detachments to the amount of one thousand, besides Indians.

None lodge in the fort but Contrecoeur and the guard, consisting of forty men and five officers; the rest lodge in bark cabins around the fort. The Indians have access day and night, and come and go when they please. If one hundred trusty Shawnees, Mingoes, and Delawares were picked out, they might surprise the fort, lodging themselves under the palisades by day, and at night secure the guard with their tomahawks, shut the sally-gate, and the fort is ours."

One part of Stobo's letter breathes a loyal and generous spirit of self-devotion. Alluding to the danger in which he and Van Braam, his fellow-hostage, might be involved, he says, "Consider the good of the expedition without regard to us. When we engaged to serve the country it was expected we were to do it with our lives. For my part, I would die a hundred deaths to have the pleasure of possessing this fort but one day. They are so vain of their success at the Meadows it is worse than death to hear them. Haste to strike."[38]

The Indian messenger carried the letter to Aughquick and delivered it into the hands of George Croghan. The Indian chiefs who were with him insisted upon his opening it. He did so, but on finding the tenor of it, transmitted it to the Governor of Pennsylvania. The secret information communicated by Stobo, may have been the cause of a project suddenly conceived by Governor Dinwiddie, of a detachment which, by a forced march across the mountains, might descend upon the French and take Fort Duquesne at a single blow; or, failing that, might build a rival fort in its vicinity. He accordingly wrote to Washington to march forthwith for Wills' Creek, with such companies as were complete, leaving orders with the officers to follow as soon as they should have enlisted men sufficient to make up their companies. "The season of the year," added he, "calls for despatch. I depend upon your usual diligence and spirit to encourage your people to be active on this occasion."

The ignorance of Dinwiddie in military affairs, and his want of forecast, led him perpetually into blunders. Washington saw the rashness of an attempt to dispossess the French with a force so inferior that it could be harassed and driven from place to place at their pleasure. Before the troops could be collected, and munitions of war provided, the season would be too far advanced. There would be no forage for the horses; the streams would be swollen

---

38   Hazard's Register of Penn., iv., 329.

117

and unfordable; the mountains rendered impassable by snow, and frost, and slippery roads. The men, too, unused to campaigning on the frontier, would not be able to endure a winter in the wilderness, with no better shelter than a tent; especially in their present condition, destitute of almost every thing. Such are a few of the cogent reasons urged by Washington in a letter to his friend William Fairfax, then in the House of Burgesses, which no doubt was shown to Governor Dinwiddie, and probably had an effect in causing the rash project to be abandoned.

The governor, in truth, was sorely perplexed about this time by contradictions and cross-purposes, both in military and civil affairs. A body of three hundred and fifty North Carolinian troops had been enlisted at high pay, and were to form the chief reinforcement of Colonel Innes at Wills' Creek. By the time they reached Winchester, however, the provincial military chest was exhausted, and future pay seemed uncertain; whereupon they refused to serve any longer, disbanded themselves tumultuously, and set off for their homes without taking leave.

The governor found the House of Burgesses equally unmanageable. His demands for supplies were resisted on what he considered presumptuous pretexts; or granted sparingly, under mortifying restrictions. His high Tory notions were outraged by such republican conduct. "There appears to me," said he, "an infatuation in all the assemblies in this part of the world." In a letter to the Board of Trade he declared that the only way effectually to check the progress of the French, would be an act of parliament requiring the colonies to contribute to the common cause, *independently of assemblies*; and in another, to the Secretary of State, he urged the policy of compelling the colonies to their duty to the king by a general poll-tax of two and sixpence a head. The worthy governor would have made a fitting counsellor for the Stuart dynasty. Subsequent events have shown how little his policy was suited to compete with the dawning republicanism of America.

In the month of October the House of Burgesses made a grant of twenty thousand pounds for the public service; and ten thousand more were sent out from England, beside a supply of firearms. The governor now applied himself to military matters with renewed spirit; increased the actual force to ten companies; and, as there had been difficulties among the different kinds of troops with regard to precedence, he reduced them all to independent companies; so that there would be no officer in a Virginia regiment above the rank of captain.

This shrewd measure, upon which Dinwiddie secretly prided himself as calculated to put an end to the difficulties in question, immediately drove Washington out of the service; considering it derogatory to his character to accept a lower commission than that under which his conduct had gained him a vote of thanks from the Legislature.

Governor Sharpe, of Maryland, appointed by the king commander-in-chief of all the forces engaged against the French, sought to secure his valuable services, and authorized Colonel Fitzhugh, whom he had placed in temporary command of the army, to write to him to that effect. The reply of Washington (15th Nov.) is full of dignity and spirit, and shows how deeply he felt his military degradation.

"You make mention," says he, "of my continuing in the service and retaining my colonel's commission. This idea has filled me with surprise; for if you think me capable of holding a commission that has neither rank nor emolument annexed to it, you must maintain a very contemptible opinion of my weakness, and believe me more empty than the commission itself." After intimating a suspicion that the project of reducing the regiment into independent companies, and thereby throwing out the higher officers, was "generated and hatched at Wills' Creek,"—in other words, was an expedient of Governor Dinwiddie, instead of being a peremptory order from England, he adds, "Ingenuous treatment and plain dealing I at least expected. It is to be hoped the project will answer; it shall meet with my acquiescence in every thing except personal services. I herewith inclose Governor Sharpe's letter, which I beg you will return to him with my acknowledgments for the favor he intended me. Assure him, sir, as you truly may, of my reluctance to quit the service, and the pleasure I should have received in attending his fortunes. Inform him, also, that it was to obey the call of honor and the advice of my friends that I declined it, and not to gratify any desire I had to leave the military line. My feelings are strongly bent to arms."

Even had Washington hesitated to take this step, it would have been forced upon him by a further regulation of government, in the course of the ensuing winter, settling the rank of officers of his majesty's forces when joined or serving with the provincial forces in North America, "which directed that all such as were commissioned by the king, or by his general commander-in-chief in North America, should take rank of all officers commissioned by the governors of the respective provinces. And further, that the general and field officers of the provincial troops should have no rank when serving with the general and field officers commissioned by the crown; but that all captains and other inferior officers of the royal troops should take rank over provincial officers of the same grade, having older commissions."

These regulations, originating in that supercilious assumption of superiority which sometimes overruns and degrades true British pride, would have been spurned by Washington, as insulting to the character and conduct of his high-minded brethren of the colonies. How much did this open disparagement of colonial honor and understanding, contribute to wean from England the affection of her American subjects, and prepare the way for their ultimate assertion of independence.

Another cause of vexation to Washington was the refusal of Governor Dinwiddie to give up the French prisoners, taken in the affair of De Jumonville, in fulfilment of the articles of capitulation. His plea was, that since the capitulation, the French had taken several British subjects, and sent them prisoners to Canada he considered himself justifiable in detaining those Frenchmen which he had in his custody. He sent a flag of truce, however, offering to return the officer Drouillon, and the two cadets, in exchange for Captains Stobo and Van Braam, whom the French held as hostages; but his offer was treated with merited disregard. Washington felt deeply mortified by this obtuseness of the governor on a point of military punctilio and honorable faith, but his remonstrances were unavailing.

The French prisoners were clothed and maintained at the public expense, and Drouillon and the cadets were allowed to go at large; the private soldiers were kept in confinement. La Force, also, not having acted in a military capacity, and having offended against the peace and security of the frontier, by his intrigues among the Indians, was kept in close durance. Washington, who knew nothing of this, was shocked on visiting Williamsburg, to learn that La Force was in prison. He expostulated with the governor on the subject, but without effect; Dinwiddie was at all times pertinacious, but particularly so when he felt himself to be a little in the wrong.

As we shall have no further occasion to mention La Force, in connection with the subject of this work, we will anticipate a page of his fortunes. After remaining two years in confinement he succeeded in breaking out of prison, and escaping into the country. An alarm was given, and circulated far and wide, for such was the opinion of his personal strength, desperate courage, wily cunning, and great influence over the Indians, that the most mischievous results were apprehended should he regain the frontier. In the mean time he was wandering about the country ignorant of the roads, and fearing to make inquiries, lest his foreign tongue should betray him. He reached King and Queen Court House, about thirty miles from Williamsburg, when a countryman was struck with his foreign air and aspect. La Force ventured to put a question as to the distance and direction of Fort Duquesne, and his broken English convinced the countryman of his being the French prisoner, whose escape had been noised about the country. Watching an opportunity he seized him, and regardless of offers of great bribes, conducted him back to the prison of Williamsburg, where he was secured with double irons, and chained to the floor of his dungeon.

The refusal of Governor Dinwiddie to fulfil the article of the capitulation respecting the prisoners, and the rigorous treatment of La Force, operated hardly upon the hostages, Stobo and Van Braam, who, in retaliation, were confined in prison in Quebec, though otherwise treated with kindness. They, also, by extraordinary efforts, succeeded in breaking prison, but found it more difficult to evade the sentries of a fortified place. Stobo managed to escape into the country; but the luckless Van Braam sought concealment under an arch of a causeway leading from the fortress. Here he remained until nearly exhausted by hunger. Seeing the Governor of Canada passing by, and despairing of being able to effect his escape, he came forth from his hiding place, and surrendered himself, invoking his clemency. He was remanded to prison, but experienced no additional severity. He was subsequently shipped by the governor from Quebec to England, and never returned to Virginia. It is this treatment of Van Braam, more than any thing else, which convinces us that the suspicion of his being in collusion with the French in regard to the misinterpretation of the articles of capitulation, was groundless. He was simply a blunderer.

CHAPTER XIV.

RETURN TO QUIET LIFE—FRENCH AND ENGLISH
PREPARE FOR HOSTILITIES—PLAN OF A CAMPAIGN—
GENERAL BRADDOCK—HIS CHARACTER—SIR JOHN
ST. CLAIR, QUARTERMASTER-GENERAL—HIS TOUR
OF INSPECTION—PROJECTED ROADS—ARRIVAL
OF BRADDOCK—MILITARY CONSULTATIONS AND
PLANS—COMMODORE KEPPEL AND HIS SEAMEN—
SHIPS AND TROOPS AT ALEXANDRIA—EXCITEMENT
OF WASHINGTON—INVITED TO JOIN THE STAFF
OF BRADDOCK—A MOTHER'S OBJECTIONS—
WASHINGTON AT ALEXANDRIA—GRAND COUNCIL
OF GOVERNORS—MILITARY ARRANGEMENTS—
COLONEL WILLIAM JOHNSON—SIR JOHN ST. CLAIR AT
FORT CUMBERLAND—HIS EXPLOSIONS OF WRATH—
THEIR EFFECTS—INDIANS TO BE ENLISTED—
CAPTAIN JACK AND HIS BAND OF BUSH-BEATERS.

Having resigned his commission, and disengaged himself from public affairs, Washington's first care was to visit his mother, inquire into the state of domestic concerns, and attend to the welfare of his brothers and sisters. In these matters he was ever his mother's adjunct and counsellor, discharging faithfully the duties of an eldest son, who should consider himself a second father to the family.

He now took up his abode at Mount Vernon, and prepared to engage in those agricultural pursuits, for which, even in his youthful days, he had as keen a relish as for the profession of arms. Scarcely had he entered upon his rural occupations, however, when the service of his country once more called him to the field.

The disastrous affair at the Great Meadows, and the other acts of French hostility on the Ohio, had roused the attention of the British ministry. Their ambassador at Paris was instructed to complain of those violations of the peace. The court of Versailles amused him with general assurances of amity, and a strict adherence to treaties. Their ambassador at the court of St. James, the Marquis de Mirepoix, on the faith of his instructions, gave the same assurances. In the mean time, however, French ships were fitted out, and troops embarked, to carry out the schemes of the government in America. So profound was the dissimulation of the court of Versailles, that even their own ambassador is said to have been kept in ignorance of their real designs, and of the hostile game they were playing, while he was exerting himself in good faith, to lull the suspicions of England, and maintain the international peace. When his eyes, however, were opened, he returned indignantly to France, and upbraided the cabinet with the duplicity of which he had been made the unconscious instrument.

The British government now prepared for military operations in America; none of them professedly aggressive, but rather to resist and counteract aggressions. A plan of campaign was devised for 1755, having four objects.

To eject the French from lands which they held unjustly, in the province of Nova Scotia.

To dislodge them from a fortress which they had erected at Crown Point, on Lake Champlain, within what was claimed as British territory.

To dispossess them of the fort which they had constructed at Niagara, between Lake Ontario and Lake Erie.

To drive them from the frontiers of Pennsylvania and Virginia, and recover the valley of the Ohio.

The Duke of Cumberland, captain-general of the British army, had the organization of this campaign; and through his patronage, Major-general Edward Braddock was intrusted with the execution of it, being appointed generalissimo of all the forces in the colonies.

Braddock was a veteran in service, and had been upwards of forty years in the guards, that school of exact discipline and technical punctilio. Cumberland, who held a commission in the guards, and was bigoted to its routine, may have considered Braddock fitted, by his skill and preciseness as a tactician, for a command in a new country, inexperienced in military science, to bring its raw levies into order, and to settle those questions of rank and etiquette apt to arise where regular and provincial troops are to act together.

The result proved the error of such an opinion. Braddock was a brave and experienced officer but his experience was that of routine, and rendered him pragmatical and obstinate, impatient of novel expedients "not laid down in the books," but dictated by emergencies in a "new country," and his military precision, which would have been brilliant on parade, was a constant obstacle to alert action in the wilderness.[39]

Braddock was to lead in person the grand enterprise of the campaign, that destined for the frontiers of Virginia and Pennsylvania; it was the enterprise in which Washington became enlisted, and, therefore, claims our especial attention.

Prior to the arrival of Braddock, came out from England Lieutenant-colonel Sir John St. Clair, deputy quartermaster-general, eager to make himself acquainted with the field of operations. He made a tour of inspection, in company with Governor Sharpe, of Maryland, and appears to have been dismayed at sight of the impracticable wilderness, the region of Washington's campaign. From Fort Cumberland, he wrote in February to Governor Morris, of Pennsylvania, to have the road cut, or repaired, toward the head of the river Youghiogeny, and another opened from Philadelphia for the transportation of supplies. "No general," writes he, "will

---

39   Horace Walpole, in his letters, relates some anecdotes of Braddock, which give a familiar picture of him in the fashionable life in which he had mingled in London, and are of value, as letting us into the private character of a man whose name has become proverbial in American history. "Braddock," says Walpole, "is a very Iroquois in disposition. He had a sister, who, having gamed away all her little fortune at Bath, hanged herself with a truly English deliberation, leaving a note on the table with these lines: 'To die is landing on some silent shore,' &c. When Braddock was told of it, he only said: 'Poor Fanny! I always thought she would play till she would be forced to tuck herself up.'"

Braddock himself had been somewhat of a spendthrift. He was touchy also, and punctilious. "He once had a duel," says Walpole, "with Colonel Glumley, Lady Bath's brother, who had been his great friend. As they were going to engage, Glumley, who had good humor and wit (Braddock had the latter) said: 'Braddock, you are a poor dog! here, take my purse, if you kill me you will be forced to run away, and then you will not have a shilling to support you.' Braddock refused the purse, insisted on the duel, was disarmed, and would not even ask for his life."

advance with an army without having a communication open to the provinces in his rear, both for the security of retreat, and to facilitate the transport of provisions, the supplying of which must greatly depend on your province."[40]

Unfortunately the governor of Pennsylvania had no money at his command, and was obliged, for expenses, to apply to his Assembly, "a set of men," writes he, "quite unacquainted with every kind of military service, and exceedingly unwilling to part with money on any terms." However, by dint of exertions, he procured the appointment of commissioners to explore the country, and survey and lay out the roads required. At the head of the commission was George Croghan, the Indian trader, whose mission to the Twightwees we have already spoken of. Times had gone hard with Croghan. The French had seized great quantities of his goods. The Indians, with whom he traded, had failed to pay their debts, and he had become a bankrupt. Being an efficient agent on the frontier, and among the Indians, he still enjoyed the patronage of the Pennsylvania government.

When Sir John St. Clair had finished his tour of inspection, he descended Wills' Creek and the Potomac for two hundred miles in a canoe to Alexandria, and repaired to Virginia to meet General Braddock. The latter had landed on the 20th of February at Hampton, in Virginia, and proceeded to Williamsburg to consult with Governor Dinwiddie. Shortly afterwards he was joined there by Commodore Keppel, whose squadron of two ships-of-war, and several transports, had anchored in the Chesapeake. On board of these ships were two prime regiments of about five hundred men each; one commanded by Sir Peter Halket, the other by Colonel Dunbar; together with a train of artillery, and the necessary munitions of war. The regiments were to be augmented to seven hundred men, each by men selected by Sir John St. Clair from Virginia companies recently raised.

Alexandria was fixed upon as the place where the troops should disembark, and encamp. The ships were accordingly ordered up to that place, and the levies directed to repair thither.

The plan of the campaign included the use of Indian allies. Governor Dinwiddie had already sent Christopher Gist, the pioneer,

40   Colonial Records, vi., 300.

Washington's guide in 1753, to engage the Cherokees and Catawbas, the bravest of the Southern tribes, who he had no doubt would take up the hatchet for the English, peace being first concluded, through the mediation of his government, between them and the Six Nations; and he gave Braddock reason to expect at least four hundred Indians to join him at Port Cumberland. He laid before him also contracts that he had made for cattle, and promises that the Assembly of Pennsylvania had made of flour; these, with other supplies, and a thousand barrels of beef on board of the transports, would furnish six months' provisions for four thousand men.

General Braddock apprehended difficulty in procuring wagons and horses sufficient to attend him in his march. Sir John St. Clair, in the course of his tour of inspection, had met with two Dutch settlers, at the foot of the Blue Ridge, who engaged to furnish two hundred waggons, and fifteen hundred carrying-horses, to be at Fort Cumberland early in May.

Governor Sharpe was to furnish above a hundred waggons for the transportation of stores, on the Maryland side of the Potomac.

Keppel furnished four cannons from his ships, for the attack on Fort Duquesne, and thirty picked seamen to assist in dragging them over the mountains; for "soldiers," said he, "cannot be as well acquainted with the nature of purchases, and making use of tackles, as seamen," They were to aid also in passing the troops and artillery on floats or in boats, across the rivers, and were under the command of a midshipman and lieutenant.[41]

"Every thing," writes Captain Robert Orme, one of the general's aides-de-camp, "seemed to promise so far the greatest success. The transports were all arrived safe, and the men in health. Provisions, Indians, carriages, and horses, were already provided; at least were to be esteemed so, considering the authorities on which they were promised to the general."

Trusting to these arrangements, Braddock proceeded to Alexandria. The troops had all been disembarked before his arrival, and the Virginia levies selected by Sir John St. Clair, to join the regiments of regulars, were arrived. There were beside two companies of hatchet men, or carpenters; six of rangers; and one troop of light horse. The levies, having been clothed, were ordered

---

41   Keppel's Life of Keppel, p. 205.

to march immediately for Winchester, to be armed, and the general gave them in charge of an ensign of the 44th, "to make them as like soldiers as possible."[42] The light horse were retained by the general as his escort and body guard.

The din and stir of warlike preparation disturbed the quiet of Mount Vernon. Washington looked down from his rural retreat upon the ships of war and transports, as they passed up the Potomac, with the array of arms gleaming along their decks. The booming of cannon echoed among his groves. Alexandria was but a few miles distant. Occasionally he mounted his horse, and rode to that place; it was like a garrisoned town, teeming with troops, and resounding with the drum and fife. A brilliant campaign was about to open under the auspices of an experienced general, and with all the means and appurtenances of European warfare. How different from the starveling expeditions he had hitherto been doomed to conduct! What an opportunity to efface the memory of his recent disaster! All his thoughts of rural life were put to flight. The military part of his character was again in the ascendant; his great desire was to join the expedition as a volunteer.

It was reported to General Braddock. The latter was apprised by Governor Dinwiddie and others, of Washington's personal merits, his knowledge of the country, and his experience in frontier service. The consequence was, a letter from Captain Robert Orme, one of Braddock's aides-de-camp, written by the general's order, inviting Washington to join his staff; the letter concluded with frank and cordial expressions of esteem on the part of Orme, which were warmly reciprocated, and laid the foundation of a soldierlike friendship between them.

A volunteer situation on the staff of General Braddock offered no emolument nor command, and would be attended with considerable expense, beside a sacrifice of his private interests, having no person in whom he had confidence, to take charge of his affairs in his absence; still he did not hesitate a moment to accept the invitation. In the position offered to him, all the questions of military rank which had hitherto annoyed him, would be obviated. He could indulge his passion for arms without any sacrifice of dignity, and he looked forward with high anticipation

---

42   Orme's Journal.

to an opportunity of acquiring military experience in a corps well organized, and thoroughly disciplined, and in the family of a commander of acknowledged skill as a tactician.

His mother heard with concern of another projected expedition into the wilderness. Hurrying to Mount Vernon, she entreated him not again to expose himself to the hardships and perils of these frontier campaigns. She doubtless felt the value of his presence at home, to manage and protect the complicated interests of the domestic connection, and had watched with solicitude over his adventurous campaigning, where so much family welfare was at hazard. However much a mother's pride may have been gratified by his early advancement and renown, she had rejoiced on his return to the safer walks of peaceful life. She was thoroughly practical and prosaic in her notions; and not to be dazzled by military glory. The passion for arms which mingled with the more sober elements of Washington's character, would seem to have been inherited from his father's side of the house; it was, in fact, the old chivalrous spirit of the De Wessyngtons.

His mother had once prevented him from entering the navy, when a gallant frigate was at hand, anchored in the waters of the Potomac; with all his deference for her, which he retained through life, he could not resist the appeal to his martial sympathies, which called him to the head-quarters of General Braddock at Alexandria.

His arrival was hailed by his young associates, Captains Orme and Morris, the general's aides-de-camp, who at once received him into frank companionship, and a cordial intimacy commenced between them, that continued throughout the campaign.

He experienced a courteous reception from the general, who expressed in flattering terms the impression he had received of his merits. Washington soon appreciated the character of the general. He found him stately and somewhat haughty, exact in matters of military etiquette and discipline, positive in giving an opinion, and obstinate in maintaining it; but of an honorable and generous, though somewhat irritable nature.

There were at that time four governors, beside Dinwiddie, assembled at Alexandria, at Braddock's request, to concert a plan of military operations; Governor Shirley, of Massachusetts; Lieutenant-governor Delancey, of New York; Lieutenant-governor Sharpe, of Maryland; Lieutenant-governor Morris, of Pennsylvania.

Washington was presented to them in a manner that showed how well his merits were already appreciated. Shirley seems particularly to have struck him as the model of a gentleman and statesman. He was originally a lawyer, and had risen not more by his talents, than by his implicit devotion to the crown. His son William was military secretary to Braddock.

A grand council was held on the 14th of April, composed of General Braddock, Commodore Keppel, and the governors, at which the general's commission was read, as were his instructions from the king, relating to a common fund, to be established by the several colonies, toward defraying the expenses of the campaign.

The governors were prepared to answer on this head, letters to the same purport having been addressed to them by Sir Thomas Robinson, one of the king's secretaries of state, in the preceding month of October. They informed Braddock that they had applied to their respective Assemblies for the establishment of such a fund, but in vain, and gave it as their unanimous opinion, that such a fund could never be established in the colonies without the aid of Parliament. They had found it impracticable, also, to obtain from their respective governments the proportions expected from them by the crown, toward military expenses in America; and suggested that ministers should find out some mode of compelling them to do it; and that, in the mean time, the general should make use of his credit upon government, for current expenses, lest the expedition should come to a stand.[43]

In discussing the campaign, the governors were of opinion that New York should be made the centre of operations, as it afforded easy access by water to the heart of the French possessions in Canada. Braddock, however, did not feel at liberty to depart from his instructions, which specified the recent establishments of the French on the Ohio as the objects of his expedition.

Niagara and Crown Point were to be attacked about the same time with Fort Duquesne, the former by Governor Shirley, with his own and Sir William Pepperell's regiments, and some New York companies; the latter by Colonel William Johnson, sole manager and director of Indian affairs; a personage worthy of especial note.

---

43   Colonial Records, vol vi., p. 366.

He was a native of Ireland, and had come out to this country in 1734, to manage the landed estates owned by his uncle, Commodore Sir Peter Warren, in the Mohawk country. He had resided ever since in the vicinity of the Mohawk River, in the province of New York. By his agency, and his dealings with the native tribes, he had acquired great wealth, and become a kind of potentate in the Indian country. His influence over the Six Nations was said to be unbounded; and it was principally with the aid of a large force of their warriors that it was expected he would accomplish his part of the campaign. The end of June, "nearly in July," was fixed upon as the time when the several attacks upon Forts Duquesne, Niagara, and Crown Point, should be carried into execution, and Braddock anticipated an easy accomplishment of his plans.

The expulsion of the French from the lands wrongfully held by them in Nova Scotia, was to be assigned to Colonel Lawrence, Lieutenant-governor of that province; we will briefly add, in anticipation, that it was effected by him, with the aid of troops from Massachusetts and elsewhere, led by Lieutenant-colonel Monckton.

The business of the Congress being finished, General Braddock would have set out for Fredericktown, in Maryland, but few waggons or teams had yet come to remove the artillery. Washington had looked with wonder and dismay at the huge paraphernalia of war, and the world of superfluities to be transported across the mountains, recollecting the difficulties he had experienced in getting over them with his nine swivels and scanty supplies. "If our march is to be regulated by the slow movements of the train," said he, "it will be tedious, very tedious, indeed." His predictions excited a sarcastic smile in Braddock, as betraying the limited notions of a young provincial officer, little acquainted with the march of armies.

In the mean while, Sir John St. Clair, who had returned to the frontier, was storming at the camp at Fort Cumberland. The road required of the Pennsylvania government had not been commenced. George Croghan and the other commissioners were but just arrived in camp. Sir John, according to Croghan, received them in a very disagreeable manner; would not look at their draughts, nor suffer any representations to be made to him in regard to the province, "but stormed like a lion rampant;" declaring that the want of the road and of the provisions promised by Pennsylvania had retarded the expedition, and might cost them, their lives from the fresh numbers of French that might be poured into the country.—"That instead of marching to the Ohio, he would in nine days march his army into Cumberland County to cut the roads, press horses, waggons, &c.—That he would not suffer a soldier to handle an axe, but by fire and sword oblige the inhabitants to do it. . . . That he would kill all kinds of cattle, and carry away the horses, burn the houses, &c.; and that if the French defeated them, by the delays of Pennsylvania, he would, with his sword drawn, pass through the province and treat the inhabitants as a parcel of traitors to his master. That he would write to England by a man-of-war; shake Mr. Penn's proprietaryship, and represent Pennsylvania as a disaffected province. . . . He told us to go to the general, if we pleased, who would give us *ten bad words for one that he had given.*"

The explosive wrath of Sir John, which was not to be appeased, shook the souls of the commissioners, and they wrote to Governor Morris, urging that people might be set at work upon the road, if the Assembly had made provision for opening it; and that flour might be sent without delay to the mouth of Canococheague River, "as being the only remedy left to prevent these threatened mischiefs."[44]

In reply, Mr. Richard Peters, Governor Morris's secretary, wrote in his name: "Get a number of hands immediately, and further the work by all possible methods. Your expenses will be paid at the next sitting of Assembly. Do your duty, and oblige the general and quartermaster if possible. Finish the road that will be wanted first, and then proceed to any other that may be thought necessary."

An additional commission, of a different kind, was intrusted to George Croghan. Governor Morris by letter requested him to convene at Aughquick, in Pennsylvania, as many warriors as possible of the mixed tribes of the Ohio, distribute among them wampum belts sent for the purpose, and engage them to meet General Braddock when on the march, and render him all the assistance in their power.

In reply, Croghan engaged to enlist a strong body of Indians, being sure of the influence of Scarooyadi, successor to the half-king, and of his adjunct, White Thunder, keeper of the speech-belts.[45] At the instance of Governor Morris, Croghan secured the services of another kind of force. This was a band of hunters,

---

44   Colonial Records, vol. vi., p. 368.
45   Colonial Records, vol. vi., p, 375.

resolute men, well acquainted with the country, and inured to hardships. They were under the command of Captain Jack, one of the most remarkable characters of Pennsylvania; a complete hero of the wilderness. He had been for many years a captive among the Indians; and, having learnt their ways, had formed this association for the protection of the settlements, receiving a commission of captain from the Governor of Pennsylvania. The band had become famous for its exploits, and was a terror to the Indians. Captain Jack was at present protecting the settlements on the Canococheague; but promised to march by a circuitous route and join Braddock with his hunters. "They require no shelter for the night," writes Croghan; "they ask no pay. If the whole army was composed of such men there would be no cause of apprehension. I shall be with them in time for duty."[46]

NOTE.

The following extract of a letter, dated August, 1750, gives one of the stories relative to this individual:

"The 'Black Hunter,' the 'Black Rifle,' the 'Wild Hunter of Juniata,' is a white man; his history is this: He entered the woods with a few enterprising companions; built his cabin; cleared a little land, and amused himself with the pleasures of fishing and hunting. He felt happy, for then he had not a care. But on an evening, when he returned from a day of sport, he found his cabin burnt, his wife and children murdered. From that moment he forsakes civilized man; hunts out caves, in which he lives; protects the frontier inhabitants from the Indians; and seizes every opportunity of revenge that offers. He lives the terror of the Indians and the consolation of the whites. On one occasion, near Juniata, in the middle of a dark night, a family were suddenly awaked from sleep by the report of a gun; they jump from their huts, and by the glimmering light from the chimney saw an Indian fall to rise no more. The open door exposed to view the wild hunter. 'I have saved your lives,' he cried, then turned and was buried in the gloom of night."—*Hazard's Register of Penn.*, vol. iv., 389.

---

46   Hazard's Register of Penn., vol. iv., p. 416.

CHAPTER XV.

WASHINGTON PROCLAIMED AIDE-DE-CAMP—
DISAPPOINTMENTS AT FREDERICKTOWN—BENJAMIN
FRANKLIN AND BRADDOCK—CONTRACTS—
DEPARTURE FOR WILLS' CREEK—ROUGH ROADS—
THE GENERAL IN HIS CHARIOT—CAMP AT FORT
CUMBERLAND—HUGH MERCER—DR. CRAIK—
MILITARY TACTICS—CAMP RULES—SECRETARY
PETERS—INDIANS IN CAMP—INDIAN BEAUTIES—
THE PRINCESS BRIGHT LIGHTNING—ERRAND
TO WILLIAMSBURG—BRADDOCK'S OPINION
OF CONTRACTORS AND INDIANS—ARRIVAL OF
CONVEYANCES.

General Braddock set out from Alexandria on the 20th of April. Washington remained behind a few days to arrange his affairs, and then rejoined him at Fredericktown, in Maryland, where, on the 10th of May, he was proclaimed one of the general's aides-de-camp. The troubles of Braddock had already commenced. The Virginian contractors failed to fulfil their engagements; of all the immense means of transportation so confidently promised, but fifteen waggons and a hundred draft-horses had arrived, and there was no prospect of more. There was equal disappointment in provisions, both as to quantity and quality; and he had to send round the country to buy cattle for the subsistence of the troops.

Fortunately, while the general was venting his spleen in anathemas against army contractors, Benjamin Franklin arrived at Fredericktown. That eminent man, then about forty-nine years of age, had been for many years member of the Pennsylvania Assembly, and was now postmaster-general for America. The Assembly understood that Braddock was incensed against them, supposing them adverse to the service of the war. They had procured Franklin to wait upon him, not as if sent by them, but as if he came in his capacity of postmaster-general, to arrange for the sure and speedy transmission of despatches between the commander-in-chief and the governors of the provinces.

He was well received, and became a daily guest at the general's table. In his autobiography, he gives us an instance of the blind confidence and fatal prejudices by which Braddock was deluded throughout this expedition. "In conversation with him one day," writes Franklin, "he was giving me some account of his intended progress. 'After taking Fort Duquesne,' said he, 'I am to proceed to Niagara; and, having taken that, to Frontenac, if the season will allow time; and I suppose it will, for Duquesne can hardly detain me above three or four days: and then I can see nothing that can obstruct my march to Niagara.'

"Having before revolved in my mind," continues Franklin, "the long line his army must make in their march by a very narrow road, to be cut for them through the woods and bushes, and also what I had heard of a former defeat of fifteen hundred French, who invaded the Illinois country, I had conceived some doubts and some fears for the event of the campaign; but I ventured only to say, 'To be sure, sir, if you arrive well before Duquesne with these fine troops, so well provided with artillery, the fort, though completely fortified, and assisted with a very strong garrison, can probably make but a short resistance. The only danger I apprehend of obstruction to your march, is from the ambuscades of the Indians, who, by constant practice, are dexterous in laying and executing them; and the slender line, nearly four miles long, which your army must make, may expose it to be attacked by surprise on its flanks, and to be cut like thread into several pieces, which, from their distance, cannot come up in time to support one another.'

"He smiled at my ignorance, and replied: 'These savages may indeed be a formidable enemy to raw American militia, but upon the king's regular and disciplined troops, sir, it is impossible they should make an impression.' I was conscious of an impropriety in my disputing with a military man in matters of his profession, and said no more."[47]

---

47   Autobiography of Franklin. Sparks' Edition, p. 190.

As the whole delay of the army was caused by the want of conveyances, Franklin observed one day to the general that it was a pity the troops had not been landed in Pennsylvania, where almost every farmer had his waggon. "Then, sir," replied Braddock, "you who are a man of interest there can probably procure them for me, and I beg you will." Franklin consented. An instrument in writing was drawn up, empowering him to contract for one hundred and fifty waggons, with four horses to each waggon, and fifteen hundred saddle or packhorses for the service of his majesty's forces, to be at Wills' Creek on or before the 20th of May, and he promptly departed for Lancaster to execute the commission.

After his departure, Braddock, attended by his staff, and his guard of light horse, set off for Wills' Creek by the way of Winchester, the road along the north side of the Potomac not being yet made. "This gave him," writes Washington, "a good opportunity to see the absurdity of the route, and of damning it very heartily."[48]

Three of Washington's horses were knocked up before they reached Winchester, and he had to purchase others. This was a severe drain of his campaigning purse; fortunately he was in the neighborhood of Greenway Court, and was enabled to replenish it by a loan from his old friend Lord Fairfax.

The discomforts of the rough road were increased with the general, by his travelling with some degree of state in a chariot which he had purchased of Governor Sharpe. In this he dashed by Dunbar's division of the troops, which he overtook near Wills' Creek; his body guard of light horse galloping on each side of his chariot, and his staff accompanying him; the drums beating the Grenadier's march as he passed. In this style, too, he arrived at Fort Cumberland, amid a thundering salute of seventeen guns.[49]

By this time the general discovered that he was not in a region fitted for such display, and his travelling chariot was abandoned at Fort Cumberland; otherwise it would soon have become a wreck among the mountains beyond.

By the 19th of May, the forces were assembled at Fort Cumberland. The two royal regiments, originally one thousand strong, now increased to fourteen hundred, by men chosen from

---

48   Draft of a letter, among Washington's papers, addressed to Major John Carlyle.
49   Journal of the Seamen's detachment.

the Maryland and Virginia levies. Two provincial companies of carpenters, or pioneers, thirty men each, with subalterns and captains. A company of guides, composed of a captain, two aids, and ten men. The troop of Virginia light horse, commanded by Captain Stewart; the detachment of thirty sailors with their officers, and the remnants of two independent companies from New York, one of which was commanded by Captain Horatio Gates, of whom, we shall have to speak much hereafter, in the course of this biography.

Another person in camp, of subsequent notoriety, and who became a warm friend of Washington, was Dr. Hugh Mercer, a Scotchman, about thirty-three years of age. About ten years previously he had served as assistant surgeon in the forces of Charles Edward, and followed his standard to the disastrous field of Culloden. After the defeat of the "chevalier," Mercer had escaped by the way of Inverness to America, and taken up his residence in Virginia. He was now with the Virginia troops, rallying under the standard of the House of Hanover, in an expedition led by a general who had aided to drive the chevalier from Scotland.[50]

Another young Scotchman in the camp was Dr. James Craik, who had become strongly attached to Washington, being about the same age, and having been with him in the affair of the Great Meadows, serving as surgeon in the Virginia regiment, to which he still belonged.

At Fort Cumberland, Washington had an opportunity of seeing a force encamped according to the plan approved of by the council of war; and military tactics, enforced with all the precision of a martinet.

The roll of each company was called over morning, noon, and night. There was strict examination of arms and accoutrements; the commanding officer of each company being answerable for their being kept in good order.

The general was very particular in regard to the appearance and drill of the Virginia recruits and companies, whom he had put under the rigorous discipline of Ensign Allen. "They performed their evolutions and firings, as well as could be expected," writes

---

50   Braddock had been an officer under the Duke of Cumberland, in his campaign against Charles Edward.

Captain Orme, "but their languid, spiritless, and unsoldier-like appearance, considered with the lowness and ignorance of most of their officers, gave little hopes of their future good behavior."[51] He doubtless echoed the opinion of the general; how completely were both to be undeceived as to their estimate of these troops!

The general held a levee in his tent every morning, from ten to eleven. He was strict as to the morals of the camp. Drunkenness was severely punished. A soldier convicted of theft was sentenced to receive one thousand lashes, and to be drummed out of his regiment. Part of the first part of the sentence was remitted. Divine service was performed every Sunday, at the head of the colors of each regiment, by the chaplain. There was the funeral of a captain who died at this encampment. A captain's guard marched before the corpse, the captain of it in the rear, the firelocks reversed, the drums beating the dead march. When near the grave, the guard formed two lines, facing each other; rested on their arms, muzzles downwards, and leaned their faces on the butts. The corpse was carried between them, the sword and sash on the coffin, and the officers following two and two. After the chaplain of the regiment had read the service, the guard fired three volleys over the grave, and returned.[52]

Braddock's camp, in a word, was a complete study for Washington, during the halt at Fort Cumberland, where he had an opportunity of seeing military routine in its strictest forms. He had a specimen, too, of convivial life in the camp, which the general endeavored to maintain, even in the wilderness, keeping a hospitable table; for he is said to have been somewhat of a *bon vivant*, and to have had with him "two good cooks, who could make an excellent ragout out of a pair of boots, had they but materials to toss them up with."[53]

There was great detention at the fort, caused by the want of forage and supplies, the road not having been finished from Philadelphia. Mr. Richard Peters, the secretary of Governor Morris, was in camp, to attend to the matter. He had to bear the brunt of Braddock's complaints. The general declared he would not stir from

---

51   Orme's Journal.
52   Orme's Journal. Journal of the Seamen's detachment.
53   Preface to Winthrop Sargent's Introductory Memoir.

Wills' Creek until he had the governor's assurance that the road would be opened in time. Mr. Peters requested guards to protect the men while at work, from attacks by the Indians. Braddock swore he would not furnish guards for the woodcutters,—"let Pennsylvania do it!" He scoffed at the talk about danger from Indians. Peters endeavored to make him sensible of the peril which threatened him in this respect. Should an army of them, led by French officers, beset him in his march, he would not be able, with all his strength and military skill, to reach Fort Duquesne without a body of rangers, as well on foot as horseback. The general, however, "despised his observations."[54] Still, guards had ultimately to be provided, or the work on the road would have been abandoned.

Braddock, in fact, was completely chagrined and disappointed about the Indians. The Cherokees and Catawbas, whom Dinwiddie had given him reason to expect in such numbers, never arrived.

George Croghan reached the camp with but about fifty warriors, whom he had brought from Aughquick. At the general's request he sent a messenger to invite the Delawares and Shawnees from the Ohio, who returned with two chiefs of the former tribe. Among the sachems thus assembled were some of Washington's former allies; Scarooyadi, alias, Monacatoocha, successor to the half-king; White Thunder, the keeper of the speech-belts, and Silver Heels, so called, probably, from being swift of foot.

Notwithstanding his secret contempt for the Indians, Braddock, agreeably to his instructions, treated them with great ceremony. A grand council was held in his tent, where all his officers attended. The chiefs, and all the warriors, came painted and decorated for war. They were received with military honors, the guards resting on their fire-arms. The general made them a speech through his interpreter, expressing the grief of their father, the great king of England, at the death of the half-king, and made them presents to console them. They in return promised their aid as guides and scouts, and declared eternal enmity to the French, following the declaration with the war song, "making a terrible noise."

The general, to regale and astonish them, ordered all the artillery to be fired, "the drums and fifes playing and beating the point of war;" the fête ended by their feasting, in their own camp,

---

54   Colonial Records, vi. 396.

on a bullock which the general had given them, following up their repast by dancing the war dance round a fire, to the sound of their uncouth drums and rattles, "making night hideous," by howls and yellings.

"I have engaged between forty and fifty Indians from the frontiers of your province to go over the mountains with me," writes Braddock to Governor Morris, "and shall take Croghan and Montour into service." Croghan was, in effect, put in command of the Indians, and a warrant given to him of captain.

For a time all went well. The Indians had their separate camp, where they passed half the night singing, dancing, and howling. The British were amused by their strange ceremonies, their savage antics, and savage decorations. The Indians, on the other hand, loitered by day about the English camp, fiercely painted and arrayed, gazing with silent admiration at the parade of the troops, their marchings and evolutions; and delighted with the horse-races, with which the young officers recreated themselves.

Unluckily the warriors had brought their families with them to Wills' Creek, and the women were even fonder than the men of loitering about the British camp. They were not destitute of attractions; for the young squaws resemble the gypsies, having seductive forms, small hands and feet, and soft voices. Among those who visited the camp was one who no doubt passed for an Indian princess. She was the daughter of the sachem, White Thunder, and bore the dazzling name of Bright Lightning.[55] The charms of these wild-wood beauties were soon acknowledged. "The squaws," writes Secretary Peters, "bring in money plenty; the officers are scandalously fond of them."[56]

The jealousy of the warriors was aroused some of them became furious. To prevent discord, the squaws were forbidden to come into the British, camp. This did not prevent their being sought elsewhere. It was ultimately found necessary, for the sake of quiet, to send Bright Lightning, with all the other women and children, back to Aughquick. White Thunder, and several of the warriors, accompanied them for their protection.

---

55   Seamen's Journal.
56   Letter of Peters to Governor Morris.

As to, the three Delaware chiefs, they returned to the Ohio, promising the general they would collect their warriors together, and meet him on his march. They never kept their word. "These people are villains, and always side with the strongest," says a shrewd journalist of the expedition.

During the halt of the troops at Wills' Creek, Washington had been sent to Williamsburg to bring on four thousand pounds for the military chest. He returned, after a fortnight's absence, escorted from Winchester by eight men, "which eight men," writes he, "were two days assembling, but I believe would not have been more than as many seconds dispersing if I had been attacked."

He found the general out of all patience and temper at the delays and disappointments in regard to horses, waggons, and forage, making no allowances for the difficulties incident to a new country, and to the novel and great demands upon its scanty and scattered resources. He accused the army contractors of want of faith, honor, and honesty; and in his moments of passion, which were many, extended the stigma to the whole country. This stung the patriotic sensibility of Washington, and overcame his usual self-command, and the proud and passionate commander was occasionally surprised by a well-merited rebuke from his aide-de-camp. "We have frequent disputes on this head," writes Washington, "which are maintained with warmth on both sides, especially on his, as he is incapable of arguing without it, or of giving up any point he asserts, be it ever so incompatible with reason or common sense."

The same pertinacity was maintained with respect to the Indians. George Croghan informed Washington that the sachems considered themselves treated with slight, in never being consulted in war matters. That he himself had repeatedly offered the services of the warriors under his command as scouts and outguards, but his offers had been rejected. Washington ventured to interfere, and to urge their importance for such purposes, especially now when they were approaching the stronghold of the enemy. As usual, the general remained bigoted in his belief of the all-sufficiency of well-disciplined troops.

Either from disgust thus caused, or from being actually dismissed, the warriors began to disappear from the camp. It is said that Colonel Innes, who was to remain in command at Fort Cumberland, advised the dismissal of all but a few to serve as guides; certain it is, before Braddock recommenced his march, none remained to accompany him but Scarooyadi, and eight of his warriors.[57]

Seeing the general's impatience at the non-arrival of conveyances, Washington again represented to him the difficulties he would encounter in attempting to traverse the mountains with such a train of wheel-carriages, assuring him it would be the most arduous part of the campaign; and recommended, from his own experience, the substitution, as much as possible, of packhorses. Braddock, however, had not been sufficiently harassed by frontier campaigning to depart from his European modes, or to be swayed in his military operations by so green a counsellor.

At length the general was relieved from present perplexities by the arrival of the horses and waggons which Franklin had undertaken to procure. That eminent man, with his characteristic promptness and unwearied exertions, and by his great personal popularity, had obtained them from the reluctant Pennsylvania farmers, being obliged to pledge his own responsibility for their being fully remunerated. He performed this laborious task out of pure zeal for the public service, neither expecting nor receiving emolument; and, in fact, experiencing subsequently great delay and embarrassment before he was relieved from the pecuniary responsibilities thus patriotically incurred.

The arrival of the conveyances put Braddock in good humor with Pennsylvania. In a letter to Governor Morris, he alludes to the threat of Sir John St. Clair to go through that province with a drawn sword in his hand. "He is ashamed of his having talked to you in the manner he did." Still the general made Franklin's contract for waggons the sole instance in which he had not experienced deceit and villany. "I hope, however, in spite of all this," adds he, "that we shall pass a merry Christmas together."

---

57 Braddock's own secretary, William Shirley, was disaffected to him. Writing about him to Governor Morris, he satirically observes: "We have a general most judiciously chosen for being disqualified for the service he is employed in, in almost every respect." And of the secondary officers: "As to them, I don't think we have much to boast. Some are insolent and ignorant; others capable, but rather aiming at showing their own abilities than making a proper use of them."—*Colonial Records*, vi., 405.

CHAPTER XVI.

MARCH FROM FORT CUMBERLAND—THE GREAT
SAVAGE MOUNTAIN—CAMP AT THE LITTLE
MEADOWS—DIVISION OF THE FORCES—CAPTAIN
JACK AND HIS BAND—SCAROOYADI IN DANGER—
ILLNESS OF WASHINGTON—HIS HALT AT THE
YOUGHIOGENY—MARCH OF BRADDOCK—THE
GREAT MEADOWS—LURKING ENEMIES—THEIR
TRACKS—PRECAUTIONS—THICKETTY RUN—
SCOUTS—INDIAN MURDERS—FUNERAL OF AN
INDIAN WARRIOR—CAMP ON THE MONONGAHELA—
WASHINGTON'S ARRIVAL THERE—MARCH FOR
FORT DUQUESNE—THE FORDING OF THE
MONONGAHELA—THE BATTLE—THE RETREAT—
DEATH OF BRADDOCK.

On the 10th of June, Braddock set off from Fort Cumberland with his aides-de-camp, and others of his staff, and his body guard of light horse. Sir Peter Halket, with his brigade, had marched three days previously; and a detachment of six hundred men, under the command of Colonel Chapman, and the supervision of Sir John St. Clair, had been employed upwards of ten days in cutting down trees, removing rocks, and opening a road.

The march over the mountains proved, as Washington had foretold, a "tremendous undertaking." It was with difficulty the heavily laden waggons could be dragged up the steep and rugged roads, newly made, or imperfectly repaired. Often they extended for three or four miles in a straggling and broken line, with the soldiers so dispersed, in guarding them, that an attack on any side would have thrown the whole in confusion. It was the dreary region of the great Savage Mountain, and the "Shades of Death" that was again made to echo with the din of arms.

What outraged Washington's notions of the abstemious frugality suitable to campaigning in the "backwoods," was the great number of horses and waggons required by the officers for the transportation of their baggage, camp equipage, and a thousand articles of artificial necessity. Simple himself in his tastes and habits, and manfully indifferent to personal indulgences, he almost doubted whether such sybarites in the camp could be efficient in the field.

By the time the advanced corps had struggled over two mountains, and through the intervening forest, and reached (16th June) the Little Meadows, where Sir John St. Clair had made a temporary camp, General Braddock had become aware of the difference between campaigning in a new country, or on the old well beaten battle-grounds of Europe. He now, of his own accord, turned to Washington for advice, though it must have been a sore trial to his pride to seek it of so young a man; but he had by this time sufficient proof of his sagacity, and his knowledge of the frontier.

Thus unexpectedly called on, Washington gave his counsel with becoming modesty, but with his accustomed clearness. There was just now an opportunity to strike an effective blow at Fort Duquesne, but it might be lost by delay. The garrison, according to credible reports, was weak; large reinforcements and supplies, which were on their way, would be detained by the drought, which rendered the river by which they must come low and unnavigable. The blow must be struck before they could arrive. He advised the general, therefore, to divide his forces; leave one part to come on with the stores and baggage, and all the cumbrous appurtenances of an army, and to throw himself in the advance with the other part, composed of his choicest troops, lightened of every thing superfluous that might impede a rapid march.

His advice was adopted. Twelve hundred men, selected out of all the companies, and furnished with ten field-pieces, were to form the first division, their provisions, and other necessaries, to be carried on packhorses. The second division, with all the stores, munitions, and heavy baggage, was to be brought on by Colonel Dunbar.

The least practicable part of the arrangement was with regard to the officers of the advance. Washington had urged a retrenchment of their baggage and camp equipage, that as many of their horses as possible might be used as packhorses. Here was the difficulty. Brought up, many of them, in fashionable and luxurious life, or the loitering indulgence of country quarters, they were so encumbered with what they considered indispensable necessaries, that out of two hundred and twelve horses generally appropriated to their use, not more than a dozen could be spared by them for the public service. Washington, in his own case, acted up to the advice he had given. He retained no more clothing and effects with him than would about half fill a portmanteau, and gave up his best steed as a packhorse,—which he never heard of afterwards.[58]

During the halt at the Little Meadows, Captain Jack and his band of forest rangers, whom Croghan had engaged at Governor Morris's suggestion, made their appearance in the camp; armed and equipped with rifle, knife, hunting-shirts, leggings and moccasins, and looking almost like a band of Indians as they issued from the woods.

The captain asked an interview with the general, by whom, it would seem, he was not expected. Braddock received him in his tent, in his usual stiff and stately manner. The "Black Rifle" spoke of himself and his followers as men inured to hardships, and accustomed to deal with Indians, who preferred stealth and stratagem to open warfare. He requested his company should be employed as a reconnoitering party, to beat up the Indians in their lurking-places and ambuscades.

Braddock, who had a sovereign contempt for the chivalry of the woods, and despised their boasted strategy, replied to the hero of the Pennsylvania settlements in a manner to which he had not been accustomed. "There was time enough," he said, "for making arrangements; and he had experienced troops, on whom he could completely rely for all purposes."

Captain Jack withdrew, indignant at so haughty a reception, and informed his leathern-clad followers of his rebuff. They forthwith shouldered their rifles, turned their backs upon the camp, and, headed by the captain, departed in Indian file through the woods,

58   Letter to J. Augustine Washington. Sparks, ii., 81.

for the usual scenes of their exploits, where men knew their value, the banks of the Juniata or the Conococheague.[59]

On the 19th of June Braddock's first division set out, with less than thirty carriages, including those that transported ammunition for the artillery, all strongly horsed. The Indians marched with the advanced party. In the course of the day, Scarooyadi and his son being at a small distance from the line of march, was surrounded and taken by some French and Indians. His son escaped, and brought intelligence to his warriors; they hastened to rescue or revenge him, but found him tied to a tree. The French had been disposed to shoot him, but their savage allies declared they would abandon them should they do so; having some tie of friendship or kindred with the chieftain, who thus rejoined the troops unharmed.

Washington was disappointed in his anticipations of a rapid march. The general, though he had adopted his advice in the main, could not carry it out in detail. His military education was in the way; bigoted to the regular and elaborate tactics of Europe, he could not stoop to the make-shift expedients of a new country, where every difficulty is encountered and mastered in a rough-and-ready style. "I found," said Washington, "that instead of pushing on with vigor, without regarding a little rough road, they were halting to level every mole hill, and to erect bridges over every brook, by which means we were four days in getting twelve miles."

For several days Washington had suffered from fever, accompanied by intense headache, and his illness increased in violence to such a degree that he was unable to ride, and had to be conveyed for a part of the time in a covered waggon. His illness continued without intermission until the 23d, "when I was relieved," says he, "by the general's absolutely ordering the physician, to give me Dr. James's powders; one of the most excellent medicines in the world. It gave me immediate relief, and removed my fever and other complaints in four days' time."

He was still unable to bear the jolting of the waggon, but it needed another interposition of the kindly-intended authority of General Braddock, to bring him to a halt at the great crossings of

59   On the Conococheague and Juniata is left the history of their exploits. At one time you may hear of the band near Fort Augusta, next at Fort Franklin, then at Loudon, then at Juniata,—rapid were the movements of this hardy band.— *Hazard's Reg. Penn.*, iv., 390; also, v., 194.

the Youghiogeny. There the general assigned him a guard, provided him with necessaries, and requested him to remain, under care of his physician, Dr. Craik, until the arrival of Colonel Dunbar's detachment, which was two days' march in the rear; giving him his word of honor that he should, at all events, be enabled to rejoin the main division before it reached the French fort.[60]

This kind solicitude on the part of Braddock, shows the real estimation in which he was held by that officer. Doctor Craik backed the general's orders, by declaring that should Washington persevere in his attempts to go on in the condition he then was, his life would be in danger. Orme also joined his entreaties, and promised, if he would remain, he would keep him informed by letter of every occurrence of moment.

Notwithstanding all the kind assurances of Braddock and his aide-de-camp Orme, it was with gloomy feelings that Washington saw the troops depart; fearful he might not be able to rejoin them in time for the attack upon the fort, which, he assured his brother aide-de-camp, he would not miss for five hundred pounds.

Leaving Washington at the Youghiogeny, we will follow the march of Braddock. In the course of the first day (June 24th), he came to a deserted Indian camp; judging from the number of wigwams, there must have been about one hundred and seventy warriors. Some of the trees about it had been stripped, and painted with threats, and bravadoes, and scurrilous taunts written on them in the French language, showing that there were white men with the savages.

The next morning at daybreak, three men venturing beyond the sentinels were shot and scalped; parties were immediately sent out to scour the woods, and drive in the stray horses.

The day's march, passed by the Great Meadows and Fort Necessity, the scene of Washington's capitulation. Several Indians were seen hovering in the woods, and the light horse and Indian allies were sent out to surround them, but did not succeed. In crossing a mountain beyond the Great Meadows, the carriages had to be lowered with the assistance of the sailors, by means of tackle. The camp for the night was about two miles beyond Fort Necessity.

---

60   Letter to John Augustine Washington. Sparks, ii., 80.

Several French and Indians endeavored to reconnoitre it, but were fired upon by the advanced sentinels.

The following day (26th) there was a laborious march of but four miles, owing to the difficulties of the road. The evening halt was at another deserted Indian camp, strongly posted on a high rock, with a steep and narrow ascent; it had a spring in the middle, and stood at the termination of the Indian path to the Monongahela. By this pass the party had come which attacked Washington the year before, in the Great Meadows. The Indians and French too, who were hovering about the army, had just left this camp. The fires they had left were yet burning. The French had inscribed their names on some of the trees with insulting bravadoes, and the Indians had designated in triumph the scalps they had taken two days previously. A party was sent out with guides, to follow their tracks and fall on them in the night, but again without success. In fact, it was the Indian boast, that throughout this march of Braddock, they saw him every day from the mountains, and expected to be able to shoot down his soldiers "like pigeons."

The march continued to be toilful and difficult; on one day it did not exceed two miles, having to cut a passage over a mountain. In cleaning their guns the men were ordered to draw the charge, instead of firing it off. No fire was to be lighted in front of the pickets. At night the men were to take their arms into the tents with them.

Further on the precautions became still greater. On the advanced pickets the men were in two divisions, relieving each other every two hours. Half remained on guard with fixed bayonets, the other half lay down by their arms. The picket sentinels were doubled.

On the 4th of July they encamped at Thicketty Run. The country was less mountainous and rocky, and the woods, consisting chiefly of white pine, were more open. The general now supposed himself to be within thirty miles of Fort Duquesne. Ever since his halt at the deserted camp on the rock beyond the Great Meadows, he had endeavored to prevail upon the Croghan Indians to scout in the direction of the fort, and bring him intelligence, but never could succeed. They had probably been deterred by the number of French and Indian tracks, and by the recent capture of Scarooyadi. This day, however, two consented to reconnoitre; and shortly after their departure, Christopher Gist, the resolute pioneer, who acted as guide to the general, likewise set off as a scout.

The Indians returned on the 6th. They had been close to Fort Duquesne. There were no additional works there; they saw a few boats under the fort, and one with a white flag coming down the Ohio; but there were few men to be seen, and few tracks of any. They came upon an unfortunate officer, shooting within half a mile of the fort, and brought a scalp as a trophy of his fate. None of the passes between the camp and fort were occupied; they believed there were few men abroad reconnoitering.

Gist returned soon after them. His account corroborated theirs; but he had seen a smoke in a valley between the camp and the fort, made probably by some scouting party. He had intended to prowl about the fort at night, but had been discovered and pursued by two Indians and narrowly escaped with his life.

On the same day, during the march, three or four men loitering in the rear of the grenadiers were killed and scalped. Several of the grenadiers set off to take revenge. They came upon a party of Indians, who held up boughs and grounded their arms, the concerted sign of amity. Not perceiving or understanding it, the grenadiers fired upon them, and one fell. It proved to be the son of Scarooyadi. Aware too late of their error, the grenadiers brought the body to the camp. The conduct of Braddock was admirable on the occasion. He sent for the father and the other Indians, and condoled with them on the lamentable occurrence; making them the customary presents of expiation. But what was more to the point, he caused the youth to be buried with the honors of war; at his request the officers attended the funeral, and a volley was fired over the grave.

These soldierlike tributes of respect to the deceased, and sympathy with the survivors, soothed the feelings and gratified the pride of the father, and attached him more firmly to the service. We are glad to record an anecdote so contrary to the general contempt for the Indians with which Braddock stands charged. It speaks well for the real kindness of his heart.

We will return now to Washington in his sick encampment on the banks of the Youghiogeny where he was left repining at the departure of the troops without him. To add to his annoyances, his servant, John Alton, a faithful Welshman, was taken ill with the same malady, and unable to render him any services. Letters from his fellow aides-de-camp showed him the kind solicitude that was felt concerning him. At the general's desire, Captain Morris wrote to him, informing him of their intended halts.

"It is the desire of every individual in the family," adds he, "and the general's positive commands to you, not to stir, but by the advice of the person [Dr. Craik] under whose care you are, till you are better, which we all hope will be very soon."

Orme, too, according to promise, kept him informed of the incidents of the march; the frequent night alarms, and occasional scalping parties. The night alarms Washington considered mere feints, designed to harass the men and retard the march; the enemy, he was sure, had not sufficient force for a serious attack; and he was glad to learn from Orme that the men were in high spirits and confident of success.

He now considered himself sufficiently recovered to rejoin the troops, and his only anxiety was that he should not be able to do it in time for the great blow. He was rejoiced, therefore, on the 3d of July, by the arrival of an advanced party of one hundred men convoying provisions. Being still too weak to mount his horse, he set off with the escort in a covered waggon; and after a most fatiguing journey, over mountain and through forest, reached Braddock's camp on the 8th of July. It was on the east side of the Monongahela, about two miles from the river in the neighborhood of the town of Queen Aliquippa, and about fifteen miles from Fort Duquesne.

In consequence of adhering to technical rules and military forms, General Braddock had consumed a month in marching little more than a hundred miles. The tardiness of his progress was regarded with surprise and impatience even in Europe; where his patron, the Duke of Brunswick, was watching the events of the campaign he had planned. "The Duke," writes Horace Walpole, "is much dissatisfied at the slowness of General Braddock, *who does not march as if he was at all impatient to be scalped.*" The insinuation of the satirical wit was unmerited. Braddock was a stranger to fear; but in his movements he was fettered by system.

Washington was warmly received on his arrival, especially by his fellow aides-de-camp, Morris and Orme. He was just in time, for the attack upon Fort Duquesne was to be made on the following day. The neighboring country had been reconnoitered to determine upon a plan of attack. The fort stood on the same side of the Monongahela with the camp; but there was a narrow pass between them of about two miles, with the river on the left and a very high mountain on the right, and in its present state quite impassable for carriages. The route determined on was to cross the Monongahela by a ford immediately opposite to the camp; proceed along the west bank of the river, for about five miles, then recross by another ford to the eastern side, and push on to the fort. The river at these fords was shallow, and the banks were not steep.

According to the plan of arrangement, Lieutenant-Colonel Gage, with the advance, was to cross the river before daybreak, march to the second ford, and recrossing there, take post to secure the passage of the main force. The advance was to be composed of two companies of grenadiers, one hundred and sixty infantry, the independent company of Captain Horatio Gates, and two six pounders.

Washington, who had already seen enough of regular troops to doubt their infallibility in wild bush-fighting, and who knew the dangerous nature of the ground they were to traverse, ventured to suggest, that on the following day the Virginia rangers, being accustomed to the country and to Indian warfare, might be thrown in the advance. The proposition drew an angry reply from the general, indignant, very probably, that a young provincial officer should presume to school a veteran like himself.

Early next morning (July 9th), before daylight, Colonel Gage crossed with the advance. He was followed, at some distance, by Sir John St. Clair, quartermaster-general, with a working party of two hundred and fifty men, to make roads for the artillery and baggage. They had with them their waggons of tools, and two six pounders. A party of about thirty savages rushed out of the woods as Colonel Gage advanced, but were put to flight before they had done any harm.

By sunrise the main body turned out in full uniform. At the beating of the general, their arms, which had been cleaned the night before, were charged with fresh cartridges. The officers were perfectly equipped. All looked as if arrayed for a fête, rather than a battle. Washington, who was still weak and unwell, mounted his horse, and joined the staff of the general, who was scrutinizing every thing with the eye of a martinet. As it was supposed the enemy would be on the watch for the crossing of the troops, it had been agreed that they should do it in the greatest order, with bayonets fixed, colors flying, and drums and fifes beating and playing.[61] They accordingly made a gallant appearance as they forded the Monongahela, and wound along its banks, and through the open forests, gleaming and glittering in morning sunshine, and stepping buoyantly to the Grenadier's March.

Washington, with his keen and youthful relish for military affairs, was delighted with their perfect order and equipment, so different from the rough bush-fighters, to which he had been accustomed. Roused to new life, he forgot his recent ailments, and broke forth in expressions of enjoyment and admiration, as he rode in company with his fellow aides-de-camp, Orme and Morris. Often, in after life, he used to speak of the effect upon him of the first sight of a well-disciplined European army, marching in high confidence and bright array, on the eve of a battle.

About noon they reached the second ford. Gage, with the advance, was on the opposite side of the Monongahela, posted according to orders; but the river bank had not been sufficiently sloped. The artillery and baggage drew up along the beach and halted until one, when the second crossing took place, drums beating, fifes playing, and colors flying, as before. When all had passed, there was again a halt close by a small stream called Frazier's Run, until the general arranged the order of march.

First went the advance, under Gage, preceded by the engineers and guides, and six light horsemen.

Then, Sir John St. Clair and the working party, with their waggons and the two six pounders. On each side were thrown out four flanking parties.

Then, at some distance, the general was to follow with the main body, the artillery and baggage preceded and flanked by light horse and squads of infantry; while the Virginian, and other provincial troops, were to form the rear guard.

The ground before them was level until about half a mile from the river, where a rising ground, covered with long grass, low bushes, and scattered trees, sloped gently up to a range of hills. The whole country, generally speaking, was a forest, with no clear

---

61   Orme's Journal.

opening but the road, which was about twelve feet wide, and flanked by two ravines, concealed by trees and thickets.

Had Braddock been schooled in the warfare of the woods, or had he adopted the suggestions of Washington, which he rejected so impatiently, he would have thrown out Indian scouts or Virginia rangers in the advance, and on the flanks, to beat up the woods and ravines; but, as has been sarcastically observed, he suffered his troops to march forward through the centre of the plain, with merely their usual guides and flanking parties, "as if in a review in St. James' Park."

It was now near two o'clock. The advanced party and the working party had crossed the plain and were ascending the rising ground. Braddock was about to follow with the main body and had given the word to march, when he heard an excessively quick and heavy firing in front. Washington, who was with the general, surmised that the evil he had apprehended had come to pass. For want of scouting parties ahead the advance parties were suddenly and warmly attacked. Braddock ordered Lieutenant-Colonel Burton to hasten to their assistance with the vanguard of the main body, eight hundred strong. The residue, four hundred, were halted, and posted to protect the artillery and baggage.

The firing continued, with fearful yelling. There was a terrible uproar. By the general's orders an aide-de-camp spurred forward to bring him an account of the nature of the attack. Without waiting for his return the general himself, finding the turmoil increase, moved forward, leaving Sir Peter Halket with the command of the baggage.[62]

The van of the advance had indeed been taken by surprise. It was composed of two companies of carpenters or pioneers to cut the road, and two flank companies of grenadiers to protect them. Suddenly the engineer who preceded them to mark out the road gave the alarm, "French and Indians!" A body of them was approaching rapidly, cheered on by a Frenchman in gaily fringed hunting-shirt, whose gorget showed him to be an officer. There was sharp firing on both sides at first. Several of the enemy fell; among them their leader; but a murderous fire broke out from among trees and a ravine on the right, and the woods resounded with unearthly

---

62   Orme's Journal.

whoops and yellings. The Indian rifle was at work, levelled by unseen hands. Most of the grenadiers and many of the pioneers were shot down. The survivors were driven in on the advance.

Gage ordered his men to fix bayonets and form in order of battle. They did so in hurry and trepidation. He would have scaled a hill on the right whence there was the severest firing. Not a platoon would quit the line of march. They were more dismayed by the yells than by the rifles of the unseen savages. The latter extended themselves along the hill and in the ravines; but their whereabouts was only known by their demoniac cries and the puffs of smoke from their rifles. The soldiers fired wherever they saw the smoke. Their officers tried in vain to restrain them until they should see their foe. All orders were unheeded; in their fright they shot at random, killing some of their own flanking parties, and of the vanguard, as they came running in. The covert fire grew more intense. In a short time most of the officers and many of the men of the advance were killed or wounded. Colonel Gage himself received a wound. The advance fell back in dismay upon Sir John St. Clair's corps, which was equally dismayed. The cannon belonging to it were deserted.

Colonel Burton had come up with the reinforcement, and was forming his men to face the rising ground on the right, when both of the advanced detachments fell back upon him, and all now was confusion.

By this time the general was upon the ground. He tried to rally the men. "They would fight," they said, "if they could see their enemy; but it was useless to fire at trees and bushes, and they could not stand to be shot down by an invisible foe."

The colors were advanced in different places to separate the men of the two regiments. The general ordered the officers to form the men, tell them off into small divisions, and advance with them; but the soldiers could not be prevailed upon either by threats or entreaties. The Virginia troops, accustomed to the Indian mode of fighting, scattered themselves, and took post behind trees, where they could pick off the lurking foe. In this way they, in some degree, protected the regulars. Washington advised General Braddock to adopt the same plan with the regulars; but he persisted in forming them into platoons; consequently they were cut down from behind logs and trees as fast as they could advance. Several attempted to take to the trees, without orders, but the general stormed at them, called them cowards, and even struck them with the flat of his sword. Several of the Virginians, who had taken post and were doing good service in this manner, were slain by the fire of the regulars, directed wherever a smoke appeared among the trees.

The officers behaved with consummate bravery; and Washington beheld with admiration those who, in camp or on the march, had appeared to him to have an almost effeminate regard for personal ease and convenience, now exposing themselves to imminent death, with a courage that kindled with the thickening horrors. In the vain hope of inspiriting the men to drive off the enemy from the flanks and regain the cannon, they would dash forward singly or in groups. They were invariably shot down; for the Indians aimed from their coverts at every one on horseback, or who appeared to have command.

Some were killed by random shot of their own men, who, crowded in masses, fired with affrighted rapidity, but without aim. Soldiers in the front ranks were killed by those in the rear. Between friend and foe, the slaughter of the officers was terrible. All this while the woods resounded with the unearthly yellings of the savages, and now and then one of them, hideously painted, and ruffling with feathered crest, would rush forth to scalp an officer who had fallen, or seize a horse galloping wildly without a rider.

Throughout this disastrous day, Washington distinguished himself by his courage and presence of mind. His brother aids, Orme and Morris, were wounded and disabled early in the action, and the whole duty of carrying the orders of the general devolved on him. His danger was imminent and incessant. He was in every part of the field, a conspicuous mark for the murderous rifle. Two horses were shot under him. Four bullets passed through his coat. His escape without a wound was almost miraculous. Dr. Craik, who was on the field attending to the wounded, watched him with anxiety as he rode about in the most exposed manner, and used to say that he expected every moment to see him fall. At one time he was sent to the main body to bring the artillery into action. All there was likewise in confusion; for the Indians had extended themselves along the ravine so as to flank the reserve and carry slaughter into the ranks. Sir Peter Halket had been shot down at the head of his regiment. The men who should have served the guns were paralyzed. Had they raked the ravines with grapeshot the day might have been saved. In his ardor Washington sprang from his horse; wheeled and pointed a brass field-piece with his own hand, and directed an effective discharge into the woods; but neither his efforts nor example were of avail. The men could not be kept to the guns.

Braddock still remained in the centre of the field, in the desperate hope of retrieving the fortunes of the day. The Virginia rangers, who had been most efficient in covering his position, were nearly all killed or wounded. His secretary, Shirley, had fallen by his side. Many of his officers had been slain within his sight, and many of his guard of Virginia light horse. Five horses had been killed under him; still he kept his ground, vainly endeavoring to check the flight of his men, or at least to effect their retreat in good order. At length a bullet passed through his right arm, and lodged itself in his lungs. He fell from his horse, but was caught by Captain Stewart of the Virginia guards, who, with the assistance of another American, and a servant, placed him in a tumbril. It was with much difficulty they got him out of the field—in his despair he desired to be left there.[63]

The rout now became complete. Baggage, stores, artillery, every thing was abandoned. The waggoners took each a horse out of his team, and fled. The officers were swept off with the men in this headlong flight. It was rendered more precipitate by the shouts and yells of the savages, numbers of whom rushed forth from their coverts, and pursued the fugitives to the river side, killing several as they dashed across in tumultuous confusion. Fortunately for the latter, the victors gave up the pursuit in their eagerness to collect the spoil.

The shattered army continued its flight after it had crossed the Monongahela, a wretched wreck of the brilliant little force that had recently gleamed along its banks, confident of victory. Out of eighty-six officers, twenty-six had been killed, and thirty-six wounded. The number of rank and file killed and wounded was upwards of seven hundred. The Virginia corps had suffered the most; one company had been almost annihilated, another, beside

---

63   Journal of the Seamen's detachment.

those killed and wounded in the ranks, had lost all its officers, even to the corporal.

About a hundred men were brought to a halt about a quarter of a mile from the ford of the river. Here was Braddock, with his wounded aides-de-camp and some of his officers; Dr. Craik dressing his wounds, and Washington attending him with faithful assiduity. Braddock was still able to give orders, and had a faint hope of being able to keep possession of the ground until reinforced. Most of the men were stationed in a very advantageous spot about two hundred yards from the road; and Lieutenant-Colonel Burton posted out small parties and sentinels. Before an hour had elapsed most of the men had stolen off. Being thus deserted, Braddock and his officers continued their retreat; he would have mounted his horse but was unable, and had to be carried by soldiers. Orme and Morris were placed on litters borne by horses. They were subsequently joined by Colonel Gage with eighty men whom he had rallied.

Washington, in the mean time, notwithstanding his weak state, being found most efficient in frontier service, was sent to Colonel Dunbar's camp, forty miles distant, with orders for him to hurry forward provisions, hospital stores, and waggons for the wounded, under the escort of two grenadier companies. It was a hard and a melancholy ride throughout the night and the following day. The tidings of the defeat preceded him, borne by the waggoners, who had mounted their horses, on Braddock's fall, and fled from the field of battle. They had arrived, haggard, at Dunbar's camp at mid-day; the Indian yells still ringing in their ears. "All was lost!" they cried. "Braddock was killed! They had seen wounded officers borne off from the field in bloody sheets! The troops were all cut to pieces!" A panic fell upon the camp. The drums beat to arms. Many of the soldiers, waggoners and attendants, took to flight; but most of them were forced back by the sentinels.

Washington arrived at the camp in the evening, and found the agitation still prevailing. The orders which he brought were executed during the night, and he was in the saddle early in the morning accompanying the convoy of supplies. At Gist's plantation, about thirteen miles off, he met Gage and his scanty force escorting Braddock and his wounded officers. Captain Stewart and a sad remnant of the Virginia light horse still accompanied the general as his guard. The captain had been unremitting in his attentions to him during the retreat. There was a halt of one day at Dunbar's camp for the repose and relief of the wounded. On the 13th they resumed their melancholy march, and that night reached the Great Meadows.

The proud spirit of Braddock was broken by his defeat. He remained silent the first evening after the battle, only ejaculating at night, "who would have thought it!" He was equally silent the following day; yet hope still seemed to linger in his breast, from another ejaculation: "We shall better know how to deal with them another time!"[64]

He was grateful for the attentions paid to him by Captain Stewart and Washington, and more than once, it is said, expressed his admiration of the gallantry displayed by the Virginians in the action. It is said, moreover, that in his last moments, he apologized to Washington for the petulance with which he had rejected his advice, and bequeathed to him his favorite charger and his faithful servant, Bishop, who had helped to convey him from the field.

Some of these facts, it is true, rest on tradition, yet we are willing to believe them, as they impart a gleam of just and generous feeling to his closing scene. He died on the night of the 13th, at the Great Meadows, the place of Washington's discomfiture in the previous year. His obsequies were performed before break of day. The chaplain having been wounded, Washington read the funeral service. All was done in sadness, and without parade, so as not to attract the attention of lurking savages, who might discover, and outrage his grave. It is doubtful even whether a volley was fired over it, that last military honor which he had recently paid to the remains of an Indian warrior. The place of his sepulture, however, is still known, and pointed out.

Reproach spared him not, even when in his grave. The failure of the expedition was attributed both in England and America to his obstinacy, his technical pedantry, and his military conceit. He had been continually warned to be on his guard against ambush and surprise, but without avail. Had he taken the advice urged on him

---

64   Captain Orme, who gave these particulars to Dr. Franklin, says that Braddock "died a few minutes after." This, according to his account, was on the second day; whereas the general survived upwards of four days. Orme, being conveyed on a litter at some distance from the general, could only speak of his moods from hearsay.

by Washington and others to employ scouting parties of Indians and rangers, he would never have been so signally surprised and defeated.

Still his dauntless conduct on the field of battle shows him to have been a man of fearless spirit; and he was universally allowed to be an accomplished disciplinarian. His melancholy end, too, disarms censure of its asperity. Whatever may have been his faults and errors, he, in a manner, expiated them by the hardest lot that can befall a brave soldier, ambitious of renown—an unhonored grave in a strange land; a memory clouded by misfortune, and a name for ever coupled with defeat.

NOTE.

In narrating the expedition of Braddock, we have frequently cited the Journals of Captain Orme and of the "Seamen's Detachment;" they were procured in England by the Hon. Joseph R. Ingersoll, while Minister at the Court of St. James, and recently published by the Historical Society of Pennsylvania: ably edited, and illustrated with an admirable Introductory Memoir by Winthrop Sargent, Esq., member of that Society.

CHAPTER XVII.

ARRIVAL AT FORT CUMBERLAND—LETTERS
OF WASHINGTON TO HIS FAMILY—PANIC OF
DUNBAR—FORTUNES OF DR. HUGH MERCER—
TRIUMPH OF THE FRENCH.

The obsequies of the unfortunate Braddock being finished, the escort continued its retreat with the sick and wounded. Washington, assisted by Dr. Craik, watched with assiduity over his comrades, Orme and Morris. As the horses which bore their litters were nearly knocked up, he despatched messengers to the commander of Fort Cumberland requesting that others might be sent on, and that comfortable quarters might be prepared for the reception of those officers.

On the 17th, the sad cavalcade reached the fort, and were relieved from the incessant apprehension of pursuit. Here, too, flying reports had preceded them, brought by fugitives from the battle; who, with the disposition usual in such cases to exaggerate, had represented the whole army as massacred. Fearing these reports might reach home, and affect his family, Washington wrote to his mother, and his brother, John Augustine, apprising them of his safety. "The Virginia troops," says he, in a letter to his mother, "showed a good deal of bravery, and were nearly all killed. . . . The dastardly behavior of those they called regulars exposed all others, that were ordered to do their duty, to almost certain death; and, at last, in despite of all the efforts of the officers to the contrary, they ran, as sheep pursued by dogs, and it was impossible to rally them."

To his brother, he writes: "As I have heard, since my arrival at this place, a circumstantial account of my death and dying speech, I take this early opportunity of contradicting the first, and of assuring you that I have not composed the latter. But, by the all-powerful dispensations of Providence, I have been protected beyond all human probability, or expectation; for I had four bullets through my coat, and two horses shot under me, yet escaped unhurt, though death was levelling my companions on every side of me!

"We have been most scandalously beaten by a trifling body of men, but fatigue and want of time prevent me from giving you any of the details, until I have the happiness of seeing you at Mount Vernon, which I now most earnestly wish for, since we are driven in thus far. A feeble state of health obliges me to halt here for two or three days to recover a little strength, that I may thereby be enabled to proceed homeward with more ease."

Dunbar arrived shortly afterward with the remainder of the army. No one seems to have shared more largely in the panic of the vulgar than that officer. From the moment he received tidings of the defeat, his camp became a scene of confusion. All the ammunition, stores, and artillery were destroyed, to prevent, it was said, their falling into the hands of the enemy; but, as it was afterwards alleged, to relieve the terror-stricken commander from all incumbrances, and furnish him with more horses in his flight toward the settlements.[65]

At Cumberland his forces amounted to fifteen hundred effective men; enough for a brave stand to protect the frontier, and recover some of the lost honor; but he merely paused to leave the sick and wounded under care of two Virginia and Maryland companies, and some of the train, and then continued his hasty march, or rather flight, through the country, not thinking himself safe, as was sneeringly intimated, until he arrived in Philadelphia, where the inhabitants could protect him.

The true reason why the enemy did not pursue the retreating army was not known until some time afterwards, and added to the disgrace of the defeat. They were not the main force of the French, but a mere detachment of 72 regulars, 146 Canadians, and 637 Indians, 855 in all, led by Captain de Beaujeu. De Contrecoeur, the commander of Fort Duquesne, had received information, through his scouts, that the English, three thousand strong, were within six leagues of his fort. Despairing of making an effectual

---

65   Franklin's Autobiography.

defence against such a superior force, he was balancing in his mind whether to abandon his fort without awaiting their arrival, or to capitulate on honorable terms. In this dilemma Beaujeu prevailed on him to let him sally forth with a detachment to form an ambush, and give check to the enemy. De Beaujeu was to have taken post at the river, and disputed the passage at the ford. For that purpose he was hurrying forward when discovered by the pioneers of Gage's advance party. He was a gallant officer, and fell at the beginning of the fight. The whole number of killed and wounded of French and Indians, did not exceed seventy.

Such was the scanty force which the imagination of the panic-stricken army had magnified into a great host, and from which they had fled in breathless terror, abandoning the whole frontier. No one could be more surprised than the French commander himself, when the ambuscading party returned in triumph with a long train of packhorses laden with booty, the savages uncouthly clad in the garments of the slain, grenadier caps, officers' gold-laced coats, and glittering epaulettes; flourishing swords and sabres, or firing off muskets, and uttering fiendlike yells of victory. But when De Contrecoeur was informed of the utter rout and destruction of the much dreaded British army, his joy was complete. He ordered the guns of the fort to be fired in triumph, and sent out troops in pursuit of the fugitives.

The affair of Braddock remains a memorable event in American history, and has been characterized as "the most extraordinary victory ever obtained, and the farthest flight ever made." It struck a fatal blow to the deference for British prowess, which once amounted almost to bigotry, throughout the provinces. "This whole transaction," observes Franklin, in his autobiography, "gave us the first suspicion, that our exalted ideas of the prowess of British regular troops had not been well founded."

CHAPTER XVIII.

COSTS OF CAMPAIGNING—MEASURES FOR PUBLIC
SAFETY—WASHINGTON IN COMMAND—HEAD-
QUARTERS AT WINCHESTER—LORD FAIRFAX AND
HIS TROOP OF HORSE—INDIAN RAVAGES—PANIC AT
WINCHESTER—CAUSE OF THE ALARM—OPERATIONS
ELSEWHERE—SHIRLEY AGAINST NIAGARA—
JOHNSON AGAINST CROWN POINT—AFFAIR AT LAKE
GEORGE—DEATH OF DIESKAU.

Washington arrived at Mount Vernon on the 26th of July, still
in feeble condition from his long illness. His campaigning, thus far,
had trenched upon his private fortune, and impaired one of the
best of constitutions.

In a letter to his brother Augustine, then a member of
Assembly at Williamsburg, he casts up the result of his frontier
experience. "I was employed," writes he, "to go a journey in the
winter, when I believe few or none would have undertaken it, and
what did I get by it?—my expenses borne! I was then appointed,
with trifling pay, to conduct a handful of men to the Ohio. What did
I get by that? Why, after putting myself to a considerable expense in
equipping and providing necessaries for the campaign, I went out,
was soundly beaten, and lost all! Came in, and had my commission
taken from me; or, in other words, my command reduced, under
pretence of an order from home (England). I then went out a
volunteer with General Braddock, and lost all my horses, and many
other things. But this being a voluntary act, I ought not to have
mentioned it; nor should I have done it, were it not to show that
I have been on the losing order ever since I entered the service,
which is now nearly two years."

What a striking lesson is furnished by this brief summary! How little was he aware of the vast advantages he was acquiring in this school of bitter experience! "In the hand of heaven he stood," to be shaped and trained for its great purpose; and every trial and vicissitude of his early life, but fitted him to cope with one or other of the varied and multifarious duties of his future destiny.

But though, under the saddening influence of debility and defeat, he might count the cost of his campaigning, the martial spirit still burned within him. His connection with the army, it is true, had ceased at the death of Braddock, but his military duties continued as adjutant-general of the northern division of the province, and he immediately issued orders for the county lieutenants to hold the militia in readiness for parade and exercise, foreseeing that, in the present defenceless state of the frontier, there would be need of their services.

Tidings of the rout and retreat of the army had circulated far and near, and spread consternation throughout the country. Immediate incursions both of French and Indians were apprehended; and volunteer companies began to form, for the purpose of marching across the mountains to the scene of danger. It was intimated to Washington that his services would again be wanted on the frontier. He declared instantly that he was ready to serve his country to the extent of his powers; but never on the same terms as heretofore.

On the 4th of August, Governor Dinwiddie convened the Assembly to devise measures for the public safety. The sense of danger had quickened the slow patriotism of the burgesses; they no longer held back supplies; forty thousand pounds were promptly voted, and orders issued for the raising of a regiment of one thousand men.

Washington's friends urged him to present himself at Williamsburg as a candidate for the command; they were confident of his success, notwithstanding that strong interest was making for the governor's favorite, Colonel Innes.

With mingled modesty and pride, Washington declined to be a solicitor. The only terms, he said, on which he would accept a command, were a certainty as to rank and emoluments, a right to appoint his field officers, and the supply of a sufficient military chest; but to solicit the command, and, at the same time, to make stipulations, would be a little incongruous, and carry with it the face of self-sufficiency. "If," added he, "the command should be offered to me, the case will then be altered, as I should be at liberty to make such objections as reason, and my small experience, have pointed out."

While this was in agitation, he received letters from his mother, again imploring him not to risk himself in these frontier wars. His answer was characteristic, blending the filial deference with which he was accustomed from childhood to treat her, with a calm patriotism of the Roman stamp.

"Honored Madam: If it is in my power to avoid going to the Ohio again, I shall; but if the command is pressed upon me by the general voice of the country, and offered upon such terms as cannot be objected against, it would reflect dishonor on me to refuse it; and that, I am sure, must, and ought, to give you greater uneasiness, than my going in an honorable command. Upon no other terms will I accept it. At present I have no proposals made to me, nor have I any advice of such an intention, except from private hands."

On the very day that this letter was despatched (Aug. 14), he received intelligence of his appointment to the command on the terms specified in his letters to his friends. His commission nominated him commander-in-chief of all the forces raised, or to be raised in the colony. The Assembly also voted three hundred pounds to him, and proportionate sums to the other officers, and to the privates of the Virginia companies, in consideration of their gallant conduct, and their losses in the late battle.

The officers next in command under him were Lieutenant-Colonel Adam Stephens, and Major Andrew Lewis. The former, it will be recollected, had been with him in the unfortunate affair at the Great Meadows; his advance in rank shows that his conduct had been meritorious.

The appointment of Washington to his present station was the more gratifying and honorable from being a popular one, made in deference to public sentiment; to which Governor Dinwiddie was obliged to sacrifice his strong inclination in favor of Colonel Innes. It is thought that the governor never afterwards regarded Washington with a friendly eye. His conduct towards him subsequently was on various occasions cold and ungracious.[66]

---

66   Sparks' Writings of Washington, vol. ii., p. 161, note.

It is worthy of note that the early popularity of Washington was not the result of brilliant achievements nor signal success; on the contrary, it rose among trials and reverses, and may almost be said to have been the fruit of defeats. It remains an honorable testimony of Virginian intelligence, that the sterling, enduring, but undazzling qualities of Washington were thus early discerned and appreciated, though only heralded by misfortunes. The admirable manner in which he had conducted himself under these misfortunes, and the sagacity and practical wisdom he had displayed on all occasions, were universally acknowledged; and it was observed that, had his modest counsels been adopted by the unfortunate Braddock, a totally different result might have attended the late campaign.

An instance of this high appreciation of his merits occurs in a sermon preached on the 17th of August by the Rev. Samuel Davis, wherein he cites him as "that heroic youth, Colonel Washington, *whom I cannot but hope Providence has hitherto preserved in so signal a manner for some important service to his country.*" The expressions of the worthy clergyman may have been deemed enthusiastic at the time; viewed in connection with subsequent events they appear almost prophetic.

Having held a conference with Governor Dinwiddie at Williamsburg, and received his instructions, Washington repaired, on the 14th of September, to Winchester, where he fixed his headquarters. It was a place as yet of trifling magnitude, but important from its position; being a central point where the main roads met, leading from north to south, and east to west, and commanding the channels of traffic and communication between some of the most important colonies and a great extent of frontier.

Here he was brought into frequent and cordial communication with his old friend Lord Fairfax. The stir of war had revived a spark of that military fire which animated the veteran nobleman in the days of his youth, when an officer in the cavalry regiment of the Blues. He was lord-lieutenant of the county. Greenway Court was his headquarters. He had organized a troop of horse, which occasionally was exercised about the lawn of his domain, and he was now as prompt to mount his steed for a cavalry parade as he ever was for a fox chase. The arrival of Washington frequently brought the old nobleman to Winchester to aid the young commander with his counsels or his sword.

His services were soon put in requisition. Washington, having visited the frontier posts, established recruiting places, and taken other measures of security, had set off for Williamsburg on military business, when an express arrived at Winchester from Colonel Stephens, who commanded at Fort Cumberland, giving the alarm that a body of Indians were ravaging the country, burning the houses, and slaughtering the inhabitants. The express was instantly forwarded after Washington; in the mean time, Lord Fairfax sent out orders for the militia of Fairfax and Prince William counties to arm and hasten to the defence of Winchester, where all was confusion and affright. One fearful account followed another. The whole country beyond it was said to be at the mercy of the savages. They had blockaded the rangers in the little fortresses or outposts provided for the protection of neighborhoods. They were advancing upon Winchester with fire, tomahawk, and scalping-knife. The country people were flocking into the town for safety— the townspeople were moving off to the settlements beyond the Blue Ridge. The beautiful valley of the Shenandoah was likely to become a scene of savage desolation.

In the height of the confusion Washington rode into the town. He had been overtaken by Colonel Stephens' express. His presence inspired some degree of confidence, and he succeeded in stopping most of the fugitives. He would have taken the field at once against the savages, believing their numbers to be few; but not more than twenty-five of the militia could be mustered for the service. The rest refused to stir—they would rather die with their wives and children.

Expresses were sent off to hurry up the militia ordered out by Lord Fairfax. Scouts were ordered out to discover the number of the foe, and convey assurances of succor to the rangers said to be blocked up in the fortresses, though Washington suspected the latter to be "more encompassed by fear than by the enemy." Smiths were set to work to furbish up and repair such firearms as were in the place, and waggons were sent off for musket balls, flints, and provisions.

Instead, however, of animated co-operation, Washington was encountered by difficulties at every step. The waggons in question had to be impressed, and the waggoners compelled by force to assist. "No orders," writes he, "are obeyed, but such as a party of soldiers or my own drawn sword enforces. Without this, not a single horse, for the most earnest occasion, can be had,—to such a pitch has the insolence of these people arrived, by having every point hitherto submitted to them. However, I have given up none, where his majesty's service requires the contrary, and where my proceedings are justified by my instructions; nor will I, unless they execute what they threaten—that is, blow out our brains."

One is tempted to smile at this tirade about the "insolence of the people," and this zeal for "his majesty's service," on the part of Washington; but he was as yet a young man and a young officer; loyal to his sovereign, and with high notions of military authority, which he had acquired in the camp of Braddock.

What he thus terms insolence was the dawning spirit of independence, which he was afterwards the foremost to cherish and promote; and which, in the present instance, had been provoked by the rough treatment from the military, which the waggoners and others of the yeomanry had experienced when employed in Braddock's campaign, and by the neglect to pay them for their services. Much of Washington's difficulties also arose, doubtlessly, from the inefficiency of the military laws, for an amendment of which he had in vain made repeated applications to Governor Dinwiddie.

In the mean time the panic and confusion increased. On Sunday an express hurried into town, breathless with haste and terror. The Indians, he said, were but twelve miles off; they had attacked the house of Isaac Julian; the inhabitants were flying for their lives. Washington immediately ordered the town guards to be strengthened; armed some recruits who had just arrived, and sent out two scouts to reconnoitre the enemy. It was a sleepless night in Winchester. Horror increased with the dawn; before the men could be paraded a second express arrived, ten times more terrified than the former. The Indians were within four miles of the town, killing and destroying all before them. He had heard the constant firing of the savages and the shrieks of their victims.

The terror of Winchester now passed all bounds. Washington put himself at the head of about forty men, militia and recruits, and pushed for the scene of carnage.

The result is almost too ludicrous for record. The whole cause of the alarm proved to be three drunken troopers, carousing, hallooing, uttering the most unheard of imprecations, and ever and anon firing off their pistols. Washington interrupted them in the midst of their revel and blasphemy, and conducted them prisoners to town.

The reported attack on the house of Isaac Julian proved equally an absurd exaggeration. The ferocious party of Indians turned out to be a mulatto and a negro in quest of cattle. They had been seen by a child of Julian, who alarmed his father, who alarmed the neighborhood.

"These circumstances," says Washington, "show what a panic prevails among the people; how much they are all alarmed at the most usual and customary cries; and yet how impossible it is to get them to act in any respect for their common safety."

They certainly present a lively picture of the feverish state of a frontier community, hourly in danger of Indian ravage and butchery; than which no kind of warfare is more fraught with real and imaginary horrors.

The alarm thus originating had spread throughout the country. A captain, who arrived with recruits from Alexandria, reported that he had found the road across the Blue Ridge obstructed by crowds of people flying for their lives, whom he endeavored in vain to stop. They declared that Winchester was in flames!

At length the band of Indians, whose ravages had produced this consternation throughout the land, and whose numbers did not exceed one hundred and fifty, being satiated with carnage, conflagration, and plunder, retreated, bearing off spoils and captives. Intelligent scouts sent out by Washington, followed their traces, and brought back certain intelligence that they had recrossed the Allegany Mountains and returned to their homes on the Ohio. This report allayed the public panic and restored temporary quiet to the harassed frontier.

Most of the Indians engaged in these ravages were Delawares and Shawnees, who, since Braddock's defeat, had been gained over by the French. A principal instigator was said to be Washington's old acquaintance, Shengis, and a reward was offered for his head.

Scarooyadi, successor to the half-king, remained true to the English, and vindicated his people to the Governor and Council of Pennsylvania from the charge of having had any share in the late massacres. As to the defeat at the Monongahela, "it was owing," he said, "to the pride and ignorance of that great general (Braddock) that came from England. He is now dead; but he was a bad man when he was alive. He looked upon us as dogs, and would never hear any thing that was said to him. We often endeavored to advise him, and tell him of the danger he was in with his soldiers; but he never appeared pleased with us, and that was the reason that a great many of our warriors left him."[67]

Scarooyadi was ready with his warriors to take up the hatchet again with their English brothers against the French. "Let us unite our strength," said he; "you are numerous, and all the English governors along your sea-shore can raise men enough; but don't let those that come from over the great seas be concerned any more. *They art unfit to fight in the woods. Let us go ourselves—we that came out of this ground.*"

No one felt more strongly than Washington the importance, at this trying juncture, of securing the assistance of these forest warriors. "It is in their power," said he, "to be of infinite use to us; and without Indians, we shall never be able to cope with these cruel foes to our country."[68]

Washington had now time to inform himself of the fate of the other enterprises included in this year's plan of military operations. We shall briefly dispose of them, for the sake of carrying on the general course of events. The history of Washington is linked with the history of the colonies. The defeat of Braddock paralyzed the expedition against Niagara. Many of General Shirley's troops, which were assembled at Albany, struck with the consternation which it caused throughout the country, deserted. Most of the batteau men, who were to transport stores by various streams, returned home. It was near the end of August before Shirley was in force at Oswego. Time was lost in building boats for the lake. Storms and head winds ensued; then sickness: military incapacity in the general completed the list of impediments. Deferring the completion of the enterprise until the following year, Shirley returned to Albany with the main part of his forces in October, leaving about seven hundred men to garrison the fortifications he had commenced at Oswego.

---

67   Hazard's Register of Penn., v., p. 252, 266.
68   Letter to Dinwiddie.

To General William Johnson, it will be recollected, had been confided the expedition against Crown Point, on Lake Champlain. Preparations were made for it in Albany, whence the troops were to march, and the artillery, ammunition, and stores to be conveyed up the Hudson to the carrying-place between that river and Lake St. Sacrament, as it was termed by the French, but Lake George, as Johnson named it, in honor of his sovereign. At the carrying-place a fort was commenced, subsequently called Fort Edward. Part of the troops remained under General Lyman, to complete and garrison it; the main force proceeded under General Johnson to Lake George, the plan being to descend that lake to its outlet at Ticonderoga, in Lake Champlain. Having to attend the arrival of batteaux forwarded for the purpose from Albany by the carrying-place, Johnson encamped at the south end of the lake. He had with him between five and six thousand troops of New York and New England, and a host of Mohawk warriors, loyally devoted to him.

It so happened that a French force of upwards of three thousand men, under the Baron de Dieskau, an old general of high reputation, had recently arrived at Quebec, destined against Oswego. The baron had proceeded to Montreal, and sent forward thence seven hundred of his troops, when news arrived of the army gathering on Lake George for the attack on Crown Point, perhaps for an inroad into Canada. The public were in consternation; yielding to their importunities, the baron took post at Crown Point for its defence. Beside his regular troops, he had with him eight hundred Canadians, and seven hundred Indians of different tribes. The latter were under the general command of the Chevalier Legardeur de St. Pierre, the veteran officer to whom Washington had delivered the despatches of Governor Dinwiddie on his diplomatic mission to the frontier. The chevalier was a man of great influence among the Indians.

In the mean time Johnson remained encamped at the south end of Lake George, awaiting the arrival of his batteaux. The camp was protected in the rear by the lake, in front by a bulwark of felled trees; and was flanked by thickly wooded swamps.

On the 7th of September, the Indian scouts brought word that they had discovered three large roads made through the forests toward Fort Edward. An attack on that post was apprehended. Adams, a hardy waggoner, rode express with orders to the commander to draw all the troops within the works. About midnight came other scouts. They had seen the French within four miles of the carrying-place. They had heard the report of a musket, and the voice of a man crying for mercy, supposed to be the unfortunate Adams. In the morning Colonel Williams was detached with one thousand men, and two hundred Indians, to intercept the enemy in their retreat.

Within two hours after their departure a heavy fire of musketry, in the midst of the forest, about three or four miles off, told of a warm encounter. The drums beat to arms; all were at their posts. The firing grew sharper and sharper, and nearer and nearer. The detachment under Williams was evidently retreating. Colonel Cole was sent with three hundred men to cover their retreat. The breastwork of trees was manned. Some heavy cannon were dragged up to strengthen the front. A number of men were stationed with a field-piece on an eminence on the left flank.

In a short time fugitives made their appearance; first singly, then in masses, flying in confusion, with a rattling fire behind them, and the horrible Indian war-whoop. Consternation seized upon the camp, especially when the French emerged from the forest in battle array, led by the Baron Dieskau, the gallant commander of Crown Point. Had all his troops been as daring as himself, the camp might have been carried by assault; but the Canadians and Indians held back, posted themselves behind trees, and took to bush-fighting.

The baron was left with his regulars (two hundred grenadiers) in front of the camp. He kept up a fire by platoons, but at too great a distance to do much mischief; the Canadians and Indians fired from their coverts. The artillery played on them in return. The camp, having recovered from its panic, opened a fire of musketry. The engagement became general. The French grenadiers stood their ground bravely for a long time, but were dreadfully cut up by the artillery and small arms. The action slackened on the part of the French, until, after a long contest, they gave way. Johnson's men and the Indians then leaped over the breastwork, and a chance medley fight ensued, that ended in the slaughter, rout, or capture of the enemy.

The Baron de Dieskau had been disabled by a wound in the leg. One of his men, who endeavored to assist him, was shot down by his side. The baron, left alone in the retreat, was found by the pursuers leaning against the stump of a tree. As they approached, he felt for his watch to insure kind treatment by delivering it up. A soldier, thinking he was drawing forth a pistol to defend himself, shot him through the hips. He was conveyed a prisoner to the camp, but ultimately died of his wounds.

The baron had really set off from Crown Point to surprise Fort Edward, and, if successful, to push on to Albany and Schenectady; lay them in ashes, and cut off all communication with Oswego. The Canadians and Indians, however, refused to attack the fort, fearful of its cannon; he had changed his plan, therefore, and determined to surprise the camp. In the encounter with the detachment under Williams, the brave Chevalier Legardeur de St. Pierre lost his life. On the part of the Americans, Hendrick, a famous old Mohawk sachem, grand ally of General Johnson, was slain.

Johnson himself received a slight wound early in the action, and retired to his tent. He did not follow up the victory as he should have done, alleging that it was first necessary to build a strong fort at his encampment, by way of keeping up a communication with Albany, and by the time this was completed, it would be too late to advance against Crown Point. He accordingly erected a stockaded fort, which received the name of William Henry; and having garrisoned it, returned to Albany. His services, although they gained him no laurel-wreath, were rewarded by government with five thousand pounds, and a baronetcy; and he was made Superintendent of Indian Affairs.[69]

---

69   Johnson's Letter to the Colonial Governors, Sept. 9th, 1753. London Mag., 1755., p. 544. Holmes' Am. Annals, vol. ii., p. 63. 4th edit., 1829.

CHAPTER XIX.

REFORM IN THE MILITIA LAWS—DISCIPLINE OF
THE TROOPS—DAGWORTHY AND THE QUESTION
OF PRECEDENCE—WASHINGTON'S JOURNEY TO
BOSTON—STYLE OF TRAVELLING—CONFERENCE
WITH SHIRLEY—THE EARL OF LOUDOUN—MILITARY
RULE FOR THE COLONIES—WASHINGTON AT NEW
YORK—MISS MARY PHILIPSE.

Mortifying experience had convinced Washington of the inefficiency of the militia laws, and he now set about effecting a reformation. Through his great and persevering efforts, an act was passed in the Virginia Legislature giving prompt operation to courts-martial; punishing insubordination, mutiny and desertion with adequate severity; strengthening the authority of a commander, so as to enable him to enforce order and discipline among officers as well as privates; and to avail himself, in time of emergency, and for the common safety, of the means and services of individuals.

This being effected, he proceeded to fill up his companies, and to enforce this newly defined authority within his camp. All gaming, drinking, quarrelling, swearing, and similar excesses, were prohibited under severe penalties.

In disciplining his men, they were instructed not merely in ordinary and regular tactics, but in all the strategy of Indian warfare, and what is called "bush-fighting,"—a knowledge indispensable in the wild wars of the wilderness. Stockaded forts, too, were constructed at various points, as places of refuge and defence, in exposed neighborhoods. Under shelter of these, the inhabitants began to return to their deserted homes. A shorter and better road, also, was opened by him between Winchester and Cumberland, for the transmission of reinforcements and supplies.

His exertions, however, were impeded by one of those questions of precedence, which had so often annoyed him, arising from the difference between crown and provincial commissions. Maryland having by a scanty appropriation raised a small militia force, stationed Captain Dagworthy, with a company of thirty men, at Fort Cumberland, which stood within the boundaries of that province. Dagworthy had served in Canada in the preceding war, and had received a king's commission. This he had since commuted for half-pay, and, of course, had virtually parted with its privileges. He was nothing more, therefore, than a Maryland provincial captain, at the head of thirty men. He now, however, assumed to act under his royal commission, and refused to obey the orders of any officer, however high his rank, who merely held his commission from a governor. Nay, when Governor, or rather Colonel Innes, who commanded at the fort, was called away to North Carolina by his private affairs, the captain took upon himself the command, and insisted upon it as his right.

Parties instantly arose, and quarrels ensued among the inferior officers; grave questions were agitated between the Governors of Maryland and Virginia, as to the fort itself; the former claiming it as within his province, the latter insisting that, as it had been built according to orders sent by the king, it was the king's fort, and could not be subject to the authority of Maryland.

Washington refrained from mingling in this dispute; but intimated that if the commander-in-chief of the forces of Virginia must yield precedence to a Maryland captain of thirty men, he should have to resign his commission, as he had been compelled to do before, by a question of military rank.

So difficult was it, however, to settle these disputes of precedence, especially where the claims of two governors came in collision, that it was determined to refer the matter to Major-General Shirley, who had succeeded Braddock in the general command of the colonies. For this purpose Washington was to go to Boston, obtain a decision from Shirley of the point in dispute, and a general regulation, by which these difficulties could be prevented in future. It was thought, also, that in a conference with the commander-in-chief he might inform himself of the military measures in contemplation.

Accordingly, on the 4th of February (1756), leaving Colonel Adam Stephen in command of the troops, Washington set out on his mission, accompanied by his aide-de-camp, Captain George Mercer of Virginia, and Captain Stewart of the Virginia light horse; the officer who had taken care of General Braddock in his last moments.

In those days the conveniences of travelling, even between our main cities, were few, and the roads execrable. The party, therefore, travelled in Virginia style, on horseback, attended by their black servants in livery.[70]

In this way they accomplished a journey of five hundred miles in the depth of winter; stopping for some days at Philadelphia and New York. Those cities were then comparatively small, and the arrival of a party of young Southern officers attracted attention. The late disastrous battle was still the theme of every tongue, and the honorable way in which these young officers had acquitted themselves in it, made them objects of universal interest. Washington's fame, especially, had gone before him; having been spread by the officers who had served with him, and by the public honors decreed him by the Virginia Legislature. "Your name," wrote his former fellow-campaigner, Gist, in a letter dated in the preceding autumn, "is more talked of in Philadelphia than that of any other person in the army, and every body seems willing to venture under your command."

---

70 We have hitherto treated of Washington in his campaigns in the wilderness, frugal and scanty in his equipments, often, very probably, in little better than hunter's garb. His present excursion through some of the Atlantic cities presents him in a different aspect. His recent intercourse with young British officers, had probably elevated his notions as to style in dress and appearance; at least we are inclined to suspect so from the following aristocratical order for clothes, sent shortly before the time in question, to his correspondent in London.

"2 complete livery suits for servants; with a spare cloak, and all other necessary trimmings for two suits more. I would have you choose the livery by our arms, only as the field of the arms is white, I think the clothes had better not be quite so, but nearly like the inclosed. The trimmings and facings of scarlet, and a scarlet waistcoat. If livery lace is not quite disused, I should be glad to have the cloaks laced. I like that fashion best, and two silver-laced hats for the above servants.

"1 set of horse furniture, with livery lace, with the Washington crest on the housings, &c. The cloak to be of the same piece and color of the clothes.

"3 gold and scarlet sword-knots. 3 silver and blue do. 1 fashionable gold-laced hat."

With these prepossessions in his favor, when we consider Washington's noble person and demeanor, his consummate horsemanship, the admirable horses he was accustomed to ride, and the aristocratical style of his equipments, we may imagine the effect produced by himself and his little cavalcade, as they clattered through the streets of Philadelphia, and New York, and Boston. It is needless to say, their sojourn in each city was a continual fête.

The mission to General Shirley was entirely successful as to the question of rank. A written order from the Commander-in-chief determined that Dagworthy was entitled to the rank of a provincial captain, only, and, of course, must on all occasions give precedence to Colonel Washington, as a provincial field officer. The latter was disappointed, however, in the hope of getting himself and his officers put upon the regular establishment, with commissions from the king, and had to remain subjected to mortifying questions of rank and etiquette, when serving in company with regular troops.

From General Shirley he learnt that the main objects of the ensuing campaign would be the reduction of Fort Niagara, so as to cut off the communication between Canada and Louisiana, the capture of Ticonderoga and Crown Point, as a measure of safety for New York, the besieging of Fort Duquesne, and the menacing of Quebec by a body of troops which were to advance by the Kennebec River.

The official career of General Shirley was drawing to a close. Though a man of good parts, he had always, until recently, acted in a civil capacity, and proved incompetent to conduct military operations. He was recalled to England, and was to be superseded by General Abercrombie, who was coming out with two regiments.

The general command in America, however, was to be held by the Earl of Loudoun, who was invested with powers almost equal to those of a viceroy, being placed above all the colonial governors. These might claim to be civil and military representatives of their sovereign, within their respective colonies; but, even there, were bound to defer and yield precedence to this their official superior. This was part of a plan devised long since, but now first brought into operation, by which the ministry hoped to unite the colonies under military rule, and oblige the Assemblies, magistrates, and people to furnish quarters and provide a general fund subject to the control of this military dictator.

Beside his general command, the Earl of Loudoun was to be governor of Virginia and colonel of a royal American regiment of four battalions, to be raised in the colonies, but furnished with officers who, like himself, had seen foreign service. The campaign would open on his arrival, which, it was expected, would be early in the spring; and brilliant results were anticipated.

Washington remained ten days in Boston, attending, with great interest, the meetings of the Massachusetts Legislature, in which the plan of military operations was ably discussed; and receiving the most hospitable attentions from the polite and intelligent society of the place, after which he returned to New York.

Tradition gives very different motives from those of business for his two sojourns in the latter city. He found there an early friend and school-mate, Beverly Robinson, son of John Robinson, speaker of the Virginia House of Burgesses. He was living happily and prosperously with a young and wealthy bride, having married one of the nieces and heiresses of Mr. Adolphus Philipse, a rich landholder, whose manor-house is still to be seen on the banks of the Hudson. At the house of Mr. Beverly Robinson, where Washington was an honored guest, he met Miss Mary Philipse, sister of and co-heiress with Mrs. Robinson, a young lady whose personal attractions are said to have rivalled her reputed wealth.

We have already given an instance of Washington's early sensibility to female charms. A life, however, of constant activity and care, passed for the most part in the wilderness and on the frontier, far from female society, had left little mood or leisure for the indulgence of the tender sentiment; but made him more sensible, in the present brief interval of gay and social life, to the attractions of an elegant woman, brought up in the polite circle of New York.

That he was an open admirer of Miss Philipse is an historical fact; that he sought her hand, but was refused, is traditional, and not very probable. His military rank, his early laurels and distinguished presence, were all calculated to win favor in female eyes; but his sojourn in New York was brief; he may have been diffident in urging his suit with a lady accustomed to the homage of society and surrounded by admirers. The most probable version of the story is, that he was called away by his public duties before he had made sufficient approaches in his siege of the lady's heart to warrant a summons to surrender. In the latter part of March we find him at Williamsburg attending the opening of the Legislature of Virginia, eager to promote measures for the protection of the frontier and the capture of Fort Duquesne, the leading object of his ambition. Maryland and Pennsylvania were erecting forts for the defence of their own borders, but showed no disposition to co-operate with Virginia in the field; and artillery, artillerymen, and engineers were wanting for an attack on fortified places. Washington urged, therefore, an augmentation of the provincial forces, and various improvements in the militia laws.

While thus engaged, he received a letter from a friend and confidant in New York, warning him to hasten back to that city before it was too late, as Captain Morris, who had been his fellow aide-de-camp under Braddock, was laying close siege to Miss Philipse. Sterner alarms, however, summoned him in another direction. Expresses from Winchester brought word that the French had made another sortie from Fort Duquesne, accompanied by a band of savages, and were spreading terror and desolation through the country. In this moment of exigency all softer claims were forgotten; Washington repaired in all haste to his post at Winchester, and Captain Morris was left to urge his suit unrivalled and carry off the prize.

CHAPTER XX.

TROUBLES IN THE SHENANDOAH VALLEY—
GREENWAY COURT AND LORD FAIRFAX IN DANGER—
ALARMS AT WINCHESTER—WASHINGTON APPEALED
TO FOR PROTECTION—ATTACKED BY THE VIRGINIA
PRESS—HONORED BY THE PUBLIC—PROJECTS FOR
DEFENCE—SUGGESTIONS OF WASHINGTON—THE
GENTLEMEN ASSOCIATORS—RETREAT OF THE
SAVAGES—EXPEDITION AGAINST KITTANNING—
CAPTAIN HUGH MERCER—SECOND STRUGGLE
THROUGH THE WILDERNESS.

Report had not exaggerated the troubles of the frontier. It was marauded by merciless bands of savages, led, in some instances, by Frenchmen. Travellers were murdered, farm-houses burnt down, families butchered, and even stockaded forts, or houses of refuge, attacked in open day. The marauders had crossed the mountains and penetrated the valley of the Shenandoah; and several persons had fallen beneath the tomahawk in the neighborhood of Winchester.

Washington's old friend, Lord Fairfax, found himself no longer safe in his rural abode. Greenway Court was in the midst of a woodland region, affording a covert approach for the stealthy savage. His lordship was considered a great chief, whose scalp would be an inestimable trophy for an Indian warrior. Fears were entertained, therefore, by his friends, that an attempt would be made to surprise him in his green-wood castle. His nephew, Colonel Martin, of the militia, who resided with him, suggested the expediency of a removal to the lower settlements, beyond the Blue Ridge. The high-spirited old nobleman demurred; his heart cleaved to the home which he had formed for himself in the wilderness. "I am an old man," said he, "and it is of little importance whether

I fall by the tomahawk or die of disease and old age; but you are young, and, it is to be hoped, have many years before you, therefore decide for us both; my only fear is, that if we retire, the whole district will break up and take to flight; and this fine country, which I have been at such cost and trouble to improve, will again become a wilderness."

Colonel Martin took but a short time to deliberate. He knew the fearless character of his uncle, and perceived what was his inclination. He considered that his lordship had numerous retainers, white and black, with hardy huntsmen and foresters to rally round him, and that Greenway Court was at no great distance from Winchester; he decided, therefore, that they should remain and abide the course of events.

Washington, on his arrival at Winchester, found the inhabitants in great dismay. He resolved immediately to organize a force, composed partly of troops from Fort Cumberland, partly of militia from Winchester and its vicinity, to put himself at its head, and "scour the woods and suspected places in all the mountains and valleys of this part of the frontier, in quest of the Indians and their more cruel associates."

He accordingly despatched an express to Fort Cumberland with orders for a detachment from the garrison; "but how," said he, "are men to be raised at Winchester, since orders are no longer regarded in the county?"

Lord Fairfax, and other militia officers with whom he consulted, advised that each captain should call a private muster of his men, and read before them an address, or "exhortation" as it was called, being an appeal to their patriotism and fears, and a summons to assemble on the 15th of April to enroll themselves for the projected mountain foray.

This measure was adopted; the private musterings occurred; the exhortation was read; the time and place of assemblage appointed; but, when the day of enrolment arrived, not more than fifteen men appeared upon the ground. In the mean time the express returned with sad accounts from Fort Cumberland. No troops could be furnished from that quarter. The garrison was scarcely strong enough for self-defence, having sent out detachments in different directions. The express had narrowly escaped with his life, having been fired upon repeatedly, his horse shot under him, and his clothes riddled with bullets. The roads, he said, were infested by savages; none but hunters, who knew how to thread the forests at night, could travel with safety.

Horrors accumulated at Winchester. Every hour brought its tale of terror, true or false, of houses burnt, families massacred, or beleaguered and famishing in stockaded forts. The danger approached. A scouting party had been attacked in the Warm Spring Mountain, about twenty miles distant, by a large body of French and Indians, mostly on horseback. The captain of the scouting party and several of his men had been slain, and the rest put to flight.

An attack on Winchester was apprehended, and the terrors of the people rose to agony. They now turned to Washington as their main hope. The women surrounded him, holding up their children, and imploring him with tears and cries to save them from the savages. The youthful commander looked round on the suppliant crowd with a countenance beaming with pity, and a heart wrung with anguish. A letter to Governor Dinwiddie shows the conflict of his feelings. "I am too little acquainted with pathetic language to attempt a description of these people's distresses. But what can I do? I see their situation; I know their danger, and participate their sufferings, without having it in my power to give them further relief than uncertain promises."—"The supplicating tears of the women, and moving petitions of the men, melt me into such deadly sorrow, that I solemnly declare, if I know my own mind, I could offer myself a willing sacrifice to the butchering enemy, provided that would contribute to the people's ease."

The unstudied eloquence of this letter drew from the governor an instant order for a militia force from the upper counties to his assistance; but the Virginia newspapers, in descanting on the frontier troubles, threw discredit on the army and its officers, and attached blame to its commander. Stung to the quick by this injustice, Washington publicly declared that nothing but the imminent danger of the times prevented him from instantly resigning a command from which he could never reap either honor or benefit. His sensitiveness called forth strong letters from his friends, assuring him of the high sense entertained at the seat of government, and elsewhere, of his merits and services. "Your good health and fortune are the toast of every table," wrote his early friend, Colonel Fairfax, at that time a member of the governor's council. "Your endeavors in the service and defence of your country must redound to your honor."

"Our hopes, dear George," wrote Mr. Robinson, the Speaker of the House of Burgesses, "are all fixed on you for bringing our affairs to a happy issue. Consider what fatal consequences to your country your resigning the command at this time may be, especially as there is no doubt most of the officers will follow your example."

In fact, the situation and services of the youthful commander, shut up in a frontier town, destitute of forces, surrounded by savage foes, gallantly, though despairingly, devoting himself to the safety of a suffering people, were properly understood throughout the country, and excited a glow of enthusiasm in his favor. The Legislature, too, began at length to act, but timidly and inefficiently. "The country knows her danger," writes one of the members, "but such is her parsimony that she is willing to wait for the rains to wet the powder, and the rats to eat the bowstrings of the enemy, rather than attempt to drive them from her frontiers."

The measure of relief voted by the Assembly was an additional appropriation of twenty thousand pounds, and an increase of the provincial force to fifteen hundred men. With this, it was proposed to erect and garrison a chain of frontier forts, extending through the ranges of the Allegany Mountains, from the Potomac to the borders of North Carolina; a distance of between three and four hundred miles. This was one of the inconsiderate projects devised by Governor Dinwiddie.

Washington, in letters to the governor and to the speaker of the House of Burgesses, urged the impolicy of such a plan, with their actual force and means. The forts, he observed, ought to be within fifteen or eighteen miles of each other, that their spies might be able to keep watch over the intervening country, otherwise the Indians would pass between them unperceived, effect their ravages, and escape to the mountains, swamps, and ravines, before the troops from the forts could be assembled to pursue them. They ought each to be garrisoned with eighty or a hundred men, so as to afford detachments of sufficient strength, without leaving the garrison too weak; for the Indians are the most stealthy and patient of spies and lurkers; will lie in wait for days together about small forts of the kind, and, if they find, by some chance prisoner, that the garrison is actually weak, will first surprise and cut off its scouting parties, and then attack the fort itself. It was evident, therefore, observed he, that to garrison properly such a line of forts, would require, at least, two thousand men. And even then, a line of such extent might be broken through at one end before the other end could yield assistance. Feint attacks, also, might be made at one point, while the real attack was made at another, quite distant; and the country be overrun before its widely-posted defenders could be alarmed and concentrated. Then must be taken into consideration the immense cost of building so many forts, and the constant and consuming expense of supplies and transportation.

His idea of a defensive plan was to build a strong fort at Winchester, the central point, where all the main roads met of a wide range of scattered settlements, where tidings could soonest be collected from every quarter, and whence reinforcements and supplies could most readily be forwarded. It was to be a grand deposit of military stores, a residence for commanding officers, a place of refuge for the women and children in time of alarm, when the men had suddenly to take the field; in a word, it was to be the citadel of the frontier.

Beside this, he would have three or four large fortresses erected at convenient distances upon the frontiers, with powerful garrisons, so as to be able to throw out, in constant succession, strong scouting parties, to range the country. Fort Cumberland he condemned as being out of the province, and out of the track of Indian incursions, insomuch that it seldom received an alarm until all the mischief had been effected.

His representations with respect to military laws and regulations were equally cogent. In the late act of the Assembly for raising a regiment, it was provided that, in cases of emergency, if recruits should not offer in sufficient number, the militia might be drafted to supply the deficiencies, but only to serve until December, and not to be marched out of the province. In this case, said he, before they have entered upon service, or got the least smattering of duty, they will claim a discharge; if they are pursuing an enemy who has committed the most unheard-of cruelties, he has only to step across the Potomac, and he is safe. Then as to the limits of service, they might just as easily have been enlisted for seventeen months, as seven. They would then have been seasoned as well as disciplined; "for we find by experience," says he, "that our poor ragged soldiers would kill the most active militia in five days' marching."

Then, as to punishments: death, it was true, had been decreed for mutiny and desertion; but there was no punishment for cowardice; for holding correspondence with the enemy; for quitting, or sleeping on one's post; all capital offences, according to the military codes of Europe. Neither were there provisions for quartering or billeting soldiers, or impressing waggons and other conveyances, in times of exigency. To crown all, no court-martial could sit out of Virginia; a most embarrassing regulation, when troops were fifty or a hundred miles beyond the frontier. He earnestly suggested amendments on all these points, as well as with regard to the soldiers' pay; which was less than that of the regular troops, or the troops of most of the other provinces.

All these suggestions, showing at this youthful age that forethought and circumspection which distinguished him throughout life, were repeatedly and eloquently urged upon Governor Dinwiddie, with very little effect. The plan of a frontier line of twenty-three forts was persisted in. Fort Cumberland was pertinaciously kept up at a great and useless expense of men and money, and the militia laws remained lax and inefficient. It was decreed, however, that the great central fort at Winchester recommended by Washington, should be erected.

In the height of the alarm, a company of one hundred gentlemen, mounted and equipped, volunteered their services to repair to the frontier. They were headed by Peyton Randolph, attorney-general, a man deservedly popular throughout the province. Their offer was gladly accepted. They were denominated the "Gentlemen Associators," and great expectations, of course, were entertained from their gallantry and devotion. They were empowered, also, to aid with their judgment in the selection of places for frontier forts.

The "Gentlemen Associators," like all gentlemen associators in similar emergencies, turned out with great zeal and spirit, and immense popular effect, but wasted their fire in preparation, and on the march. Washington, who well understood the value of such aid, observed dryly in a letter to Governor Dinwiddie, "I am heartily glad that you have fixed upon these gentlemen to point out the places for erecting forts, but regret to find, their motions so slow." There is no doubt that they would have conducted themselves gallantly, had they been put to the test; but before they arrived near the scene of danger the alarm was over. About the beginning of May, scouts brought in word that the tracks of the marauding savages tended toward Fort Duquesne, as if on the return. In a little while it was ascertained that they had recrossed the Allegany Mountain to the Ohio in such numbers as to leave a beaten track, equal to that made in the preceding year by the army of Braddock.

The repeated inroads of the savages called for an effectual and permanent check. The idea of being constantly subject to the irruptions of a deadly foe, that moved with stealth and mystery, and was only to be traced by its ravages, and counted by its footprints, discouraged all settlement of the country. The beautiful valley of the Shenandoah was fast becoming a deserted and a silent place. Her people, for the most part, had fled to the older settlements south of the mountains, and the Blue Ridge was likely soon to become virtually the frontier line of the province.

We have to record one signal act of retaliation on the perfidious tribes of the Ohio, in which a person whose name subsequently became dear to Americans, was concerned. Prisoners who had escaped from the savages reported that Shingis, Washington's faithless ally, and another sachem, called Captain Jacobs, were the two heads of the hostile bands that had desolated the frontier. That they lived at Kittanning, an Indian town, about forty miles above Fort Duquesne; at which their warriors were fitted out for incursions, and whither they returned with their prisoners and plunder. Captain Jacobs was a daring fellow, and scoffed at palisaded forts. "He could take any fort," he said, "that would catch fire."

A party of two hundred and eighty provincials, resolute men, undertook to surprise, and destroy this savage nest. It was commanded by Colonel John Armstrong; and with him went Dr. Hugh Mercer, of subsequent renown, who had received a captain's commission from Pennsylvania, on the 6th of March, 1756.

Armstrong led his men rapidly, but secretly, over mountain, and through forest, until, after a long and perilous march, they reached the Allegany. It was a moonlight night when they arrived in the neighborhood of Kittanning. They were guided to the village by whoops and yells, and the sound of the Indian drum.

The warriors were celebrating their exploits by the triumphant scalp-dance. After a while the revel ceased, and a number of fires appeared here and there in a corn-field. They were made by such of the Indians as slept in the open air, and were intended to drive off the gnats. Armstrong and his men lay down "quiet and hush," observing every thing narrowly, and waiting until the moon should set, and the warriors be asleep. At length the moon went down, the fires burned low; all was quiet. Armstrong now roused his men, some of whom, wearied by their long march, had fallen asleep. He divided his forces; part were to attack the warriors in the corn-field, part were despatched to the houses, which were dimly seen by the first streak of day. There was sharp firing in both quarters, for the Indians, though taken by surprise, fought bravely, inspired by the war-whoop of their chief, Captain Jacobs. The women and children fled to the woods. Several of the provincials were killed and wounded. Captain Hugh Mercer received a wound in the arm, and was taken to the top of a hill. The fierce chieftain, Captain Jacobs, was besieged in his house, which had port-holes; whence he and his warriors made havoc among the assailants. The adjoining houses were set on fire. The chief was summoned to surrender himself. He replied he was a man, and would not be a prisoner. He was told he would be burnt. His reply was, "he would kill four or five before he died." The flames and smoke approached. "One of the besieged warriors, to show his manhood, began to sing. A squaw at the same time was heard to cry, but was severely rebuked by the men."[71]

In the end, the warriors were driven out by the flames; some escaped, and some were shot. Among the latter was Captain Jacobs, and his gigantic son, said to be seven feet high. Fire was now set to all the houses, thirty in number. "During the burning of the houses," says Colonel Armstrong, "we were agreeably entertained with a quick succession of charged guns, gradually firing off as reached by the fire, but much more so with the vast explosion of sundry bags, and large kegs of powder, wherewith almost every house abounded." The colonel was in a strange condition to enjoy such an entertainment, having received a wound from a large musket-ball in the shoulder.

---

71   Letter from Col. Armstrong.

The object of the expedition was accomplished. Thirty or forty of the warriors were slain; their stronghold was a smoking ruin. There was danger of the victors being cut off by a detachment from Fort Duquesne. They made the best of their way, therefore, to their horses, which had been left at a distance, and set off rapidly on their march to Fort Lyttleton, about sixty miles north of Fort Cumberland.

Colonel Armstrong had reached Fort Lyttleton on the 14th of September, six days after the battle, and fears were entertained that he had been intercepted by the Indians and was lost. He, with his ensign and eleven men, had separated from the main body when they began their march, and had taken another and what was supposed a safer road. He had with him a woman, a boy, and two little girls, recaptured from the Indians. The whole party ultimately arrived safe at Fort Lyttleton, but it would seem that Mercer, weak and faint from his fractured arm, must have fallen behind, or in some way become separated from them, and had a long, solitary, and painful struggle through the wilderness, reaching the fort sick, weary, and half famished.[72] We shall have to speak hereafter of his services when under the standard of Washington, whose friend and neighbor he subsequently became.[73]

---

72   "We hear that Captain Mercer was fourteen days in getting to Fort Lyttleton. He had a miraculous escape, living ten days on two dried clams and a rattlesnake, with the assistance of a few berries."—*New York Mercury for October* 4, 1756.

73   Mercer was a Scotchman, about thirty-four years of age. About ten years previously he had served as Assistant Surgeon in the forces of Charles Edward, and followed his standard to the disastrous field of Culloden. After the defeat of the "Chevalier," he had escaped by the way of Inverness to America, and taken up his residence on the frontier of Pennsylvania.

CHAPTER XXI.

FOUNDING OF FORT LOUDOUN—WASHINGTON'S
TOUR OF INSPECTION—INEFFICIENCY OF THE MILITIA
SYSTEM—GENTLEMEN SOLDIERS—CROSS-PURPOSES
WITH DINWIDDIE—MILITARY AFFAIRS IN THE
NORTH—DELAYS OF LORD LOUDOUN—ACTIVITY OF
MONTCALM—LOUDOUN IN WINTER QUARTERS.

Throughout the summer of 1756, Washington exerted himself diligently in carrying out measures determined upon for frontier security. The great fortress at Winchester was commenced, and the work urged forward as expeditiously as the delays and perplexities incident to a badly organized service would permit. It received the name of Fort Loudoun, in honor of the commander-in-chief, whose arrival in Virginia was hopefully anticipated.

As to the sites of the frontier posts, they were decided upon by Washington and his officers, after frequent and long consultations; parties were sent out to work on them, and men recruited, and militia drafted, to garrison them. Washington visited occasionally such as were in progress, and near at hand. It was a service of some peril, for the mountains and forests were still infested by prowling savages, especially in the neighborhood of these new forts. At one time when he was reconnoitering a wild part of the country, attended merely by a servant and a guide, two men were murdered by the Indians in a solitary defile shortly after he had passed through it.

In the autumn, he made a tour of inspection along the whole line, accompanied by his friend, Captain Hugh Mercer, who had recovered from his recent wounds. This tour furnished repeated proofs of the inefficiency of the militia system. In one place he attempted to raise a force with which to scour a region infested by roving bands of savages. After waiting several days, but five men answered to his summons. In another place, where three companies had been ordered to the relief of a fort, attacked by the Indians, all that could be mustered were a captain, a lieutenant, and seven or eight men.

When the militia were drafted, and appeared under arms, the case was not much better. It was now late in the autumn; their term of service, by the act of the Legislature, expired in December,—half of the time, therefore, was lost in marching out and home. Their waste of provisions was enormous. To be put on allowance, like other soldiers, they considered an indignity. They would sooner starve than carry a few days' provisions on their backs. On the march, when breakfast was wanted, they would knock down the first beeves they met with, and, after regaling themselves, march on till dinner, when they would take the same method; and so for supper, to the great oppression of the people. For the want of proper military laws, they were obstinate, self-willed, and perverse. Every individual had his own crude notion of things, and would undertake to direct. If his advice were neglected, he would think himself slighted, abused, and injured, and, to redress himself, would depart for his home.

The garrisons were weak for want of men, but more so from indolence and irregularity. None were in a posture of defence; few but might be surprised with the greatest ease. At one fort, the Indians rushed from their lurking-place, pounced upon several children playing under the walls, and bore them off before they were discovered. Another fort was surprised, and many of the people massacred in the same manner. In the course of his tour, as he and his party approached a fort, he heard a quick firing for several minutes; concluding that it was attacked, they hastened to its relief, but found the garrison were merely amusing themselves firing at a mark, or for wagers. In this way they would waste their ammunition as freely as they did their provisions. In the mean time, the inhabitants of the country were in a wretched situation, feeling the little dependence to be put on militia, who were slow in coming to their assistance, indifferent about their preservation, unwilling to continue, and regardless of every thing but of their own ease. In short, they were so apprehensive of approaching ruin, that the whole back country was in a general motion towards the southern colonies.

From the Catawba, he was escorted along a range of forts by a colonel, and about thirty men, chiefly officers. "With this small company of irregulars," says he, "with whom order, regularity, circumspection, and vigilance were matters of derision and contempt, we set out, and, by the protection of Providence, reached Augusta court-house in seven days, without meeting the enemy; otherwise, we must have fallen a sacrifice, through the indiscretion of these whooping, hallooing, *gentlemen* soldiers!"

How lively a picture does this give of the militia system at all times, when not subjected to strict military law.

What rendered this year's service peculiarly irksome and embarrassing to Washington, was the nature of his correspondence with Governor Dinwiddie. That gentleman, either from the natural hurry and confusion of his mind, or from a real disposition to perplex, was extremely ambiguous and unsatisfactory in most of his orders and replies. "So much am I kept in the dark," says Washington, in one of his letters, "that I do not know whether to prepare for the offensive or defensive. What would be absolutely necessary for the one, would be quite useless for the other." And again: "The orders I receive are full of ambiguity. I am left like a wanderer in the wilderness, to proceed at hazard. I am answerable for consequences, and blamed, without the privilege of defence."

In nothing was this disposition to perplex more apparent than in the governor's replies respecting Fort Cumberland. Washington had repeatedly urged the abandonment of this fort as a place of frontier deposit, being within the bounds of another province, and out of the track of Indian incursion; so that often the alarm would not reach there until after the mischief had been effected. He applied, at length, for particular and positive directions from the governor on this head. "The following," says he, "is an exact copy of his answer:—'Fort Cumberland is a *king's* fort, and built chiefly at the charge of the colony, therefore properly under our direction until a new governor is appointed.' Now, whether I am to understand this aye or no to the plain simple question asked, Is the fort to be continued or removed? I know not. But in all important matters I am directed in this ambiguous and uncertain way."

Governor Dinwiddie subsequently made himself explicit on this point. Taking offence at some of Washington's comments on the military affairs of the frontier, he made the stand of a self-willed and obstinate man, in the case of Fort Cumberland; and represented it in such light to Lord Loudoun, as to draw from his lordship an order that it should be kept up: and an implied censure of the conduct of Washington in slighting a post of such paramount importance. "I cannot agree with Colonel Washington," writes his lordship, "in not drawing in the posts from the stockade forts, in order to defend that advanced one; and I should imagine much more of the frontier will be exposed by retiring your advanced posts near Winchester, where I understand he is retired; for, from your letter, I take it for granted he has before this executed his plan, without waiting for any advice. If he leaves any of the great quantity of stores behind, it will be very unfortunate, and he ought to consider that it must lie at his own door."

Thus powerfully supported, Dinwiddie went so far as to order that the garrisons should be withdrawn from the stockades and small frontier forts, and most of the troops from Winchester, to strengthen Fort Cumberland, which was now to become headquarters; thus weakening the most important points and places, to concentrate a force where it was not wanted, and would be out of the way in most cases of alarm. By these meddlesome moves, made by Governor Dinwiddie from a distance, without knowing any thing of the game, all previous arrangements were reversed, every thing was thrown into confusion, and enormous losses and expenses were incurred.

"Whence it arises, or why, I am truly ignorant," writes Washington to Mr. Speaker Robinson, "but my strongest representations of matters relative to the frontiers are disregarded as idle and frivolous; my propositions and measures as partial and selfish; and all my sincerest endeavors for the service of my country are perverted to the worst purposes. My orders are dark and uncertain; today approved, tomorrow disapproved."

Whence all this contradiction and embarrassment arose has since been explained, and with apparent reason. Governor Dinwiddie had never recovered from the pique caused by the popular elevation of Washington to the command in preference to his favorite, Colonel Innes. His irritation was kept alive by a little Scottish faction, who were desirous of disgusting Washington with the service, so as to induce him to resign, and make way for his rival. They might have carried their point during the panic at Winchester, had not his patriotism and his sympathy with the public distress been more powerful than his self-love. He determined, he said, to bear up under these embarrassments in the hope of better regulations when Lord Loudoun should arrive; to whom he looked for the future fate of Virginia.

While these events were occurring on the Virginia frontier, military affairs went on tardily and heavily at the north. The campaign against Canada, which was to have opened early in the year, hung fire. The armament coming out for the purpose, under Lord Loudoun, was delayed through the want of energy and union in the British cabinet. General Abercrombie, who was to be next in command to his lordship, and to succeed to General Shirley, set sail in advance for New York with two regiments, but did not reach Albany, the head-quarters of military operation, until the 25th of June. He billeted his soldiers upon the town, much to the disgust of the inhabitants, and talked of ditching and stockading it, but postponed all exterior enterprises until the arrival of Lord Loudoun; then the campaign was to open in earnest.

On the 12th of July, came word that the forts Ontario and Oswego, on each side of the mouth of the Oswego River, were menaced by the Drench. They had been imperfectly constructed by Shirley, and were insufficiently garrisoned, yet contained a great amount of military and naval stores, and protected the vessels which cruised on Lake Ontario.

Major-general Webb was ordered by Abercrombie to hold himself in readiness to march with one regiment to the relief of these forts, but received no further orders. Every thing awaited the arrival at Albany of Lord Loudoun, which at length took place, on the 29th of July. There were now at least ten thousand troops, regulars and provincials, loitering in an idle camp at Albany, yet relief to Oswego was still delayed. Lord Loudoun was in favor of it, but the governments of New York and New England urged the immediate reduction of Crown Point, as necessary for the security of their frontier. After much debate, it was agreed that General Webb should march to the relief of Oswego. He left Albany on the 12th of August, but had scarce reached the carrying-place, between the Mohawk River and Wood Creek, when he received news that Oswego was reduced, and its garrison captured. While the British commanders had debated, Field-marshal the Marquis De Montcalm, newly arrived from France, had acted. He was a different kind of soldier from Abercrombie or Loudoun. A capacious mind and enterprising spirit animated a small, but active and untiring frame. Quick in thought, quick in speech, quicker still in action, he comprehended every thing at a glance, and moved from point to point of the province with a celerity and secrecy that completely baffled his slow and pondering antagonists. Crown Point and Ticonderoga were visited, and steps taken to strengthen their works, and provide for their security; then hastening to Montreal, he put himself at the head of a force of regulars, Canadians, and Indians; ascended the St. Lawrence to Lake Ontario; blocked up the mouth of the Oswego by his vessels, landed his guns, and besieged the two forts; drove the garrison out of one into the other; killed the commander, Colonel Mercer, and compelled the garrisons to surrender prisoners of war. With the forts was taken an immense amount of military stores, ammunition, and provisions; one hundred and twenty-one cannon, fourteen mortars, six vessels of war, a vast number of batteaux, and three chests of money. His blow achieved, Montcalm returned in triumph to Montreal, and sent the colors of the captured forts to be hung up as trophies in the Canadian churches.

The season was now too far advanced for Lord Loudoun to enter upon any great military enterprise; he postponed, therefore, the great northern campaign, so much talked of and debated, until the following year; and having taken measures for the protection of his frontiers, and for more active operations in the spring, returned to New York, hung up his sword, and went into comfortable winter-quarters.

CHAPTER XXII.

WASHINGTON VINDICATES HIS CONDUCT TO LORD
LOUDOUN—HIS RECEPTION BY HIS LORDSHIP—
MILITARY PLANS—LORD LOUDOUN AT HALIFAX—
MONTCALM ON LAKE GEORGE—HIS TRIUMPHS—
LORD LOUDOUN'S FAILURES—WASHINGTON AT
WINCHESTER—CONTINUED MISUNDERSTANDINGS
WITH DINWIDDIE—RETURN TO MOUNT VERNON.

Circumstances had led Washington to think that Lord Loudoun "had received impressions to his prejudice by false representations of facts," and that a wrong idea prevailed at head-quarters respecting the state of military affairs in Virginia. He was anxious, therefore, for an opportunity of placing all these matters in a proper light; and, understanding that there was to be a meeting in Philadelphia in the month of March, between Lord Loudoun and the southern governors, to consult about measures of defence for their respective provinces, he wrote to Governor Dinwiddie for permission to attend it.

"I cannot conceive," writes Dinwiddie in reply, "what service you can be of in going there, as the plan concerted will, in course, be communicated to you and the other officers. However, as you seem so earnest to go, I now give you leave."

This ungracious reply seemed to warrant the suspicions entertained by some of Washington's friends, that it was the busy pen of Governor Dinwiddie which had given the "false representation of facts," to Lord Loudoun. About a month, therefore, before the time of the meeting, Washington addressed a long letter to his lordship, explanatory of military affairs in the quarter where he had commanded. In this he set forth the various defects in the militia laws of Virginia; the errors in its system of defence, and the inevitable confusion which had thence resulted.

Adverting to his own conduct: "The orders I receive," said he, "are full of ambiguity. I am left like a wanderer in the wilderness to proceed at hazard. I am answerable for consequences, and blamed, without the privilege of defence. . . . It is not to be wondered at, if, under such peculiar circumstances, I should be sick of a service which promises so little of a soldier's reward.

"I have long been satisfied of the impossibility of continuing in this service, without loss of honor. Indeed, I was fully convinced of it before I accepted the command the second time, seeing the cloudy prospect before me; and I did, for this reason, reject the offer, until I was ashamed any longer to refuse, not caring to expose my character to public censure. The solicitations of the country overcame my objections, and induced me to accept it. Another reason has of late operated to continue me in the service until now, and that is, the dawn of hope that arose, when I heard your lordship was destined, by his majesty, for the important command of his armies in America, and appointed to the government of his dominion of Virginia. Hence it was, that I drew my hopes, and fondly pronounced your lordship our patron. Although I have not the honor to be known to your lordship, yet your name was familiar to my ear, on account of the important services rendered to his majesty in other parts of the world."

The manner in which Washington was received by Lord Loudoun on arriving in Philadelphia, showed him at once, that his long, explanatory letter had produced the desired effect, and that his character and conduct were justly appreciated. During his sojourn in Philadelphia he was frequently consulted on points of frontier service, and his advice was generally adopted. On one point it failed. He advised that an attack should be made on Fort Duquesne, simultaneous with the attempts on Canada. At such time a great part of the garrison would be drawn away to aid in the defence of that province, and a blow might be struck more likely to insure the peace and safety of the southern frontier, than all its forts and defences.

Lord Loudoun, however, was not to be convinced, or at least persuaded. According to his plan, the middle and southern provinces were to maintain a merely defensive warfare; and as Virginia would be required to send four hundred of her troops to the aid of South Carolina, she would, in fact, be left weaker than before.

Washington was also disappointed a second time, in the hope of having his regiment placed on the same footing as the regular army, and of obtaining a king's commission; the latter he was destined never to hold.

His representations with respect to Fort Cumberland had the desired effect in counteracting the mischievous intermeddling of Dinwiddie. The Virginia troops and stores were ordered to be again removed to Fort Loudoun, at Winchester, which once more became head-quarters, while Fort Cumberland was left to be occupied by a Maryland garrison. Washington was instructed, likewise, to correspond and co-operate, in military affairs, with Colonel Stanwix, who was stationed on the Pennsylvania frontier, with five hundred men from the Royal American regiment, and to whom he would be, in some measure, subordinate. This proved a correspondence of friendship, as well as duty; Colonel Stanwix being a gentleman of high moral worth, as well as great ability in military affairs.

The great plan of operations at the north was again doomed to failure. The reduction of Crown Point, on Lake Champlain, which had long been meditated, was laid aside, and the capture of Louisburg substituted, as an acquisition of far greater importance. This was a place of great consequence, situated on the isle of Cape Breton, and strongly fortified. It commanded the fisheries of Newfoundland, overawed New England, and was a main bulwark to Acadia.

In the course of July, Lord Loudoun set sail for Halifax with all the troops he could collect, amounting to about six thousand men, to join with Admiral Holbourne, who had just arrived at that port with eleven ships of the line, a fire-ship, bomb-ketch, and fleet of transports, having on board six thousand men. With this united force Lord Loudoun anticipated the certain capture of Louisburg.

Scarce had the tidings of his lordship's departure reached Canada, when the active Montcalm again took the field, to follow up the successes of the preceding year. Fort William Henry, which Sir Wm. Johnson had erected on the southern shore of Lake George, was now his object; it commanded the lake, and was an important protection to the British frontier. A brave old officer, Colonel Monro, with about five hundred men, formed the garrison; more than three times that number of militia were intrenched near by. Montcalm had, early in the season, made three ineffectual attempts upon the fort; he now trusted to be more successful. Collecting his forces from Crown Point, Ticonderoga, and the adjacent posts, with a considerable number of Canadians and Indians, altogether nearly eight thousand men, he advanced up the lake, on the 1st of August, in a fleet of boats, with swarms of Indian canoes in the advance. The fort came near being surprised; but the troops encamped without it, abandoned their tents and hurried within the works. A summons to surrender was answered by a brave defiance. Montcalm invested the fort, made his approaches, and battered it with his artillery. For five days its veteran commander kept up a vigorous defence, trusting to receive assistance from General Webb, who had failed to relieve Fort Oswego in the preceding year, and who was now at Fort Edward, about fifteen miles distant, with upwards of five thousand men. Instead of this, Webb, who overrated the French forces, sent him a letter, advising him to capitulate. The letter was intercepted by Montcalm, but still forwarded to Monro. The obstinate old soldier, however, persisted in his defence, until most of his cannon were burst, and his ammunition expended. At length, in the month of August, he hung out a flag of truce, and obtained honorable terms from an enemy who knew how to appreciate his valor. Montcalm demolished the fort, carried off all the artillery and munitions of war, with vessels employed in the navigation of the lake; and having thus completed his destruction of the British defences on this frontier, returned once more in triumph with the spoils of victory, to hang up fresh trophies in the churches of Canada.

Lord Loudoun, in the mean time, formed his junction with Admiral Holbourne at Halifax, and the troops were embarked with all diligence on board of the transports. Unfortunately, the French were again too quick for them. Admiral de Bois de la Mothe had arrived at Louisburg, with a large naval and land force; it was ascertained that he had seventeen ships of the line, and three frigates, quietly moored in the harbor; that the place was well fortified and supplied with provisions and ammunition, and garrisoned with six thousand regular troops; three thousand natives, and thirteen hundred Indians.

Some hot-heads would have urged an attempt against all such array of force, but Lord Loudoun was aware of the probability of defeat, and the disgrace and ruin that it would bring upon British arms in America. He wisely, though ingloriously, returned to New York. Admiral Holbourne made a silly demonstration of his fleet off the harbor of Louisburg, approaching within two miles of the batteries, but retired on seeing the French admiral preparing to unmoor. He afterwards returned with a reinforcement of four ships of the line; cruised before Louisburg, endeavoring to draw the enemy to an engagement, which De la Mothe had the wisdom to decline; was overtaken by a hurricane, in which one of his ships was lost, eleven were dismasted, others had to throw their guns overboard, and all returned in a shattered condition to England. Thus ended the northern campaign by land and sea, a subject of great mortification to the nation, and ridicule and triumph to the enemy.

During these unfortunate operations to the north, Washington was stationed at Winchester, shorn of part of his force by the detachment to South Carolina, and left with seven hundred men to defend a frontier of more than three hundred and fifty miles in extent. The capture and demolition of Oswego by Montcalm had produced a disastrous effect. The whole country of the five nations was abandoned to the French. The frontiers of Pennsylvania, Maryland, and Virginia were harassed by repeated inroads of French and Indians, and Washington had the mortification to see the noble valley of the Shenandoah almost deserted by its inhabitants, and fast relapsing into a wilderness.

The year wore away on his part in the harassing service of defending a wide frontier with an insufficient and badly organized force, and the vexations he experienced were heightened by continual misunderstandings with Governor Dinwiddie. From the ungracious tenor of several of that gentleman's letters, and from private information, he was led to believe that some secret enemy had been making false representations of his motives and conduct, and prejudicing the governor against him. He vindicated himself warmly from the alleged aspersions, proudly appealing to the whole course of his public career in proof of their falsity. "It is uncertain," said he, "in what light my services may have appeared to your honor; but this I know, and it is the highest consolation I am capable of feeling, that no man that ever was employed in a public capacity has endeavored to discharge the trust reposed in him with greater honesty and more zeal for the country's interest than I have done; and if there is any person living who can say, with justice, that I have offered any intentional wrong to the public, I will cheerfully submit to the most ignominious punishment that an injured people ought to inflict. On the other hand, it is hard to have my character arraigned, and my actions condemned, without a hearing."

His magnanimous appeal had but little effect. Dinwiddie was evidently actuated by the petty pique of a narrow and illiberal mind, impatient of contradiction, even when in error. He took advantage of his official station to vent his spleen and gratify his petulance in a variety of ways incompatible with the courtesy of a gentleman. It may excite a grave smile at the present day to find Washington charged by this very small-minded man with looseness in his way of writing to him; with remissness in his duty towards him; and even with impertinence in the able and eloquent representations which he felt compelled to make of disastrous mismanagement in military affairs; and still more, to find his reasonable request, after a long course of severe duty, for a temporary leave of absence to attend to his private concerns peremptorily refused, and that with as little courtesy as though he were a mere subaltern seeking to absent himself on a party of pleasure.

The multiplied vexations which Washington had latterly experienced from this man, had preyed upon his spirits, and contributed, with his incessant toils and anxieties, to undermine his health. For some time he struggled with repeated attacks of dysentery and fever, and continued in the exercise of his duties; but the increased violence of his malady, and the urgent advice of his friend Dr. Craik, the army surgeon, induced him to relinquish his post towards the end of the year and retire to Mount Vernon.

The administration of Dinwiddie, however, was now at an end. He set sail for England in January, 1758, very little regretted, excepting by his immediate hangers-on, and leaving a character overshadowed by the imputation of avarice and extortion in the exaction of illegal fees, and of downright delinquency in regard to large sums transmitted to him by government to be paid over to the province in indemnification of its extra expenses; for the disposition of which sums he failed to render an account.

He was evidently a sordid, narrow-minded, and somewhat arrogant man; bustling rather than active; prone to meddle with matters of which he was profoundly ignorant, and absurdly unwilling to have his ignorance enlightened.

CHAPTER XXIII.

For several months Washington was afflicted by returns of his malady, accompanied by symptoms indicative, as he thought, of a decline. "My constitution," writes he to his friend Colonel Stanwix, "is much impaired, and nothing can retrieve it but the greatest care and the most circumspect course of life. This being the case, as I have now no prospect left of preferment in the military way, and despair of rendering that immediate service which my country may require from the person commanding its troops, I have thoughts of quitting my command and retiring from all public business, leaving my post to be filled by some other person more capable of the task, and who may, perhaps, have his endeavors crowned with better success than mine have been."

A gradual improvement in his health, and a change in his prospects, encouraged him to continue in what really was his favorite career, and at the beginning of April he was again in command at Fort Loudoun. Mr. Francis Fauquier had been appointed successor to Dinwiddie, and, until he should arrive, Mr. John Blair, president of the council, had, from his office, charge of the government. In the latter Washington had a friend who appreciated his character and services, and was disposed to carry out his plans.

The general aspect of affairs, also, was more animating. Under the able and intrepid administration of William Pitt, who had control of the British cabinet, an effort was made to retrieve the disgraces of the late American campaign, and to carry on the war with greater vigor. The instructions for a common fund were discontinued; there was no more talk of taxation by Parliament. Lord Loudoun, from whom so much had been anticipated, had disappointed by his inactivity, and been relieved from a command in which he had attempted much and done so little. His friends alleged that his inactivity was owing to a want of unanimity and co-operation in the colonial governments, which paralyzed all his well meant efforts. Franklin, it is probable, probed the matter with his usual sagacity when he characterized him as a man "entirely made up of indecision."—"Like St. George on the signs, he was always on horseback, but never rode on."

On the return of his lordship to England, the general command in America devolved on Major-general Abercrombie, and the forces were divided into three detached bodies; one, under Major-general Amherst, was to operate in the north with the fleet under Boscawen, for the reduction of Louisburg and the island of Cape Breton; another, under Abercrombie himself, was to proceed against Ticonderoga and Crown Point on Lake Champlain; and the third, under Brigadier-general Forbes, who had the charge of the middle and southern colonies, was to undertake the reduction of Fort Duquesne. The colonial troops were to be supplied, like the regulars, with arms, ammunition, tents, and provisions, at the expense of government, but clothed and paid by the colonies; for which the king would recommend to Parliament a proper compensation. The provincial officers appointed by the governors, and of no higher rank than colonel, were to be equal in command, when united in service with those who held direct from the king, according to the date of their commissions. By these wise provisions of Mr. Pitt a fertile cause of heartburnings and dissensions was removed.

It was with the greatest satisfaction Washington saw his favorite measure at last adopted, the reduction of Fort Duquesne; and he resolved to continue in the service until that object was accomplished. In a letter to Stanwix, who was now a brigadier-general, he modestly requested to be mentioned in favorable terms to General Forbes, "not," said he, "as a person who would depend upon him for further recommendation to military preferment (for I have long conquered all such inclinations, and shall serve this campaign merely for the purpose of affording my best endeavors to bring matters to a conclusion), but as a person who would gladly be distinguished in some measure from the *common run* of provincial officers, as I understand there will be a motley herd of us." He had the satisfaction subsequently of enjoying the fullest confidence of General Forbes, who knew too well the sound judgment and practical ability evinced by him in the unfortunate campaign of Braddock not to be desirous of availing himself of his counsels.

Washington still was commander-in-chief of the Virginia troops, now augmented, by an act of the Assembly, to two regiments of one thousand men each; one led by himself, the other by Colonel Byrd; the whole destined to make a part of the army of General Forbes in the expedition against Fort Duquesne.

Of the animation which he felt at the prospect of serving in this long-desired campaign, and revisiting with an effective force the scene of past disasters, we have a proof in a short letter, written during the excitement of the moment, to Major Francis Halket, his former companion in arms.

"My dear Halket:—Are we to have you once more among us? And shall we revisit together a hapless spot, that proved so fatal to many of our former brave companions? Yes; and I rejoice at it, hoping it will now be in our power to testify a just abhorrence of the cruel butcheries exercised on our friends in the unfortunate day of General Braddock's defeat; and, moreover, to show our enemies, that we can practise all that lenity of which they only boast, without affording any adequate proof."

Before we proceed to narrate the expedition against Fort Duquesne, however, we will briefly notice the conduct of the two other expeditions, which formed important parts in the plan of military operations for the year. And first, of that against Louisburg and the Island of Cape Breton.

Major-general Amherst, who conducted this expedition, embarked with between ten and twelve thousand men, in the fleet of Admiral Boscawen, and set sail about the end of May, from Halifax, in Nova Scotia. Along with him went Brigadier-general

James Wolfe, an officer young in years, but a veteran, in military experience, and destined to gain, an almost romantic celebrity. He may almost be said to have been born in the camp, for he was the son of Major-general Wolfe, a veteran officer of merit, and when a lad had witnessed the battles of Dettingen and Fontenoy. While a mere youth he had distinguished himself at the battle of Laffeldt, in the Netherlands; and now, after having been eighteen years in the service, he was but thirty-one years of age. In America, however, he was to win his lasting laurels.

On the 2d of June, the fleet arrived at the Bay of Gabarus, about seven miles to the west of Louisburg. The latter place was garrisoned by two thousand five hundred regulars, and three hundred militia, and subsequently reinforced by upwards of four hundred Canadians and Indians. In the harbor were six ships-of-the-line, and five frigates; three of which were sunk across the mouth. For several days the troops were prevented from landing by boisterous weather, and a heavy surf. The French improved that time to strengthen a chain of forts along the shore, deepening trenches, and constructing batteries.

On the 8th of June, preparations for landing were made before daybreak. The troops were embarked in boats in three divisions, under Brigadiers Wolfe, Whetmore, and Laurens. The landing was to be attempted west of the harbor, at a place feebly secured. Several frigates and sloops previously scoured the beach with their shot, after which Wolfe pulled for shore with his divisions; the other two divisions distracting the attention of the enemy, by making a show of landing in other parts. The surf still ran high, the enemy opened a fire of cannon and musketry from their batteries, many boats were upset, many men slain, but Wolfe pushed forward, sprang into the water when the boats grounded, dashed through the surf with his men, stormed the enemy's breastworks and batteries, and drove them from the shore. Among the subalterns who stood by Wolfe on this occasion, was an Irish youth, twenty-one years of age, named Richard Montgomery, whom, for his gallantry, Wolfe promoted to a lieutenancy, and who was destined, in after years, to gain an imperishable renown. The other divisions effected a landing after a severe conflict; artillery and stores were brought on shore, and Louisburg was formally invested.

The weather continued boisterous; the heavy cannon, and the various munitions necessary for a siege, were landed with difficulty. Amherst, moreover, was a cautious man, and made his approaches slowly, securing his camp by redoubts and epaulements. The Chevalier Drucour, who commanded at Louisburg, called in his outposts, and prepared for a desperate defence; keeping up a heavy fire from his batteries, and from the ships in the harbor.

Wolfe, with a strong detachment, surprised at night, and took possession of Light House Point, on the north-east side of the entrance to the harbor. Here he threw up batteries in addition to those already there, from which he was enabled greatly to annoy both town and shipping, as well as to aid Amherst in his slow, but regular and sure approaches.

On the 21st of July, the three largest of the enemy's ships were set on fire by a bombshell. On the night of the 25th two other of the ships were boarded, sword in hand, from boats of the squadron; one being aground, was burnt, the other was towed out of the harbor in triumph. The brave Drucour kept up the defence until all the ships were either taken or destroyed; forty, out of fifty-two pieces of cannon dismounted, and his works mere heaps of ruins. When driven to capitulate, he refused the terms proposed, as being too severe, and, when threatened with a general assault, by sea and land, determined to abide it, rather than submit to what he considered a humiliation. The prayers and petitions of the inhabitants, however, overcame his obstinacy. The place was surrendered, and he and his garrison became prisoners of war. Captain Amherst, brother to the general, carried home the news to England, with eleven pair of colors, taken at Louisburg. There were rejoicings throughout the kingdom. The colors were borne in triumph through the streets of London, with a parade of horse and foot, kettle drums and trumpets, and the thunder of artillery, and were put up as trophies in St. Paul's Cathedral.

Boscawen, who was a member of Parliament, received a unanimous vote of praise from the House of Commons, and the youthful Wolfe, who returned shortly after the victory to England, was hailed as the hero of the enterprise.

We have disposed of one of the three great expeditions contemplated in the plan of the year's campaign. The second was that against the French forts on Lakes George and Champlain. At the beginning of July, Abercrombie was encamped on the borders of Lake George, with between six and seven thousand regulars, and upwards of nine thousand provincials, from New England, New York, and New Jersey. Major Israel Putnam, of Connecticut, who had served on this lake, under Sir William Johnson, in the campaign in which Dieskau was defeated and slain, had been detached with a scouting party to reconnoitre the neighborhood. After his return and report, Abercrombie prepared to proceed against Ticonderoga, situated on a tongue of land in Lake Champlain, at the mouth of the strait communicating with Lake George.

On the 5th of July, the forces were embarked in one hundred and twenty-five whale-boats, and nine hundred batteaux, with the artillery on rafts. The vast flotilla proceeded slowly down the lake, with banners and pennons fluttering in the summer breeze; arms glittering in the sunshine, and martial music echoing along the wood-clad mountains. With Abercrombie went Lord Howe, a young nobleman brave and enterprising, full of martial enthusiasm, and endeared to the soldiery by the generosity of his disposition, and the sweetness of his manners.

On the first night they bivouacked for some hours at Sabbath-day Point, but re-embarked before midnight. The next day they landed on a point on the western shore, just at the entrance of the strait leading to Lake Champlain. Here they were formed into three columns, and pushed forward.

They soon came upon the enemy's advanced guard, a battalion encamped behind a log breastwork. The French set fire to their camp, and retreated. The columns kept their form, and pressed forward, but, through ignorance of their guides, became bewildered in a dense forest, fell into confusion, and blundered upon each other.

Lord Howe urged on with the van of the right centre column. Putnam, who was with him, and more experienced in forest warfare, endeavored in vain to inspire him with caution. After a time they came upon a detachment of the retreating foe, who, like themselves, had lost their way. A severe conflict ensued. Lord Howe, who gallantly led the van, was killed at the onset. His fall gave new ardor to his troops. The enemy were routed, some slain, some drowned, about one hundred and fifty taken prisoners, including five officers. Nothing further was done that day. The death of Lord Howe more than counterbalanced the defeat of the enemy. His loss was bewailed not merely by the army, but by the American people; for it is singular how much this young nobleman, in a short time, had made himself beloved. The point near which the troops had landed still bears his name; the place where he fell is still pointed out; and Massachusetts voted him a monument in Westminster Abbey.

With Lord Howe expired the master spirit of the enterprise. Abercrombie fell back to the landing-place. The next day he sent out a strong detachment of regulars, royal provincials, and batteaux men, under Lieutenant-colonel Bradstreet, of New York, to secure a saw-mill, which the enemy had abandoned. This done, he followed on the same evening with the main forces, and took post at the mill, within two miles of the fort. Here he was joined by Sir William Johnson, with between four and five hundred savage warriors from the Mohawk River.

Montcalm had called in all his forces, between three and four thousand men, and was strongly posted behind deep intrenchments and breastworks eight feet high; with an abatis, or felled trees, in front of his lines, presenting a horrid barrier, with their jagged boughs pointing outward. Abercrombie was deceived as to the strength of the French works; his engineers persuaded him they were formidable only in appearance, but really weak and flimsy. Without waiting for the arrival of his cannon, and against the opinion of his most judicious officers, he gave orders to storm the works. Never were rash orders more gallantly obeyed. The men rushed forward with fixed bayonets, and attempted to force their way through, or scramble over the abatis, under a sheeted fire of swivels and musketry. In the desperation of the moment, the officers even tried to cut their way through with their swords. Some even reached the parapet, where they were shot down. The breastwork was too high to be surmounted, and gave a secure covert to the enemy. Repeated assaults were made, and as often repelled, with dreadful havoc. The Iroquois warriors, who had arrived with Sir William Johnson, took no part, it is said, in this fierce conflict, but stood aloof as unconcerned spectators of the bloody strife of white men.

After four hours of desperate and fruitless fighting, Abercrombie, who had all the time remained aloof at the saw-mills gave up the ill-judged attempt, and withdrew once more to the landing-place, with the loss of nearly two thousand in killed and wounded. Had not the vastly inferior force of Montcalm prevented him from sallying beyond his trenches, the retreat of the British might have been pushed to a headlong and disastrous flight.

Abercrombie had still nearly four times the number of the enemy, with cannon, and all the means of carrying on a siege, with every prospect of success; but the failure of this rash assault seems completely to have dismayed him. The next day he re-embarked all his troops, and returned across that lake where his disgraced banners had recently waved so proudly.

While the general was planning fortifications on Lake George, Colonel Bradstreet obtained permission to carry into effect an expedition which he had for some time meditated, and which had been a favored project with the lamented Howe. This was to reduce Fort Frontenac, the stronghold of the French on the north side of the entrance of Lake Ontario, commanding the mouth of the St. Lawrence. This post was a central point of Indian trade, where the tribes resorted from all parts of a vast interior; sometimes a distance of a thousand miles, to traffic away their peltries with the fur-traders. It was, moreover, a magazine for the more southern posts, among which was Fort Duquesne on the Ohio.

Bradstreet was an officer of spirit. Pushing his way along the valley of the Mohawk and by the Oneida, where he was joined by several warriors of the Six Nations, he arrived at Oswego in August, with nearly three thousand men; the greater part of them provincial troops of New York and Massachusetts. Embarking at Oswego in open boats, he crossed Lake Ontario, and landed within a mile of Frontenac. The fort mounted sixty guns, and several mortars, yet though a place of such importance, the garrison consisted of merely one hundred and ten men, and a few Indians. These either fled, or surrendered at discretion. In the fort was an immense amount of merchandise and military stores; part of the latter intended for the supply of Fort Duquesne. In the harbor were nine armed vessels, some of them carrying eighteen guns; the whole of the enemy's shipping on the lake. Two of these Colonel Bradstreet freighted with part of the spoils of the fort, the others he destroyed; then having dismantled the fortifications, and laid waste every thing which he could not carry away, he recrossed the lake to Oswego, and returned with his troops to the army on Lake George.

CHAPTER XXIV.

SLOW OPERATIONS—WASHINGTON ORDERS OUT
THE MILITIA—MISSION TO WILLIAMSBURG—HALT
AT MR. CHAMBERLAYNE'S—MRS. MARTHA CUSTIS—
A BRIEF COURTSHIP—AN ENGAGEMENT—RETURN
TO WINCHESTER—THE RIFLE DRESS—INDIAN
SCOUTS—WASHINGTON ELECTED TO THE HOUSE
OF BURGESSES—TIDINGS OF AMHERST'S SUCCESS—
THE NEW ROAD TO FORT DUQUESNE—MARCH
FOR THE FORT—INDISCREET CONDUCT OF
MAJOR GRANT—DISASTROUS CONSEQUENCES—
WASHINGTON ADVANCES AGAINST FORT
DUQUESNE—END OF THE EXPEDITION—
WASHINGTON RETURNS HOME—HIS MARRIAGE.

Operations went on slowly in that part of the year's campaign
in which Washington was immediately engaged—the expedition
against Fort Duquesne. Brigadier-general Forbes, who was
commander-in-chief, was detained at Philadelphia by those delays
and cross-purposes incident to military affairs in a new country.
Colonel Bouquet, who was to command the advanced division,
took his station, with a corps of regulars, at Raystown, in the centre
of Pennsylvania. There slowly assembled troops from various parts.
Three thousand Pennsylvanians, twelve hundred and fifty South
Carolinians, and a few hundred men from elsewhere.

Washington, in the mean time, gathered together his scattered
regiment at Winchester, some from a distance of two hundred
miles, and diligently disciplined his recruits. He had two Virginia
regiments under him, amounting, when complete, to about nineteen
hundred men. Seven hundred Indian warriors, also, came lagging
into his camp, lured by the prospect of a successful campaign.

The president of the council had given Washington a discretionary power in the present juncture to order out militia for the purpose of garrisoning the fort in the absence of the regular troops. Washington exercised the power with extreme reluctance. He considered it, he said, an affair of too important and delicate a nature for him to manage, and apprehended the discontent it might occasion. In fact, his sympathies were always with the husbandmen and the laborers of the soil, and he deplored the evils imposed upon them by arbitrary drafts for military service; a scruple not often indulged by youthful commanders.

The force thus assembling was in want of arms, tents, field-equipage, and almost every requisite. Washington had made repeated representations, by letter, of the destitute state of the Virginia troops, but without avail; he was now ordered by Sir John St. Clair, the quartermaster-general of the forces, under General Forbes, to repair to Williamsburg, and lay the state of the case before the council. He set off promptly on horseback, attended by Bishop, the well-trained military servant, who had served the late General Braddock. It proved an eventful journey, though not in a military point of view. In crossing a ferry of the Pamunkey, a branch of York River, he fell in company with a Mr. Chamberlayne, who lived in the neighborhood, and who, in the spirit of Virginian hospitality, claimed him as a guest. It was with difficulty Washington could be prevailed on to halt for dinner, so impatient was he to arrive at Williamsburg, and accomplish his mission.

Among the guests at Mr. Chamberlayne's was a young and blooming widow, Mrs. Martha Custis, daughter of Mr. John Dandridge, both patrician names in the province. Her husband, John Parke Custis, had been dead about three years, leaving her with two young children, and a large fortune. She is represented as being rather below the middle size, but extremely well shaped, with an agreeable countenance, dark hazel eyes and hair, and those frank, engaging manners, so captivating in Southern women. We are not informed whether Washington had met with her before; probably not during her widowhood, as during that time he had been almost continually on the frontier. We have shown that, with all his gravity and reserve, he was quickly susceptible to female charms; and they may have had a greater effect upon him when thus casually encountered in fleeting moments snatched from the cares and perplexities and rude scenes of frontier warfare. At any rate, his heart appears to have been taken by surprise.

The dinner, which in those days was an earlier meal than at present, seemed all too short. The afternoon passed away like a dream. Bishop was punctual to the orders he had received on halting; the horses pawed at the door; but for once Washington loitered in the path of duty. The horses were countermanded, and it was not until the next morning that he was again in the saddle, spurring for Williamsburg. Happily the White House, the residence of Mrs. Custis, was in New Kent County, at no great distance from that city, so that he had opportunities of visiting her in the intervals of business. His time for courtship, however, was brief. Military duties called him back almost immediately to Winchester; but he feared, should he leave the matter in suspense, some more enterprising rival might supplant him during his absence, as in the case of Miss Philipse, at New York. He improved, therefore, his brief opportunity to the utmost. The blooming widow had many suitors, but Washington was graced with that renown so ennobling in the eyes of woman. In a word, before they separated, they had mutually plighted their faith, and the marriage was to take place as soon as the campaign against Fort Duquesne was at an end.

Before returning to Winchester, Washington was obliged to hold conferences with Sir John St. Clair and Colonel Bouquet, at an intermediate rendezvous, to give them information respecting the frontiers, and arrange about the marching of his troops. His constant word to them was forward! forward! For the precious time for action was slipping away, and he feared their Indian allies, so important to their security while on the march, might, with their usual fickleness, lose patience, and return home.

On arriving at Winchester, he found his troops restless and discontented from prolonged inaction. The inhabitants impatient of the burdens imposed on them, and of the disturbances of an idle camp; while the Indians, as he apprehended, had deserted outright. It was a great relief, therefore, when he received orders from the commander-in-chief to repair to Fort Cumberland. He arrived there on the 2d of July, and proceeded to open a road between that post and head-quarters, at Raystown, thirty miles distant, where Colonel Bouquet was stationed.

His troops were scantily supplied with regimental clothing. The weather was oppressively warm. He now conceived the idea of equipping them in the light Indian hunting garb, and even of adopting it himself. Two companies were accordingly equipped in this style, and sent under the command of Major Lewis to headquarters. "It is an unbecoming dress, I own, for an officer," writes Washington, "but convenience rather than show, I think, should be consulted. The reduction of bat-horses alone would be sufficient to recommend it; for nothing is more certain than that less baggage would be required."

The experiment was successful. "The dress takes very well here," writes Colonel Bouquet; "and, thank God, we see nothing but shirts and blankets. . . . Their dress should be one pattern for this expedition." Such was probably the origin of the American rifle dress, afterwards so much worn in warfare, and modelled on the Indian costume.

The army was now annoyed by scouting parties of Indians hovering about the neighborhood. Expresses passing between the posts were fired upon; a waggoner was shot down. Washington sent out counter-parties of Cherokees. Colonel Bouquet required that each party should be accompanied by an officer and a number of white men. Washington complied with the order, though he considered them an encumbrance rather than an advantage, "Small parties of Indians," said he, "will more effectually harass the enemy by keeping them under continual alarms, than any parties of white men can do. For small parties of the latter are not equal to the task, not being so dexterous at skulking as Indians; and large parties will be discovered by their spies early enough to have a superior force opposed to them." With all his efforts, however, he was never able fully to make the officers of the regular army appreciate the importance of Indian allies in these campaigns in the wilderness.

On the other hand, he earnestly discountenanced a proposition of Colonel Bouquet, to make an irruption into the enemy's country with a strong party of regulars. Such a detachment, he observed, could not be sent without a cumbersome train of supplies, which would discover it to the enemy, who must at that time be collecting his whole force at Fort Duquesne; the enterprise, therefore, would be likely to terminate in a miscarriage, if not in the destruction of the party. We shall see that his opinion was oracular.

As Washington intended to retire from military life at the close of this campaign, he had proposed himself to the electors of Frederick County as their representative in the House of Burgesses. The election was coming on at Winchester; his friends pressed him to attend it, and Colonel Bouquet gave him leave of absence; but he declined to absent himself from his post for the promotion of his political interests. There were three competitors in the field, yet so high was the public opinion of his merit, that, though Winchester had been his head-quarters for two or three years past, and he had occasionally enforced martial law with a rigorous hand, he was elected by a large majority. The election was carried on somewhat in the English style. There was much eating and drinking at the expense of the candidate. Washington appeared on the hustings by proxy, and his representative was chaired about the town with enthusiastic applause and huzzaing for Colonel Washington.

On the 21st of July arrived tidings of the brilliant success of that part of the scheme of the year's campaign conducted by General Amherst and Admiral Boscawen, who had reduced the strong town of Louisburg and gained possession of the Island of Cape Breton. This intelligence increased Washington's impatience at the delays of the expedition with which he was connected. He wished to rival these successes by a brilliant blow in the south. Perhaps a desire for personal distinction in the eyes of the lady of his choice may have been at the bottom of this impatience; for we are told that he kept up a constant correspondence with her throughout the campaign.

Understanding that the commander-in-chief had some thoughts of throwing a body of light troops in the advance, he wrote to Colonel Bouquet, earnestly soliciting his influence to have himself and his Virginia regiment included in the detachment. "If any argument is needed to obtain this favor," said he, "I hope, without vanity, I may be allowed to say, that from long intimacy with these woods, and frequent scouting in them, my men are at least as well acquainted with all the passes and difficulties as any troops that will be employed."

He soon learnt to his surprise, however, that the road to which his men were accustomed, and which had been worked by Braddock's troops in his campaign, was not to be taken in the present expedition, but a new one opened through the heart of

Pennsylvania, from Raystown to Fort Duquesne, on the track generally taken by the northern traders. He instantly commenced long and repeated remonstrances on the subject; representing that Braddock's road, from recent examination, only needed partial repairs, and showing by clear calculation that an army could reach Fort Duquesne by that route in thirty-four days, so that the whole campaign might be effected by the middle of October; whereas the extreme labor of opening a new road across mountains, swamps, and through a densely wooded country, would detain them so late, that the season would be over before they could reach the scene of action. His representations were of no avail. The officers of the regular service had received a fearful idea of Braddock's road from his own despatches, wherein he had described it as lying "across mountains and rocks of an excessive height, vastly steep, and divided by torrents and rivers," whereas the Pennsylvania traders, who were anxious for the opening of the new road through their province, described the country through which it would pass as less difficult, and its streams less subject to inundation; above all, it was a direct line, and fifty miles nearer. This route, therefore, to the great regret of Washington and the indignation of the Virginia Assembly, was definitively adopted, and sixteen hundred men were immediately thrown in the advance from Raystown to work upon it.

The first of September found Washington still encamped at Fort Cumberland, his troops sickly and dispirited, and the brilliant expedition which he had anticipated, dwindling down into a tedious operation of road-making. In the mean time, his scouts brought him word that the whole force at Fort Duquesne on the 13th of August, Indians included, did not exceed eight hundred men: had an early campaign been pressed forward, as he recommended, the place by this time would have been captured. At length, in the month of September, he received orders from General Forbes to join him with his troops at Raystown, where he had just arrived, having been detained by severe illness. He was received by the general with the highest marks of respect. On all occasions, both in private and at councils of war, that commander treated his opinions with the greatest deference. He, moreover, adopted a plan drawn out by Washington for the march of the army; and an order of battle which still exists, furnishing a proof of his skill in frontier warfare.

It was now the middle of September; yet the great body of men engaged in opening the new military road, after incredible toil, had not advanced above forty-five miles, to a place called Loyal Hannan, a little beyond Laurel Hill. Colonel Bouquet, who commanded the division of nearly two thousand men sent forward to open this road, had halted at Loyal Hannan to establish a military post and deposit.

He was upwards of fifty miles from Fort Duquesne, and was tempted to adopt the measure, so strongly discountenanced by Washington, of sending a party on a foray into the enemy's country. He accordingly detached Major Grant with eight hundred picked men, some of them Highlanders, others, in Indian garb, the part of Washington's Virginian regiment sent forward by him from Cumberland under command of Major Lewis.

The instructions given to Major Grant were merely to reconnoitre the country in the neighborhood of Fort Duquesne, and ascertain the strength and position of the enemy. He conducted the enterprise with the foolhardiness of a man eager for personal notoriety. His whole object seems to have been by open bravado to provoke an action. The enemy were apprised, through their scouts, of his approach, but suffered him to advance unmolested. Arriving at night in the neighborhood of the fort, he posted his men on a hill, and sent out a party of observation, who set fire to a log house near the walls and returned to the encampment. As if this were not sufficient to put the enemy on the alert, he ordered the reveille to be beaten in the morning in several places; then, posting Major Lewis with his provincial troops at a distance in the rear to protect the baggage, he marshalled his regulars in battle array, and sent an engineer, with a covering party, to take a plan of the works in full view of the garrison.

Not a gun was fired by the fort; the silence which was maintained was mistaken for fear, and increased the arrogance and blind security of the British commander. At length, when he was thrown off his guard, there was a sudden sally of the garrison, and an attack on the flanks by Indians hid in ambush. A scene now occurred similar to that at the defeat of Braddock. The British officers marshalled their men according to European tactics, and the Highlanders for some time stood their ground bravely; but the destructive fire and horrid yells of the Indians soon produced panic and confusion. Major Lewis, at the first noise of the attack, left Captain Bullitt, with fifty Virginians, to guard the baggage, and hastened with the main part of his men to the scene of action. The contest was kept up for some time, but the confusion was irretrievable. The Indians sallied from their concealment, and attacked with the tomahawk and scalping-knife. Lewis fought hand to hand with an Indian brave, whom, he laid dead at his feet, but was surrounded by others, and only saved his life by surrendering himself to a French officer. Major Grant surrendered himself in like manner. The whole detachment was put to the rout with dreadful carnage.

Captain Bullitt rallied several of the fugitives, and prepared to make a forlorn stand, as the only chance where the enemy was overwhelming and merciless. Despatching the most valuable baggage with the strongest horses, he made a barricade with the baggage waggons, behind which he posted his men, giving them orders how they were to act. All this was the thought and the work almost of a moment, for the savages, having finished the havoc and plunder of the field of battle, were hastening in pursuit of the fugitives. Bullitt suffered them to come near, when, on a concerted signal, a destructive fire was opened from behind the baggage waggons. They were checked for a time; but were again pressing forward in greater numbers, when Bullitt and his men held out the signal of capitulation, and advanced as if to surrender. When within eight yards of the enemy, they suddenly levelled their arms, poured a most effective volley, and then charged with the bayonet. The Indians fled in dismay, and Bullitt took advantage of this check to retreat with all speed, collecting the wounded and the scattered fugitives as he advanced. The routed detachment came back in fragments to Colonel Bouquet's camp at Loyal Hannan, with the loss of twenty-one officers and two hundred and seventy-three privates killed and taken. The Highlanders and the Virginians were those that fought the best and suffered the most in this bloody battle. Washington's regiment lost six officers and sixty-two privates.

If Washington could have taken any pride in seeing his presages of misfortune verified, he might have been gratified by the result of this rash "irruption into the enemy's country," which was exactly what he had predicted. In his letters to Governor Fauquier, however, he bears lightly on the error of Col Bouquet. "From all accounts I can collect," says he, "it appears very clear that this was a very ill-concerted, or a very ill-executed plan, perhaps both; but it seems to be generally acknowledged that Major Grant exceeded his orders, and that no disposition was made for engaging."

Washington, who was at Raystown when the disastrous news arrived, was publicly complimented by General Forbes, on the gallant conduct of his Virginian troops, and Bullitt's behavior was "a matter of great admiration." The latter was soon after rewarded with a major's commission.

As a further mark of the high opinion now entertained of provincial troops for frontier service, Washington was given the command of a division, partly composed of his own men, to keep in the advance of the main body, clear the roads, throw out scouting parties, and repel Indian attacks.

It was the 5th of November before the whole army assembled at Loyal Hannan. Winter was now at hand, and upwards of fifty miles of wilderness were yet to be traversed, by a road not yet formed, before they could reach Fort Duquesne. Again, Washington's predictions seemed likely to be verified, and the expedition to be defeated by delay; for in a council of war it was determined to be impracticable to advance further with the army that season. Three prisoners, however, who were brought in, gave such an account of the weak state of the garrison at Fort Duquesne, its want of provisions, and the defection of the Indians, that it was determined to push forward. The march was accordingly resumed, but without tents or baggage, and with only a light train of artillery.

Washington still kept the advance. After leaving Loyal Hannan, the road presented traces of the late defeat of Grant; being strewed with human bones, the sad relics of fugitives cut down by the Indians, or of wounded soldiers who had died on the retreat; they lay mouldering in various stages of decay, mingled with the bones of horses and of oxen. As they approached Fort Duquesne these mementoes of former disasters became more frequent; and the bones of those massacred in the defeat of Braddock, still lay scattered about the battle field, whitening in the sun.

At length the army arrived in sight of Fort Duquesne, advancing with great precaution, and expecting a vigorous defence; but that formidable fortress, the terror and scourge of the frontier, and the object of such warlike enterprise, fell without a blow. The recent successes of the English forces in Canada, particularly the capture and destruction of Fort Frontenac, had left the garrison without hope of reinforcements and supplies. The whole force, at the time, did not exceed five hundred men, and the provisions were nearly exhausted. The commander, therefore, waited only until the English army was within one day's march, when he embarked his troops at night in batteaux, blew up his magazines, set fire to the fort, and retreated down the Ohio, by the light of the flames. On the 25th of November, Washington, with the advanced guard, marched in, and planted the British flag on the yet smoking ruins.

One of the first offices of the army was to collect and bury, in one common tomb, the bones of their fellow-soldiers who had fallen in the battles of Braddock and Grant. In this pious duty it is said every one joined, from the general down to the private soldier; and some veterans assisted, with heavy hearts and frequent ejaculations of poignant feeling, who had been present in the scenes of defeat and carnage.

The ruins of the fortress were now put in a defensible state, and garrisoned by two hundred men from Washington's regiment; the name was changed to that of Fort Pitt, in honor of the illustrious British minister, whose measures had given vigor and effect to this year's campaign; it has since been modified into Pittsburg, and designates one of the most busy and populous cities of the interior.

The reduction of Fort Duquesne terminated, as Washington had foreseen, the troubles and dangers of the southern frontier. The French domination of the Ohio was at an end; the Indians, as usual, paid homage to the conquering power, and a treaty of peace was concluded with all the tribes between the Ohio and the lakes.

With this campaign ended, for the present, the military career of Washington. His great object was attained, the restoration of quiet and security to his native province; and, having abandoned all hope of attaining rank in the regular army, and his health being much impaired, he gave up his commission at the close of the year, and retired from the service, followed by the applause of his fellow-soldiers, and the gratitude and admiration of all his countrymen.

His marriage with Mrs. Custis took place shortly after his return. It was celebrated on the 6th of January, 1759, at the White House, the residence of the bride, in the good old hospitable style of Virginia, amid a joyous assemblage of relatives and friends.

CHAPTER XXV.

PLAN OF OPERATIONS FOR 1759—INVESTMENT
OF FORT NIAGARA—DEATH OF PRIDEAUX—
SUCCESS OF SIR WILLIAM JOHNSON—AMHERST AT
TICONDEROGA—WOLFE AT QUEBEC—HIS TRIUMPH
AND DEATH—FATE OF MONTCALM—CAPITULATION
OF QUEBEC—ATTEMPT OF DE LEVI TO RETAKE IT—
ARRIVAL OF A BRITISH FLEET—LAST STAND OF THE
FRENCH AT MONTREAL—SURRENDER OF CANADA.

Before following Washington into the retirement of domestic
life, we think it proper to notice the events which closed the great
struggle between England and France for empire in America. In
that struggle he had first become practised in arms, and schooled in
the ways of the world; and its results will be found connected with
the history of his later years.

General Abercrombie had been superseded as commander-
in-chief of the forces in America by Major-general Amherst, who
had gained great favor by the reduction of Louisburg. According
to the plan of operations for 1759, General Wolfe, who had risen
to fame by his gallant conduct in the same affair, was to ascend
the St. Lawrence in a fleet of ships of war, with eight thousand
men, as soon as the river should be free of ice, and lay siege to
Quebec, the capital of Canada. General Amherst, in the mean
time, was to advance, as Abercrombie had done, by Lake George,
against Ticonderoga and Crown Point; reduce those forts, cross
Lake Champlain, push on to the St. Lawrence, and co-operate with
Wolfe.

A third expedition, under Brigadier-general Prideaux, aided
by Sir William Johnson and his Indian warriors, was to attack Fort
Niagara, which controlled the whole country of the Six Nations, and

commanded the navigation of the great lakes, and the intercourse between Canada and Louisiana. Having reduced this fort, he was to traverse Lake Ontario, descend the St. Lawrence, capture Montreal, and join his forces with those of Amherst.

The last mentioned expedition was the first executed. General Prideaux embarked at Oswego on the first of July, with a large body of troops, regulars and provincials,—the latter partly from New York. He was accompanied by Sir William Johnson, and his Indian braves of the Mohawk. Landing at an inlet of Lake Ontario, within a few miles of Fort Niagara, he advanced, without being opposed, and proceeded to invest it. The garrison, six hundred strong, made a resolute defence. The siege was carried on by regular approaches, but pressed with vigor. On the 20th of July, Prideaux, in visiting his trenches, was killed by the bursting of a cohorn. Informed by express of this misfortune, General Amherst detached from the main army Brigadier-general Gage, the officer who had led Braddock's advance, to take the command.

In the mean time, the siege had been conducted by Sir William Johnson with courage and sagacity. He was destitute of military science, but had a natural aptness for warfare, especially for the rough kind carried on in the wilderness. Being informed by his scouts that twelve hundred regular troops, drawn from Detroit, Venango, and Presque Isle, and led by D'Aubry, with a number of Indian auxiliaries, were hastening to the rescue, he detached a force of grenadiers and light infantry, with some of his Mohawk warriors, to intercept them. They came in sight of each other on the road, between Niagara Falls and the fort, within the thundering sound of the one, and the distant view of the other. Johnson's "braves" advanced to have a parley with the hostile redskins. The latter received them with a war-whoop, and Frenchman and savage made an impetuous onset. Johnson's regulars and provincials stood their ground firmly, while his red warriors fell on the flanks of the enemy. After a sharp conflict, the French were broken, routed, and pursued through the woods, with great carnage. Among the prisoners taken were seventeen officers. The next day Sir William Johnson sent a trumpet, summoning the garrison to surrender, to spare the effusion of blood, and prevent outrages by the Indians. They had no alternative; were permitted to march out with the honors of war, and were protected by Sir William from his Indian allies. Thus was secured the key to the communication between Lakes Ontario and Erie, and to the vast interior region connected with them. The blow alarmed the French for the safety of Montreal, and De Levi, the second in command of their Canadian forces, hastened up from before Quebec, and took post at the fort of Oswegatchie (now Ogdensburg), to defend the passes of the St. Lawrence.

We now proceed to notice the expedition against Ticonderoga and Crown Point. In the month of July, General Amherst embarked with nearly twelve thousand men, at the upper part of Lake George, and proceeded down it, as Abercrombie had done in the preceding year, in a vast fleet of whale-boats, batteaux, and rafts, and all the glitter and parade of war. On the 22d, the army debarked at the lower part of the lake, and advanced toward Ticonderoga. After a slight skirmish with the advanced guard, they secured the old post at the saw-mill.

Montcalm was no longer in the fort; he was absent for the protection of Quebec. The garrison did not exceed four hundred men. Bourlamarque, a brave officer, who commanded, at first seemed disposed to make defence; but, against such overwhelming force, it would have been madness. Dismantling the fortifications, therefore, he abandoned them, as he did likewise those at Crown Point, and retreated down the lake, to assemble forces, and make a stand at the Isle Aux Noix, for the protection of Montreal and the province.

Instead of following him up, and hastening to co-operate with Wolfe, General Amherst proceeded to repair the works at Ticonderoga, and erect a new fort at Crown Point, though neither were in present danger of being attacked, nor would be of use if Canada were conquered. Amherst, however, was one of those cautious men, who, in seeking to be sure, are apt to be fatally slow. His delay enabled the enemy to rally their forces at Isle Aux Noix, and call in Canadian reinforcements, while it deprived Wolfe of that co-operation which, it will be shown, was most essential to the general success of the campaign.

Wolfe, with his eight thousand men, ascended the St. Lawrence in the fleet, in the month of June. With him came Brigadiers, Monckton, Townshend and Murray, youthful and brave like himself, and like himself, already schooled in arms. Monckton, it will be recollected, had signalized himself, when a colonel, in the expedition in 1755, in which the French were driven from Nova Scotia. The grenadiers of the army were commanded by Colonel Guy Carleton, and part of the light infantry by Lieutenant-Colonel William Howe, both destined to celebrity in after years, in the annals of the American Revolution. Colonel Howe was brother of the gallant Lord Howe, whose fall in the preceding year was so generally lamented. Among the officers of the fleet, was Jervis, the future admiral, and ultimately Earl St. Vincent; and the master of one of the ships, was James Cook, afterwards renowned as a discoverer.

About the end of June, the troops debarked on the large, populous, and well-cultivated Isle of Orleans, a little below Quebec, and encamped in its fertile fields. Quebec, the citadel of Canada, was strong by nature. It was built round the point of a rocky promontory, and flanked by precipices. The crystal current of the St. Lawrence swept by it on the right, and the river St. Charles flowed along on the left, before mingling with that mighty stream. The place was tolerably fortified, but art had not yet rendered it, as at the present day, impregnable.

Montcalm commanded the post. His troops were more numerous than the assailants but the greater part were Canadians, many of them inhabitants of Quebec; and he had a host of savages. His forces were drawn out along the northern shore below the city, from the river St. Charles to the Falls of Montmorency, and their position was secured by deep intrenchments.

The night after the debarkation of Wolfe's troops a furious storm caused great damage to the transports, and sank some of the small craft. While it was still raging, a number of fire-ships, sent to destroy the fleet, came driving down. They were boarded intrepidly by the British seamen, and towed out of the way of doing harm. After much resistance, Wolfe established batteries at the west point of the Isle of Orleans, and at Point Levi, on the right (or south) bank of the St. Lawrence, within cannon range of the city. Colonel Guy Carleton, commanded at the former battery; Brigadier Monckton at the latter. From Point Levi bombshells and red-hot shot were discharged; many houses were set on fire in the upper town, the lower town was reduced to rubbish; the main fort, however, remained unharmed.

Anxious for a decisive action, Wolfe, on the 9th of July, crossed over in boats from the Isle of Orleans, to the north bank of the St. Lawrence, and encamped below the Montmorency. It was an ill-judged position, for there was still that tumultuous stream, with its rocky banks, between him and the camp of Montcalm; but the ground he had chosen was higher than that occupied by the latter, and the Montmorency had a ford below the falls, passable at low tide. Another ford was discovered, three miles within land, but the banks were steep, and shagged with forest. At both fords the vigilant Montcalm had thrown up breastworks, and posted troops.

On the 18th of July, Wolfe made a reconnoitring expedition up the river, with two armed sloops, and two transports with troops. He passed Quebec unharmed, and carefully noted the shores above it. Rugged cliffs rose almost from the water's edge. Above them, he was told, was an extent of level ground, called the Plains of Abraham, by which the upper town might be approached on its weakest side; but how was that plain to be attained, when the cliffs, for the most part, were inaccessible, and every practicable place fortified?

He returned to Montmorency disappointed, and resolved to attack Montcalm in his camp, however difficult to be approached, and however strongly posted. Townshend and Murray, with their brigades, were to cross the Montmorency at low tide, below the falls, and storm the redoubt thrown up in front of the ford. Monckton, at the same time, was to cross, with part of his brigade, in boats from Point Levi. The ship Centurion, stationed in the channel, was to check the fire of a battery which commanded the ford; a train of artillery, planted on an eminence, was to enfilade the enemy's intrenchments; and two armed, flat-bottomed boats, were to be run on shore, near the redoubt, and favor the crossing of the troops.

As usual, in complicated orders, part were misunderstood, or neglected, and confusion was the consequence. Many of the boats from Point Levi ran aground on a shallow in the river, where they were exposed to a severe fire of shot and shells. Wolfe, who was on the shore, directing every thing, endeavored to stop his impatient troops until the boats could be got afloat, and the men landed. Thirteen companies of grenadiers, and two hundred provincials were the first to land. Without waiting for Brigadier Monckton and his regiments; without waiting for the co-operation of the troops under Townshend; without waiting even to be drawn up in form, the grenadiers rushed impetuously towards the enemy's intrenchments. A sheeted fire mowed them down, and drove them to take shelter behind the redoubt, near the ford, which the enemy had abandoned. Here they remained, unable to form under the galling fire to which they were exposed, whenever they ventured from their covert. Monckton's brigade at length was landed, drawn up in order, and advanced to their relief, driving back the enemy. Thus protected, the grenadiers retreated as precipitately as they had advanced, leaving many of their comrades wounded on the field, who were massacred and scalped in their sight, by the savages. The delay thus caused was fatal to the enterprise. The day was advanced; the weather became stormy; the tide began to make; at a later hour, retreat, in case of a second repulse, would be impossible, Wolfe, therefore, gave up the attack, and withdrew across the river, having lost upwards of four hundred men, through this headlong impetuosity of the grenadiers. The two vessels which had been run aground, were set on fire, lest they should fall into the hands of the enemy.[74]

Brigadier Murray was now detached with twelve hundred men, in transports, to ascend above the town, and co-operate with Rear-admiral Holmes, in destroying the enemy's shipping, and making descents upon the north shore. The shipping were safe from attack; some stores and ammunition were destroyed; some prisoners taken, and Murray returned with the news of the capture of Fort Niagara, Ticonderoga, and Crown Point, and that Amherst was preparing to attack the Isle Aux Noix.

Wolfe, of a delicate constitution and sensitive nature, had been deeply mortified by the severe check sustained at the Falls of Montmorency, fancying himself disgraced; and these successes of his fellow-commanders in other parts increased his self-upbraiding. The difficulties multiplying around him, and the delay of General Amherst in hastening to his aid, preyed incessantly on his spirits; he was dejected even to despondency, and declared he would never return without success, to be exposed, like other unfortunate commanders, to the sneers and reproaches of the populace. The

---

74   Wolfe's Letter to Pitt, Sept. 2d, 1759.

agitation of his mind, and his acute sensibility, brought on a fever, which for some time incapacitated him from taking the field.

In the midst of his illness he called a council of war, in which the whole plan of operations was altered. It was determined to convey troops above the town, and endeavor to make a diversion in that direction, or draw Montcalm into the open field. Before carrying this plan into effect, Wolfe again reconnoitred the town in company with Admiral Saunders, but nothing better suggested itself.

The brief Canadian summer was over; they were in the month of September. The camp at Montmorency was broken up. The troops were transported to Point Levi, leaving a sufficient number to man the batteries on the Isle of Orleans. On the fifth and sixth of September the embarkation took place above Point Levi, in transports which had been sent up for the purpose. Montcalm detached De Bougainville with fifteen hundred men to keep along the north shore above the town, watch the movements of the squadron, and prevent a landing. To deceive him, Admiral Holmes moved with the ships of war three leagues beyond the place where the landing was to be attempted. He was to drop down, however, in the night, and protect the landing. Cook, the future discoverer, also, was employed with others to sound the river and place buoys opposite the camp of Montcalm, as if an attack were meditated in that quarter.

Wolfe was still suffering under the effects of his late fever. "My constitution," writes he to a friend, "is entirely ruined, without the consolation of having done any considerable service to the state, and without any prospect of it." Still he was unremitting in his exertions, seeking to wipe out the fancied disgrace incurred at the Falls of Montmorency. It was in this mood he is said to have composed and sung at his evening mess that little campaigning song still linked with his name:

> Why, soldiers, why
> Should we be melancholy, boys?
> Why, soldiers, why?
> Whose business 'tis to die!

Even when embarked in his midnight enterprise, the presentiment of death seems to have cast its shadow over him. A midshipman who was present,[75] used to relate, that as Wolfe sat among his officers, and the boats floated down silently with the current, he recited, in low and touching tones, Gray's Elegy in a country churchyard, then just published. One stanza may especially have accorded with his melancholy mood.

> "The boast of heraldry, the pomp of power,
>   And all that beauty, all that wealth e'er gave,
> Await alike the inevitable hour.
>   The paths of glory lead but to the grave."

"Now, gentlemen," said he, when he had finished, "I would rather be the author of that poem than take Quebec."

The descent was made in flat-bottomed boats, past midnight, on the 13th of September. They dropped down silently with the swift current. *"Qui va la?"* (who goes there?) cried a sentinel from the shore. *"La France,"* replied a captain in the first boat, who understood the French language. *"A quel regiment?"* was the demand. *"De la Reine"* (the queen's), replied the captain, knowing that regiment was in De Bougainville's detachment. Fortunately, a convoy of provisions was expected down from De Bougainville's, which the sentinel supposed this to be. *"Passe,"* cried he, and the boats glided on without further challenge. The landing took place in a cove near Cape Diamond, which still bears Wolfe's name. He had marked it in reconnoitering, and saw that a cragged path straggled up from it to the Heights of Abraham, which might be climbed, though with difficulty, and that it appeared to be slightly guarded at top. Wolfe was among the first that landed and ascended up the steep and narrow path, where not more than two could go abreast, and which had been broken up by cross ditches. Colonel Howe, at the same time, with the light infantry and Highlanders, scrambled up the woody precipices, helping themselves by the roots and branches, and putting to flight a sergeant's guard posted at the summit. Wolfe drew up the men in order as they mounted; and by the break of day found himself in possession of the fateful Plains of Abraham.

Montcalm was thunderstruck when word was brought to him in his camp that the English were on the heights threatening

---

75   Afterwards Professor John Robison, of Edinburgh.

the weakest part of the town. Abandoning his intrenchments, he hastened across the river St. Charles and ascended the heights, which slope up gradually from its banks. His force was equal in number to that of the English, but a great part was made up of colony troops and savages. When he saw the formidable host of regulars he had to contend with, he sent off swift messengers to summon De Bougainville with his detachment to his aid; and De Vaudreuil to reinforce him, with fifteen hundred men from the camp. In the mean time he prepared to flank the left of the English line and force them to the opposite precipices. Wolfe saw his aim, and sent Brigadier Townshend to counteract him with a regiment which was formed *en potence*, and supported by two battalions, presenting on the left a double front.

The French, in their haste, thinking they were to repel a mere scouting party, had brought but three light field-pieces with them; the English had but a single gun, which the sailors had dragged up the heights. With these they cannonaded each other for a time, Montcalm still waiting for the aid he had summoned. At length, about nine o'clock, losing all patience, he led on his disciplined troops to a close conflict with small arms, the Indians to support them by a galling fire from thickets and corn-fields. The French advanced gallantly, but irregularly; firing rapidly, but with little effect. The English reserved their fire until their assailants were within forty yards, and then delivered it in deadly volleys. They suffered, however, from the lurking savages, who singled out the officers. Wolfe, who was in front of the line, a conspicuous mark, was wounded by a ball in the wrist. He bound his handkerchief round the wound and led on the grenadiers, with fixed bayonets, to charge the foe, who began to waver. Another ball struck him in the breast. He felt the wound to be mortal, and feared his fall might dishearten the troops. Leaning on a lieutenant for support; "Let not my brave fellows see me drop," said he faintly. He was borne off to the rear; water was brought to quench his thirst, and he was asked if he would have a surgeon. "It is needless," he replied; "it is all over with me." He desired those about him to lay him down. The lieutenant seated himself on the ground, and supported him in his arms. "They run! they run! see how they run!" cried one of the attendants. "Who run?" demanded Wolfe, earnestly, like one aroused from sleep. "The enemy, sir; they give way every where."

The spirit of the expiring hero flashed up. "Go, one of you, my lads, to Colonel Burton; tell him to march Webb's regiment with all speed down to Charles' River, to cut off the retreat by the bridge." Then turning on his side; "Now, God be praised, I will die in peace!" said he, and expired,[76]—soothed in his last moments by the idea that victory would obliterate the imagined disgrace at Montmorency.

Brigadier Murray had indeed broken the centre of the enemy, and the Highlanders were making deadly havoc with their claymores, driving the French into the town or down to their works on the river St. Charles. Monckton, the first brigadier, was disabled by a wound in the lungs, and the command devolved on Townshend, who hastened to re-form the troops of the centre, disordered in pursuing the enemy. By this time De Bougainville appeared at a distance in the rear, advancing with two thousand fresh troops, but he arrived too late to retrieve the day. The gallant Montcalm had received his death-wound near St. John's Gate, while endeavoring to rally his flying troops, and had been borne into the town.

Townshend advanced with a force to receive De Bougainville; but the latter avoided a combat, and retired into woods and swamps, where it was not thought prudent to follow him. The English had obtained a complete victory; slain about five hundred of the enemy; taken above a thousand prisoners, and among them several officers; and had a strong position on the Plains of Abraham, which they hastened to fortify with redoubts and artillery, drawn up the heights.

The brave Montcalm wrote a letter to General Townshend, recommending the prisoners to British humanity. When told by his surgeon that he could not survive above a few hours; "So much the better," replied he; "I shall not live to see the surrender of Quebec." To De Ramsey, the French king's lieutenant, who commanded the garrison, he consigned the defence of the city. "To your keeping," said he, "I commend the honor of France. I'll neither give orders, nor interfere any further. I have business to attend to of greater moment than your ruined garrison, and this wretched country. My time is short,—I shall pass this night with God, and prepare myself for death. I wish you all comfort; and to be happily extricated from

76   Hist. Jour. of Capt. John Knox, vol. i., p. 79.

your present perplexities." He then called for his chaplain, who, with the bishop of the colony, remained with him through the night. He expired early in the morning, dying like a brave soldier and a devout Catholic. Never did two worthier foes mingle their life blood on the battle-field than Wolfe and Montcalm.[77]

Preparations were now made by the army and the fleet to make an attack on both upper and lower town; but the spirit of the garrison was broken, and the inhabitants were clamorous for the safety of their wives and children. On the 17th of September, Quebec capitulated, and was taken possession of by the British, who hastened to put it in a complete posture of defence. A garrison of six thousand effective men was placed in it, under the command of Brigadier-general Murray, and victualled from the fleet. General Townshend embarked with Admiral Saunders, and returned to England; and the wounded General Monckton was conveyed to New York, of which he afterwards became governor.

Had Amherst followed up his success at Ticonderoga the preceding summer, the year's campaign would have ended, as had been projected, in the subjugation of Canada. His cautious delay gave De Levi, the successor of Montcalm, time to rally, concentrate the scattered French forces, and struggle for the salvation of the province.

In the following spring, as soon as the river St. Lawrence opened, he approached Quebec, and landed at Point an Tremble, about twelve miles off. The garrison had suffered dreadfully during the winter from excessive cold; want of vegetables and of fresh provisions. Many had died of scurvy, and many more were ill. Murray, sanguine and injudicious, on hearing that De Levi was advancing with ten thousand men, and five hundred Indians, sallied out with his diminished forces of not more than three thousand. English soldiers, he boasted, were habituated to victory; he had a fine train of artillery, and stood a better chance in the field than cooped up in a wretched fortification. If defeated, he would defend the place to the last extremity, and then retreat to the Isle of Orleans, and wait for reinforcements. More brave than discreet, he attacked the vanguard of the enemy; the battle which took place was fierce and sanguinary. Murray's troops had caught his own headlong valor,

---

77   Knox; Hist. Jour., vol. i., p. 77.

and fought until near a third of their number were slain. They were at length driven back into the town, leaving their boasted train of artillery on the field.

De Levi opened trenches before the town the very evening of the battle. Three French ships, which had descended the river, furnished him with cannon, mortars, and ammunition. By the 11th of May, he had one bomb battery, and three batteries of cannon. Murray, equally alert within the walls, strengthened his defences, and kept up a vigorous fire. His garrison was now reduced to two hundred and twenty effective men, and he himself, with all his vaunting spirit, was driven almost to despair, when a British fleet arrived in the river. The whole scene was now reversed. One of the French frigates was driven on the rocks above Cape Diamond; another ran on shore, and was burnt; the rest of their vessels were either taken, or destroyed. The besieging army retreated in the night, leaving provisions, implements, and artillery behind them; and so rapid was their flight, that Murray, who sallied forth on the following day, could not overtake them.

A last stand for the preservation of the colony was now made by the French at Montreal, where De Vaudreuil fixed his headquarters, fortified himself, and called in all possible aid, Canadian and Indian.

The cautious, but tardy Amherst was now in the field to carry out the plan in which he had fallen short in the previous year. He sent orders to General Murray to advance by water against Montreal, with all the force that could be spared from Quebec; he detached a body of troops under Colonel Haviland from Crown Point, to cross Lake Champlain, take possession of the Isle Aux Noix, and push on to the St. Lawrence, while he took the roundabout way with his main army by the Mohawk and Oneida rivers to Lake Ontario; thence to descend the St. Lawrence to Montreal.

Murray, according to orders, embarked his troops in a great number of small vessels, and ascended the river in characteristic style, publishing manifestoes in the Canadian villages, disarming the inhabitants, and exacting the oath of neutrality. He looked forward to new laurels at Montreal, but the slow and sure Amherst had anticipated him. That worthy general, after delaying on Lake Ontario to send out cruisers, and stopping to repair petty forts on the upper part of the St. Lawrence, which had been deserted by their

229

garrisons, or surrendered without firing a gun, arrived on the 6th of September at the island of Montreal, routed some light skirmishing parties, and presented himself before the town. Vaudreuil found himself threatened by an army of nearly ten thousand men, and a host of Indians; for Amherst had called in the aid of Sir William Johnson, and his Mohawk braves. To withstand a siege in an almost open town against such superior force, was out of the question; especially as Murray from Quebec, and Haviland from Crown Point, were at hand with additional troops. A capitulation accordingly took place on the 8th of September, including the surrender not merely of Montreal, but of all Canada.

Thus ended the contest between France and England for dominion in America, in which, as has been said, the first gun was fired in Washington's encounter with De Jumonville. A French statesman and diplomatist consoled himself by the persuasion that it would be a fatal triumph to England. It would remove the only check by which her colonies were kept in awe. "They will no longer need her protection," said he; "she will call on them to contribute toward supporting the burdens they have helped to bring on her, and *they will answer by striking off* all *dependence.*"[78]

---

78   Count de Vergennes, French ambassador at Constantinople.

CHAPTER XXVI.

WASHINGTON'S INSTALLATION IN THE HOUSE OF
BURGESSES—HIS RURAL LIFE—MOUNT VERNON
AND ITS VICINITY—ARISTOCRATICAL DAYS OF
VIRGINIA—WASHINGTON'S MANAGEMENT OF HIS
ESTATE—DOMESTIC HABITS—FOX-HUNTING—LORD
FAIRFAX—FISHING AND DUCK-SHOOTING—THE
POACHER—LYNCH LAW—AQUATIC STATE—LIFE AT
ANNAPOLIS—WASHINGTON IN THE DISMAL SWAMP.

For three months after his marriage, Washington resided with his bride at the "White House." During his sojourn there, he repaired to Williamsburg, to take his seat in the House of Burgesses. By a vote of the House, it had been determined to greet his instalment by a signal testimonial of respect. Accordingly, as soon as he took his seat, Mr. Robinson, the Speaker, in eloquent language, dictated by the warmth of private friendship, returned thanks, on behalf of the colony, for the distinguished military services he had rendered to his country.

Washington rose to reply; blushed-stammered-trembled, and could not utter a word. "Sit down, Mr. Washington," said the Speaker, with a smile; "your modesty equals your valor, and that surpasses the power of any language I possess."

Such was Washington's first launch into civil life, in which he was to be distinguished by the same judgment, devotion, courage, and magnanimity exhibited in his military career. He attended the House frequently during the remainder of the session, after which he conducted his bride to his favorite abode of Mount Vernon.

Mr. Custis, the first husband of Mrs. Washington, had left large landed property, and forty-five thousand pounds sterling in money. One third fell to his widow in her own right; two thirds were inherited equally by her two children,—a boy of six, and a girl of four years of age. By a decree of the General Court, Washington was intrusted with the care of the property inherited by the children; a sacred and delicate trust, which he discharged in the most faithful and judicious manner; becoming more like a parent, than a mere guardian to them.

From a letter to his correspondent in England, it would appear that he had long entertained a desire to visit that country. Had he done so, his acknowledged merit and military services would have insured him a distinguished reception; and it has been intimated, that the signal favor of government might have changed the current of his career. We believe him, however, to have been too pure a patriot, and too clearly possessed of the true interests of his country, to be diverted from the course which he ultimately adopted. His marriage, at any rate, had put an end to all travelling inclinations. In his letter from Mount Vernon, he writes: "I am now, I believe, fixed in this seat, with an agreeable partner for life, and I hope to find more happiness in retirement than I ever experienced in the wide and bustling world."

This was no Utopian dream transiently indulged, amid the charms of novelty. It was a deliberate purpose with him, the result of innate and enduring inclinations. Throughout the whole course of his career, agricultural life appears to have been his *beau ideal* of existence, which haunted his thoughts even amid the stern duties of the field, and to which he recurred with unflagging interest whenever enabled to indulge his natural bias.

Mount Vernon was his harbor of repose, where he repeatedly furled his sail, and fancied himself anchored for life. No impulse of ambition tempted him thence; nothing but the call of his country, and his devotion to the public good. The place was endeared to him by the remembrance of his brother Lawrence, and of the happy days he had passed here with that brother in the days of boyhood; but it was a delightful place in itself, and well calculated to inspire the rural feeling.

The mansion was beautifully situated on a swelling height, crowned with wood, and commanding a magnificent view up and down the Potomac. The grounds immediately about it were laid out somewhat in the English taste. The estate was apportioned into separate farms, devoted to different kinds of culture, each having its allotted laborers. Much, however, was still covered with wild woods, seamed with deep dells and runs of water, and indented with inlets; haunts of deer, and lurking-places of foxes. The whole woody region along the Potomac from Mount Vernon to Belvoir, and far beyond, with its range of forests and hills, and picturesque promontories, afforded sport of various kinds, and was a noble hunting-ground. Washington had hunted through it with old Lord Fairfax in his stripling days; we do not wonder that his feelings throughout life incessantly reverted to it.

"No estate in United America," observes he, in one of his letters, "is more pleasantly situated. In a high and healthy country; in a latitude between the extremes of heat and cold; on one of the finest rivers in the world; a river well stocked with various kinds of fish at all seasons of the year, and in the spring with shad, herrings, bass, carp, sturgeon, &c., in great abundance. The borders of the estate are washed by more than ten miles of tide water; several valuable fisheries appertain to it: the whole shore, in fact, is one entire fishery."

These were, as yet, the aristocratical days of Virginia. The estates were large, and continued in the same families by entails. Many of the wealthy planters were connected with old families in England. The young men, especially the elder sons, were often sent to finish their education there, and on their return brought out the tastes and habits of the mother country. The governors of Virginia were from the higher ranks of society, and maintained a corresponding state. The "established," or Episcopal church, predominated throughout the "ancient dominion," as it was termed; each county was divided into parishes, as in England,—each with its parochial church, its parsonage, and glebe. Washington was vestryman of two parishes, Fairfax and Truro; the parochial church of the former was at Alexandria, ten miles from Mount Vernon; of the latter, at Pohick, about seven miles. The church at Pohick was rebuilt on a plan of his own, and in a great measure at his expense. At one or other of these churches he attended every Sunday, when the weather and the roads permitted. His demeanor was reverential and devout. Mrs. Washington knelt during the prayers; he always stood, as was the custom at that time. Both were communicants.

Among his occasional visitors and associates were Captain Hugh Mercer and Dr. Craik; the former, after his narrow escapes from the tomahawk and scalping-knife, was quietly settled at Fredericksburg; the latter, after the campaigns on the frontier were over, had taken up his residence at Alexandria, and was now Washington's family physician. Both were drawn to him by campaigning ties and recollections, and were ever welcome at Mount Vernon.

A style of living prevailed among the opulent Virginian families in those days that has long since faded away. The houses were spacious, commodious, liberal in all their appointments, and fitted to cope with the free-handed, open-hearted hospitality of the owners. Nothing was more common than to see handsome services of plate, elegant equipages, and superb carriage horses— all imported from England.

The Virginians have always been noted for their love of horses; a manly passion which, in those days of opulence, they indulged without regard to expense. The rich planters vied with each other in their studs, importing the best English stocks. Mention is made of one of the Randolphs of Tuckahoe, who built a stable for his favorite dapple-gray horse, Shakespeare, with a recess for the bed of the negro groom, who always slept beside him at night.

Washington, by his marriage, had added above one hundred thousand dollars to his already considerable fortune, and was enabled to live in ample and dignified style. His intimacy with the Fairfaxes, and his intercourse with British officers of rank, had perhaps had their influence on his mode of living. He had his chariot and four, with black postilions in livery, for the use of Mrs. Washington and her lady visitors. As for himself, he always appeared on horseback. His stable was well filled and admirably regulated. His stud was thoroughbred and in excellent order. His household books contain registers of the names, ages, and marks of his various horses; such as Ajax, Blueskin, Valiant, Magnolia (an Arab), &c. Also his dogs, chiefly fox-hounds, Vulcan, Singer, Ringwood, Sweetlips, Forrester, Music, Rockwood, Truelove, &c.[79]

---

79 In one of his letter-books we find orders on his London agent for riding equipments. For example:

1 Man's riding-saddle, hogskin seat, large plated stirrups and every thing complete. Double reined bridle and Pelham bit, plated.

A very neat and fashionable Newmarket saddle-cloth.

A large and best portmanteau, saddle, bridle, and pillion.

A large Virginia estate, in those days, was a little empire. The mansion-house was the seat of government, with its numerous dependencies, such as kitchens, smoke-house, workshops and stables. In this mansion the planter ruled supreme; his steward or overseer was his prime minister and executive officer; he had his legion of house negroes for domestic service, and his host of field negroes for the culture of tobacco, Indian corn, and other crops, and for other out of door labor. Their quarter formed a kind of hamlet apart, composed of various huts, with little gardens and poultry yards, all well stocked, and swarms of little negroes gambolling in the sunshine. Then there were large wooden edifices for curing tobacco, the staple and most profitable production, and mills for grinding wheat and Indian corn, of which large fields were cultivated for the supply of the family and the maintenance of the negroes.

Among the slaves were artificers of all kinds, tailors, shoemakers, carpenters, smiths, wheelwrights, and so forth; so that a plantation produced every thing within itself for ordinary use: as to articles of fashion and elegance, luxuries, and expensive clothing, they were imported from London; for the planters on the main rivers, especially the Potomac, carried on an immediate trade with England. Their tobacco was put up by their own negroes, bore their own marks, was shipped on board of vessels which came up the rivers for the purpose, and consigned to some agent in Liverpool or Bristol, with whom the planter kept an account.

The Virginia planters were prone to leave the care of their estates too much to their overseers, and to think personal labor a degradation. Washington carried into his rural affairs the same method, activity, and circumspection that had distinguished him in military life. He kept his own accounts, posted up his books and balanced them with mercantile exactness. We have examined them as well as his diaries recording his daily occupations, and

---

Cloak-bag surcingle; checked saddle-cloth, holsters, &c.

A riding-frock of a handsome drab-colored broadcloth, with plain double gilt buttons.

A riding waistcoat of superfine scarlet cloth and gold lace, with buttons like those of the coat.

A blue surtout coat.

A neat switch whip, silver cap.

Black velvet cap for servant.

his letter-books, containing entries of shipments of tobacco, and correspondence with his London agents. They are monuments of his business habits.[80]

The products of his estate also became so noted for the faithfulness, as to quality and quantity, with which they were put up, that it is said any barrel of flour that bore the brand of George Washington, Mount Vernon, was exempted from the customary inspection in the West India ports.[81]

He was an early riser, often before daybreak in the winter when the nights were long. On such occasions he lit his own fire and wrote or read by candle-light. He breakfasted at seven in summer, at eight in winter. Two small cups of tea and three or four cakes of Indian meal (called hoe cakes), formed his frugal repast. Immediately after breakfast he mounted his horse and visited those parts of the estate where any work was going on, seeing to every thing with his own eyes, and often aiding with his own hand.

Dinner was served at two o'clock. He ate heartily, but was no epicure, nor critical about his food. His beverage was small beer or cider, and two glasses of old Madeira. He took tea, of which he was very fond, early in the evening, and retired for the night about nine o'clock.

If confined to the house by bad weather, he took that occasion to arrange his papers, post up his accounts, or write letters; passing part of the time in reading, and occasionally reading aloud to the family.

---

80   The following letter of Washington to his London correspondents will give an idea of the early intercourse of the Virginia planters with the mother country.

"Our goods by the Liberty, Capt. Walker, came to hand in good order and soon after his arrival, as they generally do when shipped in a vessel to this river [the Potomac], and scarce ever when they go to any others; for it don't often happen that a vessel bound to one river has goods of any consequence to another; and the masters, in these cases, keep the packages till an accidental conveyance offers, and for want of better opportunities frequently commit them to boatmen who care very little for the goods so they get their freight, and often land them wherever it suits their convenience, not where they have engaged to do so. . . . A ship from London to Virginia may be in Rappahannock or any of the other rivers three months before I know any thing of their arrival, and may make twenty voyages without my seeing or even hearing of the captain."

81   Speech of the Hon. Robert C. Winthrop on laying the corner-stone of Washington's Monument.

He treated his negroes with kindness; attended to their comforts; was particularly careful of them in sickness; but never tolerated idleness, and exacted a faithful performance of all their allotted tasks. He had a quick eye at calculating each man's capabilities. An entry in his diary gives a curious instance of this. Four of his negroes, employed as carpenters, were hewing and shaping timber. It appeared to him, in noticing the amount of work accomplished between two succeeding mornings, that they loitered at their labor. Sitting down quietly he timed their operations; how long it took them to get their cross-cut saw and other implements ready; how long to clear away the branches from the trunk of a fallen tree; how long to hew and saw it; what time was expended in considering and consulting, and after all, how much work was effected during the time he looked on. From this he made his computation how much they could execute in the course of a day, working entirely at their ease.

At another time we find him working for a part of two days with Peter, his smith, to make a plough on a new invention of his own. This, after two or three failures, he accomplished. Then, with less than his usual judgment, he put his two chariot horses to the plough, and ran a great risk of spoiling them, in giving his new invention a trial over ground thickly swarded.

Anon, during a thunderstorm, a frightened negro alarms the house with word that the mill is giving way, upon which there is a general turn out of all the forces, with Washington at their head, wheeling and shovelling gravel, during a pelting rain, to check the rushing water.

Washington delighted in the chase. In the hunting season, when he rode out early in the morning to visit distant parts of the estate, where work was going on, he often took some of the dogs with him for the chance of starting a fox, which he occasionally did, though he was not always successful in killing him. He was a bold rider and an admirable horseman, though he never claimed the merit of being an accomplished fox-hunter. In the height of the season, however, he would be out with the foxhounds two or three times a week, accompanied by his guests at Mount Vernon and the gentlemen of the neighborhood, especially the Fairfaxes of Belvoir, of which estate his friend George William Fairfax was now the proprietor. On such occasions there would be a hunting dinner at one or other of those establishments, at which convivial repasts Washington is said to have enjoyed himself with unwonted hilarity.

Now and then his old friend and instructor in the noble art of venery, Lord Fairfax, would be on a visit to his relatives at Belvoir, and then the hunting was kept up with unusual spirit.[82]

His lordship, however, since the alarms of Indian war had ceased, lived almost entirely at Greenway Court, where Washington was occasionally a guest, when called by public business to Winchester. Lord Fairfax had made himself a favorite throughout the neighborhood. As lord-lieutenant and custos rotulorum of Frederick County, he presided at county courts held at Winchester, where, during the sessions, he kept open table. He acted also as surveyor and overseer of the public roads and highways, and was unremitted in his exertions and plans for the improvement of the country. Hunting, however, was his passion. When the sport was poor near home, he would take his hounds to a distant part of the country, establish himself at an inn, and keep open house and open table to every person of good character and respectable appearance who chose to join him in following the hounds.

It was probably in quest of sport of the kind that he now and then, in the hunting season, revisited his old haunts and former companions on the banks of the Potomac, and then the beautiful woodland region about Belvoir and Mount Vernon was sure to ring at early morn with the inspiring music of the hound.

The waters of the Potomac also afforded occasional amusement in fishing and shooting. The fishing was sometimes on a grand scale, when the herrings came up the river in shoals, and the negroes of Mount Vernon were marshalled forth to draw the seine, which was generally done with great success. Canvas-back ducks abounded at the proper season, and the shooting of them was one of Washington's favorite recreations. The river border of his

82   Hunting memoranda from Washington's journal, Mount Vernon.

Nov. 22.—Hunting with Lord Fairfax and his brother, and Colonel Fairfax.

Nov. 25.—Mr. Bryan Fairfax, Mr. Grayson, and Phil. Alexander came here by sunrise. Hunted and catched a fox with these, Lord Fairfax, his brother, and Col. Fairfax,—all of whom, with Mr. Fairfax and Mr. Wilson of England, dined here. 26th and 29th.—Hunted again with the same company.

Dec. 5.—Fox-hunting with Lord Fairfax and his brother, and Colonel Fairfax. Started a fox and lost it. Dined at Belvoir, and returned in the evening.

domain, however, was somewhat subject to invasion. An oysterman once anchored his craft at the landing-place, and disturbed the quiet of the neighborhood by the insolent and disorderly conduct of himself and crew. It took a campaign of three days to expel these invaders from the premises.

A more summary course was pursued with another interloper. This was a vagabond who infested the creeks and inlets which bordered the estate, lurking in a canoe among the reeds and bushes, and making great havoc among the canvas-back ducks. He had been warned off repeatedly, but without effect. As Washington was one day riding about the estate he heard the report of a gun from the margin of the river. Spurring in that direction he dashed through the bushes and came upon the culprit just as he was pushing his canoe from shore. The latter raised his gun with a menacing look; but Washington rode into the stream, seized the painter of the canoe, drew it to shore, sprang from his horse, wrested the gun from the hands of the astonished delinquent, and inflicted on him a lesson in "Lynch law" that effectually cured him of all inclination to trespass again on these forbidden shores.

The Potomac, in the palmy days of Virginia, was occasionally the scene of a little aquatic state and ostentation among the rich planters who resided on its banks. They had beautiful barges, which, like their land equipages, were imported from England; and mention is made of a Mr. Digges who always received Washington in his barge, rowed by six negroes, arrayed in a kind of uniform of check shirts and black velvet caps. At one time, according to notes in Washington's diary, the whole neighborhood is thrown into a paroxysm of festivity, by the anchoring of a British frigate (the Boston) in the river, just in front of the hospitable mansion of the Fairfaxes. A succession of dinners and breakfasts takes place at Mount Vernon and Belvoir, with occasional tea parties on board of the frigate. The commander, Sir Thomas Adams, his officers, and his midshipmen, are cherished guests, and have the freedom of both establishments.

Occasionally he and Mrs. Washington would pay a visit to Annapolis, at that time the seat of government of Maryland, and partake of the gayeties which prevailed during the session of the legislature. The society of these seats of provincial governments was always polite and fashionable, and more exclusive than in these republican days, being, in a manner, the outposts of the English aristocracy, where all places of dignity or profit were secured for younger sons, and poor, but proud relatives. During the session of the Legislature, dinners and balls abounded, and there were occasional attempts at theatricals. The latter was an amusement for which Washington always had a relish, though he never had an opportunity of gratifying it effectually. Neither was he disinclined to mingle in the dance, and we remember to have heard venerable ladies, who had been belles in his day, pride themselves on having had him for a partner, though, they added, he was apt to be a ceremonious and grave one.[83]

In this round of rural occupation, rural amusements, and social intercourse, Washington passed several tranquil years, the halcyon season of his life. His already established reputation drew many visitors to Mount Vernon; some of his early companions in arms were his occasional guests, and his friendships and connections linked him with some of the most prominent and worthy people of the country, who were sure to be received with cordial, but simple and unpretending hospitality. His marriage was unblessed with children; but those of Mrs. Washington experienced from him parental care and affection, and the formation of their minds and manners was one of the dearest objects of his attention. His domestic concerns and social enjoyments, however, were not permitted to interfere with his public duties. He was active by nature, and eminently a man of business by habit. As judge of the county court, and member of the House of Burgesses, he had numerous calls upon his time and thoughts, and was often drawn from home; for whatever trust he undertook, he was sure to fulfil with scrupulous exactness.

About this time we find him engaged, with other men of enterprise, in a project to drain the great Dismal Swamp, and render

---

83   We have had an amusing picture of Annapolis, as it was at this period, furnished to us, some years since by an octogenarian who had resided there in his boyhood. "In those parts of the country," said he, "where the roads were too rough for carriages, the ladies used to ride on ponies, followed by black servants on horseback; in this way his mother, then advanced in life, used to travel, in a scarlet cloth riding habit, which she had procured from England. Nay, in this way, on emergencies," he added, "the young ladies from the country used to come to the balls at Annapolis, riding with their hoops arranged 'fore and aft' like lateen sails; and after dancing all night, would ride home again in the morning."

it capable of cultivation. This vast morass was about thirty miles long, and ten miles wide, and its interior but little known. With his usual zeal and hardihood he explored it on horseback and on foot. In many parts it was covered with dark and gloomy woods of cedar, cypress, and hemlock, or deciduous trees, the branches of which were hung with long drooping moss. Other parts were almost inaccessible, from the density of brakes and thickets, entangled with vines, briers, and creeping plants, and intersected by creeks and standing pools. Occasionally the soil, composed of dead vegetable fibre, was over his horse's fetlocks, and sometimes he had to dismount and make his way on foot over a quaking bog that shook beneath his tread.

In the centre of the morass he came to a great piece of water, six miles long, and three broad, called Drummond's Pond, but more poetically celebrated as the Lake of the Dismal Swamp. It was more elevated than any other part of the swamp, and capable of feeding canals, by which the whole might be traversed. Having made the circuit of it, and noted all its characteristics, he encamped for the night upon the firm land which bordered it, and finished his explorations on the following day.

In the ensuing session of the Virginia Legislature, the association in behalf of which he had acted, was chartered under the name of the Dismal Swamp Company; and to his observations and forecast may be traced the subsequent improvement and prosperity of that once desolate region.

CHAPTER XXVII.

TREATY OF PEACE—PONTIAC'S WAR—COURSE
OF PUBLIC EVENTS—BOARD OF TRADE AGAINST
PAPER CURRENCY—RESTRICTIVE POLICY OF
ENGLAND—NAVIGATION LAWS—DISCONTENTS
IN NEW ENGLAND—OF THE OTHER COLONIES—
PROJECTS TO RAISE REVENUE BY TAXATION—BLOW
AT THE INDEPENDENCE OF THE JUDICIARY—NAVAL
COMMANDERS EMPLOYED AS CUSTOM-HOUSE
OFFICERS—RETALIATION OF THE COLONISTS—
TAXATION RESISTED IN BOSTON—PASSING OF THE
STAMP ACT—BURST OF OPPOSITION IN VIRGINIA—
SPEECH OF PATRICK HENRY.

Tidings of peace gladdened the colonies in the spring of 1763.
The definitive treaty between England and France had been signed
at Fontainbleau. Now, it was trusted, there would be an end to
those horrid ravages that had desolated the interior of the country.
"The desert and the silent place would rejoice, and the wilderness
would blossom like the rose."

The month of May proved the fallacy of such hopes. In that
month the famous insurrection of the Indian tribes broke out,
which, from the name of the chief who was its prime mover and
master spirit, is commonly called Pontiac's war. The Delawares
and Shawnees, and other of those emigrant tribes of the Ohio,
among whom Washington had mingled, were foremost in this
conspiracy. Some of the chiefs who had been his allies, had now
taken up the hatchet against the English. The plot was deep laid,
and conducted with. Indian craft and secrecy. At a concerted time
an attack was made upon all the posts from Detroit to Fort Pitt
(late Fort Duquesne). Several of the small stockaded forts, the

places of refuge of woodland neighborhoods, were surprised and sacked with remorseless butchery. The frontiers of Pennsylvania, Maryland, and Virginia, were laid waste; traders in the wilderness were plundered and slain; hamlets and farmhouses were wrapped in flames, and their inhabitants massacred. Shingis, with his Delaware warriors, blockaded Fort Pitt, which, for some time, was in imminent danger. Detroit, also, came near falling into the hands of the savages. It needed all the influence of Sir William Johnson, that potentate in savage life, to keep the Six Nations from joining this formidable conspiracy; had they done so, the triumph of the tomahawk and scalping knife would have been complete; as it was, a considerable time elapsed before the frontier was restored to tolerable tranquillity.

Fortunately, Washington's retirement from the army prevented his being entangled in this savage war, which raged throughout the regions he had repeatedly visited, or rather his active spirit had been diverted into a more peaceful channel, for he was at this time occupied in the enterprise just noticed, for draining the great Dismal Swamp.

Public events were now taking a tendency which, without any political aspiration or forethought of his own, was destined gradually to bear him away from his quiet home and individual pursuits, and launch him upon a grander and wider sphere of action than any in which he had hitherto been engaged.

The prediction of the Count de Vergennes was in the process of fulfilment. The recent war of Great Britain for dominion in America, though crowned with success, had engendered a progeny of discontents in her colonies. Washington was among the first to perceive its bitter fruits. British merchants had complained loudly of losses sustained by the depreciation of the colonial paper, issued during the late war, in times of emergency, and had addressed a memorial on the subject to the Board of Trade. Scarce was peace concluded, when an order from the board declared that no paper, issued by colonial Assemblies, should thenceforward be a legal tender in the payment of debts. Washington deprecated this "stir of the merchants" as peculiarly ill-timed; and expressed an apprehension that the orders in question "would get the whole country in flames."

We do not profess, in this personal memoir, to enter into a wide scope of general history, but shall content ourselves with a glance at the circumstances and events which gradually kindled the conflagration thus apprehended by the anxious mind of Washington.

Whatever might be the natural affection of the colonies for the mother country,—and there are abundant evidences to prove that it was deep-rooted and strong,—it had never been properly reciprocated. They yearned to be considered as children; they were treated by her as changelings. Burke testifies that her policy toward them from the beginning had been purely commercial, and her commercial policy wholly restrictive. "It was the system of a monopoly."

Her navigation laws had shut their ports against foreign vessels; obliged them to export their productions only to countries belonging to the British crown; to import European goods solely from England, and in English ships; and had subjected the trade between the colonies to duties. All manufactures, too, in the colonies that might interfere with those of the mother country had been either totally prohibited, or subjected to intolerable restraints.

The acts of Parliament, imposing these prohibitions and restrictions, had at various times produced sore discontent and opposition on the part of the colonies, especially among those of New England. The interests of these last were chiefly commercial, and among them the republican spirit predominated. They had sprung into existence during that part of the reign of James I. when disputes ran high about kingly prerogative and popular privilege.

The Pilgrims, as they styled themselves, who founded Plymouth Colony in 1620, had been incensed while in England by what they stigmatized as the oppressions of the monarchy, and the established church. They had sought the wilds of America for the indulgence of freedom of opinion, and had brought with them the spirit of independence and self-government. Those who followed them in the reign of Charles I. were imbued with the same spirit, and gave a lasting character to the people of New England.

Other colonies, having been formed under other circumstances, might be inclined toward a monarchical government, and disposed to acquiesce in its exactions; but the republican spirit was ever alive in New England, watching over "natural and chartered rights," and prompt to defend them against any infringement. Its example and instigation had gradually an effect on the other colonies; a general impatience was evinced from time to time of parliamentary interference in colonial affairs, and a disposition in the various provincial Legislatures to think and act for themselves in matters of civil and religious, as well as commercial polity.

There was nothing, however, to which the jealous sensibilities of the colonies were more alive than to any attempt of the mother country to draw a revenue from them by taxation. From the earliest period of their existence, they had maintained the principle that they could only be taxed by a Legislature in which they were represented. Sir Robert Walpole, when at the head of the British government, was aware of their jealous sensibility on this point, and cautious of provoking it. When American taxation was suggested, "it must be a bolder man than himself," he replied, "and one less friendly to commerce, who should venture on such an expedient. For his part, he would encourage the trade of the colonies to the utmost; one half of the profits would be sure to come into the royal exchequer through the increased demand for British manufactures. *This*," said he, sagaciously, "*is taxing them more agreeably to their own constitution and laws.*"

Subsequent ministers adopted a widely different policy. During the progress of the French war, various projects were discussed in England with regard to the colonies, which were to be carried into effect on the return of peace. The open avowal of some of these plans, and vague rumors of others, more than ever irritated the jealous feelings of the colonists, and put the dragon spirit of New England on the alert.

In 1760, there was an attempt in Boston to collect duties on foreign sugar and molasses imported into the colonies. Writs of assistance were applied for by the custom-house officers, authorizing them to break open ships, stores, and private dwellings, in quest of articles that had paid no duty; and to call the assistance of others in the discharge of their odious task. The merchants opposed the execution of the writ on constitutional grounds. The question was argued in court, where James Otis spoke so eloquently in vindication of American rights, that all his hearers went away ready to take arms against writs of assistance. "Then and there," says John Adams, who was present, "was the first scene of opposition to the arbitrary claims of Great Britain. Then and there American Independence was born."

Another ministerial measure was to instruct the provincial governors to commission judges. Not as theretofore "during good behavior," but "during the king's pleasure." New York was the first to resent this blow at the independence of the judiciary. The lawyers appealed to the public through the press against an act which subjected the halls of justice to the prerogative. Their appeals were felt beyond the bounds of the province, and awakened a general spirit of resistance.

Thus matters stood at the conclusion of the war. One of the first measures of ministers, on the return of peace, was to enjoin on all naval officers stationed on the coasts of the American colonies the performance, under oath, of the duties of custom-house officers, for the suppression of smuggling. This fell ruinously upon a clandestine trade which had long been connived at between the English and Spanish colonies, profitable to both, but especially to the former, and beneficial to the mother country, opening a market to her manufactures.

"Men-of-war," says Burke, "were for the first time armed with the regular commissions of custom-house officers, invested the coasts, and gave the collection of revenue the air of hostile contribution. ... They fell so indiscriminately on all sorts of contraband, or supposed contraband, that some of the most valuable branches of trade were driven violently from our ports, which caused an universal consternation throughout the colonies."[84]

As a measure of retaliation, the colonists resolved not to purchase British fabrics, but to clothe themselves as much as possible in home manufactures. The demand for British goods in Boston alone was diminished upwards of £10,000 sterling in the course of a year.

In 1764, George Grenville, now at the head of government, ventured upon the policy from which Walpole had so wisely abstained. Early in March the eventful question was debated, "whether they had a right to tax America." It was decided in the affirmative. Next followed a resolution, declaring it proper to charge certain stamp duties in the colonies and plantations, but no immediate step was

---

84   Burke on the state of the nation.

taken to carry it into effect. Mr. Grenville, however, gave notice to the American agents in London, that he should introduce such a measure on the ensuing session of Parliament. In the mean time Parliament perpetuated certain duties on sugar and molasses—heretofore subjects of complaint and opposition—now reduced and modified so as to discourage smuggling, and thereby to render them more productive. Duties, also, were imposed on other articles of foreign produce or manufacture imported into the colonies. To reconcile the latter to these impositions, it was stated that the revenue thus raised was to be appropriated to their protection and security; in other words, to the support of a standing army, intended to be quartered upon them.

We have here briefly stated but a part of what Burke terms an "infinite variety of paper chains," extending through no less than twenty-nine acts of Parliament, from 1660 to 1764, by which the colonies had been held in thraldom.

The New Englanders were the first to take the field against the project of taxation. They denounced it as a violation of their rights as freemen; of their chartered rights, by which they were to tax themselves for their support and defence; of their rights as British subjects, who ought not to be taxed but by themselves or their representatives. They sent petitions and remonstrances on the subject to the king, the lords and the commons, in which they were seconded by New York and Virginia. Franklin appeared in London at the head of agents from Pennsylvania, Connecticut and South Carolina, to deprecate, in person, measures so fraught with mischief. The most eloquent arguments were used by British orators and statesmen to dissuade Grenville from enforcing them. He was warned of the sturdy independence of the colonists, and the spirit of resistance he might provoke. All was in vain. Grenville, "great in daring and little in views," says Horace Walpole, "was charmed to have an untrodden field before him of calculation and experiment." In March, 1765, the act was passed, according to which all instruments in writing were to be executed on stamped paper, to be purchased from the agents of the British government. What was more: all offences against the act could be tried in any royal, marine or admiralty court throughout the colonies, however distant from the place where the offence had been committed; thus interfering with that most inestimable right, a trial by jury.

It was an ominous sign that the first burst of opposition to this act should take place in Virginia. That colony had hitherto been slow to accord with the republican spirit of New England. Founded at an earlier period of the reign of James I., before kingly prerogative and ecclesiastical supremacy had been made matters of doubt and fierce dispute, it had grown up in loyal attachment to king, church, and constitution; was aristocratical in its tastes and habits, and had been remarked above all the other colonies for its sympathies with the mother country. Moreover, it had not so many pecuniary interests involved in these questions as had the people of New England, being an agricultural rather than a commercial province; but the Virginians are of a quick and generous spirit, readily aroused on all points of honorable pride, and they resented the stamp act as an outrage on their rights.

Washington occupied his seat in the House of Burgesses, when, on the 29th of May, the stamp act became a subject of discussion. We have seen no previous opinions of his on the subject. His correspondence hitherto had not turned on political or speculative themes; being engrossed by either military or agricultural matters, and evincing little anticipation of the vortex of public duties into which he was about to be drawn. All his previous conduct and writings show a loyal devotion to the crown, with a patriotic attachment to his country. It is probable that on the present occasion that latent patriotism received its first electric shock.

Among the Burgesses sat Patrick Henry, a young lawyer who had recently distinguished himself by pleading against the exercise of the royal prerogative in church matters, and who was now for the first time a member of the House. Rising in his place, he introduced his celebrated resolutions, declaring that the General Assembly of Virginia had the exclusive right and power to lay taxes and impositions upon the inhabitants, and that whoever maintained the contrary should be deemed an enemy to the colony.

The speaker, Mr. Robinson, objected to the resolutions, as inflammatory. Henry vindicated them, as justified by the nature of the case; went into an able and constitutional discussion of colonial rights, and an eloquent exposition of the manner in which they had been assailed; wound up by one of those daring flights of declamation for which he was remarkable, and startled the

House by a warning flash from history: "Caesar had his Brutus; Charles his Cromwell, and George the Third—('Treason! treason!' resounded from the neighborhood of the Chair)—may profit by their examples," added Henry. "Sir, if this be treason (bowing to the speaker), make the most of it!"

The resolutions were modified, to accommodate them to the scruples of the speaker and some of the members, but their spirit was retained. The Lieutenant-governor (Fauquier), startled by this patriotic outbreak, dissolved the Assembly, and issued writs for a new election; but the clarion had sounded. "The resolves of the Assembly of Virginia," says a correspondent of the ministry, "gave the signal for a general outcry over the continent. The movers and supporters of them were applauded as the protectors and assertors of American liberty."[85]

---

85   Letter to Secretary Conway, New York, Sept. 23.—*Parliamentary Register.*

CHAPTER XXVIII.

WASHINGTON'S IDEAS CONCERNING THE STAMP
ACT—OPPOSITION TO IT IN THE COLONIES—
PORTENTOUS CEREMONIES AT BOSTON AND NEW
YORK—NON-IMPORTATION AGREEMENT AMONG
THE MERCHANTS—WASHINGTON AND GEORGE
MASON—DISMISSAL OF GRENVILLE FROM THE
BRITISH CABINET—FRANKLIN BEFORE THE HOUSE
OF COMMONS—REPEAL OF THE STAMP ACT—JOY
OF WASHINGTON—FRESH CAUSES OF COLONIAL
DISSENSIONS—CIRCULAR OF THE GENERAL COURT
OF MASSACHUSETTS—EMBARKATION OF TROOPS
FOR BOSTON—MEASURES OF THE BOSTONIANS.

Washington returned to Mount Vernon full of anxious
thoughts inspired by the political events of the day, and the
legislative scene which he witnessed. His recent letters had spoken
of the state of peaceful tranquillity in which he was living; those
now written from his rural home show that he fully participated
in the popular feeling, and that while he had a presentiment of
an arduous struggle, his patriotic mind was revolving means of
coping with it. Such is the tenor of a letter written to his wife's
uncle, Francis Dandridge, then in London. "The stamp act," said
he, "engrosses the conversation of the speculative part of the
colonists, who look upon this unconstitutional method of taxation
as a direful attack upon their liberties, and loudly exclaim against the
violation. What may be the result of this, and of some other (I think
I may add ill-judged) measures, I will not undertake to determine;
but this I may venture to affirm, that the advantage accruing to
the mother country will fall greatly short of the expectation of
the ministry; for certain it is, that our whole substance already in

a manner flows to Great Britain, and that whatsoever contributes to lessen our importations must be hurtful to her manufactures. The eyes of our people already begin to be opened; and they will perceive, that many luxuries, for which we lavish our substance in Great Britain, can well be dispensed with. This, consequently, will introduce frugality, and be a necessary incitement to industry.... As to the stamp act, regarded in a single view, one of the first bad consequences attending it, is, that our courts of judicature must inevitably be shut up; for it is impossible, or next to impossible, under our present circumstances, that the act of Parliament can be complied with, were we ever so willing to enforce its execution. And not to say (which alone would be sufficient) that we have not money enough to pay for the stamps, there are many other cogent reasons which prove that it would be ineffectual."

A letter of the same date to his agents in London, of ample length and minute in all its details, shows that, while deeply interested in the course of public affairs, his practical mind was enabled thoroughly and ably to manage the financial concerns of his estate and of the estate of Mrs. Washington's son, John Parke Custis, towards whom, he acted the part of a faithful and affectionate guardian. In those days, Virginia planters were still in direct and frequent correspondence with their London factors; and Washington's letters respecting his shipments of tobacco, and the returns required in various articles for household and personal use, are perfect models for a man of business. And this may be remarked throughout his whole career, that no pressure of events nor multiplicity of cares prevented a clear, steadfast, undercurrent of attention to domestic affairs, and the interest and well-being of all dependent upon him.

In the mean time, from his quiet abode at Mount Vernon, he seemed to hear the patriotic voice of Patrick Henry, which had startled the House of Burgesses, echoing throughout the land, and rousing one legislative body after another to follow the example of that of Virginia. At the instigation of the General Court or Assembly of Massachusetts, a Congress was held in New York in October, composed of delegates from Massachusetts, Rhode Island, Connecticut, New York, New Jersey, Pennsylvania, Delaware, Maryland, and South Carolina. In this they denounced the acts of Parliament imposing taxes on them without their consent, and extending the jurisdiction of the courts of admiralty, as violations of their rights and liberties as natural born subjects of Great Britain, and prepared an address to the king, and a petition to both Houses of Parliament, praying for redress. Similar petitions were forwarded to England by the colonies not represented in the Congress.

The very preparations for enforcing the stamp act called forth popular tumults in various places. In Boston the stamp distributor was hanged in effigy; his windows were broken; a house intended for a stamp office was pulled down, and the effigy burnt in a bonfire made of the fragments. The lieutenant-governor, chief justice, and sheriff, attempting to allay the tumult, were pelted. The stamp officer thought himself happy to be hanged merely in effigy, and next day publicly renounced the perilous office.

Various were the proceedings in other places, all manifesting public scorn and defiance of the act. In Virginia, Mr. George Mercer had been appointed distributor of stamps, but on his arrival at Williamsburg publicly declined officiating. It was a fresh triumph to the popular cause. The bells were rung for joy; the town was illuminated, and Mercer was hailed with acclamations of the people.[86]

The 1st of November, the day when the act was to go into operation, was ushered in with portentous solemnities. There was great tolling of bells and burning of effigies in the New England colonies. At Boston the ships displayed their colors but half-mast high. Many shops were shut; funeral knells resounded from the steeples, and there was a grand auto-da-fe, in which the promoters of the act were paraded, and suffered martyrdom in effigy.

At New York the printed act was carried about the streets on a pole, surmounted by a death's head, with a scroll bearing the inscription, "The folly of England and ruin of America." Colden, the lieutenant-governor, who acquired considerable odium by recommending to government the taxation of the colonies, the institution of hereditary Assemblies, and other Tory measures, seeing that a popular storm was rising, retired into the fort, taking with him the stamp papers, and garrisoned it with marines from a ship of war. The mob broke into his stable; drew out his chariot;

---

86   Holmes's Annals, vol. ii., p. 138.

put his effigy into it; paraded it through the streets to the common (now the Park), where they hung it on a gallows. In the evening it was taken down, put again into the chariot, with the devil for a companion, and escorted back by torchlight to the Bowling Green; where the whole pageant, chariot and all, was burnt under the very guns of the fort.

These are specimens of the marks of popular reprobation with which the stamp act was universally nullified. No one would venture to carry it into execution. In fact no stamped paper was to be seen; all had been either destroyed or concealed. All transactions which required stamps to give them validity were suspended, or were executed by private compact. The courts of justice were closed, until at length some conducted their business without stamps. Union was becoming the watch-word. The merchants of New York, Philadelphia, Boston, and such other colonies as had ventured publicly to oppose the stamp act, agreed to import no more British manufactures after the 1st of January unless it should be repealed. So passed away the year 1765.

As yet Washington took no prominent part in the public agitation. Indeed he was never disposed to put himself forward on popular occasions, his innate modesty forbade it; it was others who knew his worth that called him forth; but when once he engaged in any public measure, he devoted himself to it with conscientiousness and persevering zeal. At present he remained a quiet but vigilant observer of events from his eagle nest at Mount Vernon. He had some few intimates in his neighborhood who accorded with him in sentiment. One of the ablest and most efficient of these was Mr. George Mason, with whom he had occasional conversations on the state of affairs. His friends the Fairfaxes, though liberal in feelings and opinions, were too strong in their devotion to the crown not to regard with an uneasy eye the tendency of the popular bias. From one motive or other, the earnest attention of all the inmates and visitors at Mount Vernon, was turned to England, watching the movements of the ministry.

The dismissal of Mr. Grenville from the cabinet gave a temporary change to public affairs. Perhaps nothing had a greater effect in favor of the colonies than an examination of Dr. Franklin before the House of Commons, on the subject of the stamp act.

"What," he was asked, "was the temper of America towards Great Britain, before the year 1763?"

"The best in the world. They submitted willingly to the government of the crown, and paid, in all their courts, obedience to the acts of Parliament. Numerous as the people are in the several old provinces, they cost you nothing in forts, citadels, garrisons, or armies, to keep them in subjection. They were governed by this country at the expense only of a little pen, ink, and paper. They were led by a thread. They had not only a respect, but an affection for Great Britain, for its laws, its customs, and manners, and even a fondness for its fashions, that greatly increased the commerce. Natives of Great Britain were always treated with particular regard; to be an Old-England man was, of itself, a character of some respect, and gave a kind of rank among us."

"And what is their temper now?"

"Oh! very much altered."

"If the act is not repealed, what do you think will be the consequences?"

"A total loss of the respect and affection the people of America bear to this country, and of all the commerce that depends on that respect and affection."

"Do you think the people of America would submit to pay the stamp duty if it was moderated?"

"No, never, unless compelled by force of arms."[87]

The act was repealed on the 18th of March, 1766, to the great joy of the sincere friends of both countries, and to no one more than to Washington. In one of his letters he observes: "Had the Parliament of Great Britain resolved upon enforcing it, the consequences, I conceive, would have been more direful than is generally apprehended, both to the mother country and her colonies. All, therefore, who were instrumental in procuring the repeal, are entitled to the thanks of every British subject, and have mine cordially."[88]

Still, there was a fatal clause in the repeal, which declared that the king, with the consent of Parliament, had power and authority

---

87   Parliamentary Register, 1766.
88   Sparks. Writings of Washington, ii., 345, note.

to make laws and statutes of sufficient force and validity to "bind the colonies, and people of America, in all cases whatsoever."

As the people of America were contending for principles, not mere pecuniary interests, this reserved power of the crown and Parliament left the dispute still open, and chilled the feeling of gratitude which the repeal might otherwise have inspired. Further aliment for public discontent was furnished by other acts of Parliament. One imposed duties on glass, pasteboard, white and red lead, painters' colors, and tea; the duties to be collected on the arrival of the articles in the colonies; another empowered naval officers to enforce the acts of trade and navigation. Another wounded to the quick the pride and sensibilities of New York. The mutiny act had recently been extended to America, with an additional clause, requiring the provincial Assemblies to provide the troops sent out with quarters, and to furnish them with fire, beds, candles, and other necessaries, at the expense of the colonies. The Governor and Assembly of New York refused to comply with, this requisition as to stationary forces, insisting that it applied only to troops on a march. An act of Parliament now suspended the powers of the governor and Assembly until they should comply. Chatham attributed this opposition of the colonists to the mutiny act to "their jealousy of being somehow or other taxed internally by the Parliament; the act," said he, "asserting the right of Parliament, has certainly spread a most unfortunate jealousy and diffidence of government here throughout America, and makes them jealous of the least distinction between this country and that, lest the same principle may be extended to taxing them."[89]

Boston continued to be the focus of what the ministerialists termed sedition. The General Court of Massachusetts, not content with petitioning the king for relief against the recent measures of Parliament, especially those imposing taxes as a means of revenue, drew up a circular, calling on the other colonial Legislatures to join with them in suitable efforts to obtain redress. In the ensuing session, Governor Sir Francis Bernard called upon them to rescind the resolution on which the circular was founded,—they refused to comply, and the General Court was consequently dissolved. The governors of colonies required of their Legislatures an assurance

---

89   Chatham's Correspondence, vol. iii., p. 189-192.

that they would not reply to the Massachusetts circular,—these Legislatures likewise refused compliance and were dissolved. All this added to the growing excitement.

Memorials were addressed to the lords, spiritual and temporal, and remonstrances to the House of Commons, against taxation for revenue, as destructive to the liberties of the colonists; and against the act suspending the legislative power of the province of New York, as menacing the welfare of the colonies in general.

Nothing, however, produced a more powerful effect upon the public sensibilities throughout the country, than certain military demonstrations at Boston. In consequence of repeated collisions between the people of that place and the commissioners of customs, two regiments were held in readiness at Halifax to embark for Boston in the ships of Commodore Hood whenever Governor Bernard, or the general, should give the word, "Had this force been landed in Boston six months ago," writes the commodore, "I am perfectly persuaded no address or remonstrances would have been sent from the other colonies, and that all would have been tolerably quiet and orderly at this time throughout America."[90]

Tidings reached Boston that these troops were embarked and that they were coming to overawe the people. What was to be done? The General Court had been dissolved, and the governor refused to convene it without the royal command. A convention, therefore, from various towns met at Boston, on the 22d of September, to devise measures for the public safety; but disclaiming all pretensions to legislative powers. While the convention was yet in session (September 28th), the two regiments arrived, with seven armed vessels. "I am very confident," writes Commodore Hood from Halifax, "the spirited measures now pursuing will soon effect order in America."

On the contrary, these "spirited measures" added, fuel to the fire they were intended to quench. It was resolved in a town meeting that the king had no right to send troops thither without the consent of the Assembly; that Great Britain had broken the original compact, and that, therefore, the king's officers had no longer any business there.[91]

---

90   Grenville Papers, vol. iv., p. 362.
91   Whately to Grenville. Gren. Papers, vol. iv., p. 389.

The "selectmen" accordingly refused to find quarters for the soldiers in the town; the council refused to find barracks for them, lest it should be construed into a compliance with the disputed clause of the mutiny act. Some of the troops, therefore, which had tents, were encamped on the common; others, by the governor's orders, were quartered in the state-house, and others in Faneuil Hall, to the great indignation of the public, who were grievously scandalized at seeing field-pieces planted in front of the state-house; sentinels stationed at the doors, challenging every one who passed; and, above all, at having the sacred quiet of the Sabbath disturbed by drum and fife, and other military music.

CHAPTER XXIX.

CHEERFUL LIFE AT MOUNT VERNON—WASHINGTON
AND GEORGE MASON—CORRESPONDENCE
CONCERNING THE NON-IMPORTATION
AGREEMENT—FEELING TOWARD ENGLAND—
OPENING OF THE LEGISLATIVE SESSION—SEMI-
REGAL STATE OF LORD BOTETOURT—HIGH-
TONED PROCEEDINGS OF THE HOUSE—SYMPATHY
WITH NEW ENGLAND—DISSOLVED BY LORD
BOTETOURT—WASHINGTON AND THE ARTICLES OF
ASSOCIATION.

Throughout these public agitations, Washington endeavored to preserve his equanimity. Removed from the heated throngs of cities, his diary denotes a cheerful and healthful life at Mount Vernon, devoted to those rural occupations in which he delighted, and varied occasionally by his favorite field sports. Sometimes he is duck-shooting on the Potomac. Repeatedly we find note of his being out at sunrise with the hounds, in company with old Lord Fairfax, Bryan Fairfax, and others; and ending the day's sport by a dinner at Mount Vernon, or Belvoir.

Still he was too true a patriot not to sympathize in the struggle for colonial rights which now agitated the whole country, and we find him gradually carried more and more into the current of political affairs.

A letter written on the 5th of April, 1769, to his friend, George Mason, shows the important stand he was disposed to take. In the previous year, the merchants and traders of Boston, Salem, Connecticut, and New York, had agreed to suspend for a time the importation of all articles subject to taxation. Similar resolutions had recently been adopted by the merchants of Philadelphia.

Washington's letter is emphatic in support of the measure. "At a time," writes he, "when our lordly masters in Great Britain will be satisfied with nothing less, than the deprivation of American freedom, it seems highly necessary that something should be done to avert the stroke, and maintain the liberty which we have derived from our ancestors. But the manner of doing it, to answer the purpose effectually, is the point in question. That no man should scruple, or hesitate a moment in defence of so valuable a blessing, is clearly my opinion; yet arms should be the last resource—the *dernier ressort*. We have already, it is said, proved the inefficacy of addresses to the throne, and remonstrances to Parliament. How far their attention to our rights and interests is to be awakened, or alarmed, by starving their trade and manufactures, remains to be tried.

"The northern colonies, it appears, are endeavoring to adopt this scheme. In my opinion, it is a good one, and must be attended with salutary effects, provided it can be carried pretty generally into execution. . . . That there will be a difficulty attending it every where from clashing interests, and selfish, designing men, ever attentive to their own gain, and watchful of every turn that can assist their lucrative views, cannot be denied, and in the tobacco colonies, where the trade is so diffused, and in a manner wholly conducted by factors for their principals at home, these difficulties are certainly enhanced, but I think not insurmountably increased, if the gentlemen in their several counties will be at some pains to explain matters to the people, and stimulate them to cordial agreements to purchase none but certain enumerated articles out of any of the stores, after a definite period, and neither import, nor purchase any themselves. . . . I can see but one class of people, the merchants excepted, who will not, or ought not, to wish well to the scheme,—namely, they who live genteelly and hospitably on clear estates. Such as these, were they not to consider the valuable object in view, and the good of others, might think it hard to be curtailed in their living and enjoyments."

This was precisely the class to which Washington belonged; but he was ready and willing to make the sacrifices required. "I think the scheme a good one," added he, "and that it ought to be tried here, with such alterations as our circumstances render absolutely necessary."

Mason, in his reply, concurred with him in opinion. "Our all is at stake," said he, "and the little conveniences and comforts of life, when set in competition with our liberty, ought to be rejected, not with reluctance, but with pleasure. Yet it is plain that, in the tobacco colonies, we cannot at present confine our importations within such narrow bounds as the northern colonies. A plan of this kind, to be practicable, must be adapted to our circumstances; for, if not steadily executed, it had better have remained unattempted. We may retrench all manner of superfluities, finery of all descriptions, and confine ourselves to linens, woollens, &c., not exceeding a certain price. It is amazing how much this practice, if adopted in all the colonies, would lessen the American imports, and distress the various trades and manufactures of Great Britain. This would awaken their attention. They would see, they would feel, the oppressions we groan under, and exert themselves to procure us redress. This, once obtained, we should no longer discontinue our importations, confining ourselves still not to import any article that should hereafter be taxed by act of Parliament for raising a revenue in America; for, however singular I may be in the opinion, *I am thoroughly convinced, that, justice and harmony happily restored, it is not the interest of these colonies to refuse British manufactures. Our supplying our mother country with gross materials, and taking her manufactures in return, is the true chain of connection between us. These are the bands which, if not broken by oppression, must long hold us together, by maintaining a constant reciprocation of interests.*"

The latter part of the above quotation shows the spirit which actuated Washington and the friends of his confidence; as yet there was no thought nor desire of alienation from the mother country, but only a fixed determination to be placed on an equality of rights and privileges with her other children.

A single word in the passage cited from Washington's letter, evinces the chord which still vibrated in the American bosom: he incidentally speaks of England as *home*. It was the familiar term with which she was usually indicated by those of English descent; and the writer of these pages remembers when the endearing phrase still lingered on Anglo-American lips even after the Revolution. How easy would it have been before that era for the mother country to have rallied back the affections of her colonial children, by a proper attention to their complaints! They asked for nothing but what they were entitled to, and what she had taught them to prize as their dearest inheritance. The spirit of liberty which they manifested had been derived from her own precept and example.

The result of the correspondence between Washington and Mason was the draft by the latter of a plan of association, the members of which were to pledge themselves not to import or use any articles of British merchandise or manufacture subject to duty. This paper Washington was to submit to the consideration of the House of Burgesses, at the approaching session in the month of May.

The Legislature of Virginia opened on this occasion with a brilliant pageant. While military force was arrayed to overawe the republican Puritans of the east, it was thought to dazzle the aristocratical descendants of the cavaliers by the reflex of regal splendor. Lord Botetourt, one of the king's lords of the bedchamber, had recently come out as governor of the province. Junius described him as "a cringing, bowing, fawning, sword-bearing courtier." Horace Walpole predicted that he would turn the heads of the Virginians in one way or other. "If his graces do not captivate them he will enrage them to fury; for I take all his *douceur* to be enamelled on iron."[92] The words of political satirists and court wits, however, are always to be taken with great distrust. However his lordship may have bowed in presence of royalty, he elsewhere conducted himself with dignity, and won general favor by his endearing manners. He certainly showed promptness of spirit in his reply to the king on being informed of his appointment. "When will you be ready to go?" asked George III. "Tonight, sir."

He had come out, however, with a wrong idea of the Americans. They had been represented to him as factious, immoral, and prone to sedition; but vain and luxurious, and easily captivated by parade and splendor. The latter foibles were aimed at in his appointment and fitting out. It was supposed that his titled rank would have its effect. Then to prepare him for occasions of ceremony, a coach of state was presented to him by the king. He was allowed, moreover, the quantity of plate usually given to ambassadors, whereupon the joke was circulated that he was going "plenipo to the Cherokees."[93]

---

92   Grenville papers, iv., note to p. 330.
93   Whately to Geo. Grenville. Grenville papers.

His opening of the session was in the style of the royal opening of Parliament. He proceeded in due parade from his dwelling to the capitol, in his state coach, drawn by six milk-white horses. Having delivered his speech according to royal form, he returned home with the same pomp and circumstance.

The time had gone by, however, for such display to have the anticipated effect. The Virginian legislators penetrated the intention of this pompous ceremonial, and regarded it with a depreciating smile. Sterner matters occupied their thoughts; they had come prepared to battle for their rights, and their proceedings soon showed Lord Botetourt how much he had mistaken them. Spirited resolutions were passed, denouncing the recent act of Parliament imposing taxes; the power to do which, on the inhabitants of this colony, "was legally and constitutionally vested in the House of Burgesses, with consent of the council and of the king, or of his governor, for the time being." Copies of these resolutions were ordered to be forwarded by the speaker to the Legislatures of the other colonies, with a request for their concurrence.

Other proceedings of the Burgesses showed their sympathy with their fellow-patriots of New England. A joint address of both Houses of Parliament had recently been made to the king, assuring him of their support in any further measures for the due execution of the laws in Massachusetts, and beseeching him that all persons charged with treason, or misprision of treason, committed within that colony since the 30th of December, 1767, might be sent to Great Britain for trial.

As Massachusetts had no General Assembly at this time, having been dissolved by government, the Legislature of Virginia generously took up the cause. An address to the king was resolved on, stating, that all trials for treason, or misprision of treason, or for any crime whatever committed by any person residing in a colony, ought to be in and before his majesty's courts within said colony; and beseeching the king to avert from his loyal subjects those dangers and miseries which would ensue from seizing and carrying beyond sea any person residing in America suspected of any crime whatever, thereby depriving them of the inestimable privilege of being tried by a jury from the vicinage, as well as the liberty of producing witnesses on such trial.

Disdaining any further application to Parliament, the House ordered the speaker to transmit this address to the colonies' agent in England, with directions to cause it to be presented to the king, and afterwards to be printed and published in the English papers.

Lord Botetourt was astonished and dismayed when he heard of these high-toned proceedings. Repairing to the capitol on the following day at noon, he summoned the speaker and members to the council chamber, and addressed them in the following words: "Mr. Speaker, and gentlemen of the House of Burgesses, I have heard of your resolves, and augur ill of their effects. You have made it my duty to dissolve you, and you are dissolved accordingly."

The spirit conjured up by the late decrees of Parliament was not so easily allayed. The Burgesses adjourned to a private house. Peyton Randolph, their late speaker, was elected moderator. Washington now brought forward a draft of the articles of association, concerted between him and George Mason. They formed the groundwork of an instrument signed by all present, pledging themselves neither to import, nor use any goods, merchandise, or manufactures taxed by Parliament to raise a revenue in America. This instrument was sent throughout the country for signature, and the scheme of non-importation, hitherto confined to a few northern colonies, was soon universally adopted. For his own part, Washington adhered to it rigorously throughout the year. The articles proscribed by it were never to be seen in his house, and his agent in London was enjoined to ship nothing for him while subject to taxation.

The popular ferment in Virginia was gradually allayed by the amiable and conciliatory conduct of Lord Botetourt. His lordship soon became aware of the erroneous notions with which he had entered upon office. His semi-royal equipage and state were laid aside. He examined into public grievances; became a strenuous advocate for the repeal of taxes; and, authorized by his despatches from the ministry, assured the public that such repeal would speedily take place. His assurance was received with implicit faith, and for a while Virginia was quieted.

CHAPTER XXX.

HOOD AT BOSTON—THE GENERAL COURT
REFUSES TO DO BUSINESS UNDER MILITARY
SWAY—RESISTS THE BILLETING ACT—EFFECT OF
THE NON-IMPORTATION ASSOCIATION—LORD
NORTH PREMIER—DUTIES REVOKED EXCEPT ON
TEA—THE BOSTON MASSACRE—DISUSE OF TEA—
CONCILIATORY CONDUCT OF LORD BOTETOURT—
HIS DEATH.

"The worst is past, and the spirit of sedition broken," writes Hood to Grenville, early in the spring of 1769.[94] When the commodore wrote this, his ships were in the harbor, and troops occupied the town, and he flattered himself that at length turbulent Boston was quelled. But it only awaited its time to be seditious according to rule; there was always an irresistible "method in its madness."

In the month of May, the General Court, hitherto prorogued, met according to charter. A committee immediately waited on the governor, stating it was impossible to do business with dignity and freedom while the town was invested by sea and land, and a military guard was stationed at the state-house, with cannon pointed at the door; and they requested the governor, as his majesty's representative, to have such forces removed out of the port and gates of the city during the session of the Assembly.

The governor replied that he had no authority over either the ships or troops. The court persisted in refusing to transact business while so circumstanced, and the governor was obliged to transfer the session to Cambridge. There he addressed a message to that

---

94   Grenville Papers, vol. iii.

body in July, requiring funds for the payment of the troops, and quarters for their accommodation. The Assembly, after ample discussion of past grievances, resolved, that the establishment of a standing army in the colony in a time of peace was an invasion of natural rights; that a standing army was not known as a part of the British constitution, and that the sending an armed force to aid the civil authority was unprecedented, and highly dangerous to the people.

After waiting some days without receiving an answer to his message, the governor sent to know whether the Assembly would, or would not, make provision for the troops. In their reply, they followed the example of the Legislature of New York, in commenting on the mutiny, or billeting act, and ended by declining to furnish funds for the purposes specified, "being incompatible with their own honor and interest, and their duty to their constituents." They were in consequence again prorogued, to meet in Boston on the 10th of January.

So stood affairs in Massachusetts. In the mean time, the non-importation associations, being generally observed throughout the colonies, produced the effect on British commerce which Washington had anticipated, and Parliament was incessantly importuned by petitions from British merchants, imploring its intervention to save them from ruin.

Early in 1770, an important change took place in the British cabinet. The Duke of Grafton suddenly resigned, and the reins of government passed into the hands of Lord North. He was a man of limited capacity, but a favorite of the king, and subservient to his narrow colonial policy. His administration, so eventful to America, commenced with an error. In the month of March, an act was passed, revoking all the duties laid in 1767, *excepting that on tea*. This single tax was continued, as he observed, "to maintain the parliamentary right of taxation,"—the very right which was the grand object of contest. In this, however, he was in fact yielding, against his better judgment, to the stubborn tenacity of the king.

He endeavored to reconcile the opposition, and perhaps himself, to the measure, by plausible reasoning. An impost of threepence on the pound could never, he alleged, be opposed by the colonists, unless they were determined to rebel against Great Britain. Besides, a duty on that article, payable in England, and amounting to nearly one shilling on the pound, was taken off on its exportation to America, so that the inhabitants of the colonies saved ninepence on the pound.

Here was the stumbling-block at the threshold of Lord North's administration. In vain the members of the opposition urged that this single exception, while it would produce no revenue, would keep alive the whole cause of contention; that so long as a single external duty was enforced, the colonies would consider their rights invaded, and would remain unappeased. Lord North was not to be convinced; or rather, he knew the royal will was inflexible, and he complied with its behests. "The properest time to exert our right of taxation," said he, "is when the right is refused. To temporize is to yield; and the authority of the mother country, if it is now unsupported, will be relinquished for ever: *a total repeal cannot be thought of, till America is prostrate at our feet.*"[95]

On the very day in which this ominous bill was passed in Parliament, a sinister occurrence took place in Boston. Some of the young men of the place insulted the military while under arms; the latter resented it; the young men, after a scuffle, were put to flight, and pursued. The alarm bells rang,—a mob assembled; the custom-house was threatened; the troops, in protecting it, were assailed with clubs and stones, and obliged to use their fire-arms, before the tumult could be quelled. Four of the populace were killed, and several wounded. The troops were now removed from the town, which remained in the highest state of exasperation; and this untoward occurrence received the opprobrious, and somewhat extravagant name of "the Boston massacre."

The colonists, as a matter of convenience, resumed the consumption of those articles on which the duties had been repealed; but continued, on principle, the rigorous disuse of tea, excepting such as had been smuggled in. New England was particularly earnest in the matter; many of the inhabitants, in the spirit of their Puritan progenitors, made a covenant to drink no more of the forbidden beverage, until the duty on tea should be repealed.

In Virginia the public discontents, which had been allayed by the conciliatory conduct of Lord Botetourt, and by his assurances,

---

95   Holmes's Amer. Annals, vol. ii., p. 173.

made on the strength of letters received from the ministry, that the grievances complained of would be speedily redressed, now broke out with more violence than ever. The Virginians spurned the mock-remedy which left the real cause of complaint untouched. His lordship also felt deeply wounded by the disingenuousness of ministers which had led him into such a predicament, and wrote home demanding his discharge. Before it arrived, an attack of bilious fever, acting upon a delicate and sensitive frame, enfeebled by anxiety and chagrin, laid him in his grave. He left behind him a name endeared to the Virginians by his amiable manners, his liberal patronage of the arts, and, above all, by his zealous intercession for their rights. Washington himself testifies that he was inclined "to render every just and reasonable service to the people whom he governed." A statue to his memory was decreed by the House of Burgesses, to be erected in the area of the capitol. It is still to be seen, though in a mutilated condition, in Williamsburg, the old seat of government, and a county in Virginia continues to bear his honored name.

CHAPTER XXXI.

EXPEDITION OF WASHINGTON TO THE OHIO, IN
BEHALF OF SOLDIERS' CLAIMS—UNEASY STATE OF
THE FRONTIER—VISIT TO FORT PITT—GEORGE
CROGHAN—HIS MISHAPS DURING PONTIAC'S WAR—
WASHINGTON DESCENDS THE OHIO—SCENES AND
ADVENTURES ALONG THE RIVER—INDIAN HUNTING
CAMP—INTERVIEW WITH AN OLD SACHEM AT THE
MOUTH OF THE KANAWHA—RETURN—CLAIMS OF
STOBO AND VAN BRAAM—LETTER TO COLONEL
GEORGE MUSE.

In the midst of these popular turmoils, Washington was
induced, by public as well as private considerations, to make
another expedition to the Ohio. He was one of the Virginia Board
of Commissioners, appointed, at the close of the late war, to settle
the military accounts of the colony. Among the claims which came
before the board, were those of the officers and soldiers who had
engaged to serve until peace, under the proclamation of Governor
Dinwiddie, holding forth a bounty of two hundred thousand acres
of land, to be apportioned among them according to rank. Those
claims were yet unsatisfied, for governments, like individuals, are
slow to pay off in peaceful times the debts incurred while in the
fighting mood. Washington became the champion of those claims,
and an opportunity now presented itself for their liquidation. The
Six Nations, by a treaty in 1768, had ceded to the British crown, in
consideration of a sum of money, all the lands possessed by them
south of the Ohio. Land offices would soon be opened for the
sale of them. Squatters and speculators were already preparing to
swarm in, set up their marks on the choicest spots, and establish
what were called pre-emption rights. Washington determined at

once to visit the lands thus ceded; affix his mark on such tracts as he should select, and apply for a grant from government in behalf of the "soldier's claim."

The expedition would be attended with some degree of danger. The frontier was yet in an uneasy state. It is true some time had elapsed since the war of Pontiac, but some of the Indian tribes were almost ready to resume the hatchet. The Delawares, Shawnees, and Mingoes, complained that the Six Nations had not given them their full share of the consideration money of the late sale, and they talked of exacting the deficiency from the white men who came to settle in what had been their hunting-grounds. Traders, squatters, and other adventurers into the wilderness, were occasionally murdered, and further troubles were apprehended.

Washington had for a companion in this expedition his friend and neighbor, Dr. Craik, and it was with strong community of feeling they looked forward peaceably to revisit the scenes of their military experience. They set out on the 5th of October with three negro attendants, two belonging to Washington, and one to the doctor. The whole party was mounted, and there was a led horse for the baggage.

After twelve days' travelling they arrived at Fort Pitt (late Fort Duquesne). It was garrisoned by two companies of royal Irish, commanded by a Captain Edmonson. A hamlet of about twenty log-houses, inhabited by Indian traders, had sprung up within three hundred yards of the fort, and was called "the town." It was the embryo city of Pittsburg, now so populous. At one of the houses, a tolerable frontier inn, they took up their quarters; but during their brief sojourn, they were entertained with great hospitality at the fort.

Here at dinner Washington met his old acquaintance, George Croghan, who had figured in so many capacities and experienced so many vicissitudes on the frontier. He was now Colonel Croghan, deputy-agent to Sir William Johnson, and had his residence—or seat, as Washington terms it—on the banks of the Allegany River, about four miles from the fort.

Croghan had experienced troubles and dangers during the Pontiac war, both from white man and savage. At one time, while he was convoying presents from Sir William to the Delawares and Shawnees, his caravan was set upon and plundered by a band of backwoodsmen of Pennsylvania—men resembling Indians in garb and habits, and fully as lawless. At another time, when encamped at the mouth of the Wabash with some of his Indian allies, a band of Kickapoos, supposing the latter to be Cherokees, their deadly enemies, rushed forth from the woods with horrid yells, shot down several of his companions, and wounded himself. It must be added, that no white men could have made more ample apologies than did the Kickapoos, when they discovered that they had fired upon friends.

Another of Croghan's perils was from the redoubtable Pontiac himself. That chieftain had heard of his being on a mission to win off, by dint of presents, the other sachems of the conspiracy, and declared, significantly, that he had a large kettle boiling in which he intended to seethe the ambassador. It was fortunate for Croghan that he did not meet with the formidable chieftain while in this exasperated mood. He subsequently encountered him when Pontiac's spirits were broken by reverses. They smoked the pipe of peace together, and the colonel claimed the credit of having, by his diplomacy, persuaded the sachem to bury the hatchet.

On the day following the repast at the fort, Washington visited Croghan at his abode on the Allegany River, where he found several of the chiefs of the Six Nations assembled. One of them, the White Mingo by name, made him a speech, accompanied, as usual, by a belt of wampum. Some of his companions, he said, remembered to have seen him in 1753, when he came on his embassy to the French commander; most of them had heard of him. They had now come to welcome him to their country. They wished the people of Virginia to consider them as friends and brothers, linked together in one chain, and requested him to inform the governor of their desire to live in peace and harmony with the white men. As to certain unhappy differences which had taken place between them on the frontiers, they were all made up, and, they hoped, forgotten.

Washington accepted the "speech-belt," and made a suitable reply, assuring the chiefs that nothing was more desired by the people of Virginia than to live with them on terms of the strictest friendship.

At Pittsburg the travellers left their horses, and embarked in a large canoe, to make a voyage down the Ohio as far as the Great Kanawha. Colonel Croghan engaged two Indians for their service, and an interpreter named John Nicholson. The colonel and some of the officers of the garrison accompanied them as far as

Logstown, the scene of Washington's early diplomacy, and his first interview with the half-king. Here they breakfasted together; after which they separated, the colonel and his companions cheering the voyagers from the shore, as the canoe was borne off by the current of the beautiful Ohio.

It was now the hunting season, when the Indians leave their towns, set off with their families, and lead a roving life in cabins and hunting-camps along the river; shifting from place to place, as game abounds or decreases, and often extending their migrations two or three hundred miles down the stream. The women were as dexterous as the men in the management of the canoe, but were generally engaged in the domestic labors of the lodge while their husbands were abroad hunting.

Washington's propensities as a sportsman had here full play. Deer were continually to be seen coming down to the water's edge to drink, or browsing along the shore; there were innumerable flocks of wild turkeys, and streaming flights of ducks and geese; so that as the voyagers floated along, they were enabled to load their canoe with game. At night they encamped on the river bank, lit their fire and made a sumptuous hunter's repast. Washington always relished this wild-wood life; and the present had that spice of danger in it, which has a peculiar charm for adventurous minds. The great object of his expedition, however, is evinced in his constant notes on the features and character of the country; the quality of the soil as indicated by the nature of the trees, and the level tracts fitted for settlements.

About seventy-five miles below Pittsburg the voyagers landed at a Mingo town, which they found in a stir of warlike preparation— sixty of the warriors being about to set off on a foray into the Cherokee country against the Catawbas.

Here the voyagers were brought to a pause by a report that two white men, traders, had been murdered about thirty-eight miles further down the river. Reports of the kind were not to be treated lightly. Indian faith was uncertain along the frontier, and white men were often shot down in the wilderness for plunder or revenge. On the following day the report moderated. Only one man was said to have been killed, and that not by Indians; so Washington determined to continue forward until he could obtain correct information in the matter.

On the 24th, about 3 o'clock in the afternoon, the voyagers arrived at Captema Creek, at the mouth of which the trader was said to have been killed. As all was quiet and no one to be seen, they agreed to encamp, while Nicholson the interpreter, and one of the Indians, repaired to a village a few miles up the creek to inquire about the murder. They found but two old women at the village. The men were all absent, hunting. The interpreter returned to camp in the evening, bringing the truth of the murderous tale. A trader had fallen a victim to his temerity, having been drowned in attempting, in company with another, to swim his horse across the Ohio.

Two days more of voyaging brought them to an Indian hunting camp, near the mouth of the Muskingum. Here it was necessary to land and make a ceremonious visit, for the chief of the hunting party was Kiashuta, a Seneca sachem, the head of the river tribes. He was noted to have been among the first to raise the hatchet in Pontiac's conspiracy, and almost equally vindictive with that potent warrior. As Washington approached the chieftain, he recognized him for one of the Indians who had accompanied him on his mission to the French in 1753.

Kiashuta retained a perfect recollection of the youthful ambassador, though seventeen years had matured him into thoughtful manhood. With hunter's hospitality he gave him a quarter of a fine buffalo just slain, but insisted that they should encamp together for the night; and in order not to retard him, moved with his own party to a good camping place some distance down the river. Here they had long talks and council-fires over night and in the morning, with all the "tedious ceremony," says Washington, "which the Indians observe in their counsellings and speeches." Kiashuta had heard of what had passed between Washington and the "White Mingo," and other sachems, at Colonel Croghan's, and was eager to express his own desire for peace and friendship with Virginia, and fair dealings with her traders; all which Washington promised to report faithfully to the governor. It was not until a late hour in the morning that he was enabled to bring these conferences to a close, and pursue his voyage.

At the mouth of the Great Kanawha the voyagers encamped for a day or two to examine the lands in the neighborhood, and Washington set up his mark upon such as he intended to claim on behalf of the soldiers' grant. It was a fine sporting country, having small lakes or grassy ponds abounding with water-fowl, such as ducks, geese, and swans. Flocks of turkeys, as usual; and, for larger game, deer and buffalo; so that their camp abounded with provisions.

Here Washington was visited by an old sachem, who approached him with great reverence, at the head of several of his tribe, and addressed him through Nicholson, the interpreter. He had heard, he said, of his being in that part of the country, and had come from a great distance to see him. On further discourse, the sachem made known that he was one of the warriors in the service of the French, who lay in ambush on the banks of the Monongahela and wrought such havoc in Braddock's army. He declared that he and his young men had singled out Washington, as he made himself conspicuous riding about the field of battle with the general's orders, and had fired at him repeatedly, but without success; whence they had concluded that he was under the protection of the Great Spirit, had a charmed life, and could not be slain in battle.

At the Great Kanawha Washington's expedition down the Ohio terminated; having visited all the points he wished to examine. His return to Fort Pitt, and thence homeward, affords no incident worthy of note. The whole expedition, however, was one of that hardy and adventurous kind, mingled with practical purposes, in which he delighted. This winter voyage down the Ohio in a canoe, with the doctor for a companion and two Indians for crew, through regions yet insecure from the capricious hostility of prowling savages, is not one of the least striking of his frontier "experiences." The hazardous nature of it was made apparent shortly afterwards by another outbreak of the Ohio tribes; one of its bloodiest actions took place on the very banks of the Great Kanawha, in which Colonel Lewis and a number of brave Virginians lost their lives.

NOTE.

In the final adjustment of claims under Governor Dinwiddie's proclamation, Washington, acting on behalf of the officers and soldiers, obtained grants for the lands he had marked out in the course of his visit to the Ohio. Fifteen thousand acres were awarded to a field-officer, nine thousand to a captain, six thousand to a subaltern, and so on. Among the claims which he entered were those of Stobo and Van Braam, the hostages in the capitulation at the Great Meadows. After many vicissitudes they were now in London, and nine thousand acres were awarded to each of them. Their domains were ultimately purchased by Washington through his London agent.

Another claimant was Colonel George Muse, Washington's early instructor in military science. His claim was admitted with difficulty, for he stood accused of having acted the part of a poltroon in the campaign, and Washington seems to have considered the charge well founded. Still he appears to have been dissatisfied with the share of land assigned him, and to have written to Washington somewhat rudely on the subject. His letter is not extant, but we subjoin Washington's reply almost entire, as a specimen of the caustic pen he could wield under a mingled emotion of scorn and indignation.

"Sir,—Your impertinent letter was delivered to me yesterday. As I am not accustomed to receive such from any man, nor would have taken the same language from you personally, without letting you feel some marks of my resentment, I advise you to be cautious in writing me a second of the same tenor; for though I understand you were drunk when you did it, yet give me leave to tell you that drunkenness is no excuse for rudeness. But for your stupidity and sottishness you might have known, by attending to the public gazette, that you had your full quantity of ten thousand acres of land allowed you; that is, nine thousand and seventy-three acres in the great tract, and the remainder in the small tract.

"But suppose you had really fallen short, do you think your superlative merit entitles you to greater indulgence than others? Or, if it did, that I was to make it good to you, when it was at the option of the governor and council to allow but five hundred acres in the whole, if they had been so inclined? If either of these should happen to be your opinion, I am very well convinced that you will be singular in it; and all my concern is that I ever engaged myself in behalf of so ungrateful and dirty a fellow as you are."

N.B.—The above is from the letter as it exists in the archives of the Department of State at Washington. It differs in two or three particulars from that published among Washington's writings.

CHAPTER XXXII.

LORD DUNMORE GOVERNOR OF VIRGINIA—PIQUES
THE PRIDE OF THE VIRGINIANS—OPPOSITION OF
THE ASSEMBLY—CORRESPONDING COMMITTEES—
DEATH OF MISS CUSTIS—WASHINGTON'S
GUARDIANSHIP OF JOHN PARKE CUSTIS—HIS
OPINIONS AS TO PREMATURE TRAVEL AND
PREMATURE MARRIAGE.

The discontents of Virginia, which had been partially soothed by the amiable administration of Lord Botetourt, were irritated anew under his successor, the Earl of Dunmore. This nobleman had for a short time held the government of New York. When appointed to that of Virginia, he lingered for several months at his former post. In the mean time, he sent his military secretary, Captain Foy, to attend to the despatch of business until his arrival; awarding to him a salary and fees to be paid by the colony.

The pride of the Virginians was piqued at his lingering at New York, as if he preferred its gayety and luxury to the comparative quiet and simplicity of Williamsburg. Their pride was still more piqued on his arrival, by what they considered haughtiness on his part. The spirit of the "Ancient Dominion" was roused, and his lordship experienced opposition at his very outset.

The first measure of the Assembly, at its opening, was to demand by what right he had awarded a salary and fees to his secretary without consulting it; and to question whether it was authorized by the crown.

His lordship had the good policy to rescind the unauthorized act, and in so doing mitigated the ire of the Assembly; but he lost no time in proroguing a body, which, from various symptoms, appeared to be too independent, and disposed to be untractable.

He continued to prorogue it from time to time, seeking in the interim to conciliate the Virginians, and soothe their irritated pride. At length, after repeated prorogations, he was compelled by circumstances to convene it on the 1st of March, 1773.

Washington was prompt in his attendance on the occasion; and foremost among the patriotic members, who eagerly availed themselves of this long wished for opportunity to legislate upon the general affairs of the colonies. One of their most important measures was the appointment of a committee of eleven persons, "whose business it should be to obtain the most clear and authentic intelligence of all such acts and resolutions of the British Parliament, or proceedings of administration, as may relate to or affect the British colonies, and to maintain with their sister colonies a correspondence and communication."

The plan thus proposed by their "noble, patriotic sister colony of Virginia,"[96] was promptly adopted by the people of Massachusetts, and soon met with general concurrence. These corresponding committees, in effect, became the executive power of the patriot party, producing the happiest concert of design and action throughout the colonies.

Notwithstanding the decided part taken by Washington in the popular movement, very friendly relations existed between him and Lord Dunmore. The latter appreciated his character, and sought to avail himself of his experience in the affairs of the province. It was even concerted that Washington should accompany his lordship on an extensive tour, which the latter intended to make in the course of the summer along the western frontier. A melancholy circumstance occurred to defeat this arrangement.

We have spoken of Washington's paternal conduct towards the two children of Mrs. Washington. The daughter, Miss Custis, had long been an object of extreme solicitude. She was of a fragile constitution, and for some time past had been in very declining health. Early in the present summer, symptoms indicated a rapid change for the worse. Washington was absent from home at the time. On his return to Mount Vernon, he found her in the last stage of consumption.

Though not a man given to bursts of sensibility, he is said on the present occasion to have evinced the deepest affliction;

---

96   Boston Town Records.

kneeling by her bedside, and pouring out earnest prayers for her recovery. She expired on the 19th of June, in the seventeenth year of her age. This, of course, put an end to Washington's intention of accompanying Lord Dunmore to the frontier; he remained at home to console Mrs. Washington in her affliction,—furnishing his lordship, however, with travelling hints and directions, and recommending proper guides. And here we will take occasion to give a few brief particulars of domestic affairs at Mount Vernon.

For a long time previous to the death of Miss Custis, her mother, despairing of her recovery, had centred her hopes in her son, John Parke Custis. This rendered Washington's guardianship of him a delicate and difficult task. He was lively, susceptible, and impulsive; had an independent fortune in his own right, and an indulgent mother, ever ready to plead in his behalf against wholesome discipline. He had been placed under the care and instruction of an Episcopal clergyman at Annapolis, but was occasionally at home, mounting his horse, and taking a part, while yet a boy, in the fox-hunts at Mount Vernon. His education had consequently been irregular and imperfect, and not such as Washington would have enforced had he possessed over him the absolute authority of a father. Shortly after the return of the latter from his tour to the Ohio, he was concerned to find that there was an idea entertained of sending the lad abroad, though but little more than sixteen years of age, to travel under the care of his clerical tutor. Through his judicious interference, the travelling scheme was postponed, and it was resolved to give the young gentleman's mind the benefit of a little preparatory home culture.

Little more than a year elapsed before the sallying impulses of the youth had taken a new direction. He was in love; what was more, he was engaged to the object of his passion, and on the high road to matrimony.

Washington now opposed himself to premature marriage as he had done to premature travel. A correspondence ensued between him and the young lady's father, Benedict Calvert, Esq. The match was a satisfactory one to all parties, but it was agreed, that it was expedient for the youth to pass a year or two previously at college. Washington accordingly accompanied him to New York, and placed him under the care of the Rev. Dr. Cooper, president of King's (now Columbia) College, to pursue his studies in that institution. All this occurred before the death of his sister. Within a year after that melancholy event, he became impatient for a union with the object of his choice. His mother, now more indulgent than ever to this, her only child, yielded her consent, and Washington no longer made opposition.

"It has been against my wishes," writes the latter to President Cooper, "that he should quit college in order that he may soon enter into a new scene of life, which I think he would be much fitter for some years hence than now. But having his own inclination, the desires of his mother, and the acquiescence of almost all his relatives to encounter, I did not care, as he is the last of the family, to push my opposition too far; I have, therefore, submitted to a kind of necessity."

The marriage was celebrated on the 3d of February, 1774, before the bridegroom was twenty-one years of age.

NOTE.

We are induced to subjoin extracts of two letters from Washington relative to young Custis. The first gives his objections to premature travel; the second to premature matrimony. Both are worthy of consideration in this country, where our young people have such a general disposition to "go ahead."

To the reverend Jonathan Boucher (the tutor of young Custis).

. . . "I cannot help giving it as my opinion, that his education, however advanced it may be for a youth of his age, is by no means ripe enough for a travelling tour; not that I think his becoming a mere scholar is a desirable education for a gentleman, but I conceive a knowledge of books is the basis upon which all other knowledge is to be built, and in travelling he is to become acquainted with men and things, rather than books. At present, however well versed he may be in the principles of the Latin language (which is not to be wondered at, as he began the study of it as soon as he could speak), he is unacquainted with several of the classic authors that might be useful to him. He is ignorant of Greek, the advantages of learning which I do not pretend to judge of; and he knows nothing of French, which is absolutely necessary to him as a traveller. He has little or no acquaintance with arithmetic, and is totally ignorant of the mathematics—than which, at least, so much of them as relates to surveying, nothing can be more essentially necessary to any man possessed of a large landed estate, the bounds of some part or other of which are always in controversy. Now whether he has time between this and next spring to acquire a sufficient knowledge of these studies, I leave you to judge; as, also, whether a boy of seventeen years old (which will be his age next November), can have any just notions of the end and design of travelling. I have already given it as my opinion that it would be precipitating this event, unless he were to go immediately to the university for a couple of years; in which case he could see nothing of America; which might be a disadvantage to him, as it is to be expected that every man, who travels with a view of observing the laws and customs of other countries, should be able to give some description of the situation and government of his own."

The following are extracts from the letter to Benedict Calvert, Esq., the young lady's father:

"I write to you on a subject of importance, and of no small embarrassment to me; My son-in-law and ward, Mr. Custis, has, as I have been informed, paid his addresses to your second daughter; and having made some progress in her affections, has solicited her in marriage. How far a union of this sort may be agreeable to you, you best can tell; but I should think myself wanting in candor, were I not to confess that Miss Nelly's amiable qualities are acknowledged on all hands, and that an alliance with your family will be pleasing to his.

"This acknowledgment being made, you must permit me to add, sir, that at this, or in any short time, his youth, inexperience, and unripened education are, and will be, insuperable obstacles, in my opinion, to the completion of the marriage. As his guardian, I conceive it my indispensable duty to endeavor to carry him through a regular course of education (many branches of which, I am sorry to say, he is totally deficient in), and to guide his youth to a more advanced age, before an event, on which his own peace and the happiness of another are to depend, takes place. . . . If the affection which they have avowed for each other is fixed upon a solid basis, it will receive no diminution in the course of two or three years; in which time he may prosecute his studies, and thereby render himself more deserving of the lady, and useful to society. If, unfortunately, as they are both young, there should be an abatement of affection on either side, or both, it had better precede than follow marriage.

"Delivering my sentiments thus freely, will not, I hope, lead you into a belief that I am desirous of breaking off the match. To postpone it is all I have in view; for I shall recommend to the young gentleman, with the warmth that becomes a man of honor, to consider himself as much engaged to your daughter, as if the indissoluble knot were tied; and as the surest means of effecting this, to apply himself closely to his studies, by which he will, in a great measure, avoid those little flirtations with other young ladies, that may, by dividing the attention, contribute not a little to divide the affection."

CHAPTER XXXIII.

LORD NORTH'S BILL FAVORING THE EXPORTATION
OF TEAS—SHIPS FREIGHTED WITH TEA TO THE
COLONIES—SENT BACK FROM SOME OF THE
PORTS—TEA DESTROYED AT BOSTON—PASSAGE OF
THE BOSTON PORT BILL—SESSION OF THE HOUSE
OF BURGESSES—SPLENDID OPENING—BURST
OF INDIGNATION AT THE PORT BILL—HOUSE
DISSOLVED—RESOLUTIONS AT THE RALEIGH
TAVERN—PROJECT OF A GENERAL CONGRESS—
WASHINGTON AND LORD DUNMORE—THE PORT
BILL GOES INTO EFFECT—GENERAL GAGE AT
BOSTON—LEAGUE AND COVENANT.

The general covenant throughout the colonies against the use
of taxed tea, had operated disastrously against the interests of the
East India Company, and produced an immense accumulation of
the proscribed article in their warehouses. To remedy this, Lord
North brought in a bill (1773), by which the company were allowed
to export their teas from England to any part whatever, without
paying export duty. This, by enabling them to offer their teas at a
low price in the colonies would, he supposed, tempt the Americans
to purchase large quantities, thus relieving the company, and at the
same time benefiting the revenue by the impost duty. Confiding in
the wisdom of this policy, the company disgorged their warehouses,
freighted several ships with tea, and sent them to various parts of
the colonies. This brought matters to a crisis. One sentiment, one
determination, pervaded the whole continent. Taxation was to
receive its definitive blow. Whoever submitted to it was an enemy
to his country. From New York and Philadelphia the ships were
sent back, unladen, to London. In Charleston the tea was unloaded,

and stored away in cellars and other places, where it perished. At Boston the action was still more decisive. The ships anchored in the harbor. Some small parcels of tea were brought on shore, but the sale of them was prohibited. The captains of the ships, seeing the desperate state of the case, would have made sail back for England, but they could not obtain the consent of the consignees, a clearance at the custom-house, or a passport from the governor to clear the fort. It was evident, the tea was to be forced upon the people of Boston, and the principle of taxation established.

To settle the matter completely, and prove that, on a point of principle, they were not to be trifled with, a number of the inhabitants, disguised as Indians, boarded the ships in the night (18th December), broke open all the chests of tea, and emptied the contents into the sea. This was no rash and intemperate proceeding of a mob, but the well-considered, though resolute act of sober, respectable citizens, men of reflection, but determination. The whole was done calmly, and in perfect order; after which the actors in the scene dispersed without tumult, and returned quietly to their homes.

The general opposition of the colonies to the principle of taxation had given great annoyance to government, but this individual act concentrated all its wrath upon Boston. A bill was forthwith passed in Parliament (commonly called the Boston port bill), by which all lading and unlading of goods, wares, and merchandise, were to cease in that town and harbor, on and after the 4th of June, and the officers of the customs to be transferred to Salem.

Another law, passed soon after, altered the charter of the province, decreeing that all counsellors, judges, and magistrates, should be appointed by the crown, and hold office during the royal pleasure.

This was followed by a third, intended for the suppression of riots; and providing that any person indicted for murder, or other capital offence, committed in aiding the magistracy, might be sent by the governor to some other colony, or to Great Britain, for trial.

Such was the bolt of Parliamentary wrath fulminated against the devoted town of Boston. Before it fell there was a session in May, of the Virginia House of Burgesses. The social position of Lord Dunmore had been strengthened in the province by the arrival of his lady, and a numerous family of sons and daughters. The old Virginia aristocracy had vied with each other in hospitable attentions to the family. A court circle had sprung up. Regulations had been drawn up by a herald, and published officially, determining the rank and precedence of civil and military officers, and their wives. The aristocracy of the Ancient Dominion was furbishing up its former splendor. Carriages and four rolled into the streets of Williamsburg, with horses handsomely caparisoned, bringing the wealthy planters and their families to the seat of government.

Washington arrived in Williamsburg on the 16th, and dined with the governor on the day of his arrival, having a distinguished position in the court circle, and being still on terms of intimacy with his lordship. The House of Burgesses was opened in form, and one of its first measures was an address of congratulation to the governor, on the arrival of his lady. It was followed up by an agreement among the members to give her ladyship a splendid ball, on the 27th of the month.

All things were going on smoothly and smilingly, when a letter, received through the corresponding committee, brought intelligence of the vindictive measure of Parliament, by which the port of Boston was to be closed on the approaching 1st of June.

The letter was read in the House of Burgesses, and produced a general burst of indignation. All other business was thrown aside, and this became the sole subject of discussion. A protest against this and other recent acts of Parliament was entered upon the journal of the House, and a resolution was adopted, on the 24th of May, setting apart the 1st of June as a day of fasting, prayer, and humiliation; in which the divine interposition was to be implored, to avert the heavy calamity threatening destruction to their rights, and all the evils of civil war; and to give the people one heart and one mind in firmly opposing every injury to American liberties.

On the following morning, while the Burgesses were engaged in animated debate, they were summoned to attend Lord Dunmore in the council chamber, where he made them the following laconic speech: "Mr. Speaker, and Gentlemen of the House of Burgesses: I have in my hand a paper, published by order of your House, conceived in such terms, as reflect highly upon his majesty, and the

Parliament of Great Britain, which makes it necessary for me to dissolve you, and you are dissolved accordingly."

As on a former occasion, the Assembly, though dissolved, was not dispersed. The members adjourned to the long room of the old Raleigh tavern, and passed resolutions, denouncing the Boston port bill as a most dangerous attempt to destroy the constitutional liberty and rights of all North America; recommending their countrymen to desist from the use, not merely of tea, but of all kinds of East Indian commodities: pronouncing an attack on one of the colonies, to enforce arbitrary taxes, an attack on all; and ordering the committee of correspondence to communicate with the other corresponding committees, on the expediency of appointing deputies from the several colonies of British America, to meet annually in GENERAL CONGRESS, at such place as might be deemed expedient, to deliberate on such measures as the united interests of the colonies might require.

This was the first recommendation of a General Congress by any public assembly, though it had been previously proposed in town meetings at New York and Boston. A resolution to the same effect was passed in the Assembly of Massachusetts before it was aware of the proceedings of the Virginia Legislature. The measure recommended met with prompt and general concurrence throughout the colonies, and the fifth day of September next ensuing was fixed upon for the meeting of the first Congress, which was to be held at Philadelphia.

Notwithstanding Lord Dunmore's abrupt dissolution of the House of Burgesses, the members still continued on courteous terms with him, and the ball which they had decreed early in the session in honor of Lady Dunmore, was celebrated on the 27th with unwavering gallantry.

As to Washington, widely as he differed from Lord Dunmore on important points of policy, his intimacy with him remained uninterrupted. By memorandums in his diary it appears that he dined and passed the evening at his lordship's on the 25th, the very day of the meeting at the Raleigh tavern. That he rode out with him to his farm, and breakfasted there with him on the 26th, and on the evening of the 27th attended the ball given to her ladyship. Such was the well-bred decorum that seemed to quiet the turbulence of popular excitement, without checking the full and firm expression of popular opinion.

On the 29th, two days after the ball, letters arrived from Boston giving the proceedings of a town meeting, recommending that a general league should be formed throughout the colonies suspending all trade with Great Britain. But twenty-five members of the late House of Burgesses, including Washington, were at that time remaining in Williamsburg. They held a meeting on the following day, at which Peyton Randolph presided as moderator. After some discussion it was determined to issue a printed circular, bearing their signatures, and calling a meeting of all the members of the late House of Burgesses, on the 1st of August, to take into consideration this measure of a general league. The circular recommended them, also, to collect, in the mean time, the sense of their respective counties.

Washington was still at Williamsburg on the 1st of June, the day when the port bill was to be enforced at Boston. It was ushered in by the tolling of bells, and observed by all true patriots as a day of fasting and humiliation. Washington notes in his diary that he fasted rigidly, and attended the services appointed in the church. Still his friendly intercourse with the Dunmore family was continued during the remainder of his sojourn in Williamsburg, where he was detained by business until the 20th, when he set out on his return to Mount Vernon.

In the mean time the Boston port bill had been carried into effect. On the 1st of June the harbor of Boston was closed at noon, and all business ceased. The two other parliamentary acts altering the charter of Massachusetts were to be enforced. No public meetings, excepting the annual town meetings in March and May, were to be held without permission of the governor.

General Thomas Gage had recently been appointed to the military command of Massachusetts, and the carrying out of these offensive acts. He was the same officer who, as lieutenant-colonel, had led the advance guard on the field of Braddock's defeat. Fortune had since gone well with him. Rising in the service, he had been governor of Montreal, and had succeeded Amherst in the command of the British forces on this continent. He was linked to the country also by domestic ties, having married into one of the most respectable families of New Jersey. In the various situations in which he had hitherto been placed he had won esteem, and rendered himself popular. Not much was expected from him in his present post by those who knew him well. William Smith, the historian, speaking of him to Adams, "Gage," said he, "was a good-natured, peaceable, sociable man while here (in New York), but altogether unfit for a governor of Massachusetts. He will lose all the character he has acquired as a man, a gentleman, and a general, and dwindle down into a mere scribbling governor—a mere Bernard or Hutchinson."

With all Gage's experience in America, he had formed a most erroneous opinion of the character of the people. "The Americans," said he to the king, "will be lions only as long as the English are lambs;" and he engaged, with five regiments, to keep Boston quiet!

The manner in which his attempts to enforce the recent acts of Parliament were resented, showed how egregiously he was in error. At the suggestion of the Assembly, a paper was circulated through the province by the committee of correspondence, entitled "a solemn league and covenant," the subscribers to which bound themselves to break off all intercourse with Great Britain from the 1st of August, until the colony should be restored to the enjoyment of its chartered rights; and to renounce all dealings with those who should refuse to enter into this compact.

The very title of league and covenant had an ominous sound, and startled General Gage. He issued a proclamation, denouncing it as illegal and traitorous. Furthermore, he encamped a force of infantry and artillery on Boston Common, as if prepared to enact the lion. An alarm spread through the adjacent country. "Boston is to be blockaded! Boston is to be reduced to obedience by force or famine!" The spirit of the yeomanry was aroused. They sent in word to the inhabitants promising to come to their aid if necessary; and urging them to stand fast to the faith. Affairs were coming to a crisis. It was predicted that the new acts of Parliament would bring on "a most important and decisive trial."

CHAPTER XXXIV.

WASHINGTON CHAIRMAN OF A POLITICAL MEETING—CORRESPONDENCE WITH BRYAN FAIRFAX—PATRIOTIC RESOLUTIONS—WASHINGTON'S OPINIONS ON PUBLIC AFFAIRS—NON-IMPORTATION SCHEME—CONVENTION AT WILLIAMSBURG—WASHINGTON APPOINTED A DELEGATE TO THE GENERAL CONGRESS—LETTER FROM BRYAN FAIRFAX—PERPLEXITIES OF GENERAL GAGE AT BOSTON.

Shortly after Washington's return to Mount Vernon, in the latter part of June, he presided as moderator at a meeting of the inhabitants of Fairfax County, wherein, after the recent acts of Parliament had been discussed, a committee was appointed, with himself as chairman, to draw up resolutions expressive of the sentiments of the present meeting, and to report the same at a general meeting of the county, to be held in the court-house on the 18th of July.

The course that public measures were taking shocked the loyal feelings of Washington's valued friend, Bryan Fairfax, of Tarlston Hall, a younger brother of George William, who was absent in England. He was a man of liberal sentiments, but attached to the ancient rule; and, in a letter to Washington, advised a petition to the throne, which would give Parliament an opportunity to repeal the offensive acts.

"I would heartily join you in your political sentiments," writes Washington in reply, "as far as relates to a humble and dutiful petition to the throne, provided there was the most distant hope of success. But have we not tried this already? Have we not addressed the lords, and remonstrated to the commons? And to what end?

Does it not appear as clear as the sun in its meridian brightness that there is a regular, systematic plan to fix the right and practice of taxation upon us? . . . Is not the attack upon the liberty and property of the people of Boston, before restitution of the loss to the India Company was demanded, a plain and self-evident proof of what they are aiming at? Do not the subsequent bills for depriving the Massachusetts Bay of its charter, and for transporting offenders to other colonies or to Great Britain for trial, where it is impossible, from the nature of things, that justice can be obtained, convince us that the administration is determined to stick at nothing to carry its point? Ought we not, then, to put our virtue and fortitude to the severest tests?"

The committee met according to appointment, with Washington as chairman. The resolutions framed at the meeting insisted, as usual, on the right of self-government, and the principle that taxation and representation were in their nature inseparable. That the various acts of Parliament for raising revenue; taking away trials by jury; ordering that persons might be tried in a different country from that in which the cause of accusation originated; closing the port of Boston; abrogating the charter of Massachusetts Bay, &c., &c.,—were all part of a premeditated design and system to introduce arbitrary government into the colonies. That the sudden and repeated dissolutions of Assemblies whenever they presumed to examine the illegality of ministerial mandates, or deliberated on the violated rights of their constituents, were part of the same system, and calculated and intended to drive the people of the colonies to a state of desperation, and to dissolve the compact by which their ancestors bound themselves and their posterity to remain dependent on the British crown. The resolutions, furthermore, recommended the most perfect union and co-operation among the colonies; solemn covenants with respect to non-importation and non-intercourse, and a renunciation of all dealings with any colony, town, or province, that should refuse to agree to the plan adopted by the General Congress.

They also recommended a dutiful petition and remonstrance from the Congress to the king, asserting their constitutional rights and privileges; lamenting the necessity of entering into measures that might be displeasing; declaring their attachment to his person, family, and government, and their desire to continue in dependence upon Great Britain; beseeching him not to reduce his faithful subjects of America to desperation, and to reflect, that *from our sovereign there can be but one appeal.*

These resolutions are the more worthy of note, as expressive of the opinions and feelings of Washington at this eventful time, if not being entirely dictated by him. The last sentence is of awful import, suggesting the possibility of being driven to an appeal to arms.

Bryan Fairfax, who was aware of their purport, addressed a long letter to Washington, on the 17th of July, the day preceding that in which they were to be reported by the committee, stating his objections to several of them, and requesting that his letter might be publicly read. The letter was not received until after the committee had gone to the court-house on the 18th, with the resolutions revised, corrected, and ready to be reported. Washington glanced over the letter hastily, and handed it round to several of the gentlemen present. They, with one exception, advised that it should not be publicly read, as it was not likely to make any converts, and was repugnant, as some thought, to every principle they were contending for. Washington forbore, therefore, to give it any further publicity.

The resolutions reported by the committee were adopted, and Washington was chosen a delegate to represent the county at the General Convention of the province, to be held at Williamsburg on the 1st of August. After the meeting had adjourned, he felt doubtful whether Fairfax might not be dissatisfied that his letter had not been read, as he requested, to the county at large; he wrote to him, therefore, explaining the circumstances which prevented it; at the same time replying to some of the objections which Fairfax had made to certain of the resolutions. He reiterated his belief that an appeal would be ineffectual. "What is it we are contending against?" asked he; "Is it against paying the duty of threepence per pound on tea because burdensome? No, it is the right only, that we have all along disputed; and to this end, we have already petitioned his majesty in as humble and dutiful a manner as subjects could do. Nay, more, we applied to the House of Lords and House of Commons in their different legislative capacities, setting forth that, as Englishmen, we could not be deprived of this essential and valuable part of our constitution. . . .

"The conduct of the Boston people could not justify the rigor of their measures, unless there had been a requisition of payment, and refusal of it; nor did that conduct require an act to deprive the government of Massachusetts Bay of their charter, or to exempt offenders from trial in the places where offences were committed, as there was not, nor could there be, a single instance produced to manifest the necessity of it. Are not all these things evident proofs of a fixed and uniform plan to tax us? If we want further proofs, do not all the debates in the House of Commons serve to confirm this? And has not General Gage's conduct since his arrival, in stopping the address of his council, and publishing a proclamation, more becoming a Turkish bashaw than an English governor, declaring it treason to associate in any manner by which the commerce of Great Britain is to be affected,—has not this exhibited an unexampled testimony of the most despotic system of tyranny that ever was practised in a free government?"

The popular measure on which Washington laid the greatest stress as a means of obtaining redress from government, was the non-importation scheme; "for I am convinced," said he, "as much as of my existence, that there is no relief for us but in their distress; and I think—at least I hope—that there is public virtue enough left among us to deny ourselves every thing but the bare necessaries of life to accomplish this end." At the same time, he forcibly condemned a suggestion that remittances to England should be withheld. "While we are accusing others of injustice," said he, "we should be just ourselves; and how this can be whilst we owe a considerable debt, and refuse payment of it to Great Britain is to me inconceivable: nothing but the last extremity can justify it."

On the 1st of August, the convention of representatives from all parts of Virginia assembled at Williamsburg. Washington appeared on behalf of Fairfax County, and presented the resolutions, already cited, as the sense of his constituents. He is said, by one who was present, to have spoken in support of them in a strain of uncommon eloquence, which shows how his latent ardor had been excited on the occasion, as eloquence was not in general among his attributes. It is evident, however, that he was roused to an unusual pitch of enthusiasm, for he is said to have declared that he was ready to raise one thousand men, subsist them at his own expense, and march at their head to the relief of Boston.[97]

The Convention was six days in session. Resolutions, in the same spirit with those passed in Fairfax County, were adopted, and Peyton Randolph, Richard Henry Lee, George Washington, Patrick Henry, Richard Bland, Benjamin Harrison, and Edmund Pendleton, were appointed delegates, to represent the people of Virginia in the General Congress.

Shortly after Washington's return from Williamsburg, he received a reply from Bryan Fairfax, to his last letter. Fairfax, who was really a man of liberal views, seemed anxious to vindicate himself from any suspicions of the contrary. In adverting to the partial suppression of his letter by some of the gentlemen of the committee: "I am uneasy to find," writes he, "that any one should look upon the letter sent down as repugnant to the principles we are contending for; and, therefore, when you have leisure, I shall take it as a favor if you will let me know wherein it was thought so. I beg leave to look upon you as a friend, and it is a great relief to unbosom one's thoughts to a friend. Besides, the information, and the correction of my errors, which I may obtain from a correspondence, are great inducements to it. For I am convinced that no man in the colony wishes its prosperity more, would go greater lengths to serve it, or is, at the same time, a better subject to the crown. Pray excuse these compliments, they may be tolerable from a friend."[98]

The hurry of various occupations prevented Washington, in his reply, from entering into any further discussion of the popular theme. "I can only in general add," said he, "that an innate spirit of freedom first told me that the measures which the administration have for some time been, and now are violently pursuing, are opposed to every principle of natural justice; whilst much abler heads than my own have fully convinced me, that they are not only repugnant to natural right, but subversive of the laws and constitution of Great Britain itself. . . . I shall conclude with remarking that, if you disavow the right of Parliament to tax us, unrepresented as we

---

97   See information given to the elder Adams, by Mr. Lynch of South Carolina.—
       Adams's Diary.

98   Sparks. Washington's Writings, vol. ii., p. 329.

are, we only differ in the mode of opposition, and this difference principally arises from your belief that they (the Parliament I mean), want a decent opportunity to repeal the acts; whilst I am fully convinced that there has been a regular systematic plan to enforce them, and that nothing but unanimity and firmness in the colonies, which they did not expect, can prevent it. By the best advices from Boston, it seems that General Gage is exceedingly disconcerted at the quiet and steady conduct of the people of the Massachusetts Bay, and at the measures pursuing by the other governments. I dare say he expected to force those oppressed people into compliance, or irritate them to acts of violence before this, for a more colorable pretence of ruling that, and the other colonies, with a high hand."

Washington had formed a correct opinion of the position of General Gage. From the time of taking command at Boston, he had been perplexed how to manage its inhabitants. Had they been hot-headed, impulsive, and prone to paroxysm, his task would have been comparatively easy; but it was the cool, shrewd common sense, by which all their movements were regulated, that confounded him.

High-handed measures had failed of the anticipated effect. Their harbor had been thronged with ships; their town with troops. The port bill had put an end to commerce; wharves were deserted, warehouses closed; streets grass-grown and silent. The rich were growing poor, and the poor were without employ; yet the spirit of the people was unbroken. There was no uproar, however; no riots; every thing was awfully systematic and according to rule. Town meetings were held, in which public rights and public measures were eloquently discussed by John Adams, Josiah Quincy, and other eminent men. Over these meetings Samuel Adams presided as moderator; a man clear in judgment, calm in conduct, inflexible in resolution; deeply grounded in civil and political history, and infallible on all points of constitutional law.

Alarmed at the powerful influence of these assemblages, government issued an act prohibiting them after the 1st of August. The act was evaded by convoking the meetings before that day, and *keeping them alive* indefinitely. Gage was at a loss how to act. It would not do to disperse these assemblages by force of arms; for, the people who composed them mingled the soldier with the polemic; and, like their prototypes, the covenanters of yore, if prone to argue, were as ready to fight. So the meetings continued to be held portinaciously. Faneuil Hall was at times unable to hold them, and they swarmed from that revolutionary hive into old South Church. The liberty tree became a rallying place for any popular movement, and a flag hoisted on it was saluted by all processions as the emblem of the popular cause.

Opposition to the new plan of government assumed a more violent aspect at the extremity of the province, and was abetted by Connecticut. "It is very high," writes Gage, (August 27th,) "in Berkshire County, and makes way rapidly to the rest. At Worcester they threaten resistance, purchase arms, provide powder, cast balls, and threaten to attack any troops who may oppose them. I apprehend I shall soon have to march a body of troops into that township."

The time appointed for the meeting of the General Congress at Philadelphia was now at hand. Delegates had already gone on from Massachusetts. "It is not possible to guess," writes Gage, "what a body composed of such heterogeneous matter will determine; but the members from hence, I am assured, will promote the most haughty and insolent resolves; for their plan has ever been, by threats and high-sounding sedition, to terrify and intimidate."

CHAPTER XXXV.

MEETING OF THE FIRST CONGRESS—OPENING
CEREMONIES—ELOQUENCE OF PATRICK HENRY AND
HENRY LEE—DECLARATORY RESOLUTION—BILL
OF RIGHTS—STATE PAPERS—CHATHAM'S OPINIONS
OF CONGRESS—WASHINGTON'S CORRESPONDENCE
WITH CAPT. MACKENZIE—VIEWS WITH RESPECT
TO INDEPENDENCE—DEPARTURE OF FAIRFAX FOR
ENGLAND.

When the time approached for the meeting of the General
Congress at Philadelphia, Washington was joined at Mount Vernon
by Patrick Henry and Edmund Pendleton, and they performed
the journey together on horseback. It was a noble companionship.
Henry was then in the youthful vigor and elasticity of his bounding
genius; ardent, acute, fanciful, eloquent. Pendleton, schooled in
public life, a veteran in council, with native force of intellect, and
habits of deep reflection. Washington, in the meridian of his days,
mature in wisdom, comprehensive in mind, sagacious in foresight.
Such were the apostles of liberty, repairing on their august pilgrimage
to Philadelphia from all parts of the land, to lay the foundations of
a mighty empire. Well may we say of that eventful period, "There
were giants in those days."

Congress assembled on Monday, the 5th of September, in
a large room in Carpenter's Hall. There were fifty-one delegates,
representing all the colonies excepting Georgia.

The meeting has been described as "awfully solemn." The
most eminent men of the various colonies, were now for the first
time brought together; they were known to each other by fame,
but were, personally, strangers. The object which had called them
together, was of incalculable magnitude. The liberties of no less

than three millions of people, with that of all their posterity, were staked on the wisdom and energy of their councils.[99]

"It is such an assembly," writes John Adams, who was present, "as never before came together on a sudden, in any part of the world. Here are fortunes, abilities, learning, eloquence, acuteness, equal to any I ever met with in my life. Here is a diversity of religions, educations, manners, interests, such as it would seem impossible to unite in one plan of conduct."

There being an inequality in the number of delegates from the different colonies, a question arose as to the mode of voting; whether by colonies, by the poll, or by interests.

Patrick Henry scouted the idea of sectional distinctions or individual interests. "All America," said he, "is thrown into one mass. Where are your landmarks—your boundaries of colonies? They are all thrown down. The distinctions between Virginians, Pennsylvanians, New Yorkers and New Englanders, are no more. *I am not a Virginian, but an American.*"[100]

After some debate, it was determined that each colony should have but one vote, whatever might be the number of its delegates. The deliberations of the House were to be with closed doors, and nothing but the resolves promulgated, unless by order of the majority.

To give proper dignity and solemnity to the proceedings of the House, it was moved on the following day, that each morning the session should be opened by prayer. To this it was demurred, that as the delegates were of different religious sects, they might not consent to join in the same form of worship.

Upon this, Mr. Samuel Adams arose and said: "He would willingly join in prayer with any gentleman of piety and virtue, whatever might be his cloth, provided he was a friend of his country;" and he moved that the reverend Mr. Duché, of Philadelphia, who answered to that description, might be invited to officiate as chaplain. This was one step towards unanimity of feeling, Mr. Adams being a strong Congregationalist, and Mr. Duché an eminent Episcopalian clergyman. The motion was carried into effect; the invitation was given and accepted.

---

99   Wirt's Life of Patrick Henry, p. 224.

100   J. Adams' Diary.

In the course of the day, a rumor reached Philadelphia that Boston had been cannonaded by the British. It produced a strong sensation; and when Congress met on the following morning (7th), the effect was visible in every countenance. The delegates from the east were greeted with a warmer grasp of the hand by their associates from the south.

The reverend Mr. Duché, according to invitation, appeared in his canonicals, attended by his clerk. The morning service of the Episcopal church was read with great solemnity, the clerk making the responses. The Psalter for the 7th day of the month includes the 35th Psalm, wherein David prays for protection against his enemies. "Plead my cause, O Lord, with them that strive with me: fight against them that fight against me.

"Take hold of shield and buckler and stand up for my help.

"Draw out, also, the spear, and stop the way of them that persecute me. Say unto my soul, I am thy salvation," &c., &c.

The imploring words of this psalm, spoke the feelings of all hearts present; but especially of those from New England. John Adams writes in a letter to his wife: "You must remember this was the morning after we heard the horrible rumor of the cannonade of Boston. I never saw a greater effect upon an audience. It seemed as if heaven had ordained that psalm to be read on that morning. After this, Mr. Duché unexpectedly struck out into an extemporary prayer, which filled the bosom of every man present. Episcopalian as he is, Dr. Cooper himself never prayed with such fervor, such ardor, such earnestness and pathos, and in language so eloquent and sublime, for America, for the Congress, for the province of Massachusetts Bay, and especially the town of Boston. It has had an excellent effect upon every body here."[101]

It has been remarked that Washington was especially devout on this occasion—kneeling, while others stood up. In this, however, each, no doubt, observed the attitude in prayer to which he was accustomed. Washington knelt, being an Episcopalian.

The rumored attack upon Boston, rendered the service of the day deeply affecting to all present. They were one political family, actuated by one feeling, and sympathizing with the weal and woe of each individual member. The rumor proved to be erroneous; but it

---

101   John Adams' Correspondence and Diary.

had produced a most beneficial effect in calling forth and quickening the spirit of union, so vitally important in that assemblage.

Owing to closed doors, and the want of reporters, no record exists of the discussions and speeches made in the first Congress. Mr. Wirt, speaking from tradition, informs us that a long and deep silence followed the organization of that august body; the members looking round upon each other, individually reluctant to open a business so fearfully momentous. This "deep and deathlike silence" was beginning to become painfully embarrassing, when Patrick Henry arose. He faltered at first, as was his habit; but his exordium was impressive; and as he launched forth into a recital of colonial wrongs he kindled with his subject, until he poured forth one of those eloquent appeals which had so often shaken the House of Burgesses and gained him the fame of being the greatest orator of Virginia. He sat down, according to Mr. Wirt, amidst murmurs of astonishment and applause, and was now admitted, on every hand, to be the first orator of America. He was followed by Richard Henry Lee, who, according to the same writer, charmed the house with a different kind of eloquence, chaste and classical; contrasting, in its cultivated graces, with the wild and grand effusions of Henry. "The superior powers of these great men, however," adds he, "were manifested only in debate, and while general grievances were the topic; when called down from the heights of declamation to that severer test of intellectual excellence, the details of business, they found themselves in a body of cool-headed, reflecting, and most able men, by whom they were, in their turn, completely thrown into the shade."[102]

The first public measure of Congress was a resolution declaratory of their feelings with regard to the recent acts of Parliament, violating the rights of the people of Massachusetts, and of their determination to combine in resisting any force that might attempt to carry those acts into execution.

A committee of two from each province reported a series of resolutions, which were adopted and promulgated by Congress, as a "declaration of colonial rights." In this were enumerated their natural rights to the enjoyment of life, liberty, and property; and their rights as British subjects. Among the latter was participation

---

102   Wirt's Life of Patrick Henry.

in legislative councils. This they could not exercise through representatives in Parliament; they claimed, therefore, the power of legislating in their provincial assemblies; consenting, however, to such acts of Parliament as might be essential to the regulation of trade; but excluding all taxation, internal or external, for raising revenue in America.

The common law of England was claimed as a birthright, including the right of trial by a jury of the vicinage; of holding public meetings to consider grievances; and of petitioning the king. The benefits of all such statutes as existed at the time of the colonization were likewise claimed; together with the immunities and privileges granted by royal charters, or secured by provincial laws.

The maintenance of a standing army in any colony in time of peace, without the consent of its legislature, was pronounced contrary to law. The exercise of the legislative power in the colonies by a council appointed during pleasure by the crown, was declared to be unconstitutional, and destructive to the freedom of American legislation.

Then followed a specification of the acts of Parliament, passed during the reign of George III., infringing and violating these rights. These were: the sugar act; the stamp act; the two acts for quartering troops; the tea act; the act suspending the New York legislature; the two acts for the trial in Great Britain of offences committed in America; the Boston port bill; the act for regulating the government of Massachusetts, and the Quebec act.

"To these grievous acts and measures," it was added, "Americans cannot submit; but in hopes their fellow subjects in Great Britain will, on a revision of them, restore us to that state in which both countries found happiness and prosperity, we have, for the present, only resolved to pursue the following peaceable measures:

"1st. To enter into a non-importation, non-consumption, and non-exportation agreement, or association.

"2d. To prepare an address to the people of Great Britain, and a memorial to the inhabitants of British America.

"3d. To prepare a loyal address to his majesty."

The above-mentioned association was accordingly formed, and committees were to be appointed in every county, city, and town, to maintain it vigilantly and strictly.

Masterly state papers were issued by Congress in conformity to the resolutions: viz., a petition to the king, drafted by Mr. Dickinson, of Philadelphia; an address to the people of Canada by the same hand, inviting them to join the league of the colonies; another to the people of Great Britain, drafted by John Jay, of New York; and a memorial to the inhabitants of the British colonies by Richard Henry Lee, of Virginia.[103]

The Congress remained in session fifty-one days. Every subject, according to Adams, was discussed "with a moderation, an acuteness, and a minuteness equal to that of Queen Elizabeth's privy council."[104] The papers issued by it have deservedly been pronounced masterpieces of practical talent and political wisdom. Chatham, when speaking on the subject in the House of Lords, could not restrain his enthusiasm. "When your lordships," said he, "look at the papers transmitted to us from America; when you consider their decency, firmness, and wisdom, you cannot but respect their cause, and wish to make it your own. For myself, I must declare and avow that, in the master states of the world, I know not the people, or senate, who, in such a complication of difficult circumstances, can stand in preference to the delegates of America assembled in General Congress at Philadelphia."

From the secrecy that enveloped its discussions, we are ignorant of the part taken by Washington in the debates; the similarity of the resolutions, however, in spirit and substance to those of the Fairfax County meeting, in which he presided, and the coincidence of the measures adopted with those therein recommended, show that he had a powerful agency in the whole proceedings of this eventful assembly. Patrick Henry, being asked, on his return home, whom he considered the greatest man in Congress, replied: "If you speak of eloquence, Mr. Rutledge, of South Carolina, is by far the greatest orator; but if you speak of solid information and sound judgment, Colonel Washington is unquestionably the greatest man on that floor."

How thoroughly and zealously he participated in the feelings which actuated Congress in this memorable session, may be gathered from his correspondence with a friend enlisted in the

103   See Correspondence and Diary of J. Adams, vols. ii. and ix.
104   Letter to William Tudor, 29th Sept., 1774.

royal cause. This was Captain Robert Mackenzie, who had formerly served under him in his Virginia regiment during the French war, but now held a commission in the regular army, and was stationed among the British troops at Boston.

Mackenzie, in a letter, had spoken with loyal abhorrence of the state of affairs in the "unhappy province" of Massachusetts, and the fixed aim of its inhabitants at "total independence." "The rebellious and numerous meetings of men in arms," said he, "their scandalous and ungenerous attacks upon the best characters in the province, obliging them to save themselves by flight, and their repeated, but feeble threats, to dispossess the troops, have furnished sufficient reasons to General Gage to put the town in a formidable state of defence, about which we are now fully employed, and which will be shortly accomplished to their great mortification."

"Permit me," writes Washington in reply, "with the freedom of a friend (for you know I always esteemed you), to express my sorrow that fortune should place you in a service that must fix curses, to the latest posterity, upon the contrivers, and, if success (which, by the by, is impossible) accompanies it, execrations upon all those who have been instrumental in the execution. . . . When you condemn the conduct of the Massachusetts people, you reason from effects, not causes, otherwise you would not wonder at a people, who are every day receiving fresh proofs of a systematic assertion of an arbitrary power, deeply planned to overturn the laws and constitution of their country, and to violate the most essential and valuable rights of mankind, being irritated, and with difficulty restrained, from acts of the greatest violence and intemperance.

"For my own part, I view things in a very different point of light from the one in which you seem to consider them; and though you are led to believe, by venal men, that the people of Massachusetts are rebellious, setting up for independency, and what not, give me leave, my good friend, to tell you that you are abused, grossly abused. . . . I think I can announce it as a fact, that it is not the wish or interest of that government, or any other upon this continent, separately or collectively, to set up for independence; but this you may at the same time rely on, that none of them will ever submit to the loss of their valuable rights and privileges, which are essential to the happiness of every free state, and without which, life, liberty, and property, are rendered totally insecure.

"These, sir, being certain consequences, which must naturally result from the late acts of Parliament relative to America in general, and the government of Massachusetts in particular, is it to be wondered at that men who wish to avert the impending blow, should attempt to oppose its progress, or prepare for their defence, if it cannot be averted? Surely I may be allowed to answer in the negative; and give me leave to add, as my opinion, that more blood will be spilled on this occasion, if the ministry are determined to push matters to extremity, than history has ever yet furnished instances of in the annals of North America; and such a vital wound will be given to the peace of this great country, as time itself cannot cure, or eradicate the remembrance of."

In concluding, he repeats his views with respect to independence: "I am well satisfied that no such thing is desired by any thinking man in all North America; on the contrary, that it is the ardent wish of the warmest advocates for liberty, that peace and tranquillity, upon constitutional grounds, may be restored, and the horrors of civil discord prevented."[105]

This letter we have considered especially worthy of citation, from its being so full and explicit a declaration of Washington's sentiments and opinions at this critical juncture. His views on the question of independence are particularly noteworthy, from his being at this time in daily and confidential communication with the leaders of the popular movement, and among them with the delegates from Boston. It is evident that the filial feeling still throbbed toward the mother country, and a complete separation from her had not yet entered into the alternatives of her colonial children.

On the breaking up of Congress, Washington hastened back to Mount Vernon, where his presence was more than usually important to the happiness of Mrs. Washington, from the loneliness caused by the recent death of her daughter, and the absence of her son. The cheerfulness of the neighborhood had been diminished of late by the departure of George William Fairfax for England, to take possession of estates which had devolved to him in that kingdom. His estate of Belvoir, so closely allied with that of Mount Vernon by family ties and reciprocal hospitality, was left in charge

---

105   Sparks. Washington's Writings, vol. ii., p. 899.

of a steward, or overseer. Through some accident the house took fire, and was burnt to the ground. It was never rebuilt. The course of political events which swept Washington from his quiet home into the current of public and military life, prevented William Fairfax, who was a royalist, though a liberal one, from returning to his once happy abode, and the hospitable intercommunion of Mount Vernon and Belvoir was at an end for ever.

CHAPTER XXXVI.

GAGE'S MILITARY MEASURES—REMOVAL OF
GUNPOWDER FROM THE ARSENAL—PUBLIC
AGITATION—ALARMS IN THE COUNTRY—CIVIL
GOVERNMENT OBSTRUCTED—BELLIGERENT
SYMPTOMS—ISRAEL PUTNAM AND GENERAL
CHARLES LEE, THEIR CHARACTERS AND STORIES—
GENERAL ELECTION—SELF-CONSTITUTED
CONGRESS—HANCOCK PRESIDENT—ADJOURNS
TO CONCORD—REMONSTRANCE TO GAGE—HIS
PERPLEXITIES—GENERALS ARTEMAS WARD AND
SETH POMEROY—COMMITTEE OF SAFETY—
COMMITTEE OF SUPPLIES—RESTLESSNESS
THROUGHOUT THE LAND—INDEPENDENT
COMPANIES IN VIRGINIA—MILITARY TONE AT
MOUNT VERNON—WASHINGTON'S MILITARY
GUESTS—MAJOR HORATIO GATES—ANECDOTES
CONCERNING HIM—GENERAL CHARLES LEE—HIS
PECULIARITIES AND DOGS—WASHINGTON AT THE
RICHMOND CONVENTION—WAR SPEECH OF PATRICK
HENRY—WASHINGTON'S MILITARY INTENTIONS.

The rumor of the cannonading of Boston, which had
thrown such a gloom over the religious ceremonial at the opening
of Congress, had been caused by measures of Governor Gage.
The public mind, in Boston and its vicinity, had been rendered
excessively jealous and sensitive by the landing and encamping of
artillery upon the Common, and Welsh Fusiliers on Fort Hill, and
by the planting of four large field-pieces on Boston Neck, the only
entrance to the town by land. The country people were arming
and disciplining themselves in every direction, and collecting and

depositing arms and ammunition in places where they would be at hand in case of emergency. Gage, on the other hand, issued orders that the munitions of war in all the public magazines should be brought to Boston. One of these magazines was the arsenal in the north-west part of Charlestown, between Medford and Cambridge. Two companies of the king's troops passed silently in boats up Mystic River in the night; took possession of a large quantity of gunpowder deposited there, and conveyed it to Castle Williams. Intelligence of this sacking of the arsenal flew with lightning speed through the neighborhood. In the morning several thousands of patriots were assembled at Cambridge, weapon in hand, and were with difficulty prevented from marching upon Boston to compel a restitution of the powder. In the confusion and agitation, a rumor stole out into the country that Boston was to be attacked; followed by another that the ships were cannonading the town, and the soldiers shooting down the inhabitants. The whole country was forthwith in arms. Numerous bodies of the Connecticut people had made some marches before the report was contradicted.[106]

To guard against any irruption from the country, Gage encamped the 59th regiment on Boston Neck, and employed the soldiers in intrenching and fortifying it.

In the mean time the belligerent feelings of the inhabitants were encouraged, by learning how the rumor of their being cannonaded had been received in the General Congress, and by assurances from all parts that the cause of Boston would be made the common cause of America. "It is surprising," writes General Gage, "that so many of the other provinces interest themselves so much in this. They have some warm friends in New York, and I learn that the people of Charleston, South Carolina, are as mad as they are here."[107]

The commissions were arrived for those civil officers appointed by the crown under the new modifications of the charter: many, however, were afraid to accept of them. Those who did soon resigned, finding it impossible to withstand the odium of the people. The civil government throughout the province became obstructed in all its operations. It was enough for a man to be supposed of the governmental party to incur popular ill-will.

---

106   Holmes's Annals, ii., 191.—Letter of Gage to Lord Dartmouth.
107   Gage to Dartmouth, Sept. 20.

Among other portentous signs, war-hawks began to appear above the horizon. Mrs. Cushing, wife to a member of Congress, writes to her husband, "Two of the greatest military characters of the day are visiting this distressed town. General Charles Lee, who has served in Poland, and Colonel Israel Putnam, whose bravery and character need no description." As these two men will take a prominent part in coming events, we pause to give a word or two concerning them.

Israel Putnam was a soldier of native growth. One of the military productions of the French war; seasoned and proved in frontier campaigning. He had served at Louisburg, Fort Duquesne, and Crown Point; had signalized himself in Indian warfare; been captured by the savages, tied to a stake to be tortured and burnt, and had only been rescued by the interference, at the eleventh hour, of a French partisan of the Indians.

Since the peace, he had returned to agricultural life, and was now a farmer at Pomfret, in Connecticut, where the scars of his wounds and the tales of his exploits rendered him a hero in popular estimation. The war spirit yet burned within him. He was now chairman of a committee of vigilance, and had come to Boston in discharge of his political and semi-belligerent functions.

General Charles Lee was a military man of a different stamp; an Englishman by birth, and a highly cultivated production of European warfare. He was the son of a British officer, Lieutenant-colonel John Lee, of the dragoons, who married the daughter of Sir Henry Bunbury, Bart., and afterwards rose to be a general. Lee was born in 1731, and may almost be said to have been cradled in the army, for he received a commission by the time he was eleven years of age. He had an irregular education; part of the time in England, part on the continent, and must have scrambled his way into knowledge; yet by aptness, diligence and ambition, he had acquired a considerable portion, being a Greek and Latin scholar, and acquainted with modern languages. The art of war was his especial study from his boyhood, and he had early opportunities of practical experience. At the age of twenty-four, he commanded a company of grenadiers in the 44th regiment, and served in the French war in America, where he was brought into military companionship with Sir William Johnson's Mohawk warriors, whom he used to extol for their manly beauty, their dress, their graceful carriage and good breeding. In fact, he rendered himself so much of a favorite among them, that they admitted him to smoke in their councils, and adopted him into the tribe of the Bear, giving him an Indian name, signifying "Boiling Water."

At the battle of Ticonderoga, where Abercrombie was defeated, he was shot through the body, while leading his men against the French breastworks. In the next campaign, he was present at the siege of Fort Niagara, where General Prideaux fell, and where Sir William Johnson, with his British troops and Mohawk warriors, eventually won the fortress. Lee had, probably, an opportunity on this occasion of fighting side by side with some of his adopted brethren of the Bear tribe, as we are told he was much exposed during the engagement with the French and Indians, and that two balls grazed his hair. A military errand, afterwards, took him across Lake Erie, and down the northern branch of the Ohio to Fort Duquesne, and thence by a long march of seven hundred miles to Crown Point, where he joined General Amherst. In 1760, he was among the forces which followed that general from Lake Ontario down the St. Lawrence; and was present at the surrender of Montreal, which completed the conquest of Canada.

In 1762, he bore a colonel's commission, and served under Brigadier-general Burgoyne in Portugal, where he was intrusted with an enterprise against a Spanish post at the old Moorish castle of Villa Velha, on the banks of the Tagus. He forded the river in the night, pushed his way through mountain passes, and at 2 o'clock in the morning, rushed with his grenadiers into the enemy's camp before daylight, where every thing was carried at the point of the bayonet, assisted by a charge of dragoons. The war over, he returned to England, bearing testimonials of bravery and good conduct from his commander-in-chief, the Count de la Lippe, and from the king of Portugal.[108]

Wielding the pen as well as the sword, Lee undertook to write on questions of colonial policy, relative to Pontiac's war, in which he took the opposition side. This lost him the favor of the ministry, and with it all hope of further promotion.

---

108   Life of Charles Lee, by Jared Sparks. Also, Memoirs of Charles Lee; published in London, 1792.

He now determined to offer his services to Poland, supposed to be on the verge of a war. Recommendations from his old commander, the Count de la Lippe, procured him access to some of the continental courts. He was well received by Frederick the Great, and had several conversations with him, chiefly on American affairs. At Warsaw, his military reputation secured him the favor of Poniatowsky, recently elected king of Poland, with the name of Stanislaus Augustus, who admitted him to his table, and made him one of his aides-de-camp. Lee was disappointed in his hope of active service. There was agitation in the country, but the power of the king was not adequate to raise forces sufficient for its suppression. He had few troops, and those not trustworthy; and the town was full of the disaffected. "We have frequent alarms," said Lee, "and the pleasure of sleeping every night with our pistols on our pillows."

By way of relieving his restlessness, Lee, at the suggestion of the king, set off to accompany the Polish ambassador to Constantinople. The latter travelled too slow for him; so he dashed ahead when on the frontiers of Turkey, with an escort of the grand seignior's treasure; came near perishing with cold and hunger among the Bulgarian mountains, and after his arrival at the Turkish capital, ran a risk of being buried under the ruins of his house in an earthquake.

Late in the same year (1766), he was again in England, an applicant for military appointment, bearing a letter from king Stanislaus to king George. His meddling pen is supposed again to have marred his fortunes, having indulged in sarcastic comments on the military character of General Townshend and Lord George Sackville. "I am not at all surprised," said a friend to him, "that you find the door shut against you by a person who has such unbounded credit, as you have ever too freely indulged in a liberty of declaiming, which many invidious persons have not failed to inform him of. The principle on which you thus freely speak your mind, is honest and patriotic, but not politic."

The disappointments which Lee met with during a residence of two years in England, and a protracted attendance on people in power, rankled in his bosom, and embittered his subsequent resentment against the king and his ministers.

In 1768, he was again on his way to Poland, with the design of performing a campaign in the Russian service. "I flatter myself," said he, "that a little more practice will make me a good soldier. If not, it will serve to talk over my kitchen fire in my old age, which will soon come upon us all."

He now looked forward to spirited service. "I am to have a command of Cossacks and Wallacks," writes he, "a kind of people I have a good opinion of. I am determined not to serve in the line. One might as well be a churchwarden."

The friendship of king Stanislaus continued. "He treats me more like a brother than a patron," said Lee. In 1769, the latter was raised to the rank of major-general in the Polish army, and left Warsaw to join the Russian force, which was crossing the Dniester and advancing into Moldavia. He arrived in time to take part in a severe action between the Russians and Turks, in which the Cossacks and hussars were terribly cut up by the Turkish cavalry, in a ravine near the city of Chotzim. It was a long and doubtful conflict, with various changes; but the rumored approach of the grand vizier, with a hundred and seventy thousand men, compelled the Russians to abandon the enterprise and recross the Dniester.

Lee never returned to Poland, though he ever retained a devoted attachment to Stanislaus. He for some time led a restless life about Europe—visiting Italy, Sicily, Malta, and the south of Spain; troubled with attacks of rheumatism, gout, and the effects of a "Hungarian fever." He had become more and more cynical and irascible, and had more than one "affair of honor," in one of which he killed his antagonist. His splenetic feelings, as well as his political sentiments, were occasionally vented in severe attacks upon the ministry, full of irony and sarcasm. They appeared in the public journals, and gained him such reputation, that even the papers of Junius were by some attributed to him.

In the questions which had risen between England and her colonies, he had strongly advocated the cause of the latter; and it was the feelings thus excited, and the recollections, perhaps, of his early campaigns, that had recently brought him to America. Here he had arrived in the latter part of 1773, had visited various parts of Pennsylvania, Maryland and Virginia, taking an active part in the political agitations of the country. His caustic attacks upon the ministry; his conversational powers and his poignant sallies, had gained him great reputation; but his military renown rendered him especially interesting at the present juncture. A general, who had served in the famous campaigns of Europe, commanded Cossacks, fought with Turks, talked with Frederick the Great, and been aide-de-camp to the king of Poland, was a prodigious acquisition to the patriot cause! On the other hand, his visit to Boston was looked upon with uneasiness by the British officers, who knew his adventurous character. It was surmised that he was exciting a spirit of revolt, with a view to putting himself at its head. These suspicions found their way into the London papers, and alarmed the British cabinet. "Have an attention to his conduct," writes Lord Dartmouth to Gage, "and take every legal method to prevent his effecting any of those dangerous purposes he is said to have in view."

Lee, when subsequently informed of these suspicions, scoffed at them in a letter to his friend, Edmund Burke, and declared that he had not the "temerity and vanity" to aspire to the aims imputed to him.

"To think myself qualified for the most important charge that ever was committed to mortal man," writes he, "is the last stage of presumption; nor do I think the Americans would, or ought to confide in a man, let his qualifications be ever so great, who has no property among them. It is true, I most devoutly wish them success in the glorious struggle; that I have expressed my wishes both in writing and *viva voce*, but my errand to Boston was mere curiosity to see a people in so singular circumstances; and I had likewise an ambition to be acquainted with some of their leading men; with them only I associated during my stay in Boston. Our ingenious gentlemen in the camp, therefore, very naturally concluded my design was to put myself at their head."

To resume the course of events at Boston. Gage on the 1st of September, before this popular agitation, had issued writs for an election of an assembly to meet at Salem in October; seeing, however, the irritated state of the public mind, he now countermanded the same by proclamation. The people, disregarding the countermand, carried the election, and ninety of the new members thus elected met at the appointed time. They waited a whole day for the governor to attend, administer the oaths, and open the session; but as he did not make his appearance, they voted themselves a provincial

Congress, and chose for president of it John Hancock,—a man of great wealth, popular, and somewhat showy talents, and ardent patriotism; and eminent from his social position.

This self-constituted body adjourned to Concord, about twenty miles from Boston; quietly assumed supreme authority, and issued a remonstrance to the governor, virtually calling him to account for his military operations in fortifying Boston Neck, and collecting warlike stores about him, thereby alarming the fears of the whole province, and menacing the lives and property of the Bostonians.

General Gage, overlooking the irregularity of its organization, entered into explanations with the Assembly, but failed to give satisfaction. As winter approached, he found his situation more and more critical. Boston was the only place in Massachusetts that now contained British forces, and it had become the refuge of all the *"tories"* of the province; that is to say, of all those devoted to the British government. There was animosity between them and the principal inhabitants, among whom revolutionary principles prevailed. The town itself, almost insulated by nature, and surrounded by a hostile country, was like a place besieged.

The provincial Congress conducted its affairs with the order and system so formidable to General Gage. Having adopted a plan for organizing the militia, it had nominated general officers, two of whom, Artemas Ward and Seth Pomeroy, had accepted.

The executive powers were vested in a committee of safety. This was to determine when the services of the militia were necessary; was to call them forth,—to nominate their officers to the Congress,—to commission them, and direct the operations of the army. Another committee was appointed to furnish supplies to the forces when called out; hence, named the Committee of Supplies.

Under such auspices, the militia went on arming and disciplining itself in every direction. They associated themselves in large bodies, and engaged, verbally or by writing, to assemble in arms at the shortest notice for the common defence, subject to the orders of the committee of safety.

Arrangements had been made for keeping up an active correspondence between different parts of the country, and spreading an alarm in case of any threatening danger. Under the direction of the committees just mentioned, large quantities of military stores had been collected and deposited at Concord and Worcester.

This semi-belligerent state of affairs in Massachusetts produced a general restlessness throughout the land. The weakhearted apprehended coming troubles; the resolute prepared to brave them. Military measures, hitherto confined to New England, extended to the middle and southern provinces, and the roll of the drum resounded through the villages.

Virginia was among the first to buckle on its armor. It had long been a custom among its inhabitants to form themselves into independent companies, equipped at their own expense, having their own peculiar uniform, and electing their own officers, though holding themselves subject to militia law. They had hitherto been self-disciplined; but now they continually resorted to Washington for instruction and advice; considering him the highest authority on military affairs. He was frequently called from home, therefore, in the course of the winter and spring, to different parts of the country to review independent companies; all of which were anxious to put themselves under his command as field-officer.

Mount Vernon, therefore, again assumed a military tone as in former days, when he took his first lessons there in the art of war. He had his old campaigning associates with him occasionally, Dr. Craik and Captain Hugh Mercer, to talk of past scenes and discuss the possibility of future service. Mercer was already bestirring himself in disciplining the militia about Fredericksburg, where he resided.

Two occasional and important guests at Mount Vernon, in this momentous crisis, were General Charles Lee, of whom we have just spoken, and Major Horatio Gates. As the latter is destined to occupy an important page in this memoir, we will give a few particulars concerning him. He was an Englishman by birth, the son of a captain in the British army. Horace Walpole, whose Christian name he bore, speaks of him in one of his letters as his godson, though some have insinuated that he stood in filial relationship of a less sanctified character. He had received a liberal education, and, when but twenty-one years of age, had served as a volunteer under General Edward Cornwallis, Governor of Halifax. He was afterwards captain of a New York independent company, with which, it may be remembered, he marched in the campaign of Braddock, in which he was severely wounded. For two or three subsequent years he was with his company in the western part of the province of New York, receiving the appointment of brigade major. He accompanied General Monckton as aide-de-camp to the West Indies, and gained credit at the capture of Martinico. Being despatched to London with tidings of the victory, he was rewarded by the appointment of major to a regiment of foot; and afterwards, as a special mark of royal favor, a majority in the Royal Americans. His promotion did not equal his expectations and fancied deserts. He was married, and wanted something more lucrative; so he sold out on half-pay and became an applicant for some profitable post under government, which he hoped to obtain through the influence of General Monckton and some friends in the aristocracy. Thus several years were passed, partly with his family in retirement, partly in London, paying court to patrons and men in power, until, finding there was no likelihood of success, and having sold his commission and half-pay, he emigrated to Virginia in 1772, a disappointed man; purchased an estate in Berkeley County, beyond the Blue Ridge; espoused the popular cause, and renewed his old campaigning acquaintance with Washington.

He was now about forty-six years of age, of a florid complexion and goodly presence, though a little inclined to corpulency; social, insinuating, and somewhat specious in his manners, with a strong degree of self-approbation. A long course of solicitation; haunting public offices and antechambers, and "knocking about town," had taught him, it was said, how to wheedle and flatter, and accommodate himself to the humors of others, so as to be the boon companion of gentlemen, and "hail fellow well met" with the vulgar.

Lee, who was an old friend and former associate in arms, had recently been induced by him to purchase an estate in his neighborhood in Berkeley County, with a view to making it his abode, having a moderate competency, a claim to land on the Ohio, and the half-pay of a British colonel. Both of these officers, disappointed in the British service, looked forward probably to greater success in the patriot cause.

Lee had been at Philadelphia since his visit to Boston, and had made himself acquainted with the leading members of Congress during the session. He was evidently cultivating an intimacy with every one likely to have influence in the approaching struggle.

To Washington, the visits of these gentlemen were extremely welcome at this juncture, from their military knowledge and experience, especially as much of it had been acquired in America, in the same kind of warfare, if not the very same campaigns in which he himself had mingled. Both were interested in the popular cause. Lee was full of plans for the organization and disciplining of the militia, and occasionally accompanied Washington in his attendance on provincial reviews. He was subsequently very efficient at Annapolis in promoting and superintending the organization of the Maryland militia.

It is doubtful whether the visits of Lee were as interesting to Mrs. Washington as to the general. He was whimsical, eccentric, and at times almost rude; negligent also, and slovenly in person and attire; for though he had occasionally associated with kings and princes, he had also campaigned with Mohawks and Cossacks, and seems to have relished their "good breeding." What was still more annoying in a well regulated mansion, he was always followed by a legion of dogs, which shared his affections with his horses, and took their seats by him when at table. "I must have some object to embrace," said he misanthropically. "When I can be convinced that men are as worthy objects as dogs, I shall transfer my benevolence, and become as staunch a philanthropist as the canting Addison affected to be."[109]

In his passion for horses and dogs, Washington, to a certain degree, could sympathize with him, and had noble specimens of both in his stable and kennel, which Lee doubtless inspected with a learned eye. During the season in question, Washington, according to his diary, was occasionally in the saddle at an early hour following the fox-hounds. It was the last time for many a year that he was to gallop about his beloved hunting-grounds of Mount Vernon and Belvoir.

In the month of March the second Virginia convention was held at Richmond. Washington attended as delegate from Fairfax County. In this assembly, Patrick Henry, with his usual ardor and eloquence, advocated measures for embodying, arming and

---

109   Lee to Adams. Life and Works of Adams, ii., 414.

disciplining a militia force, and providing for the defence of the colony. "It is useless," said he, "to address further petitions to government, or to await the effect of those already addressed to the throne. The time for supplication is past; the time for action is at hand. We must fight, Mr. Speaker," exclaimed he emphatically; "I repeat it, sir, we must fight! An appeal to arms, and to the God of Hosts, is all that is left us!"

Washington joined him in the conviction, and was one of a committee that reported a plan for carrying those measures into effect. He was not an impulsive man to raise the battle cry, but the executive man to marshal the troops into the field, and carry on the war.

His brother, John Augustine, was raising and disciplining an independent company; Washington offered to accept the command of it, *should occasion require it to be drawn out*. He did the same with respect to an independent company at Richmond. "It is my full intention, if needful," writes he to his brother, *"to devote my life and fortune to the cause."*[110]

---

110   Letter to John Augustine. Sparks, ii., 405.

CHAPTER XXXVII.

INFATUATION IN BRITISH COUNCILS—COLONEL
GRANT, THE BRAGGART—COERCIVE MEASURES—
EXPEDITION AGAINST THE MILITARY MAGAZINE AT
CONCORD—BATTLE OF LEXINGTON—THE CRY OF
BLOOD THROUGH THE LAND—OLD SOLDIERS OF
THE FRENCH WAR—JOHN STARK—ISRAEL PUTNAM—
RISING OF THE YEOMANRY—MEASURES OF LORD
DUNMORE IN VIRGINIA—INDIGNATION OF THE
VIRGINIANS—HUGH MERCER AND THE FRIENDS OF
LIBERTY—ARRIVAL OF THE NEWS OF LEXINGTON
AT MOUNT VERNON—EFFECT ON BRYAN FAIRFAX,
GATES, AND WASHINGTON.

While the spirit of revolt was daily gaining strength and
determination in America, a strange infatuation reigned in the
British councils. While the wisdom and eloquence of Chatham
were exerted in vain in behalf of American rights, an empty
braggadocio, elevated to a seat in Parliament, was able to captivate
the attention of the members, and influence their votes by gross
misrepresentations of the Americans and their cause. This was no
other than Colonel Grant, the same shallow soldier who, exceeding
his instructions, had been guilty of a foolhardy bravado before the
walls of Fort Duquesne, which brought slaughter and defeat upon
his troops. From misleading the army, he was now promoted to
a station where he might mislead the councils of his country. We
are told that he entertained Parliament, especially the ministerial
side of the House, with ludicrous stories of the cowardice of
Americans. He had served with them, he said, and knew them well,
and would venture to say they would never dare to face an English
army; that they were destitute of every requisite to make good

soldiers, and that a very slight force would be sufficient for their complete reduction. With five regiments, he could march through all America!

How often has England been misled to her cost by such slanderous misrepresentations of the American character! Grant talked of having served with the Americans; had he already forgotten that in the field of Braddock's defeat, when the British regulars fled, it was alone the desperate stand of a handful of Virginians, which covered their disgraceful flight, and saved them from being overtaken and massacred by the savages?

This taunting and braggart speech of Grant was made in the face of the conciliatory bill of the venerable Chatham, devised with a view to redress the wrongs of America. The councils of the arrogant and scornful prevailed; and instead of the proposed bill, further measures of a stringent nature were adopted, coercive of some of the middle and southern colonies, but ruinous to the trade and fisheries of New England.

At length the bolt, so long suspended, fell! The troops at Boston had been augmented to about four thousand men. Goaded on by the instigations of the tories, and alarmed by the energetic measures of the whigs, General Gage now resolved to deal the latter a crippling blow. This was to surprise and destroy their magazine of military stores at Concord, about twenty miles from Boston. It was to be effected on the night of the 18th of April, by a force detached for the purpose.

Preparations were made with great secrecy. Boats for the transportation of the troops were launched, and moored under the sterns of the men-of-war. Grenadiers and light infantry were relieved from duty, and held in readiness. On the 18th, officers were stationed on the roads leading from Boston, to prevent any intelligence of the expedition getting into the country. At night orders were issued by General Gage that no person should leave the town. About ten o'clock, from eight to nine hundred men, grenadiers, light infantry, and marines, commanded by Lieutenant-colonel Smith, embarked in the boats at the foot of Boston Common, and crossed to Lechmere Point, in Cambridge, whence they were to march silently, and without beat of drum, to the place of destination.

The measures of General Gage had not been shrouded in all the secrecy he imagined. Mystery often defeats itself by the suspicions it awakens. Dr. Joseph Warren, one of the committee of safety, had observed the preparatory disposition of the boats and troops, and surmised some sinister intention. He sent notice of these movements to John Hancock and Samuel Adams, both members of the provincial Congress, but at that time privately sojourning with a friend at Lexington. A design on the magazine at Concord was suspected, and the committee of safety ordered that the cannon collected there should be secreted, and part of the stores removed.

On the night of the 18th, Dr. Warren sent off two messengers by different routes to give the alarm that the king's troops were actually sallying forth. The messengers got out of Boston just before the order of General Gage went into effect, to prevent any one from leaving the town. About the same time a lantern was hung out of an upper window of the north church, in the direction of Charlestown. This was a preconcerted signal to the patriots of that place, who instantly despatched swift messengers to rouse the country.

In the mean time, Colonel Smith set out on his nocturnal march from Lechmere Point by an unfrequented path across marshes, where at times the troops had to wade through water. He had proceeded but a few miles when alarm guns, booming through the night air, and the clang of village bells, showed that the news of his approach was travelling before him, and the people were rising. He now sent back to General Gage for a reinforcement, while Major Pitcairne was detached with six companies to press forward, and secure the bridges at Concord.

Pitcairn advanced rapidly, capturing every one that he met, or overtook. Within a mile and half of Lexington, however, a horseman was too quick on the spur for him, and galloping to the village, gave the alarm that the redcoats were coming. Drums were beaten; guns fired. By the time that Pitcairn entered the village, about seventy or eighty of the yeomanry, in military array, were mustered on the green near the church. It was a part of the "constitutional army," pledged to resist by force any open hostility of British troops. Besides these, there were a number of lookers on, armed and unarmed.

The sound of drum, and the array of men in arms, indicated a hostile determination. Pitcairn halted his men within a short distance of the church, and ordered them to prime and load. They then advanced at double quick time. The major, riding forward, waved his sword, and ordered the rebels, as he termed them, to disperse. Other of the officers echoed his words as they advanced: "Disperse, ye villains! Lay down your arms, ye rebels, and disperse!" The orders were disregarded. A scene of confusion ensued, with firing on both sides; which party commenced it, has been a matter of dispute. Pitcairn always maintained that, finding the militia would not disperse, he turned to order his men to draw out, and surround them, when he saw a flash in the pan from the gun of a countryman posted behind a wall, and almost instantly the report of two or three muskets. These he supposed to be from the Americans, as his horse was wounded, as was also a soldier close by him. His troops rushed on, and a promiscuous fire took place, though, as he declared, he made repeated signals with his sword for his men to forbear.

The firing of the Americans was irregular, and without much effect; that of the British was more fatal. Eight of the patriots were killed, and ten wounded, and the whole put to flight. The victors formed on the common, fired a volley, and gave three cheers for one of the most inglorious and disastrous triumphs ever achieved by British arms.

Colonel Smith soon arrived with the residue of the detachment, and they all marched on towards Concord, about six miles distant.

The alarm had reached that place in the dead hour of the preceding night. The church bell roused the inhabitants. They gathered together in anxious consultation. The militia and minute men seized their arms, and repaired to the parade ground, near the church. Here they were subsequently joined by armed yeomanry from Lincoln, and elsewhere. Exertions were now made to remove and conceal the military stores. A scout, who had been sent out for intelligence, brought word that the British had fired upon the people at Lexington, and were advancing upon Concord. There was great excitement and indignation. Part of the militia marched down the Lexington road to meet them, but returned, reporting their force to be three times that of the Americans. The whole of the militia now retired to an eminence about a mile from the centre of the town, and formed themselves into two battalions.

About seven o'clock, the British came in sight, advancing with quick step, their arms glittering in the morning sun. They entered in two divisions by different roads. Concord is traversed by a river of the same name, having two bridges, the north and the south. The grenadiers and light infantry took post in the centre of the town, while strong parties of light troops were detached to secure the bridges, and destroy the military stores. Two hours were expended in the work of destruction without much success, so much of the stores having been removed, or concealed. During all this time the yeomanry from the neighboring towns were hurrying in with such weapons as were at hand, and joining the militia on the height, until the little cloud of war gathering there numbered about four hundred and fifty.

About ten o'clock, a body of three hundred undertook to dislodge the British from the north bridge. As they approached, the latter fired upon them, killing two, and wounding a third. The patriots returned the fire with spirit and effect. The British retreated to the main body, the Americans pursuing them across the bridge.

By this time all the military stores which could be found had been destroyed; Colonel Smith, therefore, made preparations for a retreat. The scattered troops were collected, the dead were buried, and conveyances procured for the wounded. About noon he commenced his retrograde march for Boston. It was high time. His troops were jaded by the night march, and the morning's toils and skirmishings.

The country was thoroughly alarmed. The yeomanry were hurrying from every quarter to the scene of action. As the British began their retreat, the Americans began the work of sore and galling retaliation. Along the open road, the former were harassed incessantly by rustic marksmen, who took deliberate aim from behind trees, or over stone fences. Where the road passed through woods, the British found themselves between two fires, dealt by unseen foes, the minute men having posted themselves on each side among the bushes. It was in vain they threw out flankers, and endeavored to dislodge their assailants; each pause gave time for other pursuers to come within reach, and open attacks from different quarters. For several miles they urged their way along woody defiles, or roads skirted with fences and stone walls, the retreat growing more and more disastrous; some were shot down, some gave out through mere exhaustion; the rest hurried on, without stopping to aid the fatigued, or wounded. Before reaching Lexington, Colonel Smith received a severe wound in the leg, and the situation of the retreating troops was becoming extremely critical, when, about two o'clock, they were met by Lord Percy, with a brigade of one thousand men, and two field-pieces. His lordship had been detached from Boston about nine o'clock by General Gage, in compliance with Colonel Smith's urgent call for a reinforcement, and had marched gaily through Roxbury to the tune of "Yankee Doodle," in derision of the "rebels." He now found the latter a more formidable foe than he had anticipated. Opening his brigade to the right and left, he received the retreating troops into a hollow square; where, fainting and exhausted, they threw themselves on the ground to rest. His lordship showed no disposition to advance upon their assailants, but contented himself with keeping them at bay with his field-pieces, which opened a vigorous fire from an eminence.

Hitherto the Provincials, being hasty levies, without a leader, had acted from individual impulse, without much concert; but now General Heath was upon the ground. He was one of those authorized to take command when the minute men should be called out. That class of combatants promptly obeyed his orders, and he was efficacious in rallying them, and bringing them into military order, when checked and scattered by the fire of the field-pieces.

Dr. Warren, also, arrived on horseback, having spurred from Boston on receiving news of the skirmishing. In the subsequent part of the day, he was one of the most active and efficient men in the field. His presence, like that of General Heath, regulated the infuriated ardor of the militia, and brought it into system.

Lord Percy, having allowed the troops a short interval for repose and refreshment, continued the retreat toward Boston. As soon as he got under march, the galling assault by the pursuing yeomanry was recommenced in flank and rear. The British soldiery, irritated in turn, acted as if in an enemy's country. Houses and shops were burnt down in Lexington; private dwellings along the road were plundered, and their inhabitants maltreated. In one instance, an unoffending invalid was wantonly slain in his own house. All this increased the exasperation of the yeomanry. There was occasional sharp skirmishing, with bloodshed on both sides, but in general a dogged pursuit, where the retreating troops were galled at every step. Their march became more and more impeded by the number of their wounded. Lord Percy narrowly escaped death from a musket-ball, which struck off a button of his waistcoat. One of his officers remained behind wounded in West Cambridge. His ammunition was failing as he approached Charlestown. The provincials pressed upon him in rear, others were advancing from Roxbury, Dorchester, and Milton; Colonel Pickering, with the Essex militia, seven hundred strong, was at hand; there was danger of being intercepted in the retreat to Charlestown. The field-pieces were again brought into play, to check the ardor of the pursuit; but they were no longer objects of terror. The sharpest firing of the provincials was near Prospect Hill, as the harassed enemy hurried along the Charlestown road, eager to reach the Neck, and get under cover of their ships. The pursuit terminated a little after sunset, at Charlestown Common, where General Heath brought the minute men to a halt. Within half an hour more, a powerful body of men, from Marblehead and Salem, came up to join in the chase. "If the retreat," writes Washington, "had not been as precipitate as it was,—and God knows it could not well have been more so,—the ministerial troops must have surrendered, or been totally cut off."

The distant firing from the mainland had reached the British at Boston. The troops which, in the morning, had marched through Roxbury, to the tune of Yankee Doodle, might have been seen at sunset, hounded along the old Cambridge road to Charlestown Neck, by mere armed yeomanry. Gage was astounded at the catastrophe. It was but a short time previous that one of his officers, in writing to friends in England, scoffed at the idea of the Americans taking up arms. "Whenever it comes to blows," said he, "he that can run the fastest, will think himself well off, believe me. Any two regiments here ought to be decimated, if they did not beat in the field the whole force of the Massachusetts province." How frequently, throughout this Revolution, had the English to pay the penalty of thus undervaluing the spirit they were provoking!

In this memorable affair, the British loss was seventy-three killed, one hundred and seventy-four wounded, and twenty-six missing. Among the slain were eighteen officers. The loss of the

Americans was forty-nine killed, thirty-nine wounded, and five missing. This was the first blood shed in the revolutionary struggle; a mere drop in amount, but a deluge in its effects,—rending the colonies for ever from the mother country.

The cry of blood from the field of Lexington, went through the land. None felt the appeal more than the old soldiers of the French war. It roused John Stark, of New Hampshire—a trapper and hunter in his youth, a veteran in Indian warfare, a campaigner under Abercrombie and Amherst, now the military oracle of a rustic neighborhood. Within ten minutes after receiving the alarm, he was spurring towards the sea-coast, and on the way stirring up the volunteers of the Massachusetts borders, to assemble forthwith at Bedford, in the vicinity of Boston.

Equally alert was his old comrade in frontier exploits, Colonel Israel Putnam. A man on horseback, with a drum, passed through his neighborhood in Connecticut, proclaiming British violence at Lexington. Putnam was in the field ploughing, assisted by his son. In an instant the team was unyoked; the plough left in the furrow; the lad sent home to give word of his father's departure; and Putnam, on horseback, in his working garb, urging with all speed to the camp. Such was the spirit aroused throughout the country. The sturdy yeomanry, from all parts, were hastening toward Boston with such weapons as were at hand; and happy was he who could command a rusty fowling-piece and a powder-horn.

The news reached Virginia at a critical moment. Lord Dunmore, obeying a general order issued by the ministry to all the provincial governors, had seized upon the military munitions of the province. Here was a similar measure to that of Gage. The cry went forth that the subjugation of the colonies was to be attempted. All Virginia was in combustion. The standard of liberty was reared in every county; there was a general cry to arms. Washington was looked to, from various quarters, to take command. His old comrade in arms, Hugh Mercer, was about marching down to Williamsburg at the head of a body of resolute men, seven hundred strong, entitled "The friends of constitutional liberty and America," whom he had organized and drilled in Fredericksburg, and nothing but a timely concession of Lord Dunmore, with respect to some powder which he had seized, prevented his being beset in his palace.

Before Hugh Mercer and the Friends of Liberty disbanded themselves, they exchanged a mutual pledge to reassemble at a moment's warning, whenever called on to defend the liberty and rights of this or any other sister colony.

Washington was at Mount Vernon, preparing to set out for Philadelphia as a delegate to the second Congress, when he received tidings of the affair at Lexington. Bryan Fairfax and Major Horatio Gates were his guests at the time. They all regarded the event as decisive in its consequences; but they regarded it with different feelings. The worthy and gentle-spirited Fairfax deplored it deeply. He foresaw that it must break up all his pleasant relations in life; arraying his dearest friends against the government to which, notwithstanding the errors of its policy, he was loyally attached and resolved to adhere.

Gates, on the contrary, viewed it with the eye of a soldier and a place-hunter—hitherto disappointed in both capacities. This event promised to open a new avenue to importance and command, and he determined to enter upon it.

Washington's feelings were of a mingled nature. They may be gathered from a letter to his friend and neighbor, George William Fairfax, then in England, in which he lays the blame of this "deplorable affair" on the ministry and their military agents; and concludes with the following words, in which the yearnings of the patriot give affecting solemnity to the implied resolve of the soldier: "Unhappy it is to reflect that a brother's sword has been sheathed in a brother's breast; and that the once happy and peaceful plains of America, are to be either drenched with blood or inhabited by slaves. Sad alternative! *But can a virtuous man hesitate in his choice?*"

CHAPTER XXXVIII.

ENLISTING OF TROOPS IN THE EAST—CAMP AT
BOSTON—GENERAL ARTEMAS WARD—SCHEME
TO SURPRISE TICONDEROGA—NEW HAMPSHIRE
GRANTS—ETHAN ALLEN AND THE GREEN
MOUNTAIN BOYS—BENEDICT ARNOLD—AFFAIR OF
TICONDEROGA AND CROWN POINT—A DASH AT ST.
JOHN'S.

At the eastward, the march of the Revolution went on
with accelerated speed. Thirty thousand men had been deemed
necessary for the defence of the country. The provincial Congress
of Massachusetts resolved to raise thirteen thousand six hundred,
as its quota. Circular letters, also, were issued by the committee of
safety, urging the towns to enlist troops with all speed, and calling
for military aid from the other New England provinces.

Their appeals were promptly answered. Bodies of militia, and
parties of volunteers from New Hampshire, Rhode Island and
Connecticut, hastened to join the minute men of Massachusetts in
forming a camp in the neighborhood of Boston. With the troops of
Connecticut, came Israel Putnam; having recently raised a regiment
in that province, and received from its Assembly the commission of
brigadier-general. Some of his old comrades in French and Indian
warfare, had hastened to join his standard. Such were two of his
captains, Durkee and Knowlton. The latter, who was his especial
favorite, had fought by his side when a mere boy.

The command of the camp was given to General Artemas
Ward, already mentioned. He was a native of Shrewsbury, in
Massachusetts, and a veteran of the seven years' war—having
served as lieutenant-colonel under Abercrombie. He had, likewise,
been a member of the legislative bodies, and had recently been

made, by the provincial Congress of Massachusetts, commander-in-chief of its forces.

As affairs were now drawing to a crisis, and war was considered inevitable, some bold spirits in Connecticut conceived a project for the outset. This was the surprisal of the old forts of Ticonderoga and Crown Point, already famous in the French war. Their situation on Lake Champlain gave them the command of the main route to Canada; so that the possession of them would be all-important in case of hostilities. They were feebly garrisoned and negligently guarded, and abundantly furnished with artillery and military stores, so much needed by the patriot army.

This scheme was set on foot in the purlieus, as it were, of the provincial Legislature of Connecticut, then in session. It was not openly sanctioned by that body, but secretly favored, and money lent from the treasury to those engaged in it. A committee was appointed, also, to accompany them to the frontier, aid them in raising troops, and exercise over them, a degree of superintendence and control.

Sixteen men were thus enlisted in Connecticut, a greater number in Massachusetts, but the greatest accession of force, was from what was called the "New Hampshire Grants." This was a region having the Connecticut River on one side, and Lake Champlain and the Hudson River on the other—being, in fact, the country forming the present State of Vermont. It had long been a disputed territory, claimed by New York and New Hampshire. George II. had decided in favor of New York; but the Governor of New Hampshire had made grants of between one and two hundred townships in it, whence it had acquired the name of the New Hampshire Grants. The settlers on those grants resisted the attempts of New York to eject them, and formed themselves into an association, called "The Green Mountain Boys." Resolute, strong-handed fellows they were, with Ethan Allen at their head, a native of Connecticut, but brought up among the Green Mountains. He and his lieutenants, Seth Warner and Remember Baker, were outlawed by the Legislature of New York, and rewards offered for their apprehension. They and their associates armed themselves, set New York at defiance, and swore they would be the death of any one who should attempt their arrest.

Thus Ethan Allen was becoming a kind of Robin Hood among the mountains, when the present crisis changed the relative position of things as if by magic. Boundary feuds were forgotten amid the great questions of colonial rights. Ethan Allen at once stepped forward, a patriot, and volunteered with his Green Mountain Boys to serve in the popular cause. He was well fitted for the enterprise in question, by his experience as a frontier champion, his robustness of mind and body, and his fearless spirit. He had a kind of rough eloquence, also, that was very effective with his followers. "His style," says one, who knew him personally, "was a singular compound of local barbarisms, scriptural phrases, and oriental wildness; and though unclassic, and sometimes ungrammatical, was highly animated and forcible." Washington, in one of his letters, says there was "an original something in him which commanded admiration."

Thus reinforced, the party, now two hundred and seventy strong, pushed forward to Castleton, a place within a few miles of the head of Lake Champlain. Here a council of war was held on the 2d of May. Ethan Allen was placed at the head of the expedition, with James Easton and Seth Warner as second and third in command. Detachments were sent off to Skenesborough (now Whitehall), and another place on the lake, with orders to seize all the boats they could find and bring them to Shoreham, opposite Ticonderoga, whither Allen prepared to proceed with the main body.

At this juncture, another adventurous spirit arrived at Castleton. This was BENEDICT ARNOLD, since so sadly renowned. He, too, had conceived the project of surprising Ticonderoga and Crown Point; or, perhaps, had caught the idea from its first agitators in Connecticut,—in the militia of which province he held a captain's commission. He had proposed the scheme to the Massachusetts committee of safety. It had met with their approbation. They had given him a colonel's commission, authorized him to raise a force in Western Massachusetts, not exceeding four hundred men, and furnished him with money and means. Arnold had enlisted but a few officers and men when he heard of the expedition from Connecticut being on the march. He instantly hurried on with one attendant to overtake it, leaving his few recruits to follow, as best they could: in this way he reached Castleton just after the council of war.

Producing the colonel's commission received from the Massachusetts committee of safety, he now aspired to the supreme command. His claims were disregarded by the Green Mountain Boys; they would follow no leader but Ethan Allen. As they formed the majority of the party, Arnold was fain to acquiesce, and serve as a volunteer, with the rank, but not the command of colonel.

The party arrived at Shoreham, opposite Ticonderoga, on the night of the 9th of May. The detachment sent in quest of boats had failed to arrive. There were a few boats at hand, with which the transportation was commenced. It was slow work; the night wore away; day was about to break, and but eighty-three men, with Allen and Arnold, had crossed. Should they wait for the residue, day would dawn, the garrison wake, and their enterprise might fail. Allen drew up his men, addressed them in his own emphatic style, and announced his intention to make a dash at the fort without waiting for more force. "It is a desperate attempt," said he, "and I ask no man to go against his will. I will take the lead, and be the first to advance. You that are willing to follow, poise your firelocks." Not a firelock but was poised.

They mounted the hill briskly, but in silence, guided by a boy from the neighborhood. The day dawned as Allen arrived at a sally port. A sentry pulled trigger on him, but his piece missed fire. He retreated through a covered way. Allen and his men followed. Another sentry thrust at Easton with his bayonet, but was struck down by Allen, and begged for quarter. It was granted on condition of his leading the way instantly to the quarters of the commandant, Captain Delaplace, who was yet in bed. Being arrived there, Allen thundered at the door, and demanded a surrender of the fort. By this time his followers had formed into two lines on the parade-ground, and given three hearty cheers. The commandant appeared at his door half-dressed, "the frightened face of his pretty wife peering over his shoulder." He gazed at Allen in bewildered astonishment. "By whose authority do you act?" exclaimed he. "In the name of the great Jehovah, and the Continental Congress!" replied Allen, with a flourish of his sword, and an oath which we do not care to subjoin.

There was no disputing the point. The garrison, like the commander, had been startled from sleep, and made prisoners as they rushed forth in their confusion. A surrender accordingly took place. The captain, and forty-eight men, which composed his garrison, were sent prisoners to Hartford, in Connecticut. A great supply of military and naval stores, so important in the present crisis, was found in the fortress.

Colonel Seth Warner, who had brought over the residue of the party from Shoreham, was now sent with a detachment against Crown Point, which surrendered on the 12th of May, without firing a gun; the whole garrison being a sergeant and twelve men. Here were taken upward of a hundred cannon.

Arnold now insisted vehemently on his right to command Ticonderoga; being, as he said, the only officer invested with legal authority. His claims had again to yield to the superior popularity of Ethan Allen, to whom the Connecticut committee, which had accompanied the enterprise, gave an instrument in writing, investing him with the command of the fortress, and its dependencies, until he should receive the orders of the Connecticut Assembly, or the Continental Congress. Arnold, while forced to acquiesce, sent a protest, and a statement of his grievances to the Massachusetts Legislature. In the mean time, his chagrin was appeased by a new project. The detachment originally sent to seize upon boats at Skenesborough, arrived with a schooner, and several bateaux. It was immediately concerted between Allen and Arnold to cruise in them down the lake, and surprise St. John's, on the Sorel River, the frontier post of Canada. The schooner was accordingly armed with cannon from the fort. Arnold, who had been a seaman in his youth, took the command of her, while Allen and his Green Mountain Boys embarked in the bateaux.

Arnold outsailed the other craft, and arriving at St. John's, surprised and made prisoners of a sergeant and twelve men; captured a king's sloop of seventy tons, with two brass six-pounders and seven men; took four bateaux, destroyed several others, and then, learning that troops were on the way from Montreal and Chamblee, spread all his sails to a favoring breeze, and swept up the lake with his prizes and prisoners, and some valuable stores, which he had secured.

He had not sailed far when he met Ethan Allen and the bateaux. Salutes were exchanged; cannon on one side, musketry on the other. Allen boarded the sloop; learnt from Arnold the particulars of his success, and determined to push on, take possession of St. John's, and garrison it with one hundred of his Green Mountain Boys. He was foiled in the attempt by the superior force which had arrived; so he returned to his station at Ticonderoga.

Thus a partisan band, unpractised in the art of war, had, by a series of daring exploits, and almost without the loss of a man, won for the patriots the command of Lakes George and Champlain, and thrown open the great highway to Canada.

CHAPTER XXXIX.

SECOND SESSION OF CONGRESS—JOHN
HANCOCK—PETITION TO THE KING—FEDERAL
UNION—MILITARY MEASURES—DEBATES ABOUT
THE ARMY—QUESTION AS TO COMMANDER-IN-
CHIEF—APPOINTMENT OF WASHINGTON—OTHER
APPOINTMENTS—LETTERS OF WASHINGTON TO
HIS WIFE AND BROTHER—PREPARATIONS FOR
DEPARTURE.

The second General Congress assembled at Philadelphia on
the 10th of May. Peyton Randolph was again elected as president;
but being obliged to return, and occupy his place as speaker of the
Virginia Assembly, John Hancock, of Massachusetts, was elevated
to the chair.

A lingering feeling of attachment to the mother country,
struggling with the growing spirit of self-government, was
manifested in the proceedings of this remarkable body. Many of
those most active in vindicating colonial rights, and Washington
among the number, still indulged the hope of an eventual
reconciliation, while few entertained, or, at least, avowed the idea
of complete independence.

A second "humble and dutiful" petition to the king was
moved, but met with strong opposition. John Adams condemned it
as an imbecile measure, calculated to embarrass the proceedings of
Congress. He was for prompt and vigorous action. Other members
concurred with him. Indeed, the measure itself seemed but a mere
form, intended to reconcile the half-scrupulous; for subsequently,
when it was carried, Congress, in face of it, went on to assume and
exercise the powers of a sovereign authority. A federal union was
formed, leaving to each colony the right of regulating its internal

affairs according to its own individual constitution, but vesting in Congress the power of making peace or war; of entering into treaties and alliances; of regulating general commerce; in a word, of legislating on all such matters as regarded the security and welfare of the whole community.

The executive power was to be vested in a council of twelve, chosen by Congress from among its own members, and to hold office for a limited time. Such colonies as had not sent delegates to Congress, might yet become members of the confederacy by agreeing to its conditions. Georgia, which had hitherto hesitated, soon joined the league, which thus extended from Nova Scotia to Florida.

Congress lost no time in exercising their federated powers. In virtue of them, they ordered the enlistment of troops, the construction of forts in various parts of the colonies, the provision of arms, ammunition, and military stores; while to defray the expense of these, and other measures, avowedly of self-defence, they authorized the emission of notes to the amount of three millions of dollars, bearing the inscription of "The United Colonies;" the faith of the confederacy being pledged for their redemption.

A retaliating decree was passed, prohibiting all supplies of provisions to the British fisheries; and another, declaring the province of Massachusetts Bay absolved from its compact with the crown, by the violation of its charter; and recommending it to form an internal government for itself.

The public sense of Washington's military talents and experience, was evinced in his being chairman of all the committees appointed for military affairs. Most of the rules and regulations for the army, and the measures for defence, were devised by him.

The situation of the New England army, actually besieging Boston, became an early and absorbing consideration. It was without munitions of war, without arms, clothing, or pay; in fact, without legislative countenance or encouragement. Unless sanctioned and assisted by Congress, there was danger of its dissolution. If dissolved, how could another be collected? If dissolved, what would there be to prevent the British from sallying out of Boston, and spreading desolation throughout the country?

All this was the subject of much discussion out of doors. The disposition to uphold the army was general; but the difficult question was, who should be commander-in-chief? Adams, in his diary, gives us glimpses of the conflict of opinions and interests within doors. There was a southern party, he said, which could not brook the idea of a New England army, commanded by a New England general. "Whether this jealousy was sincere," writes he, "or whether it was mere pride, and a haughty ambition of furnishing a southern general to command the northern army, I cannot say; but the intention was very visible to me, that Colonel Washington was their object; and so many of our stanchest men were in the plan, that we could carry nothing without conceding to it. There was another embarrassment, which was never publicly known, and which was carefully concealed by those who knew it: the Massachusetts and other New England delegates were divided. Mr. Hancock and Mr. Cushing hung back; Mr. Paine did not come forward, and even Mr. Samuel Adams was irresolute. Mr. Hancock himself had an ambition to be appointed commander-in-chief. Whether he thought an election a compliment due to him, and intended to have the honor of declining it, or whether he would have accepted it, I know not. To the compliment, he had some pretensions; for, at that time, his exertions, sacrifices, and general merits in the cause of his country, had been incomparably greater than those of Colonel Washington. But the delicacy of his health, and his entire want of experience in actual service, though an excellent militia officer, were decisive objections to him in my mind."

General Charles Lee was at that time in Philadelphia. His former visit had made him well acquainted with the leading members of Congress. The active interest he had manifested in the cause was well known, and the public had an almost extravagant idea of his military qualifications. He was of foreign birth, however, and it was deemed improper to confide the supreme command to any but a native-born American. In fact, if he was sincere in what we have quoted from his letter to Burke, he did not aspire to such a signal mark of confidence.

The opinion evidently inclined in favor of Washington; yet it was promoted by no clique of partisans or admirers. More than one of the Virginia delegates, says Adams, were cool on the subject of this appointment; and particularly Mr. Pendleton, was clear and full against it. It is scarcely necessary to add, that Washington in this, as in every other situation in life, made no step in advance to clutch the impending honor.

Adams, in his diary, claims the credit of bringing the members of Congress to a decision. Rising in his place, one day, and stating briefly, but earnestly, the exigencies of the case, he moved that Congress should adopt the army at Cambridge, and appoint a general. Though this was not the time to nominate the person, "yet," adds he, "as I had reason to believe this was a point of some difficulty, I had no hesitation to declare, that I had but one gentleman in my mind for that important command, and that was a gentleman from Virginia, who was among us and very well known to all of us; a gentleman, whose skill and experience as an officer, whose independent fortune, great talents, and excellent universal character would command the approbation of all America, and unite the cordial exertions of all the colonies better than any other person in the Union. Mr. Washington, who happened to sit near the door, as soon as he heard me allude to him, from his usual modesty, darted into the library-room. Mr. Hancock, who was our president, which gave me an opportunity to observe his countenance, while I was speaking on the state of the colonies, the army at Cambridge, and the enemy, heard me with visible pleasure; but when I came to describe Washington for the commander, I never remarked a more sudden and striking change of countenance. Mortification and resentment were expressed as forcibly as his face could exhibit them."

"When the subject came under debate, several delegates opposed the appointment of Washington; not from personal objections, but because the army were all from New England, and had a general of their own, General Artemas Ward, with whom they appeared well satisfied; and under whose command they had proved themselves able to imprison the British army in Boston; which was all that was to be expected or desired."

The subject was postponed to a future day. In the interim, pains were taken out of doors to obtain a unanimity, and the voices were in general so clearly in favor of Washington, that the dissentient members were persuaded to withdraw their opposition.

On the 15th of June, the army was regularly adopted by Congress, and the pay of the Commander-in-chief fixed at five hundred dollars a month. Many still clung to the idea, that in all these proceedings they were merely opposing the measures of the ministry, and not the authority of the crown, and thus the army before Boston was designated as the Continental Army, in contradistinction to that under General Gage, which was called the Ministerial Army.

In this stage of the business Mr. Johnson, of Maryland, rose, and nominated Washington for the station of commander-in-chief. The election was by ballot, and was unanimous. It was formally announced to him by the president, on the following day, when he had taken his seat in Congress. Rising in his place, he briefly expressed his high and grateful sense of the honor conferred on him, and his sincere devotion to the cause. "But," added he, "lest some unlucky event should happen unfavorable to my reputation, I beg it may be remembered by every gentleman in the room, that I this day declare, with the utmost sincerity, I do not think myself equal to the command I am honored with. As to pay, I beg leave to assure the Congress that, as no pecuniary consideration could have tempted me to accept this arduous employment, at the expense of my domestic ease and happiness, I do not wish to make any profit of it. I will keep an exact account of my expenses. Those, I doubt not, they will discharge, and that is all I desire."

"There is something charming to me in the conduct of Washington," writes Adams to a friend; "a gentleman of one of the first fortunes upon the continent, leaving his delicious retirement, his family and friends, sacrificing his ease, and hazarding all, in the cause of his country. His views are noble and disinterested. He declared, when he accepted the mighty trust, that he would lay before us an exact account of his expenses, and not accept a shilling of pay."

Four major-generals were to be appointed. Among those specified were General Charles Lee and General Ward. Mr. Mifflin, of Philadelphia, who was Lee's especial friend and admirer, urged that he should be second in command. "General Lee," said he, "would serve cheerfully under Washington; but considering his rank, character, and experience, could not be expected to serve under any other. He must be *aut secundus, aut nullus.*"

Adams, on the other hand, as strenuously objected that it would be a great deal to expect that General Ward, who was actually in command of the army in Boston, should serve under any man; but under a stranger he ought not to serve. General Ward, accordingly, was elected the second in command, and Lee the third. The other two major-generals were, Philip Schuyler, of New York, and Israel Putnam, of Connecticut. Eight brigadier-generals were likewise appointed; Seth Pomeroy, Richard Montgomery, David Wooster, William Heath, Joseph Spencer, John Thomas, John Sullivan, and Nathaniel Greene.

Notwithstanding Mr. Mifflin's objection to having Lee ranked under Ward, as being beneath his dignity and merits, he himself made no scruple to acquiesce; though, judging from his supercilious character, and from circumstances in his subsequent conduct, he no doubt considered himself vastly superior to the provincial officers placed over him.

At Washington's express request, his old friend, Major Horatio Gates, then absent at his estate in Virginia, was appointed adjutant-general, with the rank of brigadier.

Adams, according to his own account, was extremely loth to admit either Lee or Gates into the American service, although he considered them officers of great experience and confessed abilities. He apprehended difficulties, he said, from the "natural prejudices and virtuous attachment of our countrymen to their own officers." "But," adds he, "considering the earnest desire of General Washington to have the assistance of those officers, the extreme attachment of many of our best friends in the southern colonies to them, the reputation they would give to our arms in Europe, and especially with the ministerial generals and army in Boston, as well as the real American merit of both, I could not withhold my vote from either."

The reader will possibly call these circumstances to mind when, on a future page, he finds how Lee and Grates requited the friendship to which chiefly they owed their appointments.

In this momentous change in his condition, which suddenly altered all his course of life, and called him immediately to the camp, Washington's thoughts recurred to Mount Vernon, and its rural delights, so dear to his heart, whence he was to be again exiled. His chief concern, however, was on account of the distress it might cause to his wife. His letter to her on the subject is written in a tone of manly tenderness. "You may believe me," writes he, "when I assure you, in the most solemn manner, that, so far from seeking this appointment, I have used every endeavor in my power to avoid it, not only from my unwillingness to part with you and the family, but from a consciousness of its being a trust too great for my capacity; and I should enjoy more real happiness in one month with you at home than I have the most distant prospect of finding abroad, if my stay were to be seven times seven years. But as it has been a kind of destiny that has thrown me upon this service, I shall hope that my undertaking it is designed to answer some good purpose. . . .

"I shall rely confidently on that Providence which has heretofore preserved, and been bountiful to me, not doubting but that I shall return safe to you in the Fall. I shall feel no pain from the toil or danger of the campaign; my unhappiness will flow from the uneasiness I know you will feel from being left alone. I therefore beg that you will summon your whole fortitude, and pass your time as agreeably as possible. Nothing will give me so much sincere satisfaction as to hear this, and to hear it from your own pen."

And to his favorite brother, John Augustine, he writes: "I am now to bid adieu to you, and to every kind of domestic ease, for a while. I am embarked on a wide ocean, boundless in its prospect, and in which, perhaps, no safe harbor is to be found. I have been called upon by the unanimous voice of the colonies to take the command of the continental army; an honor I neither sought after, nor desired, as I am thoroughly convinced that it requires great abilities, and much more experience, than I am master of." And subsequently, referring to his wife: "I shall hope that my friends will visit, and endeavor to keep up the spirits of my wife as much as they can, for my departure will, I know, be a cutting stroke upon her; and on this account alone I have many disagreeable sensations."

On the 20th of June, he received his commission from the president of Congress. The following day was fixed upon for his departure for the army. He reviewed previously, at the request of their officers, several militia companies of horse and foot. Every one was anxious to see the new commander, and rarely has the public *beau ideal* of a commander been so fully answered. He was now in the vigor of his days, forty-three years of age, stately in person, noble in his demeanor, calm and dignified in his deportment; as he sat his horse, with manly grace, his military presence delighted every eye, and wherever he went the air rang with acclamations.

CHAPTER XL.

MORE TROOPS ARRIVE AT BOSTON—GENERALS
HOWE, BURGOYNE, AND CLINTON—PROCLAMATION
OF GAGE—NATURE OF THE AMERICAN ARMY—
SCORNFUL CONDUCT OF THE BRITISH OFFICERS—
PROJECT OF THE AMERICANS TO SEIZE UPON BREED'S
HILL—PUTNAM'S OPINION OF IT—SANCTIONED
BY PRESCOTT—NOCTURNAL MARCH OF THE
DETACHMENT—FORTIFYING OF BUNKER'S HILL—
BREAK OF DAY, AND ASTONISHMENT OF THE ENEMY.

While Congress had been deliberating on the adoption of the
army, and the nomination of a commander-in-chief, events had
been thickening and drawing to a crisis in the excited region about
Boston. The provincial troops which blockaded the town prevented
supplies by land, the neighboring country refused to furnish them
by water; fresh provisions and vegetables were no longer to be
procured, and Boston began to experience the privations of a
besieged city.

On the 25th of May, arrived ships of war and transports from
England, bringing large reinforcements, under Generals Howe,
Burgoyne, and Henry Clinton, commanders of high reputation.

As the ships entered the harbor, and the "rebel camp" was
pointed out, ten thousand yeomanry beleaguering a town garrisoned
by five thousand regulars, Burgoyne could not restrain a burst of
surprise and scorn. "What!" cried he, "ten thousand peasants keep
five thousand king's troops shut up! Well, let us get in, and we'll
soon find elbow-room."

Inspirited by these reinforcements, General Gage determined
to take the field. Previously, however, in conformity to instructions
from Lord Dartmouth, the head of the war department, he issued

a proclamation (12th June), putting the province under martial law, threatening to treat as rebels and traitors all malcontents who should continue under arms, together with their aiders and abettors; but offering pardon to all who should lay down their arms, and return to their allegiance. From this proffered amnesty, however, John Hancock and Samuel Adams were especially excepted; their offences being pronounced "too flagitious not to meet with condign punishment."

This proclamation only served to put the patriots on the alert against such measures as might be expected to follow, and of which their friends in Boston stood ready to apprise them. The besieging force, in the mean time, was daily augmented by recruits and volunteers, and now amounted to about fifteen thousand men distributed at various points. Its character and organization were peculiar. As has well been observed, it could not be called a national army, for, as yet, there was no nation to own it; it was not under the authority of the Continental Congress, the act of that body recognizing it not having as yet been passed, and the authority of that body itself not having been acknowledged. It was, in fact, a fortuitous assemblage of four distinct bodies of troops, belonging to different provinces, and each having a leader of its own election. About ten thousand belonged to Massachusetts, and were under the command of General Artemas Ward, whose head-quarters were at Cambridge. Another body of troops, under Colonel John Stark, already mentioned, came from New Hampshire. Rhode Island furnished a third, under the command of General Nathaniel Greene. A fourth was from Connecticut, under the veteran Putnam.

These bodies of troops, being from different colonies, were independent of each other, and had their several commanders. Those from New Hampshire were instructed to obey General Ward as commander-in-chief; with the rest, it was a voluntary act, rendered in consideration of his being military chief of Massachusetts, the province which, as allies, they came to defend. There was, in fact, but little organization in the army. Nothing kept it together, and gave it unity of action, but a common feeling of exasperated patriotism.

The troops knew but little of military discipline. Almost all were familiar with the use of fire-arms in hunting and fowling; many had served in frontier campaigns against the French, and in "bush-fighting" with the Indians; but none were acquainted with regular service or the discipline of European armies. There was a regiment of artillery, partly organized by Colonel Gridley, a skilful engineer, and furnished with nine field-pieces; but the greater part of the troops were without military dress or accoutrements; most of them were hasty levies of yeomanry, some of whom had seized their rifles and fowling-pieces, and turned out in their working clothes and homespun country garbs. It was an army of volunteers, subordinate through inclination and respect to officers of their own choice, and depending for sustenance on supplies sent from, their several towns.

Such was the army spread over an extent of ten or twelve miles, and keeping watch upon the town of Boston, containing at that time a population of seventeen thousand souls, and garrisoned with more than ten thousand British troops, disciplined and experienced in the wars of Europe.

In the disposition of these forces, General Ward had stationed himself at Cambridge, with the main body of about nine thousand men and four companies of artillery. Lieutenant-general Thomas, second in command, was posted, with five thousand Massachusetts, Connecticut and Rhode Island troops, and three or four companies of artillery, at Roxbury and Dorchester, forming the right wing of the army; while the left, composed in a great measure of New Hampshire troops, stretched through Medford to the hills of Chelsea.

It was a great annoyance to the British officers and soldiers, to be thus hemmed in by what they termed a rustic rout with calico frocks and fowling-pieces. The same scornful and taunting spirit prevailed among them, that the cavaliers of yore indulged toward the Covenanters. Considering episcopacy as the only loyal and royal faith, they insulted and desecrated the "sectarian" places of worship. One was turned into a riding school for the cavalry, and the fire in the stove was kindled with books from the library of its pastor. The Provincials retaliated by turning the Episcopal church at Cambridge into a barrack, and melting down its organ-pipes into bullets.

Both parties panted for action; the British through impatience of their humiliating position, and an eagerness to chastise what they considered the presumption of their besiegers; the Provincials through enthusiasm in their cause, a thirst for enterprise and exploit, and, it must be added, an unconsciousness of their own military deficiencies.

We have already mentioned the peninsula of Charlestown (called from a village of the same name), which lies opposite to the north side of Boston. The heights, which swell up in rear of the village, overlook the town and shipping. The project was conceived in the besieging camp to seize and occupy those heights. A council of war was held upon the subject. The arguments in favor of the attempt were, that the army was anxious to be employed; that the country was dissatisfied with its inactivity, and that the enemy might thus be drawn out to ground where they might be fought to advantage. General Putnam was one of the most strenuous in favor of the measure.

Some of the more wary and judicious, among whom were General Ward and Dr. Warren, doubted the expediency of intrenching themselves on those heights, and the possibility of maintaining so exposed a post, scantily furnished, as they were, with ordnance and ammunition. Besides, it might bring on a general engagement, which it was not safe to risk.

Putnam made light of the danger. He was confident of the bravery of the militia if intrenched, having seen it tried in the old French war. "The Americans," said he, "are never afraid of their heads; they only think of their legs; shelter them, and they'll fight for ever." He was seconded by General Pomeroy, a leader of like stamp, and another veteran of the French war. He had been a hunter in his time; a dead shot with a rifle, and was ready to lead troops against the enemy, "with five cartridges to a man."

The daring councils of such men are always captivating to the inexperienced; but in the present instance, they were sanctioned by one whose opinion in such matters, and in this vicinity, possessed peculiar weight. This was Colonel William Prescott, of Pepperell, who commanded a regiment of minute men. He, too, had seen service in the French war, and acquired reputation as a lieutenant of infantry at the capture of Cape Breton. This was sufficient to constitute him an oracle in the present instance. He was now about fifty years of age, tall and commanding in his appearance, and retaining the port of a soldier. What was more, he had a military garb; being equipped with a three-cornered hat, a top wig, and a single-breasted blue coat, with facings and lapped up at the skirts.

All this served to give him consequence among the rustic militia officers with whom he was in council.

His opinion, probably, settled the question; and it was determined to seize on and fortify Bunker's Hill and Dorchester Heights. In deference, however, to the suggestions of the more cautious, it was agreed to postpone the measure until they were sufficiently supplied with the munitions of war to be able to maintain the heights when seized.

Secret intelligence hurried forward the project. General Gage, it was said, intended to take possession of Dorchester Heights on the night of the 18th of June. These heights lay on the opposite side of Boston, and the committee were ignorant of their localities. Those on Charlestown Neck, being near at hand, had some time before been reconnoitered by Colonel Richard Gridley, and other of the engineers. It was determined to seize and fortify these heights on the night of Friday, the 16th of June, in anticipation of the movement of General Gage. Troops were draughted for the purpose from the Massachusetts regiments of Colonels Prescott, Frye and Bridges. There was also a fatigue party of about two hundred men from Putnam's Connecticut troops, led by his favorite officer, Captain Knowlton; together with a company of forty-nine artillery men, with two field-pieces, commanded by Captain Samuel Gridley.

A little before sunset the troops, about twelve hundred in all, assembled on the common, in front of General Ward's quarters. They came provided with packs, blankets and provisions for four-and-twenty hours, but ignorant of the object of the expedition. Being all paraded, prayers were offered up by the reverend President Langdon, of Harvard College; after which they all set forward on their silent march.

Colonel Prescott, from his experience in military matters, and his being an officer in the Massachusetts line, had been chosen by General Ward to conduct the enterprise. His written orders were to fortify Bunker's Hill, and defend the works until he should be relieved. Colonel Richard Gridley, the chief engineer, who had likewise served in the French war, was to accompany him and plan the fortifications. It was understood that reinforcements and refreshments would be sent to the fatigue party in the morning.

The detachment left Cambridge about 9 o'clock, Colonel Prescott taking the lead, preceded by two sergeants with dark lanterns. At Charlestown Neck they were joined by Major Brooks, of Bridges' regiment, and General Putnam; and here were the waggons laden with intrenching tools, which first gave the men an indication of the nature of the enterprise.

Charlestown Neck is a narrow isthmus, connecting the peninsula with the main land; having the Mystic River, about half a mile wide, on the north, and a large embayment of Charles River on the south or right side.

It was now necessary to proceed with the utmost caution, for they were coming on ground over which the British kept jealous watch. They had erected a battery at Boston on Copp's Hill, immediately opposite to Charlestown. Five of their vessels of war were stationed so as to bear upon the peninsula from different directions, and the guns of one of them swept the isthmus, or narrow neck just mentioned.

Across this isthmus, Colonel Prescott conducted the detachment undiscovered, and up the ascent of Bunker's Hill. This commences at the Neck, and slopes up for about three hundred yards to its summit, which is about one hundred and twelve feet high. It then declines toward the south, and is connected by a ridge with Breed's Hill, about sixty or seventy feet high. The crests of the two hills are about seven hundred yards apart.

On attaining the heights, a question rose which of the two they should proceed to fortify. Bunker's Hill was specified in the written orders given to Colonel Prescott by General Ward, but Breed's Hill was much nearer to Boston, and had a better command of the town and shipping. Bunker's Hill, also, being on the upper and narrower part of the peninsula, was itself commanded by the same ship which raked the Neck. Putnam was clear for commencing at Breed's Hill, and making the principal work there, while a minor work might be thrown up at Bunker's Hill, as a protection in the rear, and a rallying point, in case of being driven out of the main work. Others concurred with this opinion, yet there was a hesitation in deviating from the letter of their orders. At length Colonel Gridley became impatient; the night was waning; delay might prostrate the whole enterprise. Breed's Hill was then determined on. Gridley marked out the lines for the fortifications; the men stacked their guns; threw off their packs; seized their trenching tools, and set to work with great spirit; but so much time had been wasted in discussion, that it was midnight before they struck the first spade into the ground.

Prescott, who felt the responsibility of his charge, almost despaired of carrying on these operations undiscovered. A party was sent out by him silently to patrol the shore at the foot of the heights, and watch for any movement of the enemy. Not willing to trust entirely to the vigilance of others, he twice went down during the night to the water's edge; reconnoitering every thing scrupulously, and noting every sight and sound. It was a warm, still, summer's night; the stars shone brightly, but every thing was quiet. Boston was buried in sleep. The sentry's cry of "All's well" could be heard distinctly from its shores, together with the drowsy calling of the watch on board of the ships of war, and then all would relapse into silence. Satisfied that the enemy were perfectly unconscious of what was going on upon the hill, he returned to the works, and a little before daybreak called in the patrolling party.

So spiritedly, though silently, had the labor been carried on, that by morning a strong redoubt was thrown up as a main work, flanked on the left by a breastwork, partly cannon-proof, extending down the crest of Breed's Hill to a piece of marshy ground called the Slough. To support the right of the redoubt, some troops were thrown into the village of Charlestown, at the southern foot of the hill. The great object of Prescott's solicitude was now attained, a sufficient bulwark to screen his men before they should be discovered; for he doubted the possibility of keeping raw recruits to their post, if openly exposed to the fire of artillery, and the attack of disciplined troops.

At dawn of day, the Americans at work were espied by the sailors on board of the ships of war, and the alarm was given. The captain of the Lively, the nearest ship, without waiting for orders, put a spring upon her cable, and bringing her guns to bear, opened a fire upon the hill. The other ships and a floating battery followed his example. Their shot did no mischief to the works, but one man, among a number who had incautiously ventured outside, was killed. A subaltern reported his death to Colonel Prescott, and asked what was to be done. "Bury him," was the reply. The chaplain gathered some of his military flock around him, and was proceeding to perform suitable obsequies over the "first martyr," but Prescott ordered that the men should disperse to their work, and the deceased be buried immediately. It seemed shocking to men accustomed to the funeral solemnities of peaceful life to bury a man without prayers, but Prescott saw that the sight of this man suddenly shot down had agitated the nerves of his comrades, unaccustomed to scenes of war. Some of them, in fact, quietly left the hill, and did not return to it.

To inspire confidence by example, Prescott now mounted the parapet, and walked leisurely about, inspecting the works, giving directions, and talking cheerfully with the men. In a little while they got over their dread of cannon-balls, and some even made them a subject of joke, or rather bravado; a species of sham courage occasionally manifested by young soldiers, but never by veterans.

The cannonading roused the town of Boston. General Gage could scarcely believe his eyes when he beheld on the opposite hill a fortification full of men, which had sprung up in the course of the night. As he reconnoitered it through a glass from Copp's Hill, the tall figure of Prescott, in military garb, walking the parapet, caught his eye. "Who is that officer who appears in command?" asked he. The question was answered by Counsellor Willard, Prescott's brother-in-law, who was at hand, and recognized his relative. "Will he fight?" demanded Gage, quickly. "Yes, sir! he is an old soldier, and will fight to the last drop of blood; but I cannot answer for his men."

"The works must be carried!" exclaimed Gage.

He called a council of war. The Americans might intend to cannonade Boston from this new fortification; it was unanimously resolved to dislodge them. How was this to be done? A majority of the council, including Clinton and Grant, advised that a force should be landed on Charlestown Neck, under the protection of their batteries, so as to attack the Americans in rear, and cut off their retreat. General Gage objected that it would place his troops between two armies; one at Cambridge, superior in numbers, the other on the heights, strongly fortified. He was for landing in front of the works, and pushing directly up the hill; a plan adopted through a confidence that raw militia would never stand their ground against the assault of veteran troops; another instance of undervaluing the American spirit, which was to cost the enemy a lamentable loss of life.

CHAPTER XLI.

BATTLE OF BUNKER'S HILL.

The sound of drum and trumpet, the clatter of hoofs, the rattling of gun-carriages, and all the other military din and bustle in the streets of Boston, soon apprised the Americans on their rudely fortified height of an impending attack. They were ill fitted to withstand it, being jaded by the night's labor, and want of sleep; hungry and thirsty, having brought but scanty supplies, and oppressed by the heat of the weather. Prescott sent repeated messages to General Ward, asking reinforcements and provisions. Putnam seconded the request in person, urging the exigencies of the case. Ward hesitated. He feared to weaken his main body at Cambridge, as his military stores were deposited there, and it might have to sustain the principal attack. At length, having taken advice of the council of safety, he issued orders for Colonels Stark and Read, then at Medford, to march to the relief of Prescott with their New Hampshire regiments. The orders reached Medford about 11 o'clock. Ammunition was distributed in all haste; two flints, a gill of powder, and fifteen balls to each man. The balls had to be suited to the different calibres of the guns; the powder to be carried in powder-horns, or loose in the pocket, for there were no cartridges prepared. It was the rude turn out of yeoman soldiery destitute of regular accoutrements.

In the mean while, the Americans on Breed's Hill were sustaining the fire from the ships, and from the battery on Copp's Hill, which opened upon them about ten o'clock. They returned an occasional shot from one corner of the redoubt, without much harm to the enemy, and continued strengthening their position until about 11 o'clock, when they ceased to work, piled their intrenching tools in the rear, and looked out anxiously and impatiently for the anticipated reinforcements and supplies.

About this time General Putnam, who had been to headquarters, arrived at the redoubt on horseback. Some words passed between him and Prescott with regard to the intrenching tools, which have been variously reported. The most probable version is, that he urged to have them taken from their present place, where they might fall into the hands of the enemy, and carried to Bunker's Hill, to be employed in throwing up a redoubt, which was part of the original plan, and which would be very important should the troops be obliged to retreat from Breed's Hill. To this Prescott demurred that those employed to convey them, and who were already jaded with toil, might not return to his redoubt. A large part of the tools were ultimately carried to Bunker's Hill, and a breastwork commenced by order of General Putnam. The importance of such a work was afterwards made apparent.

About noon the Americans descried twenty-eight barges crossing from Boston in parallel lines. They contained a large detachment of grenadiers, rangers, and light infantry, admirably equipped, and commanded by Major-general Howe. They made a splendid and formidable appearance with their scarlet uniforms, and the sun flashing upon muskets and bayonets, and brass fieldpieces. A heavy fire from the ships and batteries covered their advance, but no attempt was made to oppose them, and they landed about 1 o'clock at Moulton's Point, a little to the north of Breed's Hill.

Here General Howe made a pause. On reconnoitering the works from this point, the Americans appeared to be much more strongly posted than he had imagined. He descried troops also hastening to their assistance. These were the New Hampshire troops, led on by Stark. Howe immediately sent over to General Gage for more forces, and a supply of cannon-balls; those brought by him being found, through some egregious oversight, too large for the ordnance. While awaiting their arrival, refreshments were served out to the troops, with "grog," by the bucketful; and tantalizing it was, to the hungry and thirsty provincials, to look down from their ramparts of earth, and see their invaders seated in groups upon the grass eating and drinking, and preparing themselves by a hearty meal for the coming encounter. Their only consolation was to take advantage of the delay, while the enemy were carousing, to strengthen their position. The breast-work on the left of the redoubt extended to what was called the Slough, but beyond this, the ridge of the hill, and the slope toward Mystic River, were undefended, leaving a pass by which the enemy might turn the left flank of the position, and seize upon Bunker's Hill. Putnam ordered his chosen officer, Captain Knowlton, to cover this pass with the Connecticut troops under his command. A novel kind of rampart, savoring of rural device, was suggested by the rustic general. About six hundred feet in the rear of the redoubt, and about one hundred feet to the left of the breastwork, was a post and rail-fence, set in a low foot-wall of stone, and extending down to Mystic River. The posts and rails of another fence were hastily pulled up, and set a few feet in behind this, and the intermediate space was filled up with new mown hay from the adjacent meadows. This double fence, it will be found, proved an important protection to the redoubt, although there still remained an unprotected interval of about seven hundred feet.

While Knowlton and his men were putting up this fence, Putnam proceeded with other of his troops to throw up the work on Bunker's Hill, despatching his son, Captain Putnam, on horseback, to hurry up the remainder of his men from Cambridge. By this time his compeer in French and Indian warfare, the veteran Stark, made his appearance with the New Hampshire troops, five hundred strong. He had grown cool and wary with age, and his march from Medford, a distance of five or six miles, had been in character. He led his men at a moderate pace to bring them into action fresh and vigorous. In crossing the Neck, which was enfiladed by the enemy's ships and batteries, Captain Dearborn, who was by his side, suggested a quick step. The veteran shook his head: "One fresh man in action is worth ten tired ones," replied he, and marched steadily on.

Putnam detained some of Stark's men to aid in throwing up the works on Bunker's Hill, and directed him to reinforce Knowlton with the rest. Stark made a short speech to his men now that they were likely to have warm work. He then pushed on, and did good service that day at the rustic bulwark.

About 2 o'clock, Warren arrived on the heights, ready to engage in their perilous defence, although he had opposed the scheme of their occupation. He had recently been elected a major-general, but had not received his commission; like Pomeroy, he came to serve in the ranks with a musket on his shoulder. Putnam offered him the command at the fence; he declined it, and merely asked where he could be of most service as a volunteer. Putnam pointed to the redoubt, observing that there he would be under cover. "Don't think I seek a place of safety," replied Warren, quickly; "where will the attack be hottest?" Putnam still pointed to the redoubt. "That is the enemy's object; if that can be maintained, the day is ours."

Warren was cheered by the troops as he entered the redoubt. Colonel Prescott tendered him the command. He again declined. "I have come to serve only as a volunteer, and shall be happy to learn from a soldier of your experience." Such were the noble spirits assembled on these perilous heights.

The British now prepared for a general assault. An easy victory was anticipated; the main thought was, how to make it most effectual. The left wing, commanded by General Pigot, was to mount the hill and force the redoubt, while General Howe, with the right wing, was to push on between the fort and Mystic River, turn the left flank of the Americans, and cut off their retreat.

General Pigot, accordingly, advanced up the hill under cover of a fire from field-pieces and howitzers planted on a small height near the landing-place on Moulton's Point. His troops commenced a discharge of musketry while yet at a long distance from the redoubts. The Americans within the works, obedient to strict command, retained their fire until the enemy were within thirty or forty paces, when they opened upon them with a tremendous volley. Being all marksmen, accustomed to take deliberate aim, the slaughter was immense, and especially fatal to officers. The assailants fell back in some confusion; but, rallied on by their officers, advanced within pistol shot. Another volley, more effective than the first, made them again recoil. To add to their confusion, they were galled by a flanking fire from the handful of Provincials posted in Charlestown. Shocked at the carnage, and seeing the confusion of his troops, General Pigot was urged to give the word for a retreat.

In the mean while, General Howe, with the right wing, advanced along Mystic River toward the fence where Stark, Read and Knowlton were stationed, thinking to carry this slight breastwork with ease, and so get in the rear of the fortress. His artillery proved of little avail, being stopped by a swampy piece of ground, while his columns suffered from two or three fieldpieces with which Putnam had fortified the fence. Howe's men kept up a fire of musketry as they advanced; but, not taking aim, their shot passed over the heads of the Americans. The latter had received the same orders with those in the redoubt, not to fire until the enemy should be within thirty paces. Some few transgressed the command. Putnam rode up and swore he would cut down the next man that fired contrary to orders. When the British arrived within the stated distance a sheeted fire opened upon them from rifles, muskets, and fowling-pieces, all levelled with deadly aim. The carnage, as in the other instance, was horrible. The British were thrown into confusion and fell back; some even retreated to the boats.

There was a general pause on the part of the British. The American officers availed themselves of it to prepare for another attack, which must soon be made. Prescott mingled among his men in the redoubt, who were all in high spirits at the severe check they had given "the regulars." He praised them for their steadfastness in maintaining their post, and their good conduct in reserving their fire until the word of command, and exhorted them to do the same in the next attack.

Putnam rode about Bunker's Hill and its skirts, to rally and bring on reinforcements which had been checked or scattered in crossing Charlestown Neck by the raking fire from the ships and batteries. Before many could be brought to the scene of action the British had commenced their second attack. They again ascended the hill to storm the redoubt; their advance was covered as before by discharges of artillery. Charlestown, which had annoyed them on their first attack by a flanking fire, was in flames, by shells thrown from Copp's Hill, and by marines from the ships. Being built of wood, the place was soon wrapped in a general conflagration. The thunder of artillery from batteries and ships, the bursting of bomb-shells; the sharp discharges of musketry; the shouts and yells of the combatants; the crash of burning buildings, and the dense volumes of smoke, which obscured the summer sun, all formed a tremendous spectacle. "Sure I am," said Burgoyne in one of his letters,—"Sure I am nothing ever has or ever can be more dreadfully terrible than what was to be seen or heard at this time. The most incessant discharge of guns that ever was heard by mortal ears."

The American troops, although unused to war, stood undismayed amidst a scene where it was bursting upon them with all its horrors. Reserving their fire, as before, until the enemy was close at hand, they again poured forth repeated volleys with the fatal aim of sharpshooters. The British stood the first shock, and continued to advance; but the incessant stream of fire staggered them. Their officers remonstrated, threatened, and even attempted to goad them on with their swords, but the havoc was too deadly; whole ranks were mowed down; many of the officers were either slain or wounded, and among them several of the staff of General Howe. The troops again gave way and retreated down the hill.

All this passed under the eye of thousands of spectators of both sexes and all ages, watching from afar every turn of a battle in which the lives of those most dear to them were at hazard. The British soldiery in Boston gazed with astonishment and almost incredulity at the resolute and protracted stand of raw militia whom they had been taught to despise, and at the havoc made among their own veteran troops. Every convoy of wounded brought over to the town increased their consternation, and General Clinton, who had watched the action from Copp's Hill, embarking in a boat, hurried over as a volunteer, taking with him reinforcements.

A third attack was now determined on, though some of Howe's officers remonstrated, declaring it would be downright butchery. A different plan was adopted. Instead of advancing in front of the redoubt, it was to be taken in flank on the left, where the open space between the breastwork and the fortified fence presented a weak point. It having been accidentally discovered that the ammunition of the Americans was nearly expended, preparations were made to carry the works at the point of the bayonet; and the soldiery threw off their knapsacks, and some even their coats, to be more light for action.

General Howe, with the main body, now made a feint of attacking the fortified fence; but, while a part of his force was thus engaged, the rest brought some of the field-pieces to enfilade the breastwork on the left of the redoubt. A raking fire soon drove the Americans out of this exposed place into the enclosure. Much damage, too, was done in the latter by balls which entered the sallyport.

The troops were now led on to assail the works; those who flinched were, as before, goaded on by the swords of the officers. The Americans again reserved their fire until their assailants were close at hand, and then made a murderous volley, by which several officers were laid low, and General Howe himself was wounded in the foot. The British soldiery this time likewise reserved their fire and rushed on with fixed bayonet. Clinton and Pigot had reached the southern and eastern sides of the redoubt, and it was now assailed on three sides at once. Prescott ordered those who had no bayonets to retire to the back part of the redoubt and fire on the enemy as they showed themselves on the parapet. The first who mounted exclaimed in triumph, "The day is ours!" He was instantly shot down, and so were several others who mounted about the same time. The Americans, however, had fired their last round, their ammunition was exhausted; and now succeeded a desperate and deadly struggle, hand to hand, with bayonets, stones, and the stocks of their muskets. At length, as the British continued to pour in, Prescott gave the order to retreat. His men had to cut their way through two divisions of the enemy who were getting in rear of the redoubt, and they received a destructive volley from those who had formed on the captured works. By that volley fell the patriot Warren, who had distinguished himself throughout the action. He was among the last to leave the redoubt, and had scarce done so when he was shot through the head with a musket-ball, and fell dead on the spot.

While the Americans were thus slowly dislodged from the redoubt, Stark, Read and Knowlton maintained their ground at the fortified fence; which, indeed, had been nobly defended throughout the action. Pomeroy distinguished himself here by his sharpshooting until his musket was shattered by a ball. The resistance at this hastily constructed work was kept up after the troops in the redoubt had given way, and until Colonel Prescott had left the hill; thus defeating General Howe's design of cutting off the retreat of the main body; which would have produced a scene of direful confusion and slaughter. Having effected their purpose, the brave associates at the fence abandoned their weak outpost, retiring slowly, and disputing the ground inch by inch, with a regularity remarkable in troops many of whom had never before been in action.

The main retreat was across Bunker's Hill, where Putnam had endeavored to throw up a breastwork. The veteran, sword in hand, rode to the rear of the retreating troops, regardless of the balls whistling about him. His only thought was to rally them at the unfinished works. "Halt! make a stand here!" cried he, "we can check them yet. In God's name, form and give them one shot more."

Pomeroy, wielding his shattered musket as a truncheon, seconded him in his efforts to stay the torrent. It was impossible, however, to bring the troops to a stand. They continued on down the hill to the Neck and across it to Cambridge, exposed to a raking fire from the ships and batteries, and only protected by a single piece of ordnance. The British were too exhausted to pursue them; they contented themselves with taking possession of Bunker's Hill, were reinforced from Boston, and threw up additional works during the night.

We have collected the preceding facts from various sources, examining them carefully, and endeavoring to arrange them with scrupulous fidelity. We may appear to have been more minute in the account of the battle than the number of troops engaged would warrant; but it was one of the most momentous conflicts in our revolutionary history. It was the first regular battle between the British and the Americans, and most eventful in its consequences. The former had gained the ground for which they contended; but, if a victory, it was more disastrous and humiliating to them than an ordinary defeat. They had ridiculed and despised their enemy, representing them as dastardly and inefficient; yet here their best troops, led on by experienced officers, had repeatedly been repulsed by an inferior force of that enemy,—mere yeomanry,—from works thrown up in a single night, and had suffered a loss rarely paralleled in battle with the most veteran soldiery; for, according to their own returns, their killed and wounded, out of a detachment of two thousand men, amounted to one thousand and fifty four, and a large proportion of them officers. The loss of the Americans did not exceed four hundred and fifty.

To the latter this defeat, if defeat it might be called, had the effect of a triumph. It gave them confidence in themselves and consequence in the eyes of their enemies. They had proved to themselves and to others that they could measure weapons with the disciplined soldiers of Europe, and inflict the most harm in the conflict.

Among the British officer's slain was Major Pitcairn, who, at Lexington, had shed the first blood in the Revolutionary war.

In the death of Warren the Americans had to lament the loss of a distinguished patriot and a most estimable man. It was deplored as a public calamity. His friend Elbridge Gerry had endeavored to dissuade him from risking his life in this perilous conflict, "Dulce et decorum est pro patria mori," replied Warren, as if he had foreseen his fate—a fate to be envied by those ambitious of an honorable fame. He was one of the first who fell in the glorious cause of his country, and his name has become consecrated in its history.

There has been much discussion of the relative merits of the American officers engaged in this affair—a difficult question where no one appears to have had the general command. Prescott conducted the troops in the night enterprise; he superintended the building of the redoubt, and defended it throughout the battle; his name, therefore, will ever shine most conspicuous, and deservedly so, on this bright page of our Revolutionary history.

Putnam also was a leading spirit throughout the affair; one of the first to prompt and of the last to maintain it. He appears to have been active and efficient at every point; sometimes fortifying; sometimes hurrying up reinforcements; inspiriting the men by his presence while they were able to maintain their ground, and fighting gallantly at the outpost to cover their retreat. The brave old man, riding about in the heat of the action, on this sultry day, "with a hanger belted across his brawny shoulders, over a waistcoat without sleeves," has been sneered at by a contemporary, as "much fitter to head a band of sickle men or ditchers than musketeers." But this very description illustrates his character, and identifies him with the times and the service. A yeoman warrior fresh from the plough, in the garb of rural labor; a patriot brave and generous, but rough and ready, who thought not of himself in time of danger, but was ready to serve in any way, and to sacrifice official rank and self-glorification to the good of the cause. He was eminently a soldier for the occasion. His name has long been a favorite one with young and old; one of the talismanic names of the Revolution, the very mention of which is like the sound of a trumpet. Such names are the precious jewels of our history, to be garnered up among the treasures of the nation, and kept immaculate from the tarnishing breath of the cynic and the doubter.

NOTE.—In treating of the battle of Bunker's Hill, and of other occurrences about Boston at this period of the Revolution, we have had repeated occasion to consult the History of the Siege of Boston, by Richard Frothingham, Jr.; a work abounding with facts as to persons and events, and full of interest for the American reader.

CHAPTER XLII.

DEPARTURE FROM PHILADELPHIA—ANECDOTES OF
GENERAL SCHUYLER—OF LEE—TIDINGS OF BUNKER
HILL—MILITARY COUNCILS—POPULATION OF NEW
YORK—THE JOHNSON FAMILY—GOVERNOR TRYON—
ARRIVAL AT NEW YORK—MILITARY INSTRUCTIONS TO
SCHUYLER—ARRIVAL AT THE CAMP.

In a preceding chapter we left Washington preparing to
depart from Philadelphia for the army before Boston. He set out
on horseback on the 21st of June, having for military companions
of his journey Major-generals Lee and Schuyler, and being
accompanied for a distance by several private friends. As an escort
he had a "gentleman troop" of Philadelphia, commanded by
Captain Markoe; the whole formed a brilliant cavalcade.

General Schuyler was a man eminently calculated to sympathize
with Washington in all his patriotic views and feelings, and became
one of his most faithful coadjutors. Sprung from one of the earliest
and most respectable Dutch families which colonized New York, all
his interests and affections were identified with the country. He had
received a good education; applied himself at an early age to the
exact sciences, and became versed in finance, military engineering,
and political economy. He was one of those native born soldiers
who had acquired experience in that American school of arms, the
old French war. When but twenty-two years of age he commanded
a company of New York levies under Sir William Johnson, of
Mohawk renown, which gave him an early opportunity of becoming
acquainted with the Indian tribes, their country and their policy.
In 1758 he was in Abercrombie's expedition against Ticonderoga,
accompanying Lord Viscount Howe as chief of the commissariat
department; a post well qualified to give him experience in the

business part of war. When that gallant young nobleman fell on the banks of Lake George, Schuyler conveyed his corpse back to Albany and attended to his honorable obsequies. Since the close of the French war he had served his country in various civil stations, and been one of the most zealous and eloquent vindicators of colonial rights. He was one of the "glorious minority" of the New York General Assembly; George Clinton, Colonel Woodhull, Colonel Philip Livingston and others; who, when that body was timid and wavering, battled nobly against British influence and oppression. His last stand had been recently as a delegate to Congress, where he had served with Washington on the committee to prepare rules and regulations for the army, and where the latter had witnessed his judgment, activity, practical science, and sincere devotion to the cause.

Many things concurred to produce perfect harmony of operation between these distinguished men. They were nearly of the same age, Schuyler being one year the youngest. Both were men of agricultural, as well as military tastes. Both were men of property, living at their ease in little rural paradises; Washington on the grove-clad heights of Mount Vernon, Schuyler on the pastoral banks of the upper Hudson, where he had a noble estate at Saratoga, inherited from an uncle; and the old family mansion, near the city of Albany, half hid among ancestral trees. Yet both were exiling themselves from these happy abodes, and putting life and fortune at hazard in the service of their country.

Schuyler and Lee had early military recollections to draw them together. Both had served under Abercrombie in the expedition against Ticonderoga. There was some part of Lee's conduct in that expedition which both he and Schuyler might deem it expedient at this moment to forget. Lee was at that time a young captain, naturally presumptuous, and flushed with the arrogance of military power. On his march along the banks of the Hudson, he acted as if in a conquered country, impressing horses and oxen, and seizing upon supplies, without exhibiting any proper warrant. It was enough for him, "they were necessary for the service of his troops." Should any one question his right, the reply was a volley of execrations.

Among those who experienced this unsoldierly treatment was Mrs. Schuyler, the aunt of the general; a lady of aristocratical station, revered throughout her neighborhood. Her cattle were impressed, herself insulted. She had her revenge. After the unfortunate affair at Ticonderoga, a number of the wounded were brought down along the Hudson to the Schuyler mansion. Lee was among the number. The high-minded mistress of the house never alluded to his past conduct. He was received like his brother officers with the kindest sympathy. Sheets and tablecloths were torn up to serve as bandages. Every thing was done to alleviate their sufferings. Lee's cynic heart was conquered. "He swore in his vehement manner that he was sure there would be a place reserved for Mrs. Schuyler in heaven, though no other woman should be there, and that he should wish for nothing better than to share her final destiny!"[111]

Seventeen years had since elapsed, and Lee and the nephew of Mrs. Schuyler were again allied in military service, but under a different banner; and recollections of past times must have given peculiar interest to their present intercourse. In fact, the journey of Washington with his associate generals, experienced like him in the wild expeditions of the old French war, was a revival of early campaigning feelings.

They had scarcely proceeded twenty miles from Philadelphia when they were met by a courier, spurring with all speed, bearing despatches from the army to Congress, communicating tidings of the battle of Bunker's Hill. Washington eagerly inquired particulars; above all, how acted the militia? When told that they stood their ground bravely; sustained the enemy's fire—reserved their own until at close quarters, and then delivered it with deadly effect; it seemed as if a weight of doubt and solicitude were lifted from his heart. "The liberties of the country are safe!" exclaimed he.

The news of the battle of Bunker's Hill had startled the whole country; and this clattering cavalcade, escorting the commander-in-chief to the army, was the gaze and wonder of every town and village.

The journey may be said to have been a continual council of war between Washington and the two generals. Even the contrast in character of the two latter made them regard questions from different points of view. Schuyler, a warm-hearted patriot, with every thing staked on the cause; Lee, a soldier of fortune, indifferent to the ties

---

111   Memoirs of an American Lady (Mrs. Grant, of Laggan), vol. ii., chap. ix.

of home and country, drawing his sword without enthusiasm; more through resentment against a government which had disappointed him, than zeal for liberty or for colonial rights.

One of the most frequent subjects of conversation was the province of New York. Its power and position rendered it the great link of the confederacy; what measures were necessary for its defence, and most calculated to secure its adherence to the cause? A lingering attachment to the crown, kept up by the influence of British merchants, and military and civil functionaries in royal pay, had rendered it slow in coming into the colonial compact; and it was only on the contemptuous dismissal of their statement of grievances, unheard, that its people had thrown off their allegiance, as much in sorrow as in anger.

No person was better fitted to give an account of the interior of New York than General Schuyler; and the hawk-eyed Lee during a recent sojourn had made its capital somewhat of a study; but there was much yet for both of them to learn.

The population of New York was more varied in its elements than that of almost any other of the provinces, and had to be cautiously studied. The New Yorkers were of a mixed origin, and stamped with the peculiarities of their respective ancestors. The descendants of the old Dutch and Huguenot families, the earliest settlers, were still among the soundest and best of the population. They inherited the love of liberty, civil and religious, of their forefathers, and were those who stood foremost in the present struggle for popular rights. Such were the Jays, the Bensons, the Beekmans, the Hoffmans, the Van Hornes, the Roosevelts, the Duyckinks, the Pintards, the Yateses, and others whose names figure in the patriotic documents of the day. Some of them, doubtless, cherished a remembrance of the time when their forefathers were lords of the land, and felt an innate propensity to join in resistance to the government by which their supremacy had been overturned. A great proportion of the more modern families, dating from the downfall of the Dutch government in 1664, were English and Scotch, and among these were many loyal adherents to the crown. Then there was a mixture of the whole, produced by the intermarriages of upwards of a century, which partook of every shade of character and sentiment. The operations of foreign commerce, and the regular communications with the mother country through packets and ships of war, kept these elements in constant action, and contributed to produce that mercurial temperament, that fondness for excitement, and proneness to pleasure, which distinguished them from their neighbors on either side—the austere Puritans of New England, and the quiet "Friends" of Pennsylvania.

There was a power, too, of a formidable kind within the interior of the province, which was an object of much solicitude. This was the "Johnson Family." We have repeatedly had occasion to speak of Sir William Johnson, his majesty's general agent for Indian affairs, of his great wealth, and his almost sovereign sway over the Six Nations. He had originally received that appointment through the influence of the Schuyler family. Both Generals Schuyler and Lee, when young men, had campaigned with him; and it was among the Mohawk warriors, who rallied under his standard, that Lee had beheld his vaunted models of good-breeding.

In the recent difficulties between the crown and colonies, Sir William had naturally been in favor of the government which had enriched and honored him, but he had viewed with deep concern the acts of Parliament which were goading the colonists to armed resistance. In the height of his solicitude, he received despatches ordering him, in case of hostilities, to enlist the Indians in the cause of government. To the agitation of feelings produced by these orders many have attributed a stroke of apoplexy, of which he died, on the 11th of July, 1774, about a year before the time of which we are treating.

His son and heir, Sir John Johnson, and his sons-in-law, Colonel Guy Johnson and Colonel Claus, felt none of the reluctance of Sir William to use harsh measures in support of royalty. They lived in a degree of rude feudal style in stone mansions capable of defence, situated on the Mohawk River and in its vicinity; they had many Scottish Highlanders for tenants; and among their adherents were violent men, such as the Butlers of Tryon County, and Brant, the Mohawk sachem, since famous in Indian warfare. They had recently gone about with armed retainers, overawing and breaking up patriotic assemblages, and it was known they could at any time bring a force of warriors in the field.

Recent accounts stated that Sir John was fortifying the old family hall at Johnstown with swivels, and had a hundred and fifty

Roman Catholic Highlanders quartered in and about it, all armed and ready to obey his orders.

Colonel Guy Johnson, however, was the most active and zealous of the family. Pretending to apprehend a design on the part of the New England people to surprise and carry him off, he fortified his stone mansion on the Mohawk, called Guy's Park, and assembled there a part of his militia regiment, and other of his adherents, to the number of five hundred. He held a great Indian council there, likewise, in which the chiefs of the Six Nations recalled the friendship and good deeds of the late Sir William Johnson, and avowed their determination to stand by and defend every branch of his family.

As yet it was uncertain whether Colonel Guy really intended to take an open part in the appeal to arms. Should he do so, he would carry with him a great force of the native tribes, and might almost domineer over the frontier.

Tryon, the governor of New York, was at present absent in England, having been called home by the ministry to give an account of the affairs of the province, and to receive instructions for its management. He was a tory in heart, and had been a zealous opponent of all colonial movements, and his talents and address gave him great influence over an important part of the community. Should he return with hostile instructions, and should he and the Johnsons co-operate, the one controlling the bay and harbor of New York and the waters of the Hudson by means of ships and land forces; the others overrunning the valley of the Mohawk and the regions beyond Albany with savage hordes, this great central province might be wrested from the confederacy, and all intercourse broken off between the eastern and southern colonies.

All these circumstances and considerations, many of which came under discussion in the course of this military journey, rendered the command of New York a post of especial trust and importance, and determined Washington to confide it to General Schuyler. He was peculiarly fitted for it by his military talents, his intimate knowledge of the province and its concerns, especially what related to the upper parts of it, and his experience in Indian affairs.

At Newark, in the Jerseys, Washington was met on the 25th by a committee of the provincial Congress, sent to conduct him to the city. The Congress was in a perplexity. It had in a manner usurped and exercised the powers of Governor Tryon during his absence, while at the same time it professed allegiance to the crown which had appointed him. He was now in the harbor, just arrived from England, and hourly expected to land. Washington, too, was approaching. How were these double claims to ceremonious respect happening at the same time to be managed?

In this dilemma a regiment of militia was turned out, and the colonel instructed to pay military honors to whichever of the distinguished functionaries should first arrive. Washington was earlier than the governor by several hours, and received those honors. Peter Van Burgh Livingston, president of the New York Congress, next delivered a congratulatory address, the latter part of which evinces the cautious reserve with which, in these revolutionary times, military power was intrusted to an individual:—

"Confiding in you, sir, and in the worthy generals immediately under your command, we have the most flattering hopes of success in the glorious struggle for American liberty, and the fullest assurances that *whenever this important contest shall be decided by that fondest wish of each American soul, an accommodation with our mother country, you will cheerfully resign the important deposit committed into your hands, and reassume the character of our worthiest citizen.*"

The following was Washington's reply, in behalf of himself and his generals, to this part of the address.

"As to the fatal, but necessary operations of war, when we assumed the soldier, we did not lay aside the citizen; and we shall most sincerely rejoice with you in that happy hour, when the establishment of American liberty on the most firm and solid foundations, shall enable us to return to our private stations, in the bosom of a free, peaceful, and happy country."

The landing of Governor Tryon took place about eight o'clock in the evening. The military honors were repeated; he was received with great respect by the mayor and common council, and transports of loyalty by those devoted to the crown. It was unknown what instructions he had received from the ministry, but it was rumored that a large force would soon arrive from England, subject to his directions. At this very moment a ship of war, the Asia, lay anchored opposite the city; its grim batteries bearing upon it, greatly to the disquiet of the faint-hearted among its inhabitants.

In this situation of affairs Washington was happy to leave such an efficient person as General Schuyler in command of the place. According to his instructions, the latter was to make returns once a month, and oftener, should circumstances require it, to Washington, as commander-in-chief, and to the Continental Congress, of the forces under him, and the state of his supplies; and to send the earliest advices of all events of importance. He was to keep a wary eye on Colonel Guy Johnson, and to counteract any prejudicial influence he might exercise over the Indians. With respect to Governor Tryon, Washington hinted at a bold and decided line of conduct. "If forcible measures are judged necessary respecting the person of the governor, I should have no difficulty in ordering them, if the Continental Congress were not sitting; but as that is the case, *and the seizing of a governor quite a new thing*, I must refer you to that body for direction."

Had Congress thought proper to direct such a measure, Schuyler certainly would have been the man to execute it.

At New York, Washington had learned all the details of the battle of Bunker's Hill; they quickened his impatience to arrive at the camp. He departed, therefore, on the 26th, accompanied by General Lee, and escorted as far as Kingsbridge, the termination of New York Island, by Markoe's Philadelphia light horse, and several companies of militia.

In the mean time the provincial Congress of Massachusetts, then in session at Watertown, had made arrangements for the expected arrival of Washington. According to a resolve of that body, the president's house in Cambridge, excepting one room reserved by the president for his own use, was to be taken, cleared, prepared, and furnished for the reception of the Commander-in-Chief and General Lee. The Congress had likewise sent on a deputation which met Washington at Springfield, on the frontiers of the province, and provided escorts and accommodations for him along the road. Thus honorably attended from town to town, and escorted by volunteer companies and cavalcades of gentlemen, he arrived at Watertown on the 2d of July, where he was greeted by Congress with a congratulatory address, in which, however, was frankly stated the undisciplined state of the army he was summoned to command. An address of cordial welcome was likewise made to General Lee.

The ceremony over, Washington was again in the saddle; and, escorted by a troop of light horse and a cavalcade of citizens, proceeded to the head-quarters provided for him at Cambridge, three miles distant. As he entered the confines of the camp the shouts of the multitude and the thundering of artillery gave note to the enemy beleaguered in Boston of his arrival.

His military reputation had preceded him and excited great expectations. They were not disappointed. His personal appearance, notwithstanding the dust of travel, was calculated to captivate the public eye. As he rode through the camp, amidst a throng of officers, he was the admiration of the soldiery and of a curious throng collected from the surrounding country. Happy was the countryman who could get a full view of him to carry home an account of it to his neighbors. "I have been much gratified this day with a view of General Washington," writes a contemporary chronicler, "His excellency was on horseback, in company with several military gentlemen. It was not difficult to distinguish him from all others. He is tall and well-proportioned, and his personal appearance truly noble and majestic."[112]

The fair sex were still more enthusiastic in their admiration, if we may judge from the following passage of a letter written by the intelligent and accomplished wife of John Adams to her husband: "Dignity, ease, and complacency, the gentleman and the soldier, look agreeably blended in him. Modesty marks every line and feature of his face. Those lines of Dryden instantly occurred to me:

'Mark his majestic fabric! He's a temple
Sacred by birth, and built by hands divine;
His soul's the deity that lodges there;
Nor is the pile unworthy of the God.'"

With Washington, modest at all times, there was no false excitement on the present occasion; nothing to call forth emotions of self-glorification. The honors and congratulations with which he was received, the acclamations of the public, the cheerings of the army, only told him how much was expected from him; and when he looked round upon the raw and rustic levies he

---

112   Thacher.—Military Journal.

was to command, "a mixed multitude of people, under very little discipline, order, or government," scattered in rough encampments about hill and dale, beleaguering a city garrisoned by veteran troops, with ships of war anchored about its harbor, and strong outposts guarding it, he felt the awful responsibility of his situation, and the complicated and stupendous task before him. He spoke of it, however, not despondingly nor boastfully and with defiance; but with that solemn and sedate resolution, and that hopeful reliance on Supreme Goodness, which belonged to his magnanimous nature. The cause of his country, he observed, had called him to an active and dangerous duty, but *he trusted that Divine Providence, which wisely orders the affairs of men, would enable him to discharge it with fidelity and success.*[113]

END OF VOL. I.

---

113   Letter to Governor Trumbull.—Sparks, iii., 31.

BIBLIOBAZAAR

The essential book market!

Did you know that you can get any of our titles in large print?

Did you know that we have an ever-growing collection of books in many languages?

Order online:
www.bibliobazaar.com

Find all of your favorite classic books!

Stay up to date with the latest government reports!

At BiblioBazaar, we aim to make knowledge more accessible by making thousands of titles available to you- *quickly and affordably*.

Contact us:
BiblioBazaar
PO Box 21206
Charleston, SC 29413

47523576R00203

Made in the USA
Middletown, DE
08 June 2019